OUTRUNNING HITLER

By

HARVEY ARDMAN

Interior Layout: Brian Schwartz

r25-0725

Dedication

Thanks to all of the members of my NightWriters critique group, for their keen eyes and good suggestions:

David Brandin
Leonard Carpenter
Michele Turner
Jim Livingstone
CA Sharp

Other Books
in the Series

Outrunning Hitler, vol. 4, a fact-based novelization of Jesse Owen's role in the 1936 Berlin Olympics, with David Nathan assigned to protect the famous runner from Nazi plots.

The other three:

The Billionaires' Conspiracy, vol. 1, a fact-based novelization of the 1934 attempt by some of America's richest men to overthrow Franklin Roosevelt, an attempt thwarted by David Nathan.

Lion at Bay, vol. 2, a fact-based novelization of Emperor Haile Selassie's attempt to stop Mussolini from seizing Ethiopia in 1936, with the aid of David Nathan.

The Final Crossing, vol. 3 is book four of a series of historical thrillers involving Detective David Nathan, working on assignment from President Roosevelt.

All of these books are available at Amazon.com,
as e-books and as paperbacks.

Prologue

July 10, 1936

David Nathan's right knee was killing him. He'd been kneeling behind a big, olive-drab mailbox on the rough concrete sidewalk for better than forty-five minutes. There'd been hardly any automobile traffic since one a.m., much less a big moving truck. He was beginning to doubt his informant.

His attention was focused on a building about one hundred and fifty feet away, 508 W. 38th Street, just a couple blocks from the Hudson River. It was a nondescript structure eight stories tall, with walls of concrete and brick, windowless and without an identifying sign, just one more anonymous New York warehouse among a multitude.

As it happened, however, this particular structure contained the greatest concentration of wealth in New York City outside of the Federal Reserve vaults on Wall Street and Tiffany's safe. It held the mink coats, the sables, the chinchillas, the foxes and the ermines, thousands of them, that, in season, graced the shoulders of the richest socialites in a fifty-mile radius.

This was the summer residence for furs taken to exclusive shops and fine dry cleaners throughout the metropolitan area. It was the finest fur storage facility in the area, temperature-controlled to between 40 and 50 degrees, with humidity at 45-55%, fireproof, lightproof and waterproof, insect and vermin-free, fully insured, and totally anonymous.

The fur warehouse had but a single door, a thick, galvanized, corrugated, reinforced, double-wide steel rectangle with a row of deadbolts on each side fitted into a steel frame two inches thick, on which it was hung with industrial-size piano hinges. Timed locks controlled entry.

Between Nathan and the fur vault stood three other warehouses, all smaller, as well as a construction site where earth movers had been excavating and piling the resulting rocks and boulders into a huge dump truck.

Lampposts stood at both ends of the block, shedding cones of dim yellow light on nearby warehouse buildings. The lamppost in the middle of the street was dark. Attached to it was a rusty police call box.

A vehicle turned onto 38th St. from 10th Ave. and slowly approached. At first, all Nathan could see were the headlights. His grip on his police revolver tightened and every muscle in his body tensed. But this was not a truck. It was a taxi, empty except for the driver. Probably heading toward Times Square, Nathan thought. The driver sure wasn't very likely to find a fare here.

As the cab went by, Nathan decided he'd better get closer to the warehouse. He got to his feet—not without difficulty—and jogged down the street to the excavation site, taking cover behind a dump truck, which was about seventy-five feet from the building he had his eye on.

And here he waited.

Nathan hadn't wanted to stake out this site all by his lonely, but he couldn't convince Commander Conyingham to lend him a couple of uniforms for reinforcements. "I know Al Joad was one of your father's informants," Conyingham had said, "but he's a drunk and he has bats in his belfry. We give him fins and he gives us yesterday's news. The odds that he'd know anything about a big time fur heist are somewhere between zip and zero."

Nathan saw it differently. He'd known Al Joad for years. His Dad had brought the old man home for dinner more than once, given him pin money, played cards with him, let him play catch with his son. Yeah, Joad was a drunk. And a lot of the time he didn't know what day it was. But his warning to Nathan had been lucid, urgent and believable.

So here he was, playing solo, waiting for what Joad had assured him would be a "very big truck, like an interstate moving van, and a gang of thugs determined to stuff it full of a few million bucks worth of fur coats." But how much longer should he wait?

A few minutes after taking up residence behind the dump truck, Nathan spotted another pair of headlights coming down 10th and started tracking it. Like the taxi, it slowed up as it approached 39th Street, then turned onto the block he was staking out.

This one was no taxi.

It was a big, a very big moving van, the kind New Yorkers rent when, foolishly, they move to California. As it passed under the streetlamp, he looked for a name on the cargo box or the cab's door. Totally blank. No one was taking credit for owning this baby.

The truck slowly crept down 38th Street, heading east, coming to a hissing stop just before it reached the fur warehouse. The headlights immediately blinked out, and Nathan heard the rear door slide up and open. Feet hit the pavement. He counted ten men, eleven if you included the driver. One against eleven.

Well, this was going to be interesting, he thought, considering his Colt Police Positive Special held just six shots. How was he going to corral ten men—some, no doubt, carrying hardware of their own—and live to tell the tale?

In the dim light, Nathan watched two men sidle up to the warehouse entrance, one of them lugging what looked like a doctor's satchel. While the other crooks hung back, this pair knelt at the steel door, took something out of the bag and began fiddling with it.

Nathan couldn't see what they were doing, but he had a pretty good idea. Nitro. They weren't going to crack the lock or jimmy the door, they were going to blow it open—one sharp bang, which would go largely unnoticed in this neighborhood, since it wasn't residential, not legally anyhow, and no one who heard the noise would want to get involved.

That's why there were ten gangsters. Manpower was a necessity. One man—the driver—was the look-out. The other ten would do the pilfering. They would rush in, grab as many coats as they could, hustle out and stash them in the van. They'd each make four or five trips, then jump into the truck and drive off before anyone knew they were there.

Except him.

Nathan waited. The two bomb guys at the door continued to fiddle with the apparatus they'd taken from the bag. Then they both stood and quickly backed away. Nathan felt himself tense up. Nothing happened for much too long, nothing whatever.

Then, BANG! A sudden, bright burst of light, followed by a brief rumbling, and a little smoke. Someone switched on a flashlight. The warehouse door was down, lying on the sidewalk, grotesquely bent. The crooks hesitated a moment, waiting for the debris to settle, then scampered through the entrance, impatient to get on with it.

Nathan checked out the windows in the nearby warehouses. No signs of life. No lights suddenly appeared in the windows. No sounds at all now, except for the rumble of distant traffic from Times Square. And that was odd—the building's alarm should have been clanging wildly. So should the Precinct 13 alarm board, but Nathan was sure it was silent too. What we have here, Nathan realized, is an inside job.

Nathan took a deep breath and asked himself the logical question: what now?

The big van's door opened and the driver stepped out and lit up a cigarette. He was carrying a pistol and looking very nervous, like every other lookout in the history of crime. They'd put him in some kind of uniform, no doubt hoping he'd look official enough to stave off any questions that might come his way once they got on the road.

Nathan waited behind the truck. He didn't like the math. He remembered that his mother was the beneficiary of his life insurance policy. But he couldn't just let the bad guys grab the loot and skedaddle. He was a cop, not an innocent bystander. A detective no less, his father would be proud. What would Dad have done? he wondered. Dad would have found a way.

Nathan checked his watch, pleased that his Gruen had luminous hands. He figured the crooks had been in the building maybe five minutes. They'd take the low-hanging fruit this time, the first-floor stuff. They'd get to the second floor on the next trip. The dowagers whose furs were stored on the top floor might luck out.

Five minutes later, the thieves reappeared, one by one, each of them with a death grip on at least a dozen coats. The driver met them at the back of the truck, helping them dump the furs into the cargo box. Nathan couldn't see inside, but he figured they probably had racks in the truck and were hanging the coats to prevent schmooshing.

Empty-handed now, the burglars scampered back over the fallen steel door and into the warehouse again. Ten minutes, Nathan figured, maybe a little more this time. He'd better not dawdle. As the last man disappeared through the entrance, he hopped up on the van's running board, opened the door and slithered inside. The dome light flashed on for half a second, then went out again.

Well, this wasn't going to be easy. Not in the dark. Give him some daylight and he was pretty good at it: stick your head underneath the dash, find the two electrical wires, hopefully red, twist them together, then touch them to the ignition wire, hopefully brown or black, rum-

rum and there you go. But in the dark? Without electrocuting yourself? Where was Helen Keller when you needed her?

Nathan bent down and nearly put out an eye on the gearshift knob. He decided his sense of touch might be a better bet. He reached a hand under the dash, only to jerk it away when he encountered a sharp edge. He tried it again, gingerly, feeling around, wasting precious seconds. No success.

If this had been a common sedan—a DeSoto, a Hupmobile, even a LaSalle, he would have the engine humming by now. He'd learned on the streets. And when his father found out what he and his pals had been doing, he got a walloping he still remembered. But he'd never tried to hotwire a moving van in the dead of night, sans flashlight.

Nathan stuck his hand under the dash again, this time closer to the steering column, and he resumed his search, trying to be methodical about it. After a moment, he found one electrical wire. And then the other. He closed his fist around them and pulled. They didn't give.

He tried again, bracing himself against the seat and jerking the wires as hard as he could manage, putting every last one of his 160 pounds behind it. This time, the wires came loose, and Nathan tumbled across the front seat, banging his head on the passenger window, barely hanging on to the wires.

Now there were two questions: One—did he have the right wires? And two--could he twist them together in dark? At that moment, his hand brushed against something on the steering column. God damn it! The truck keys! He felt like an idiot. The driver had left the keys in the ignition. Nathan cursed himself for not checking before trying to hot-wire the truck. Still, the keys solved his problem. He looked toward the warehouse. The driver was nervously pacing, oblivious. He checked his watch again. The crooks had been inside for about seven minutes. There wasn't enough time to pull off the maneuver. The wise guys might be moving faster this trip.

Four minutes later, the crooks started exiting the building, loaded down with more armloads of fur. They hurried to the back of the truck and shed their cargo. One of the men who'd set the nitro—the leader, apparently—checked his watch. He held up three fingers and made sure everyone saw the signal. Three more trips, Nathan figured. But not if he had anything to do with it.

He waited until all the crooks had disappeared into the warehouse again and then turned the truck key. The vehicle's big engine roared into life. Nathan glanced through the windshield. The lookout hadn't noticed the dome light, but the noisy engine sure caught his attention. He looked sharply toward the truck, wondering what was going on. Well, he was about to find out.

Nathan hit the accelerator, stripping half the transmission gears, nonetheless managing to pull out of the construction site and into 38th Street. By now, the lookout had zeroed in on him and was staring in disbelief, stupified—at least momentarily.

Now Nathan did a quick two-point version of a three-point turn. He drove the truck right up to the stoop of the building opposite the warehouse, then managed to shift into reverse, stripping the remaining gears. With the gearbox screaming, he swiftly backed up, straight toward the warehouse entrance.

He crashed the truck directly into the open door, totally blocking the entrance. Suddenly, a gunshot. A bullet shattered the van's windshield. The lookout driver had come out of his stupor and was going to make a fight of it. But David Nathan was one of the NYPD's better shots. Thanks to his father, he'd been a marksman before he was out of grade school.

Nathan fired once, winging the truck driver in his shooting arm. Then he hopped out of the truck and disarmed the guy, a short, black-haired ruddy-faced fireplug of a man. Using the single pair of handcuffs he'd stuffed in his jacket pocket, Nathan shackled the man to the truck's front bumper.

"Jesus Christ! You shot me!" the look-out complained in classic Brooklynese, sounding hurt and surprised.

"Well, yes I did," Nathan said. "Better you than me."

"Who da fuck are ya?"

"NYPD." He showed him the gold shield, which got the briefest glance.

"Yeah? So where are da rest of ya?"

"Don't worry. You're surrounded."

The crook looked around, straining his neck. "I don't see nobody else."

"That's because they're invisible," Nathan told him. "I'll be right back."

"Invisible?" said the crook, baffled.

Nathan jogged across the street to the police call box, praying that for a change, this one would work. He picked up the receiver.

"Police Central," said a gruff male voice.

"Dispatch, this is Detective David Nathan badge #95762. I need a couple of paddy wagons and a dozen uniforms at call box"—he checked the number—"105."

"You need what?"

"Two paddy wagons and a dozen cops," Nathan said. "Soon as I can get 'em."

"Listen, Detective, I'm not sure you've noticed, but it's 2:30 in the morning. Where do you expect me to get a dozen cops at this hour?"

"Dispatch," Nathan said, "I don't care if you have to import them from Jersey City. I got ten burglars here and I'm all alone."

"You're shitting me, Detective. You got ten burglars collared?"

"Not exactly, but close enough."

"Jay-sus. I think I can get the paddy wagons and maybe half a dozen uniforms. But it could take a half hour or so. Can you hold on?"

Nathan looked over at the -battered truck sitting on the warehouse's fallen door and sealing off the building's entrance. "Don't make me wait too long, Dispatch. I bore easily."

"I'll do my damndest, Detective. Play it safe if you have to."

"Thanks, Dispatch." Nathan hung up and strolled back to his captive.

"You better get outta here," the crook said.

"Oh really?" Nathan said. "Why is that?"

"You're gonna have company in just a minute and they won't be friendly, if you get my meaning."

Nathan made a point of turning toward the truck wedged into the doorway. Muffled shouts could be heard from within. "I'm not so sure of that," he said. "Your friends seem delayed."

'I don't know what you're talking about."

Nathan took a closer look at his captive. His ill-fitting uniform was embroidered with the words "I. J. Fox"—one of New York's best known fur stores

"I. J. Fox, eh?" Nathan said. "You think anybody would believe you work there?"

"What?"

"Your uniform, Sluggo."

The crook glanced at the embroidery on his jacket. "Oh yeah, that. That's right, I'm an employee. Here to move some coats up to the Westchester storage building."

Nathan laughed. "How about the guys in the warehouse? More furriers?"

"Never saw 'em before."

"Your boss in there?"

"You kiddin? He never goes on jobs."

"By the way," Nathan said, "what's his name again?"

"Very funny," the crook said, "Hey, I gotta drain the dragon. How 'bout lettin' me loose fer a minute?"

A siren cut through the quiet night, getting louder, closer. In a minute, a paddy wagon rounded the corner at 38th and 9th Ave., wailing at the top of its lungs and flying a flashing red light on the roof. It screeched to a stop in front of the warehouse and its rear doors flew open, disgorging half a dozen confused coppers. It looked like a scene from a Mac Sennett comedy.

A tall Irishman with a genuine handlebar mustache, a captain, rushed up to Nathan, revolver in one hand, billy club in the other. "Where's the gang?" he asked, breathless.

Nathan pointed toward the wrecked truck. "Thataway," he said.

The captain gave him a look. "All of 'em?"

"Yeah, except for the lookout. That's him, cuffed to the bumper."

Another paddy wagon turned onto 38th St., this one coming from 10th Ave. It pulled up behind its twin and, to Nathan's shock, Commander Conyingham himself—the Cardinal, as he was known in the NYPD—exited the passenger side and took in the scene. He was a stiff, domineering man, bald as an egg, with fierce blue eyes and a mouth without visible lips. Uncharacteristically, his uniform jacket was misbuttoned and he needed a shave.

"What the hell is going on here, Detective?" The tone of voice was intended to make Nathan quail.

"That robbery Joad warned me about?" Nathan said. "Well, I interrupted it."

"And got me out of bed in the middle of the night—for what?"

"For the ten crooks trapped in the fur warehouse," Nathan said.

Conyingham looked at Nathan in disbelief. "Ten?"

"I counted them when they walked in."

The Cardinal studied the scene for a few moments, trying to get a handle on what had happened. He eyed the wrecked van. Finally, he looked back at Nathan. "You drove the truck?"

"I did."

"And the crooks are trapped in the warehouse?"

"Yep. All ten of them, except for the lookout." Ne nodded toward the cuffed man.

"You never cease to amaze me, Nathan."

"Thank you, sir."

"Don't get a swelled head."

One of the uniforms approached Commander Conyingham and pointed a thumb at the boulders. "What do we do now, boss?"

Conyingham thought a moment. "Well, Lt. Abahazi, I think we'd better send for a bulldozer."

Chapter One

Franklin Delano Roosevelt stood, with the help of his sturdy, ever-present Naval aide, Captain Paul Bastido, and wobbled slightly. The two men locked Roosevelt's steel leg braces and, on the arm of Capt. Bastido, Roosevelt took three tortured paces forward. He reached out, tightly grasped both edges of the podium, and grinned at his audience, looking quite dapper in his crisp, tan summer suit.

Behind him on the dais was a gaggle of New York borough Presidents and other VIPs, including Mayor Fiorello LaGuardia, New York Governor Herbert Lehman, Secretary of the Interior Harold Ickes and New York City Parks Commissioner Robert Moses. They were all protected from the scorching July sun by a temporary white canvas awning, erected on Randall's Island for just this occasion.

The occasion was the dedication of Robert Moses' latest and greatest project, the Y-shaped Triborough Bridge, which spanned the juncture of the East and Harlem Rivers and connected, as one might expect, three of New York City's boroughs, Manhattan, Queens and the Bronx, not to mention Randall's Island itself. At Harold Ickes' suggestion, the President had delayed his Maine vacation to speak at the event and to remind voters that it was Federal largesse that had made this bridge possible.

The venue for the dedication ceremonies, little Randall's Island, lay between Queens and Manhattan, under the Manhattan branch of the bridge. It was the former site of a potters' field and a psychiatric hospital, now covered by brown crabgrass, sandy bare patches and low bushes struggling to survive. Beaming with his customary self-confidence and bonhomie, FDR gazed out at his audience, a thousand people sprawled over the Randall's Island crabgrass, sweltering in the 95 degree heat. They applauded, he waved. He glanced down at the speech Capt. Bastido had placed on the podium. It was short, thank God, twelve paragraphs. He waved again, to turn off the applause. When it had subsided, he began.

"Many of you who are here today, old people like myself," he said, striking a folksy tone, "can remember that when we were boys and girls, the greater part of what is now the Boroughs of the Bronx and

Queens was cultivated as farmland. A little further back, but not much more than a hundred years ago, my own great-grandfather owned a farm in Harlem, right across there" he pointed, "close to the Manhattan approach of this bridge. But I am quite sure, Bob Moses, that he never dreamed of this magnificent bridge."

Roosevelt looked back over his shoulder, grinning at Robert Moses, a dour-looking man with deep-set eyes and a permanent frown, wearing a lopsided polka-dot bow tie. Among Moses' several public offices, he was head of the Triborough Bridge Authority. He chuckled politely at FDR's reference.

The President turned back to the crowd and began reading again, gesturing, smiling and joking as though he were actually paying attention to what he was saying. But something had caught his eye: the only real structure on the island, a small, low, hastily-constructed stadium just a few hundred yards away. On the field of play, athletes were racing, jumping, hurdling, vaulting, closely watched by officials with stop-watches and notepads. A small crowd sat in the stands, occasionally applauding an outstanding performance.

The President lost his place, but quickly recovered. "This Triborough Bridge was neither in its conception nor in its building a matter of purely local concern," he said, the words booming out in his patrician accent, "Nation, State and city, each in its own way, have contributed to the gigantic undertaking. And it will serve the people not only in all the boroughs of this largest of cities; it will serve also the people of Long Island, of up-state New York and our neighbors of Connecticut and New Jersey..."

Roosevelt once again found his eyes drifting toward the little makeshift stadium nearby. Men in racing attire had lined up at one of the cinder tracks carved into the crabgrass. They crouched, in that peculiar runner's crouch. Then, a faint shot—and they were off.

The President turned back toward his audience, not missing a beat. "At a time of great suffering, the construction of this bridge was undertaken among the very first of tens of thousands of projects launched by States and counties and municipalities and financed in part with Federal funds..."

He continued talking, on automatic pilot now, but watching the race. The runners were both black and white, but one of the black athletes flashed past the rest of the field, feet barely touching the cinders, muscles working in perfect synchronization. He won going away.

FDR caught up with himself again. "I am grateful to you workers, skilled and unskilled, here at the site and those workers in the mills and shops many miles distant, without whose strong arms, willing hands and clear heads there would be no celebration here today."

He paused for dramatic effect. "May the Triborough Bridge, in the years to come, justify our efforts and our hopes by serving truly the city, the State and the Nation!"

The crowd stood, applauding, a few of them cheering. Roosevelt nodded and waved in response, grinning in satisfaction.

Capt. Bastido moved up from his place at the back of the dais, waited for the applause to die out, then, offering an arm as strong as a steel beam, helped the President walk back to his seat, gracefully turning him, simultaneously unlocking his leg braces.

FDR sat down heavily, then turned to Robert Moses, "Robert, can you tell me what's going on over there?" FDR asked, pointing to the athletic field.

"Olympic trials," said Moses. "The winners are going to Berlin, heaven help them."

"You have something against Berlin?" the President inquired.

"I have something against Hitler," Moses told him.

The President nodded. He shaded his eyes and looked toward the stadium, where another race was underway. He leaned toward Capt. Bastido. "Is that Jesse Owens?" he asked, pointing.

Bastido followed his gaze. "I believe so, sir."

They both watched, as Owens pulled away from the field and easily won the race.

"Amazing athlete, that boy," said FDR. "Broke five world records in an hour at Michigan last year, you know."

"Yes, sir, I know," Bastido said.

He handed Roosevelt a big, white, broad-brimmed Panama hat, and the President put it on, giving it a jaunty tilt. "I'll wager he wins us some Gold Medals in Berlin," he said.

"No question of it, sir," said Bastido. "Ready to go to the car, now?"

Roosevelt was thoughtful. He imagined Jesse Owens in Berlin, winning spectacularly, puncturing Hitler's racial superiority balloon for the whole world to see. It would be like giving *der Führer* a public slap in the face.

FDR had been hoping to find some way to take *der Führer* down a peg since they both came into office, in 1933. The man was a miscreant, a villain, leading a cadre of thugs of the worst kind. A danger to world peace. But the President of the United States couldn't even say what he thought about Hitler, at least not in public. The Neutrality Act and the power of the Senate isolationists had him thoroughly handcuffed.

So Jesse Owens was a Godsend. He offered an innocent but effective way to get under Hitler's skin, to embarrass him in public, to expose him for what he was. Then Roosevelt had a more ominous thought. Would Hitler let Owens triumph at the Olympics? Maybe he would find some devious or even violent way to thwart the young man. My God, FDR thought, there's a very real chance that Owens trip to the Berlin Olympics could cost him his life.

"Mr. President?"

Roosevelt looked up to see Capt. Bastido standing over him, looking concerned.

"Paul, is Stephen Early anywhere nearby?" FDR asked.

Bastido looked behind the dais, spotted Early talking with Harold Ickes. Early was a tall man with a naturally severe expression. Bastido waggled a finger at him and he came over to the President. "Sir?"

"Stephen, could you ask David Nathan to come see me at the 65th street townhouse tomorrow morning, say around 10?"

"Nathan?"

"Yes. I have a job for him."

Early raised an eyebrow. "You know it's barely been six weeks since the Haile Selassie business. Nathan's been back only a month. I don't think it's fair to ask him to go out again so soon."

The President frowned. "You have a point, Stephen. It's a lot to ask. But I trust him. He's exactly the right man for the job I have in mind."

***

FDR's brownstone was a three-story grey structure, one of a row of them. It stood at mid-block, on the north side of E. 65th between Fifth and Madison, behind two pathetically small but well-leafed trees which emerged from a grill in the sidewalk.

Until Steven Early's call yesterday, David Nathan hadn't even known that the President had an apartment in New York. Now he was here. The question is, why? What did Roosevelt want this time? "That's for himself to tell you," Early had said.

Two remarkably conspicuous Secret Service men were standing at the door. They examined Nathan's police ID and pronounced him kosher. He lifted the gleaming brass door knocker and let it fall.

The door opened so quickly it seemed that someone must have been standing on the other side. That someone was a stooped, grey-haired black man in a business suit. The butler, Nathan guessed. "May I hep you, sir?"

"I'm David Nathan. I have an appoint…"

"Yes, sir. Mr. Roosevelt is waiting for you." The butler led the way to a small library in the back of the house, which was positively stuffed with books, on shelves, in piles on the floor and even on chairs. Standing in a corner, a walnut console radio, a Philco, was turned on, volume low. Bing Crosby was singing "You Must Have Been a Beautiful Baby."

Stephen Early and President Roosevelt were waiting for him, Early relaxing on an upholstered rocking chair, a copy of *Fortune* magazine on his lap, the President behind his desk, in a wheelchair, using a small silver tweezers to place a stamp in an ancient, leather-covered album. He wore glasses.

"Ah, David," said the President, extending a hand. "It's good to see you again. I hope you're well."

"Very well, Mr. President," Nathan said, shaking the Presidential hand, "and I hope you're the same."

"Couldn't be better," Roosevelt said. "David, I want to congratulate you and thank you again for rescuing Haile Selassie from Mussolini's army. I know of no one else who could have pulled it off."

"Thank you, sir," Nathan said. The Ethiopian adventure had taken a lot out of him and he was glad to be back in New York, where he could rest up and risk his life arresting ordinary thieves, mobsters and trigger men.

Roosevelt carefully put the stamp in place and closed the album. He took off his glasses, slipped a cigarette out of the pack lying on his desk, put it into one of his famous onyx-colored cigarette holders and lit up. "I'm going to get right to the point, David. What do you know about Jesse Owens?"

Nathan thought a moment. "Owens? The Negro track star who broke all those world records? Just what I've read in the papers."

"That's the man," said the President. "Well, yesterday he won all of his events at the Olympics trials. He'll be heading to Berlin in a few days."

Nathan tried to guess what was coming, but nothing occurred to him. "I'm sure he'll win some medals for us."

"No doubt," said FDR. "Listen, David, I'd like you to go along and keep an eye on him." He looked directly at Nathan and took a deep drag on his cigarette.

"What? To Berlin? You mean like a bodyguard?"

"Well, nothing official and certainly nothing conspicuous," FDR said. "Just being prudent."

"You think Owens is in danger?"

Roosevelt took another puff on his cigarette. "I'd like to think not. Owens is an American, after all, black or not. But Hitler and his confederates—they're nothing more than a collection of thugs and murderers. They can't be trusted."

"Can't argue with that," Nathan said. "But a bodyguard…"

"I know. But I'd rather not take any chances," Roosevelt said. "I'd be more comfortable if you were there, privately. Anonymously. Just to play it safe."

Nathan nodded, thinking. "If you feel it's that important…" He glanced toward Early, who shrugged, as if to say sorry I got you into this.

The President leaned forward and regarded the young detective with great intensity. "I know it's a lot to ask. But we have to do anything we can to discredit Hitler's claim that Aryans are superior to everyone else, and nothing would be more convincing than an actual demonstration with *der Führer* as an eyewitness."

Won't change Hitler's mind, Nathan thought. "I understand," he said, but FDR continued, warming to his subject.

"An Owens victory would be a small but telling reminder that we are all equal in the eyes of God. So we must protect him, for the sake of humanity." Roosevelt concluded.

"And to stick a finger in Hitler's eye," Early chimed in.

Nathan couldn't resist a smile. "Mr. President, by 'we', you mean…"

FDR returned the grin. "Yes, David, I mean you. If you're willing. I know I'm asking a lot to suggest you go abroad again so soon. But if we're lucky, this trip will not be as arduous as the last. The danger to Owens may be nothing more than my overheated imagination. You might even enjoy yourself. I wish *I* could go."

Nathan was silent for a moment. "I'm not sure I'm the right man for the mission," he said. "I think I should remind you that I'm Jewish. Considering Germany's attitude toward Jews, I could draw trouble to myself—and Owens."

Roosevelt leaned back in his chair, took another drag, then stubbed out his cigarette on a crystal ashtray. "Yes. I understand what you're saying, but it shouldn't be a problem. With that mop of dark hair, those brown eyes and those craggy features, you could just as easily be Italian or Greek or even a Czech. Anyhow, that's not important. You're an *American*, after all, with a US passport in the name of— what was the name we decided on, Stephen?"

"I think you liked 'Michael Novak,' Mr. President," Early said. He almost said something else, but instead opened the *Fortune* magazine and idly flipped through the pages.

"That was the one," said FDR.

Nathan tried it out. "Michael Novak. Novak. Could be from any one of a dozen different European countries."

"Yes," Roosevelt said, "but also typically American."

"But American what?" Nathan said. "Cop? Businessman?"

"Journalist," said the President. "We felt that would be best. Right, Stephen?"

The President's Press Secretary closed his magazine. "It isn't exactly a new idea," he said, "but it should work. You'll be reporting on the Olympics for the *Cleveland Plain Dealer*. That should get you into places forbidden to ordinary tourists."

"Never been to Cleveland," Nathan said.

"No worries," Early said. "I'll get you a guidebook. "If anyone asks, tell them this is your first assignment. You got the job as a favor to your father, who's a big advertiser."

"Ah, I'm going to be a neophyte."

"*I* don't think of you as a neophyte, David," FDR assured him. "In fact, I think of you as an expert in your trade."

Nathan allowed himself to be buttered up, because it felt very good to be buttered up by the President of the United States.

"One more thing," FDR said, exchanging the cigarette stub in his holder with an unsmoked one. "I believe it would be better if Owens doesn't know you're there to protect him. I don't want him thinking he's in danger. That's best kept a secret, don't you agree? Just stay near him, befriend him, protect him if…well, I don't have to tell you your business."

Nathan was well aware the President assumed he'd accept the job. He'd assumed that even before Early summoned him. Well, it was a reasonable assumption. There was no way, really, he could refuse—even though he suspected Roosevelt was overreacting. On the other hand, there were worse ways to spend a couple of weeks in summer than going to the Olympics.

The President lit his cigarette. "I'll tell our Ambassador to Germany about you—William Dodd. Good man, solid liberal. But he'll be the only person in Berlin who will know your true mission. Check in with him. If you need assistance of any kind he'll help you. If he can."

"When do the Olympics begin?" Nathan asked.

"First day of August," Stephen Early said. "But the team is leaving for Europe on the *S.S. Manhattan* on the 16th."

Nathan was incredulous. "That's in four days!"

"I know it's a bit of a rush," Roosevelt said, "but we learned only yesterday that Owens would be on the US team."

"I'll see to it that you get enough *reichsmarks* to keep you well-fed on your trip," Early said, almost apologetically. "And I'll send along some information about Berlin and the Olympics."

"Never been to Berlin either," Nathan said, thinking of how he'd feel to be in Hitler's Germany. "Should be interesting."

"When you come back, I want you to come to the White House and tell me all about it," FDR said, knowing Nathan would relish the invitation.

Nathan and Early exchanged glances. "Have fun," said the President's Press Secretary.

Chapter Two

"It still looks too small," Hitler said, frowning "Not at all impressive."
He might have been talking about himself. He was a man of about
5'8", 200 pounds, with fine hair and thin skin, wearing a belted leather
trench coat and a brown military cap. His eyelids were a bit heavy and
from the set of his mouth, under the toothbrush mustache, it looked as
though he'd had trouble with his teeth.

Hitler was talking about Berlin's new stadium, where, in a few
days, the games of the XI Olympiad, the eleventh modern Olympic
Games, would take place. It had been constructed on the site of an
earlier stadium and it incorporated some of that building's steel
structure and the underground passageways which would allow VIPs
to go to their boxes without having to mix with the common folk.

Today, on his first real inspection of the Olympic facilities, Hitler
was accompanied by six other men: The architect Werner March, a
large bald fellow with heavy eyebrows and a substantial nose, who
was eagerly seeking Hitler's approval of his masterwork; Reich Sports
Leader and SA *Oberst*, Hans von Tschammer und Osten, a slim,
distinguished gentleman, born to a family of landed gentry, whose
chief job was to eliminate Jews from German sports; and Dr. Theodor
Lewald, the head of the German Olympics organization, a dignified
older man whose position had become somewhat tenuous when it was
discovered that his paternal grandfather was, as some Nazi wit had put
it, "a Red Sea pedestrian."

The other three were among Hitler's chief partners in the creation
and ascendancy of Nazi Germany: Luftwaffe chief Hermann Göring,
a portly, wavy-haired megalomaniac with a penchant for morphine and
fine art; Propaganda Minister Joseph Goebbels, small, clever, mordant
and club-footed; and the head of the Gestapo, the tall, handsome,
imperious Reinhold Heydrich, known, behind his back, as "Hitler's
hangman."

"I can't imagine how that building can seat 100,000 people," Hitler
continued, fixing an icy blue gaze on his architect.

"Ah, but it will, *mein Führer*," said Werner March. "Inside the
stadium, we have excavated the playing field by forty feet. This has

allowed us to build five additional tiers of seating. Come, I will show you."

March started toward the stadium and Hitler trailed behind him. "You'll see," said Dr. Lewald, scurrying to keep up. "It was the perfect solution to the problem." Hitler did not acknowledge the remark.

They entered at the main gate, passing through a neoclassical colonnade of rectangular, unadorned grey stone columns at the structure's outer wall and paused just inside. Hitler surveyed the building with a critical eye. "Half of it is below ground level," he observed, surprised.

"Exactly," said Werner March. He beamed.

"Very clever," Hitler allowed. He scanned the stands. It was a cool day for July, threatening rain.

"Imagine 100,000 people, cheering for our athletes," Goebbels suggested, "People from all over the world. It will be a triumph for the Third Reich, for the Aryan race."

"Where will I be sitting?" *der Führer* inquired.

"There," said Werner March, pointing at a slightly protruding section of the stands, which extended toward the sports field. "That's the honor loge, the best view in the stadium. You will be able to see everything."

"And everyone will be able to see you," Goering added.

Hitler smiled.

"Not all of our athletes will be Aryan, of course," Heydrich noted.

The smile died. Hitler turned to von Tschammer und Osten. "How many have we agreed to accept, Hans?"

"I am pleased to tell you, *mein Führer*, that not a single full-blooded Jew will be on the German Olympics team, as I promised," said the Reich sports chief.

Goebbels interrupted. "But, *mein Führer*, as we have discussed," he said, "to avoid an American boycott, we have accepted two *mischlings:* Helene Mayer, the fencer, whose mother is Aryan, and Rudi Ball, a hockey player, also half-Jewish. One other, Gretel Bergmann, the high jumper, fully Jewish, was allowed to train and compete in the trials, but she will not be on the German team."

Hitler waved a hand in dismissal. "Yes, yes," he said. "A necessary evil."

They walked onto the open field. A small group of workers up in the stands caught Hitler's eye. "A final clean-up," March said, anticipating *der Führer's* question.

Hitler turned to Goebbels. "And the *other* clean-up?"

"We are in the last stages, *mein Führer*. All of the Berlin signs and posters that might offend foreigners or non-Aryans are gone, and we're nearly finished cleaning up the outlying areas and other big cities. Nothing will be visible by the time the athletes and the tourists get here."

"Signs hidden or destroyed?"

"Hidden, *mein Führer*. They will go back up as soon as the games are over."

"Let's give it a full month, until all the outlanders have gone home."

"Of course. As you wish."

"How about you, *Obergruppenführer* Heydrich?" Hitler said. "You have given the necessary orders to the *Sicherheitsdienst,* the *Schutzstaffel,* the *Gestapo* and the *KRIPO?*"

"Yes," Heydrich said, in his incongruously high-pitched voice. He was a tall, haughty-looking man with limp, dark-blond hair, a long, narrow face and pale blue eyes. "The Brownshirts, the Stormtroopers, the Gestapo and the criminal police will be polite to everyone. While the games are going on."

"Good," said Hitler. "Let them exercise a little patience. In time, they will have the opportunity to express their strongest patriotic and racial passions."

Heydrich smiled, the smile of a cat who has been promised an endless supply of slow-moving mice.

Hitler strolled over to one of the racing tracks, bent down and scooped up a handful of the fine reddish cinders. "They run on this?"

"Yes," said *Oberst* von Tschammer und Osten. "They run very fast."

Hitler looked from one end of the track to the other, then a thought occurred to him. "Joseph, the newspapers—in the kiosks and the newsstands. I'm thinking especially of our friend Julius Streicher's publication. Tourists might consider it, well, inflammatory. The headlines can be quite sensational, as you know."

Goebbels nodded. "He is a fierce champion of racial purity, a crusader, but perhaps too raw for foreign visitors."

"Just so," said Hitler. "So let's keep *Der Sturmer* off the newsstands during the games. But see to it that delivery to my office is not interrupted."

"Yes, *mein Führer*," Goebbels said. "I will take care of it personally."

"As for the other newspapers, it would be a good time to fill the front pages with stories about happy families and contented workers," Hitler said.

"Yes. I will see to it."

Hitler poured the cinders back onto the track, brushed off his palms and walked on, hands clasped behind his back.

Luftwaffe Chief Hermannn Göring took a step toward Hitler's special box. He was wearing a splendid, medal-bedecked uniform, carefully tailored to his design (and his rotund body) from many yards of fine, pearl-grey woolen worsted, summer weight.

"Is the box of honor large enough to accommodate any guests *der Führer* might decide to invite, *Herr* March?"

"Yes, *Reichsmarshall*," said Werner March. "It will seat fifteen in comfort. It is the size of four ordinary boxes. There will be special chairs."

Göring seemed satisfied with this, but his question had reminded Hitler of his presence. "*Reichsmarshall*, I assume you have arranged for the appearance of the *Hindenburg*?"

"Yes, *mein Führer*," Göring said. "It will overfly the stadium just as you come into view."

Goebbels interrupted. "Nothing should interfere with *der Führer*'s entrance," he said. "The overflight must take place either well before he appears or after he is seated." He smiled at Göring, as though he had scored a point. Göring looked toward Hitler for help.

"After I am seated," Hitler decreed.

"Of course, *mein Führer*," Göring said, sounding like this is what he'd always intended.

"And the birds?" Hitler asked. "When will you release them?"

"We will release the pigeons after you are seated, of course," Göring said.

"They are not pigeons," Goebbels said. "They are doves."

"Pigeons," Göring insisted. "Twenty thousand of them."

"Doves," said Goebbels. "We got them from dovecotes all over the country."

Göring stepped closer to the smaller man, using his bulk to intimidate him. "Homing pigeons," he said. "From the army's stocks."

Heydrich, tallest of the three, stepped between Goering and Goebbels. "Doves and pigeons are biologically identical," he said. "I should know. I've shot enough of them."

"Doves are a symbol of peace," Hitler said, smiling at his squabbling associates. "So we will call them doves."

"Good idea. The word pigeon has a somewhat different connotation," *Obergruppenführer* Heydrich pointed out.

"Whatever we call them, they will still be *pigeons*," Göring insisted. He chuckled belatedly, trying to make a joke out of it. *Der Führer* walked toward one of the scoring tables. "The judges will sit here?" he asked, for the first time directing a question toward Dr. Lewald.

"Yes *mein Führer*," Lewald said, almost before the words were out of Hitler's mouth. "There will be three judges at each table, all from different countries. All told, we will have hundreds of judges."

"Hundreds of judges," Hitler said. "And thousands of spectators, enough to fill all the seats, I trust." It was meant to be a little joke, but no one laughed.

"It will be standing room only, I assure you," Goebbels said.

Hitler regarded his propaganda chief with his pale blue eyes. "You will guarantee that?"

"*Mein Führer*," Goebbels said, clearing his throat, "I will guarantee it. In the last six months, we have conducted an unprecedented promotional campaign throughout the world. Interest in the Olympics—and, if I may say so, in Germany—is intense. The trains and the hotels are sold out. People are coming from all over the world and when they get here, they will see a new Germany, a Germany stronger and more united than ever before, a Germany ready to lead the world. They will see the future."

"Yes," Hitler said, musing, "the future. Joseph, I have an idea. The 1940 Olympics are scheduled for Tokyo but after that, we will bring them back here, and they will remain here permanently, an eternal declaration of our heritage and our destiny."

"Brilliant idea, *mein Führer!*" Goebbels proclaimed. "The world should know that Germany is the true inheritor of the Olympic tradition. Today's Greeks have nothing to do with it."

Lewald thought he saw an opening. "The Olympics," he proclaimed, "will show the world how truly peaceful Germany is. They'll forget about the reoccupation of the Rhineland, which was rightfully ours of course, and the nullification of the shameful and unjust Treaty of Versailles."

"That's something the world had better not forget," Hitler said. "But you are right. The Olympics is a proclamation of German leadership, a demonstration of our strength and unity, never a defeated weakling."

It occurred to Hitler that he was beginning to orate, which was inappropriate for his audience. He stopped speaking and walked on, pausing at the broad-jump runway, stuck a tentative toe in the sand pit, and looked up at Tshcammer und Osten, a question in his eyes.

"*Mein Führer*, the competitors come down the runway, gathering speed, then, when they reach the starting board embedded in the ground, they leap," Tshcammer und Osten explained. "They land in the sand pit."

Hitler absorbed the information. "And if they pass the starting board before they jump…"

"They are disqualified. For that jump. They get three chances."

"I see" said Hitler. He continued on to the pole-vaulting station, shaking the upright standard until the crossbar wobbled. Tshcammer und Osten stood ready to explain, but Hitler walked on, to the shot-put station. A shot was lying on the ground and, with some effort, *der Führer* picked it up and hefted it experimentally.

"Just a bit over sixteen *pfund*," Tshcammer und Osten told him.

"Must have originated on the battlefield," Hitler said. "Soldiers throwing cannonballs."

"No doubt," said Tshcammer und Osten. "Then it became a sporting event. It's said that Henry VIII often won such competitions."

"This time, let it be a German," Hitler said.

"We have an excellent chance, *mein Führer*."

Hitler dropped the shot back on the ground. "Hans, how many medals did Germany win last time?"

Tshcammer und Osten thought a moment. "Germany won twenty medals at the 1932 Olympics in Los Angeles, *mein Führer*. We placed ninth. The Americans won, with over one hundred. I believe they won forty-one Golds."

"That must not happen this time," Hitler said. "This time, *we* must be the victors. And that is *your* responsibility, Col. Tshcammer und Osten."

"We will field the best team in German history," said Tshcammer und Osten. "Even so, I cannot *guarantee* victory. After all, we will be competing against the world's best athletes. The American track stars…"

"Such as Jesse Owens," said *Obergruppenführer* Heydrich.

Hitler's jaw tightened. "They have *no* shame," he said. "It is disgusting."

"Beg pardon?" Tshcammer und Osten asked, confused.

"It is a racial crime to permit the blacks to compete against white Aryans," *Obergruppenführer* Heydrich explained "They are a primitive people, not as evolved as Caucasians in general, and Aryans in particular. Theirs is nothing more than the strength of animals."

"When the Olympics returns to Germany," Hitler said, "they will have no place."

"But this time…" said *Obergruppenführer* Heydrich.

Hitler glared at his Gestapo chief. "This time," he said, his voice hard with barely controlled revulsion, "this time there is nothing we can do about it."

Chapter Three

The parcel arrived at the last minute, just as he was packing. It was brought by an elderly courier with a limp no less, just the man for the job, Nathan thought. It came in the form of a battered brown valise, which bore the fading embossed initials "S.E." That meant everything inside would have to be repacked into *his* suitcase. Early had an odd sense of humor, but he took his job seriously. Maybe he should do the same, Nathan thought, but the whole thing still seemed like a lot of fuss over not very much.

He poured the bag's contents on his bed: a fat envelope stuffed with enough *reichsmarks* paper money to wallpaper his bedroom, a little red *Baedecker's Guide to Berlin*, a pocket map of the city, an ex-library copy of *Mein Kampf,* the *Short History of the Olympic Games*, a well-used US passport with his picture, in the name of Michael Novak, a Press Pass from the *Cleveland Plain Dealer*, a folder of Jesse Owens newspaper clippings, a blank reporter's notebook, a packet of ship and train tickets and, finally, a blued .38 caliber Colt Super with scored walnut grips, nestled in a worn shoulder holster, plus three full magazines.

Nathan hefted the pistol. It was one of the most powerful handguns available, each magazine holding nine rounds. Ideal if you were contemplating armed robbery or a hostage rescue. He pulled his little Colt Police Positive Special out of his suitcase, re-holstered the Super and dropped it in, next to his copy of *Lost Horizon,* the new James Hilton. The Police Special went into a steel box in the closet, which he locked.

Nathan managed to stuff most of his clothing into the beat-up black suitcase his father had given him. Then, somehow, he closed it. He looked around—a few dishes in the sink, but they would keep. He locked up the room, then hauled the suitcase down three flights to stairs and found a cab. "Pier Sixty, please."

"You inna hurry?"

Nathan checked his watch—9:30. He had an hour until sailing time. "Not particularly. Why?"

"Lotta traffic there today. Crowds coming to send off the 'Lympic team."

"I heard."

The cab driver adjusted his mirror and strained his neck, the better to see his passenger. "You some kinda athlete?"

Nathan laughed.

Pier Sixty was on Manhattan's West Side, at 23rd Street. It was the New York home of the *S.S. Manhattan*, the largest liner ever built in America, except for her identical sister ship, the *S.S. Washington*. Today, the pier was jammed with taxis, private cars and pedestrians, the crowd there to glimpse their favorite athletes and throw confetti.

"This is as close as I can get," the cabbie said. They were at 21st Street and 11th Avenue, at the edge of the meatpacking district. Nathan tossed him a couple of bucks, then lugged his bags to the pier, shouldering his way through the crowd as politely as he could.

He finally got to the gangplank and joined the line of boarding passengers. A pimply young man in uniform took his tickets, handed him a room key and an information packet and tagged his bag, which a smiling Negro porter whisked away.

The pier-side rail of the enormous, black, slab-sided ship was jammed with happy travelers, waving gaily. Their opposite number lined the pier, by the thousands, also waving, but going nowhere. They were chanting "Hoo-Ray! Hoo-Ray! For the USA," and "A-M-E-R-I-C-A!" and throwing confetti and colored crepe paper streamers. Airplanes and dirigibles circled overhead.

Nathan's gaze slid along the ship's rail, as he studied the crowd like the good cop he was. It was a boatload of innocents, men, women, and children. But there were exceptions. His eye stopped on a small, furtive man trying to hide his face with his hat—a small-time card shark. Nathan recognized him from a police lineup.

Not far away was a stocky man, slightly bulging eyes, bad five o'clock shadow—he knew this thug. A Mafia enforcer. Better he was leaving the US than arriving. Two dowagers, one wearing a fox fur stole, the other proceeded by a tiny beige chihuahua, sauntered past the thug, oblivious. The thug maliciously stuck out a foot, hoping to trip the dog, who growled, then sunk his tiny teeth deep into the man's pant leg.

"Down, Daphne!" The dog-owning grande dame instructed brusquely. She swept the little beast up to her well-upholstered chest.

Then she skewered the thug with a look that made him cringe, and walked on, regal as ever. The lout belatedly scrutinized his torn pant leg with helpless dismay.

Down the rail a bit further, Nathan noticed a small, slender man in his early forties, well-dressed, graying hair perfectly combed, handsome, but with a yellowish pallor, eyes darting everywhere, studying the crowd just as Nathan was. The man unexpectedly looked directly at Nathan, who glanced away as quickly as he could. Something about this guy he didn't like, something precise and cold. Someone worth watching?

But where were the athletes? Nathan's gaze kept sliding down the rail, past hundreds of smartly dressed young men and women in straw boaters, white trousers and skirts and blue blazers bedecked with the Olympic shield. His eye caught on a trio of young Negro men in their midst, shouting toward friends on the dock, carefree and excited. One of these, he thought, must be the celebrated running champion. But which?

His question was answered in short order when a gaggle of middle-school boys pushed through the crowd waving paper and pencils, seeking autographs. Like ants heading for a gumdrop, they converged on one of the Negro men, the one with the broadest smile.

Nathan appraised his charge. Jesse Owens was not a towering figure. He was an average-sized man, about 5' 10', maybe 160 pounds, but something about him radiated power and energy. He was lean and compact, well-muscled, alert, sharp-featured. He handled the autograph-seeking boys with humility and good humor. Nathan liked him.

A question occurred to him: when did his job begin? Now, before the ship left? On the voyage? When they got to Berlin? But Nathan was just playing games with himself. He knew when his job began. It began the moment he'd spotted his charge. In other words, now.

"Take you to your stateroom, sir?" The question came from a young steward with apple-red cheeks, wearing a natty blue uniform and a silly little white pillbox cap.

"Yes, thank you," Nathan said. He wondered what kind of a room Steve Early had booked for him—it surely wouldn't be something in First Class.

The steward checked his ticket. "You're in Second Class," he said, as though he'd been reading Nathan's mind. "But with your press badge, you'll have access to the entire ship."

Nathan followed the steward down several flights of stairs, through a bewildering multitude of tunnel-like hallways, past cabin doors open and closed, the occupants settling in for the voyage.

"Just up here," the steward said, "in the corridor with all the newspaper people."

He was in stateroom number 438, an inside double room, and it wasn't much. Not even a porthole. If this was a stateroom, Nathan thought, he was on the good ship Lilliput. At least his bag was already there, lying on one of the narrow beds. Nathan checked the suitcase latches. No sign of tampering. Sprawled on the second bed was a tall young American, by all appearances a college student, all long legs and khaki, wearing a sweater with the letter "W," looking like a child of privilege. The young man sat up, grinned and extended a hand. "Dick Helms," he said. "United Press."

"You're a reporter?" Nathan asked. "You look…"

"I know, too young," Helms said. "But I graduated from Williams last year and I've been in London, working for the UP ever since."

"Ever since?"

"Well, they let me go home to see my folks, but I'm headed back to Europe now, to Germany, to cover the Olympics."

"Yeah," Nathan said. "Me too. For the *Cleveland Plain Dealer*. First assignment. I'm Mike Novak. So, we're sharing the room?"

Helms grinned. "Cabin made for two looks like. But it's the same for most of the journalists. Not a lot of papers willing to pick up the tab for singles or First Class, old man."

"No, guess not," Nathan said. Well, at least it helps with my cover, he thought. "Meet any others yet, the reporters?"

"Just a couple, in passing," Helms said. "But everyone's gathering at the grill room as soon as the ship sails."

The *S. S. Manhattan* chose that moment to sound off—a loud, two-note toot, followed by three chimes broadcast over the public address system, then an announcement: "This is the captain speaking. All visitors should be going ashore now. We'll be casting off in half an hour."

****

Nathan did a perfunctory job of unpacking, and Helms followed his example. Then he told Nathan he was going down the corridor, to the "head." "The john," Helms explained, when he saw Nathan's puzzled look. With Helms gone for the moment, Nathan slipped off his tweedy sports jacket, retrieved the holstered pistol from his suitcase and strapped it on. It would be his constant companion until the Olympics were over and Owens was safely home. He'd just managed to put the jacket back on before Helms reappeared.

After more tooting and announcements, the engine thrumming picked up and the ship ponderously backed out of Pier Sixty, pushed and pulled by a quartet of muscular tugboats. A flotilla of other boats, large and small, waited in the Hudson to escort America's Olympic team out of the harbor and on its way to Berlin.

"Time to go to the grill room, old man," Helms said.

The thought wouldn't have occurred to Nathan, who wasn't hungry, but it was time to blend in. "Which way?"

"No idea. We'll ask."

They waylaid their next-door neighbor, Alan Gould, an old hand with the Associated Press. He led them to the restaurant in question— a low-ceilinged room on the promenade deck, with picture windows in every direction, fitted out with little glass-and-chrome tables and chrome-and-leather chairs, passable American knock-offs of Bauhaus designs.

Nathan had imagined finding a dozen or so people munching on hamburgers and French fries, but no one was eating here. They were drinking, no longer needing to wait until the ship passed the three-mile limit. Twenty or thirty men and a couple of women, most of them in their mid-thirties or early forties, had gathered in little knots, laughing, arguing, expounding, everyone armed with a glass and a cigarette. The room was hazy with smoke. Some of the men were playing gin rummy. It was like a big fraternity party and Nathan didn't feel like a member. That would not do.

"See anybody you know?" he asked Helms, hopefully.

"Yes. Well, I don't *know* them know them," Helms said, "but I know who they are." He pointed them out discreetly, one by one. "The man in the grey suit, smoking a pipe, that's Paul Gallico. Writes for the *Washington Post*. Two guys he's talking to are Grantland Rice…"

"Sports writer for the *Herald-Tribune*," Nathan put in. "I read his stuff."

"Yes, and the other one is Bill Corum of the *New York Journal*."

"Anyone else?"

"The big guy at the left end of the bar, the curly haired guy who's laughing, that's Quentin Reynolds, of the Hearst News Service. He's talking with one of my colleagues at the AP—the short, balding guy, Louis Lochner. Louie's a good guy," Helms added. "He'll introduce us around."

"What about the two women at the other end of the bar?"

Helms peered through the smoky haze. "The taller one is Janet Flanner. She writes the 'Genet' columns for the *New Yorker*. The tough-looking one with the short hair is Sigrid Schultz. Works for the *Chicago Tribune*. Does radio commentary too."

"Formidable-looking woman," Nathan said.

Helms laughed. "I hear the Nazi bigwigs call her the dragon of Chicago."

At that moment, Louie Lochner spotted Helms and waved. "Dick, come on over. I want you to meet a friend of mine." Helms made his way to his colleague, Nathan tagging along. Then the introductions began.

They followed a pattern. The newspaper people accepted Helms, although they treated him like he was just out of high school. But every time Nathan said he was with the *Cleveland Plain Dealer*, he got flak.

"How come you're here instead of Alvin Silverman?" asked Fred Birchall of the *New York Times*. "Isn't Silverman their chief sports writer?"

"Actually, they weren't going to send anyone," Nathan said. "Too much money. They were going to use the wire service reports. But Dad was willing to fund the trip, if they gave me the assignment."

"Your father?" The question came from the United Press correspondent, Webb Miller, a tall, bespectacled man with thinning brown hair and buck teeth.

Nathan offered a deprecating smile. "Yeah. You see, Dad's a big advertiser with the *Plain Dealer*," he said. "And my job with the family department store wasn't working out. So we both thought, what with my interest in sports and journalism, that reporting on the Olympics would be great experience, make a great springboard for a new career."

Webb and Birchall exchanged world-weary glances. "Well, that's one way to get into journalism," Birchall said, taking a long sip of his drink.

It was more or less the same every time Nathan got himself introduced. They saw him as a tyro, an interloper, a scrounger. That was fine with him. They didn't have to love him. They had to believe him. And believe him they did, because they figured no one would volunteer for a biography like that if it weren't true.

Before long, word of Nathan's "press credentials" had spread throughout the shipboard watering hole to almost every newspaperman there, reporters from the *Baltimore Sun*, the *Washington Post*, and the *Brooklyn Eagle*, as well as eight different New York newspapers and even the *Daily Worker*. He—and to a lesser extent, Helms—found himself getting the cold shoulder at every turn.

They were saved by one of the best-liked journalists aboard, H. R. Knickerbocker, better known as "Red," a hard-charging red-haired Texan who wrote for the *New York Evening Post* and was quite well-watered that afternoon.

"Boys," he said loudly, putting one arm around Nathan's shoulder and the other around Helms'. "Come 'ere and have a drink with your Uncle Red. I wanna welcome you both to our honored and besotted profession. Bartender, set up these lads with the best Scotch in the house, on the boat, I mean."

"Don't mind if I do," said Richard Helms, with boyish enthusiasm.

"Thank you," Nathan said, embarrassed but trapped.

The bartender, a big man in his late fifties who had been with the *Manhattan,* and before that, the *Leviathan* for nearly a decade, and who had seen just about everything in his time, poured the drinks as directed, refilling Red's glass as well.

Red took drink in hand and turned toward the crowded tables. "Ladies and gennelmun," he called out. "I want you all to welcome two greenhorns—that is, *cub* reporters, to our ink-stained world, new initiates to our profession, in the hope that they come to enjoy its long hours and meager wages as much as we do. Here's to…what's your names again?"

"Richard Helms and Michael Novak," Helms said.

"…to Dick and Mike," Red concluded with a belch. He clinked glasses with them, and glasses clinked throughout the room in response. "Three cheers," the Texan boomed out, "Hip! Hip! Hooray!" The rest of the room joined in, reluctant but resigned to it.

For a moment, Nathan considered jumping overboard.

Chapter Four

Early in the morning of the third day out, the *S.S. Manhattan* ran into a storm, quite literally. She plowed directly into a huge, black, angry-looking cloud formation nearly sitting on the ocean. Its waves had roiled the waters into towering white caps, sending nearly solid sheets of ocean froth crashing into the superstructure and drenching the upper decks. And along with the rain and the waves came the wind—gale-level gusts, hitting the ship broadside, all seven hundred and five feet of her.

Faced with this pounding, the *Manhattan*—never one of the Atlantic's steadiest liners—began to roll, first to port, hanging at the extreme, then slowly back to the starboard, hanging again, as if making an agonizing decision—whether to roll back or capsize and head for the bottom.

The ship rolled nearly twenty degrees each way, like a lazy windshield wiper, terrifying everyone on the ship except those few who were sure, pretty sure, that she could take another five or maybe even seven degrees without turning turtle.

Most of the passengers, athletes included, were seasick and retching. Nathan was not among them. For reasons he could not fathom, he felt fine, physically. Mentally was a different matter. He couldn't help imagining the worst. He could almost read the headlines in his mind's eye: "*SS Manhattan* Sinks; Entire US Olympics Team Drowns; New York Cop Also Lost." So much for protecting Jesse Owens.

No one died, although practically everyone had expected to, either by vomiting out their internal organs or going down with the ship. Outside of a few bumped heads and a passenger's broken arm, damages were limited to everything that wasn't bolted down—china settings, ash trays, chairs, glassware, and the entire contents of practically every closet and dresser on board.

Sometime around the middle of the afternoon, the squall began to let up. By five o'clock, the seas were calm, the sun was shining, the skies were blue, the vomit had been cleaned up and the broken crockery swept overboard.

At dinnertime, Nathan roused Helms, who'd stopped retching, but was still pale and dehydrated. "Let's get something to eat, Dick. You'll feel better."

"Do I have to?" Helms asked.

Nathan offered a hand and pulled him out of bed. They made their way to the dining room, Helms wobbling a bit, and found that it was half-empty. One of those present, however, was the sallow-faced man, who was sitting alone, making notes of some kind, apparently unperturbed by the rough weather.

Helms and Nathan took seats at a distant table. "Do you know that guy?" Nathan asked.

"Which guy?"

Nathan pointed as discreetly as he could. Helms looked around the room, his eyes momentarily stopping at the sallow-faced man. "Nope."

"Not one of the press corps?"

"Not that I know of."

Nathan's gaze swept the room again and he took another look at the man. "Something odd about him."

"He seems to be traveling alone," Helms said. "That's a little unusual."

"Could you take a guess on his nationality?"

Helms glanced at the man again. "European, I'd say. Fork in the left hand. French. Or maybe German. Why are you so interested in him?"

"Not sure," Nathan said. He wasn't about to tell Helms he thought the guy might be an assassin. "If you had to guess his occupation, what would you say?"

Helms was amused. He took another look, just a glance. "Let's see now. Expensive clothing. Fashionable coiffure. Middle forties. Writes left-handed. A secret agent, no question of it."

"What? What makes you say that?"

"You do, old man" Helms said, laughing. "You're so suspicious of him. He's probably a glove salesman. Or maybe an architect. Now, if he wore a cloak and carried a dagger…"

Nathan managed a laugh of his own. "Just pulling your leg, Dick."

"Well, you got me," Helms said, grinning. "Good one."

The waiter appeared, a little man in a white uniform. Nathan ordered roast turkey, Helms asked for a steak. While they ate, the dining room slowly filled with passengers, some still pale after their morning tussle with *mal de mer*.

Nathan resisted the very strong urge to look at the sallow-faced stranger, to try to get a better handle on him. Finally, when he and Helms were drinking coffee and sharing a piece of Boston cream pie, he glanced toward the man's table. It was empty. Nathan stood.

"Going somewhere?" Helms asked.

"Thought I'd check out the movie," Nathan said.

"No action there," Helms responded. "Come with me to the First Class bar. Wine, women and song await."

Nathan surveyed the room, hoping to see the sallow-faced man. But he was gone. "Okay," he said, because he couldn't think of a way to say no.

The First Class bar, it turned out was directly above the Grill Room where the newspapermen hung out. It was a big room, lots of mirrored walls, decorated with mahogany and leather instead of chrome and glass.

By the time Nathan and Helms got there, the bar was mobbed with privileged passengers, most in their 40s and 50s, most in evening wear, all smoking and drinking, intent on proving that their partying urges had survived the storm. The ship's officers looked on, bemused, having seen it all before.

Helms and Nathan surveyed the room, looking for likely conversations to join, taking stock of the unattached females, and in Nathan's case, checking the place for miscreants. The sallow-faced man was nowhere to be seen.

"Uh-oh," Helms said, under his breath.

"Something's wrong?"

"Look at the little group near the right end of the bar."

Nathan looked. "Two men, two girls. The blonde one very pretty."

"The taller of the two men, the elegant one with the thinning hair? That, I believe, is the playwright Charles MacArthur." Helms said.

"MacArthur?"

"Yes, he wrote that play about the newspaper business, *The Front Page*."

Nathan nodded. "You know him?"

"No. But I know he's married to Helen Hayes, the actress. And I know that blonde girl is not Helen Hayes—that's Eleanor Holm, the Olympic swimmer I interviewed the other day."

"Uh-oh," Nathan said. "Brundage is going to have apoplexy if he sees her here."

"Even worse, old man, she's married—to the band leader Al Jarrett."

Nathan took a closer look at the girl. She was what the British call "smashing"—lithe, lively, playful, mischievous eyes, deep dark blonde hair that swung when she turned her head, a big, broad smile and a kittenish little laugh that would have disarmed any man. Nathan found her terrifying.

As he watched, she polished off a glass of champagne, only to have it immediately refilled by a roving waiter with a keen eye. She downed that one too and the waiter, who'd anticipated her needs, filled her glass again, while she pulled out a Lucky Strike out of a pack she'd found in her purse. MacArthur lit it with gold Alfred Dunhill lighter.

At that point, the little band that had played in the Grand Lounge the night before—a cellist, a violinist, a drummer, a clarinetist and what may have been the world's oldest piano player—reassembled in the First Class bar, and launched into a schmaltzy version of *Someone to Watch Over Me*. MacArthur whispered a few words to Eleanor Holm and the two of them strolled out onto the tiny parquet dance floor, still smoking, and slid into a slow foxtrot. Other couples soon joined them.

"Should we say something to her?" Nathan asked.

"Say something?" Helms asked. "Not me. I'm going to dance with her." He walked onto the dance floor, audacious as a carnival barker, tapped MacArthur on the shoulder and took over. But one dance was all she gave him.

Before the evening was over, Eleanor Holm had danced with half the men in the bar. It wasn't just that she was beautiful, although she surely was. It was that expressive face of hers. She had an astonishing repertoire of smiles—flirtatious smiles, wheedling smiles, mischievous smiles, mocking smiles, knowing smiles, pouting smiles, sexy smiles, tolerant smiles, challenging smiles and, simply, gay, carefree smiles of pure delight.

Nathan just sat back and watched, not just Eleanor but all of them, the whole slice of society that had gathered here, a Whitman's sampler of the high born and *nouveau riche*, in elegant gowns and tuxes. He studied them like the policeman he was, picking out the cons, the liars and the opportunists, male and female.

And sure enough, the sallow-skinned man showed up, briefly. He stood at the door on the other side of the room, scanned the room like a birdwatcher, and apparently finding nothing or no one of interest, and disappeared into the hallway shadows.

The evening went on. The orchestra got sloppy. The passengers got drunker and began to leave. Helms departed. Eleanor finally started running of gas. She walked to a table, a little uncertain on her feet, and sat down. A young waiter was at her side instantly, ready to refill her glass, but she waved him off and lit another Lucky Strike.

The room was more than half empty now and Nathan was ready to retreat to his cabin. But he sat, thinking of Jesse Owens. Roosevelt had given him a devil of an assignment—guard a man's life without ever letting him know he was being guarded. Was that even possible?

Across the room, a fat man in a tux with slicked-back black hair, wearing a star sapphire pinky ring on his left hand, hauled himself out of his seat and lumbered toward Eleanor Holm, weaving as he walked. He had something in mind and Nathan wondered how Eleanor would deal with him when she heard what it was. He watched the little tableau play itself out.

The fat man sidled up to Holm and put an arm around the back of her chair. She finally looked up at him, in curiosity. He said something to her. She laughed a little and shook her head. He let his arm slip over her shoulders. She tried to disengage, without success. Now she looked at him more sternly and Nathan didn't need to be a lip reader to know what she said: "Please go away," perhaps, or something less polite. This did not have the intended result. In fact, the fat man reached down and put a paw on her hand.

Nathan found himself walking in their direction, determined to do something, he had no idea what. As he approached them, he called out, "Hi, Eleanor, I'm sorry I'm late." Both the girl and the fat man looked at him in surprise. "Hello," Nathan said, sticking a hand out toward the fat man. "I'm Mike Novak, *Cleveland Plain Dealer*."

The fat man regarded Nathan with confusion, but withdrew his paw from Eleanor's hand and shook Nathan's. "Jim Moss," he said, slurring the double s. "Moss Oldsmobile. Dearborn, Michigan."

"Nice to meet you," Nathan said. "Eleanor, we'd better go. They're waiting for us upstairs."

Eleanor smiled up at him and rose. "Well then, um, Mike, I guess we'd better get goin'." Her speech was pretty slurred too. "Nice t'meetcha, Mr. Moss," she said. Nathan casually detached Moss's arm from Eleanor's chair and walked her away from the table.

When they were out of range of the fat man, Eleanor turned to Nathan. "First, thank you," she said, her tongue stumbling on the 'th.' Second, who are you again?"

"Mike Novak," Nathan said. "I'm a journalist covering the Olympics for the *Cleveland Plain Dealer*."

"Hah!" She said drunkenly, "like Hell you are."

"Well, to be truthful, this is my first assignment and I…"

"I'll bet you've never even read the *Cleveland Plain Dealer*."

"Every morning, since I was twelve," he said.

She stood back and appraised him with a knowing grin. "You're no journalist. You're a flatfoot. I know flatfeet when I see them. My brother is a flatfoot. And I'll bet that lump in your jacket is a gun. So what are you doing on the boat? You're no tourist. No athlete either. Are you chasing a bad guy? Or maybe protecting somebody?"

"I'm a newspaper man," Nathan insisted. "And you don't want to be a news story, do you?"

Before he could stop her, Eleanor slipped a hand under his jacket lapel. She wrapped her fingers around the pistol. "They're arming journalists now?" She said. "Hey, look everyone," she called out. "Take a look at the…"

Nathan pulled her into the hallway before she could finish her sentence. "Would you mind shutting up?" he hissed.

She responded with a coquettish smile. "Would you mind telling me who you really are?" She gave the pistol a mischievous little tug. "You're a cop aren't you?"

The only way to shut her up, Nathan decided, was to tell her the truth, at least a little of it. "Yes, on a confidential mission."

"A secret mission?" Eleanor said, eyes wide. "Tell me!"

"I said 'confidential,'" Nathan said. "And I *can't* tell you. It's *confidential*."

"Hey, look everyone!" She tugged on the gun, serious this time.

"Stop that!" Nathan said, trying to pull away from her.

"Tell."

Half a dozen stories flitted through Nathan's mind—he was chasing an escaped convict, he was a private dick tracking down an unfaithful spouse, he was an FBI agent on the trail of a saboteur. She wouldn't believe any of them. Worse, they would gain him nothing.

On the other hand, if he swore her to secrecy and maybe even asked her help getting close to Owens and keeping an eye on him, it was just possible she could be useful. But could she be trusted—this brash, brazen, mercurial beauty, this dizzy, audacious dame? Or in the end, would she need more rescuing?

"Please?" Eleanor said, and she batted her eyelashes at him.

It was a simple choice: keeping mum and risking being exposed to everyone on board, including the athletes, or inviting this creature to be a co-conspirator and hoping he could control her. Some choice.

Nathan found a chair, sat her down on it and took a deep breath. "All right, I'll tell you what I can, Eleanor. I'm on a top secret assignment from the government…"

"Oh yeah?"

Top secret wasn't going to work, not with this one. He had only one choice. "Listen, Eleanor," he said. "Are you a patriot? Can I count on you?"

She looked directly into his eyes, serious for a moment. "You can say a lot about me, Mike, but I love my country. You can count on that."

Nathan took another deep breath, then plunged ahead. "Okay. Here's the truth: I'm working for the President himself. He's asked me to make sure nothing happens to Jesse Owens during the Olympics." He regretted telling her even as the words were coming out of his mouth, but there was no taking back what he'd said.

Eleanor tried to focus. "Jesse Owens the runner?"

"Jesse Owens the runner. The *Negro* runner. The man who, Roosevelt hopes, will show Hitler and the world that this Aryan superiority nonsense is just that: nonsense."

She stared at him for a moment, as if trying to comprehend what he was saying. "This is the secret?"

"Yes. FDR wants me to stay entirely in the background, not to attract any attention, and not to worry Owens. So I haven't told him. The only person I've told is you. I'm trusting you, God knows why. Can you keep it to yourself?"

"Has Owens been threatened?"

"No. But the President doesn't want to take any chances. Can you keep the secret?" That was the question Nathan should have asked her before he spilled the beans, he told himself.

For a moment, Eleanor turned serious. "Of course I can. No one's better than I am at keeping secrets. I'm keeping dozens of them right now. I've kept secrets since I was thirteen. It's a habit, Mike."

"Good habit," Nathan said, telling himself that if he'd gone this far, he might as well go the whole way. "One other thing." Nathan said. "It's not Mike Novak. It's David Nathan. I'm a New York City cop."

"I knew it," she said, triumphant. "An *at-flay-ootfay*."

Nathan offered a lukewarm smile. "*Icksnay* on the *at-flay-ootfay* stuff," he said.

"Sorry," she said. She briefly buried her head in her hands. "I'm a little dizzy."

"Time to get you back to your room, I think."

"But the secret…"

"We can talk more about that tomorrow. What's your room number?"

Eleanor laughed. "They put me in Third Class, wouldya believe it?"

"I think all the athletes…D deck?"

"Damned if I know," she said.

"Got your key?"

She opened her purse and fumbled around with such incompetence that he took it from her. "D deck. Room 134," he said, reading the key. "Come on. I think I know where it is."

It took them fifteen minutes to get to the room, partly because Nathan had trouble finding it, partly because Eleanor could barely walk.

As they approached the room, they bumped into a battleship of a woman with a halo of sparse, steel-grey hair. "What's going on here?" She demanded.

"None your bidness," Eleanor explained.

"You're quite mistaken, young lady. It *is* most definitely my business. I am Mrs. Ada T. Sackett, chaperone of the US women's swimming team. And just who are you?"

"I," said Eleanor, doing her very best to stand up straight, "I am Mrs. Eleanor Holm Jarrett. And *I* am a *member* of the Olympic swim team. Do you swim?"

Nathan winced. "Eleanor, I think it's time for you to go to bed."

"Oh? Bedtime already?" she asked, slurring every word.

"Evidently, Mrs. Jarrett, you have been drinking intoxicating spirits," Mrs. Sackett announced. She could have been accusing the girl of premeditated murder.

"A just little bit," Nathan allowed. "There was a party in the First Class bar…"

"The hussy was in the First Class bar?"

'Probably by mistake," Nathan said.

Mrs. Sackett snatched the key from his hand and knocked on the door of Room 134. It opened almost immediately and two other girls popped their heads out of the tiny cabin. Seeing Eleanor's condition, and clearly horrified by it, they pulled her inside and closed the door.

Mrs. Sackett fixed Nathan with a Medusa-like gaze. "What is your name, young man?"

"Mike Novak. I'm a reporter for the *Cleveland Plain Dealer*."

"What were you doing with Mrs. Jarrett? Fraternizing is against the rules."

"I wasn't with her. I was just seeing her back to her room."

Mrs. Sackett looked at Nathan as if she were examining a particularly ugly bug. "You haven't heard the last of this, Mr. Novak. You can count on that."

She looked him up and down one last time, then turned on her heel and strode away, as though hoping to find more victims to eviscerate.

"But I…" Nathan protested. She kept walking.

Nathan briefly considered checking on Eleanor, finally deciding it was not a good idea. He had no business getting involved with Eleanor Holm Jarrett. He'd let himself be swayed by a pretty face. And now he was going to pay a price for it. The only question was: how much?

Chapter Five

Reichsminister Joseph Goebbels watched them get into their big, open-topped Mercedes—Hitler, Heydrich, Göring and the others. He liked being last. He was self-conscious about his limp and this way no one got an opportunity to observe him.

They thought he'd been born with it, a club foot. But that wasn't it at all. He had no birth defects. He'd had a childhood run-in with osteomyelitis—a bone infection. As a result, one leg was shorter than the other. Surgery had only made it worse. So he wore a metal brace and a special shoe. Some people thought he'd been wounded in the Great War. He didn't correct them.

Goebbels knew he wasn't a prepossessing figure—a few inches over five feet tall, slender, with a narrow, deeply-creased face, a slash of a mouth and deep set eyes. But he had an exceptionally subtle mind, and he considered himself the only man in Hitler's inner circle with a sense of humor.

Aside from *der Führer* himself, Goebbels was the party's foremost orator. He could play the masses like a piano, he liked to say, not by shouting and exhorting, although he had his passions, but by cynically appealing to their basest instincts: racism, xenophobia and class envy. He could turn them into puppets at will, making them sing, stand up, chant *Seig Heil*, raise their arms to salute Hitler and parrot oaths. Franz Mesmer had nothing to teach him.

Goebbels climbed into the deeply-cushioned back seat of the gleaming, black *Grosser* Mercedes and told his chauffeur to take him to his headquarters, the Ministry of Propaganda, which occupied the 18th-century Leopold Palace on *Wilhelmstrasse*, just across from Hitler's offices in the Reich Chancellery. It was only a fifteen-minute drive from the Olympic stadium.

As he rode along *Bismarckstrasse*, past the tree-lined streets and elegant houses of Charlottenburg and through Berlin's great park, the Tiergarten, with its equestrian paths and rows of patriotic statutes, he considered Hitler's words at the stadium, his remarks about *der* Nigger runner, Owens. 'There is nothing we can do about it," he'd said. But was that really true?

Hitler's comment tugged at Goebbels' memory, vaguely reminding him of something he'd heard while getting his Ph.D. from Heidelberg, something the English King, Henry II, had murmured about the Archbishop of Canterbury, Thomas a' Becket, in 1170 or so, "Will no one rid me of this troublesome priest?"

As Goebbels recalled, four of Henry's knights had overheard that remark and they'd known what the King meant. He wanted Becket dead. And they'd fulfilled his wish. Now, he was in a position to fulfill Hitler's wish—not to kill Jesse Owens, which would be injudicious, but to thwart his effort to win any gold medals.

The chauffeur brought Goebbels' Mercedes to a gentle stop in front of the Ministry, got out, and opened the door for him. "Park the machine in the back," said the Propaganda Minister. "I won't be needing it for the rest of the day."

Goebbels stood at the curb for a moment and surveyed his domain. It was an attractive, good-sized two-story gray stone building, with a wide, handsome colonnade at the front door, a fairly unremarkable structure in a city, and especially a street lined with monumental buildings.

But it was in this building that he was directing the total makeover of Germany's cultural, intellectual, and even emotional life. It was from his office in this building that he was controlling every newspaper, book, novel, play, movie, radio broadcast, demonstration, parade, celebration and even band concert, from national enterprises to local weeklies and village choirs.

It had been, he reflected, a titanic effort. When he'd left the *Reichstag* and taken office three years ago, for instance, Germany had some 3500 newspapers, and only 120 supported Hitler. Out of this chaos, he had created a German press that spoke with a single voice. The same was true of every other means of transmitting culture and information. And now, such was the power of self-censorship that he was free to focus his efforts on what really counted this summer: the Olympics.

Goebbels squared his shoulders and walked into the Ministry, where he was immediately *Heil*ed by half a dozen underlings who happened to be walking by. It was a good group, he told himself. Seven hundred hand-picked young men, over half of them with some university education. The annual budget was $35 million reichsmarks, equivalent to about $3.5 million US, and it was growing fast. All told, a very powerful machine. And he was very pleased to be driving it.

But now he had business to take care of, an idea to pursue, a project that would gain him even more favor with *der Führer* than he had already. He headed down the hallway toward his office, automatically responding to the gauntlet of *Heil* Hitlers coming from passing assistants, secretaries, and clerks.

The *Reichsminister's* office was not the equal of Göring's gaudy monstrosity in the Air Ministry building just down the street, but Goebbels didn't mind. The office reflected the man and his was modest in size but organized to the point of genius, visually noteworthy only because of a beautiful chestnut parquet floor and an Aubusson rug that would have been at home in Versailles.

"*Heil* Hitler!" said Trudy Dingfelder, his secretary, blonde, red-lipped, big-busted, pretty in a vulgar way, and really too dumb for this job.

Goebbels did the *Heil* Hitler again. He'd had his fill of Trudy in every way that he'd cared to. It was time to make her dreams come true and send her off to the movie studios. Maybe they could do something with her, other than what he'd already done. He needed someone new—perhaps a brunette this time. Ah, women. Every man deserved at least one indulgence and this was his.

"Trudy," Goebbels said, "Ask State Secretary Essen and Deputy State Secretary Funk to come to my office, please." He sat down behind his desk, a custom-made walnut expanse with a plate glass top and enough secret drawers and cubbyholes to accommodate the complete espionage files of a small Balkan nation.

"Now?" Trudy asked. Her distinct Saxon accent was distinctly low class, almost harsh.

"What do you mean?"

"Should I call them now, or do you want to see them now?"

Goebbels smiled. "Both, I think."

"Oh," she said. "I forgot. Otto Griessing is here. He asked to see you as soon as you came in. He's brought a new *Volksempfänger.*"

"Ah. Tell him to come in. And call the others."

Otto Griessing, an electrical engineer, was a thin, pale, diffident-looking fellow, wearing delicate, wire-rimmed glasses with octagonal lenses. He was carrying—with some effort—a large brown Bakelite table radio, with a prominent round speaker, three knobs, and a frequency indicator on the front.

"Come in, Otto. Put the radio on my desk."

Griessing did as he was told. "This is the VE 301 Wn, *Reichsminister*," he said. "A great improvement over the current model. I'll demonstrate."

Goebbels nodded.

The engineer found an outlet, plugged in the radio and turned one of the knobs until it clicked. The dial slowly began to glow with a faint orange light. A hiss emerged from the speaker. Greissing fiddled with another knob and the hiss turned into Wagner's *Parcival*, apparently the third act.

Goebbels held up a hand and produced a grim smile. "I think that's enough."

He had to repeat himself before Greissing got the idea and turned off the instrument.

Goebbels stood and briefly examined the thing. "Looks a lot like its predecessor," he said, disappointed. "What makes this one better?"

"The most important improvement is that the antenna doesn't have to be removed every time you change the frequency. It's easier for ordinary people to use."

"Good."

"And the dial has the station names."

Goebbels nodded. "Anything to simplify operation," he said. "And the sensitivity?"

"Low. Not enough to receive foreign stations clearly, even on our borders, as you directed."

"Excellent. How much will it cost?"

"We've got it down to *RM* 87."

Goebbels considered this, then shook his head. "That won't do," he said. "That's at almost three weeks' wages for the average worker. I want them in every home, every restaurant, every barbershop, every store. When Hitler speaks, *everyone* must hear him."

Greissing cleared his throat, his nerves showing. "With a cheaper cabinet," he said, "We might be able to cut the price by, say *RM* 20."

Goebbels sat back in his chair and folded his arms across his chest and gazed at Greissing without expression. "Cheaper," he said.

"But, but…"

"*Much* cheaper."

Little beads of sweat broke out on Greissing's forehead. "Perhaps, if we changed the rectifier and switched to a wooden cabinet, we might be able to reduce the price to *RM* 50, but…"

"It must cost no more than one week's average wages, *Herr* Greissing. *RM* 35," Goebbels said, then he had another thought. "How much do *you* earn each week?"

"Um, well, about *RM* 150, Minister Goebbels."

"I see," said Goebbels. He opened a drawer, found a pencil and made some notes. Then he looked up with a friendly smile. "Now, if we were to cut your salary down to *RM* 50 and use the rest to defray the cost of the radio, what would it cost?"

Greissing's mouth fell open. "Cut my salary?" He managed to gasp.

"Yes, and if we eliminated your company's profit…"

"Eliminate the profit?"

"Of course. You don't expect to make a profit on the People's Radio do you? Some might consider that …unpatriotic."

"No, of course not," Greissing stammered. "I just forgot to subtract the profit."

"Totally understandable," Goebbels said. He was smiling and his eyes were glittering. "So, shall we say *RM* 30?"

"It cost us *RM 36* to make!" Greissing objected, then realized what he'd said.

Goebbels smiled again. "*RM* 36. That sounds just right. You'll have my authorization for mass production on your desk tomorrow morning." He stood and extended a hand. Greissing took it and shook, weakly. Then he unplugged his radio, tucked it under one arm and left, shoulders sagging.

As he walked out, Trudy stuck her blonde head inside. "State Secretaries Esser and Funk are here."

"Show them in."

Although he was a fat man, Hermann Essen looked a bit like Hitler. He wore his black hair slicked down and combed to one side, and he affected a mustache that shamelessly imitated *der Führer's.* He'd joined the Nazi party in 1920, along with Hitler, and had become editor of the Nazi paper, *Völkischer Beobachter.* He had a well-known and apparently insatiable appetite for underage girls, but Hitler forgave him his foibles.

Walther Funk was a bald, burley, moon-faced man, a self-anointed intellectual who had also had a journalistic background, having once edited the center-right financial newspaper the *Berliner Börsenzeitung* and he had served as the Nazi party's chief press officer. His specialty now was economics.

"*Meine Herrens*," Goebbels said, indicating his office's guest chairs, "please have a seat."

They sat, and regarded him quizzically.

"I've summoned you to help me with a very special project," he said, "a secret project. It's outside of your usual fields of expertise, but you're the most able people I have and I'm hoping the three of us can find a way to give our leader a little present."

Both readily agreed to help any way they could, and Goebbels explained what he had in mind—making sure Jesse Owens never won an event at the Berlin Olympics.

"I don't see the problem," said Hermann Essen. "A sharpshooter in the right place, at the right time, a bomb in his room at the Olympic Village…"

"Poison in his food," Funk said, joining in. "Kidnapping—and discreet disposal. Almost any SS unit could do the job. Take him from his bed at night. Or we could…"

"Gentlemen, gentlemen," Goebbels said, scolding, "if that's what I wanted, I would have consulted *Herr* Heydrich, not you."

"Heydrich?" Essen chuckled and Funk looked at him in horror. "What are you laughing at?"

"I don't know," Essen said with a shrug, "It just seemed to me…"

"The reason I summoned you two," Goebbels said, "is that I'm looking for a *subtle* way to stop Owens. It would be easy enough, I suppose, to have him assassinated, but that would make Germany a pariah for decades to come. We want the Olympics to glorify Germany, not vilify it."

"So, no beatings, no kidnappings, no assassinations," Funk said.

"Exactly," said Goebbels.

"Well," Essen said, gazing out the window, pursing his lips and then looking back at Goebbels with a sly smile. "We could easily arrange to look blameless. *Herr* Owens could suffer from a fatal beating or a bullet in the head and we could discover that the perpetrator was a known Communist thug. We could be appropriately horrified. We could execute the assassin.

"What?" Funk said, objecting, "we already did that with the Reichstag fire and the Dutch Communist fall guy. I think no one would believe us this time."

"I agree, Walther," Goebbels said. "And we should consider something else as well. 'The Night of the Long Knives,' as the foreign press called it, is still fresh in people's memory. You can't murder one hundred people—even if they are traitors—without sowing doubt and discontent."

"It was only eighty people," Essen said.

"It was just over three hundred, if you're being a stickler for accuracy," Goebbels said, "Not only Hitler's old 'friends' Ernst Röhm and Gregor Strasser and the rest of the SA leaders, but all of his other enemies."

"That was two years ago," Essen pointed out.

"Still, we do not wish to remind anyone of that event. It made us seem brutal."

"Which has been very useful," Funk said. "Let us not forget that."

"Perhaps. But we do not wish to remind the rest of the world, especially at the Olympics," Goebbels said. "So, if we are to stop *ein Schwarzer*, we must be ingenious and sophisticated."

Goebbels pulled open one of his innumerable desk drawers and extracted a thick folder." These are clippings about *Herr* Owens, which I have been studying," he said. He handed it to Essen, who leafed through the pages.

"And what have you learned?" Funk asked. He took the folder from Essen and did his own browsing.

"Owens is an innocent creature, not very bright. Charmingly superstitious," Goebbels said. "And since he is of a lower order, he is a man of high emotion, easily shaken. I am convinced if we can upset him sufficiently, that would ensure his failure. That is his fatal flaw." Goebbels cast an inquisitive glance at Essen, then at Funk. "Any thoughts on how to capitalize on that?"

Chapter Six

Reichsminister Hermann Göring, Commander-in-Chief of the *Luftwaffe*, the German Air Force, paused for a moment in front of his headquarters. The Air Force Ministry, largest of all of the government buildings on *Wilhelmstrasse,* was, in fact, the largest building in Berlin, with two thousand rooms. a five-story limestone and concrete structure of block-like, interlocking rectangles, reminiscent of a prison. It was the first Nazi structure to be completed since Hitler took power three years earlier.

Göring was a man whose boyhood dreams had come true, and more spectacularly than he could have imagined. When he won the Blue Max and took over von Richthoven's Flying Circus in 1918, after the British finally managed to shoot down the Red Baron, it seemed as though fortune had decided to smile on him.

But now he had Hitler on his side as well, and that had given him command of more than one thousand of the world's most advanced war planes, the funds to double their number within the next three years, and had put him in charge of a research and development program unmatched anywhere in the world, with seven thousand men at his beck and call.

Göring saw himself as a big man, a very big man, and for more reasons than one. He was physically large, of course—two hundred and seventy pounds and heading up. He had a large appetite, not only for food and drink, and for fine art—but most of all, for *power*. And his efforts had been rewarded. He was one of the rulers of the Third Reich, the most capable man in the government, with the possible exception of Hitler, certainly more important than the little crippled weasel Goebbels, the clever one on the other side of *Wilhelmstrasse,* he was sure.

Göring strode into the building, feeling full of himself. He had come a long way since the 1923 failed 'Beer Hall Putsch," during which Hitler was arrested and Göring wounded, suffering injuries that lead to a lifetime love of morphine.

Göring's aide, *Oberst* Otto Katzenzimmer, stood at the back door to the *Reichsmarshall's* office, a well-built young man with a strong, Aryan features and wavy blond hair the color of corn silk.

Katzenzimmer wore the *Luftwaffe's* standard dress uniform—a white shirt and a black tie, under a four-pocket dark grey worsted tunic with gold braid on the right shoulder and a curio case's worth of medals on the chest. He *Heil*ed as Göring approached and the *Reichsmarshall* responded perfunctorily.

"Is Hans-Dietrich Knoetzsch here yet?" Göring asked.

"In the ante-room. Shall I send him in?"

"Give me a minute," said the *Reichsmarshall*. He slipped into his office and briefly inspected it. The gold-colored silk drapes were open and the sun illuminated the westwall on which he'd hung a Monet, a Cezanne and a Manet. He'd filched them from the *Alte Nationalgalerie*, and now considered them his permanent possessions. On the opposite wall, momentarily in the shadows, was a gigantic, almost overpowering gilt-framed portrait of Hitler, looking warm and benevolent. At Hitler's feet was Blondi, his German Shepard.

The marble floor, Göring was pleased to see, had been freshly waxed and it appeared that the intricate Persian rug pilfered from the Pergamon Museum had been vacuumed that morning. Someone had also dusted his desk, a huge, ultra-modern affair made of machined aircraft aluminum panels and rods, and topped with a slab of rose quartz two inches thick. It was covered with stacks of paper and reports.

Göring settled heavily into his thickly-cushioned, armchair, more a throne than a piece of office furniture. He thumbed through the papers on his desk, pushing some to one side, stacking others in the middle for more immediate attention. Then he pressed the little buzzer under the desktop. A few seconds later, he heard a soft knock on his office door. "Come," he said, sitting up straight, in hopes of disguising his belly.

The man who entered Göring's office was a tall, rakish, mustachioed figure, with a sly, engaging smile, bursting with self-confidence. He was Hans-Dietrich "Bubi" Knoetzsch, chief test pilot of the *Bayerische Flugzeugwerke,* the Bavarian Aircraft Works.

As was his custom, Bubi was dressed in a pilot's outfit—gray cap, long gray coat with pockets down most of its length, and puffy gray gaiters over a pair of scuffed black boots. He had greasy hands and dirty fingernails

"Bubi, Bubi," the *Reichmarshal* said, extending his hand despite the grease and offering a warm smile. "It is so good to see you again. Please, sit, sit."

"Thank you, Hermann," said Knoetzsch, who considered himself on a first-name basis with everyone but Hitler. He sat down in the larger of the two red leather guest chairs, took the crystal ashtray off Göring's desk, laid it in his lap and lit a Reetsma cigarette.

"So, Bubi. You are well? Willy Messerschmitt's plane—it's keeping you busy?"

"I am enjoying myself, as usual."

You've had the Bf-109 for about a week now…"

"Actually, three weeks."

"Yes, good. Tell me what you think of it. If it passes muster, I plan to make it our chief fighter-interceptor. We'll build thousands of them."

Knoetzsch took a deep drag and slowly exhaled. "I like it," he said, the 'but' hanging heavily in the air, unsaid.

"Good," said Göring. He clapped his hands together.

"Of course it has flaws," Knoetzsch went on. "The rudder is too small. It's not good at controlling the propeller slipstream at the beginning of the takeoff roll."

"But *you* can control it," Göring prompted.

"Of course. But inexperienced pilots…if they don't, that will create a high load on the wheel opposite to the swing. The landing gear could collapse."

Using a gold pen, Göring made a note on a small pad. "That can be fixed."

"I hope so," Knoetzsch said. "Also, the plane has a very large ground angle. When you're in the cockpit, all you can see is sky. To see the runway, you have look out the side window and swerve from side to side as you taxi."

"I see," Göring said, making another note.

"And all that swerving—that puts a lot of stress on the landing gear. A taller tail wheel would help both problems." Knoetzsch took another drag on his cigarette.

"We can see about modifying later models," Göring said, continuing to write.

"We'd better—or we're going to lose pilots."

"But it performs well?"

Knoetzsch chuckled. "Not with the current engine." Göring's face fell and the test pilot noticed it. "Don't worry, it will be better when we get the Jumo 210A engine in October. Then it will climb faster and have better maneuverability than anything else I've ever flown. A higher top speed too—perhaps 640 kilometers an hour."

"In a dive?"

"No. In level flight."

"Impressive," Göring said, sliding back in his chair. He felt the impulse to put his feet on his desk, and in the old days, he might have done it. Now he had this stomach. "How does it compare to the best foreign aircraft?"

"Hah! The Americans." Knoetzsch smiled with contempt. "They have nothing. Neither do the French, so far as I know. The British— well, they have a project that might give us problems. The Spitfire. But they're at least a year behind us. Right now, the Bf-109 is the best fighter in the world. Potentially."

Göring nodded, pleased. "I'm going to make it a top priority," he said.

"And fix the flaws," Knoetzsch reminded him. "Especially the ground angle."

"Of course," Göring said, leaning forward. "Tell me, Bubi, is the prototype in good enough shape for a public demonstration?"

"Possibly. But why would you want to draw attention to it? No reason to show it to our friends in Britain and France."

Göring smiled. "There is no longer a reason to hide it, Bubi. And there *is* a reason to show it in public. It's called *intimidation.* Let them know how far behind they are."

"Okay," the pilot said, "if you say so. What did you have in mind?" He stubbed out his cigarette in the crystal ashtray, which he replaced on Göring's desk.

Göring smiled. "How about a fly-over at the opening of the Olympics?"

Knoetzsch raised an eyebrow. "I think that could be arranged."

"Good. Arrange it." Göring resumed inspecting the papers on his desk.

"As you wish," Knoetzsch said, realizing the interview was over.

"Excellent," Göring said. "Keep me informed of your progress."

They shook hands again and Göring was once more alone in his office. He continued to fiddle with the stack of papers, but his heart wasn't in it. He'd gotten an idea at the Olympic stadium that morning and it wouldn't go away.

A single dark cloud hovered over the games, *dark* indeed Göring thought, pleased with his pun. And if he could dispel the cloud, Hitler would be delighted, in particular, delighted with *him*. He could imagine Hitler's smile, his handshake of congratulations. And he could imagine Goebbels' defeated expression. How satisfying it would be to thwart that crippled weasel.

But how to do it, that was the question. A serious injury would probably be enough. Of course, it would be simpler to kill the American sprinter, but if he did that, it could backfire. No, injury was the way to go. Something that looked like an accident, or a random attack that couldn't be traced back to him or the government, something Hitler would understand.

Göring reached down to a lower desk drawer and slid it open. There were two objects inside: a cellophane bag of *Lustschbonbons*, his favorite candy fruit drops, and a small wooden box. He opened the box. It contained several small glass vials and a syringe. After a moment's hesitation, he closed the box and took out the candy bag. He poured out half its contents on his desktop, unwrapped a dozen pieces, shoveled them into his mouth and began sucking and crunching.

He would need a good man, he told himself. Someone clever, decisive and, not to be coy about it, brutal; someone who knew how to keep a secret; someone absolutely unstoppable. He thought back, remembering his Nazi colleagues from his old days. He considered the best of his *Luftwaffe* officers and the Stormtroopers and Brownshirts he knew.

One name kept coming up: *Oberstleutnant* Alfred von Falkenhorst, a big, yellow-haired man with whom he'd often hunted and ridden, a man of impeccable breeding, an athlete and a fine shot, a man with an unconventional mind, a casually cruel man, as courageous as a lion. Yes, von Falkenhorst was perfect for the job.

Göring picked up his ivory-colored telephone.

Chapter Seven

The *Fliegender Hamburger* rolled into the grand, barrel-vaulted steel and glass shed of Berlin's *Lehrter Bahnhof,* at 11:35 a.m., ten minutes ahead of schedule. But the station was ready. Hundreds of eager Germans crowded the platforms and concourses impatient to welcome the American Olympics team, waving US flags and cheering, throwing flowers and frequently shouting *Yes-see, Yes-see Ons* at the US superstar Long red Nazi banners with bold black swastikas hung from the walls, interspersed with big Olympic flags. Several Gestapo officers in long, black leather overcoats looked of, their expressions unreadable.

Nathan caught Knickerbocker's eye. "They seem happy to see us," he said.

"They do," the reporter admitted. "Not quite what I expected."

After going through customs with their luggage, the Americans passed through a corridor of torch-bearing German youths, to the accompaniment of cheers and live music from a uniformed marching band, followed by three thankfully short speeches by the local officials,

Nathan hung back with Eleanor and Richard Helms, trying to keep an eye on Owens, and nervously scanning the throng. This would be the perfect moment for it, he thought—noise, confusion, crowds. Someone could take a shot or slip a knife into Owens' guts and simply melt into the mob. And Nathan wouldn't even know it had happened until Jesse was down.

Suddenly, someone pushed past, jostling him. It was the man with the sallow face, perhaps the last man off the train, and this time, his eyes met Nathan's and caught. He smiled, at least with the lower half of his face. "Excuse me, sir," he said, his voice strangely sibilant. "I am in a great hurry."

Nathan backed out of his way. "Sorry."

The man doffed his white Panama hat, looked at Nathan as if they shared some kind of secret, then walked quickly away from the athletes, toward the station's grandiose main entrance. He soon disappeared into the moving mass of people.

Nathan turned to Eleanor. "What do you make of that guy?" He asked.

"Which one, the guy who just pushed past us?"

'Yeah," Nathan said. "Something a little off about him."

"You think so?" Eleanor asked. "I think he looks like one of those export-import types who bribe customs."

That isn't it, Nathan thought. But he nodded.

By this time, uniformed chaperones had taken charge of the Olympic athletes and were herding them toward the station's east side door, where convoys of red double-decker busses were waiting to take them to their quarters in the Olympic Village.

"I'm going with the athletes," Nathan told his friends.

"There'll be plenty of time for that," Helms said. "We need to check in at our hotels, old man."

Eleanor flashed a conspiratorial smile at Nathan. "Maybe I should come with…"

Nathan wanted to inspect the Olympic Village thoroughly but not with a female hanging around, especially this one. He wanted to appraise Owen's living arrangements and get closer to him. "Oh, I'll catch up with you later, Eleanor, maybe this evening. You're at the Adlon, right?"

"Yes. Where will you be staying?"

Nathan checked his travel papers. "I'll be at the *Furstenhof*, on *Potsdamer Platz*."

"Same here," Helms said. "That's Lochner's hotel too."

Nathan offered a little wave goodbye and strode off, leaving Richard Helms and Eleanor Holm standing there. Along with a few other journalists, the eager beavers, he managed to get on the bus Owens had chosen, taking a seat on the top level, right in front of Owens and Coach Snyder. He tried to catch Owens' eye, but the sprinter was staring out the window, getting his first look at Berlin.

The bus engine rattled into life and the big red vehicle rolled away from the neo-classical *Lehrter Bahnhof*, with its beautiful glazed tile exterior, and into the bustling streets of Berlin, crossing the wandering River Spree at *Paulstrasse*, and cutting across the vast, thickly-treed oasis in central Berlin, the *Tiergarten*.

While he watched Berlin pass by, Nathan thought about his mission. He told himself he'd been too casual about protecting Owens on the voyage across the Atlantic, too easily distracted, too ready to come to the aid of a damsel in distress. Now he found himself smack dab in the midst of the Third Reich. It was past time to cede the damsel rescuing to Helms, who seemed to have an interest in it, and get serious about his real assignment.

Somehow, Nathan realized, he ought to get closer to the American runner, spend time with him, make him a pal, if possible. He had to be at Owens' side when and if the Nazis tried anything. But given Coach Snyder's protective attitude, that wouldn't be easy.

Nathan's thoughts were interrupted when a sudden shadow fell across the upper deck of the bus. He looked up into the bright blue sky. Only a few hundred feet above, the *Graf Zeppelin* floated by, a silvery cigar the size of an ocean liner, swastikas decorating its fins. Nathan watched it until it disappeared over the tree line, thinking it seemed like an apparition, a chilling apparition. Such vessels, he remembered, had bombed London in 1915.

The bus convoy turned west on *Bismarckstrasse*, heading toward the Olympic Village, in Doeberitz, a small town about twenty miles from Berlin. It had been built to house the athletes—the male athletes, that is. The females would be taken to a more modest facility, *Friesenhaus,* adjacent to the *Reichssportsfeld,* arena where there was little chance they might tempt the men or vice versa.

Nathan soon found himself riding through tree-lined streets, past rows of whitewashed mansions, occasionally interrupted by theaters, fine restaurants and cabarets. He pulled out the pocket-sized Berlin map Steve Early had given him. This, he discovered, was Charlottenburg, home to most of the country's great industrialists—the men who supported Hitler's rise to power.

Charlottenburg was even less like the Germany he'd imagined than the picture-perfect villages he'd seen from the train. Germany, or at least this part of it, was rich and powerful. There was no civilian unrest here—just the opposite. The people he saw on the street were well-dressed and happy, evidently quite pleased with themselves.

And that scene in the station, the band, the cheering, the shouts of *Yes-see, Yes-see!* Was this a country that wished harm on Jesse Owens? It certainly didn't seem so. And yet there were the reports—the 1934 Night of the Long Knives, when the Nazis killed their SA rivals, the brutal beatings in the streets, the outrageous racist propaganda and the 1935 anti-Semitic Nuremberg laws.

Back in the United States, it had all seemed pretty obvious. The Nazis were thugs of the worst sort and Hitler was their nefarious leader. Roosevelt had reason to fear for Jesse Owens, maybe good reason. But here in Germany, looking out of the train window or sitting on the upper deck of the bus as it passed through Berlin's residential neighborhoods, well, it was not obvious at all.

The bus pulled into the Olympic Village just after noon. In its way, it was just as perfect and picturesque as the towns Nathan had seen from the train. It was on rolling parkland and bordered by a small forest of silver birches, firs and pines, all new growth. Small lakes and ponds dotted the landscape, along with flower beds. Rabbits, hares, squirrels and snow-white ducks abounded. Heaven itself could hardly have been better landscaped.

Nathan got off and looked around, trying to orient himself. The place was awash with people—athletes, coaches and officials from all over the world, thousands of them, and an amazing number of men in uniform—army guards assigned to every team—bilingual guides—all of them *heiling* each other incessantly, which many of the athletes found quite entertaining.

Nathan surveyed the compound—where to start? He headed toward the curving streets and the rows of little concrete houses, all white, one-story buildings, with red-tiled roofs, where the athletes would sleep. But he was stopped by a young man, a cherubic blond, blue-eyed boy wearing what at first glance he took for a Boy Scout uniform. Then he noticed the boy's armband, red with a black swastika on a white field.

"*Heil* Hitler," the boy said, saluting.

Nathan nodded awkwardly.

"May I be of service, sir?" The boy asked, with barely a trace of a German accent.

"Oh, I'm just sightseeing," Nathan lied. "Enjoying your beautiful Olympic Village." Checking your security, looking for potential assassins, he thought.

"I'm sorry sir," the boy said with what sounded like genuine regret. "Tourists are not permitted in the Village." He gave a meaningful glance at one of the soldiers standing nearby.

Nathan casually displayed his press badge. He knew how to handle a challenge like this. "I'm a reporter, American. Mike Novak," he said. *"Cleveland Plain Dealer*," he added, knowing there was no chance the boy had ever heard of it.

"A newspaperman? Yes sir! Welcome to the Olympic Village. I would be most pleased to give you a tour of the facilities."

"Well, if you don't mind," Nathan said, "I'd just as soon wander around by myself."

"Oh, but it would be no inconvenience," the boy said. "I have been trained to do it. It's my job. Did you know that the Olympic Village covers one hundred and thirty-six acres? It has one hundred and forty-two residences, each partitioned into two-man sleeping quarters, and connected by hallways, each with a shower, a wash basin and a toilet. Every residence can accommodate between sixteen and twenty-four men."

"I'm sure the press releases describe…"

"In addition to the residences," said the boy, reciting, undeterred by the interruption, "the Village has a dining hall, an assembly hall for evening entertainments, a cinema, a gymnasium, a running track, a soccer field, a glass-walled swimming pool and even a Finnish sauna."

"A sauna, eh?" Nathan said, trying to think of a way to detach himself from this little robot. "Listen, if you don't mind, I'd just like to explore on my own, wander around, you understand."

The boy was disappointed. "Of course, sir, if that's what you prefer. But please put your press badge on your lapel. If you don't, you will be stopped frequently."

"Thank you." Nathan did as he was told and walked off toward the residences. His first order of business was to find out where Jesse Owens would be staying. It wasn't long before he located the American contingent and a US athlete pointed out the sprinter's building. Another of Hitler's many Boy Scouts carefully examined his ID, then let him pass.

Nathan poked a head inside. Owens was putting his clothes away, under Snyder's watchful eye. "Hey, Jesse," Nathan said, trying for familiarity and friendliness, "I see you're getting settled. How do you like your quarters?"

Owens looked up, surprised. "Oh, hello Mr. Novak. I think it's a beautiful place."

"Looks very comfortable," Nathan said.

"Yes," said Jesse, "and everyone has been very hospitable."

Coach Snyder gave him the evil eye. "Why don't you give us a little privacy, Novak. We'll all be at the stadium tomorrow."

"Yes, of course, sorry. See you later, Jesse," Nathan said, backing out. As he came out of Owens' room, he almost bumped into a big, square-jawed, red-headed man in a generously bemedaled SS uniform, someone of obvious rank and stature, but with vaguely threatening features. He was standing in the hallway, jotting down some notes on a small pad.

Nathan glanced at the SS man as he passed him. This was not one of the ubiquitous armed guards. This was a member of the Nazi elite. And his ice-blue eyes were fiercely focused on Owens, as if he could take Leica pictures with that gaze. In his concentration, he'd hardly seemed to notice Nathan edging past.

With that rank, he might be commander of the entire Olympic Nazi guard detachment. Or maybe he was a ranking Nazi from Hitler's inner circle, making sure the athletes were pleased with their accommodations. Or maybe he was an assassin, a man dressed to look as though he belonged, but actually a plant, there to scrutinize his assigned victim.

Nathan didn't like thinking this way, but it was part of the job, especially this job. Helms and the other newspaper people might see him as a journalist. He certainly hoped they did. But he was a cop, born and bred. Suspicion was his default attitude toward everyone.

Nathan slowly walked down the hallway, occasionally glancing back at the note-taker. But after a moment, the man slipped notepad and pencil into a pocket and casually strolled off in a different direction, apparently to examine another location. If he was planning something, it wasn't going to happen now. This was only a dry run. But it had served to alert Nathan to someone who might well be his adversary, someone to be looked out for.

Nathan realized he was sweating. He took a deep breath. Maybe his imagination was working overtime—that was a classic cop's disease, especially in unfamiliar territory. It was the "every man's a killer" delusion.

With a conscious effort he wrenched wrench his thoughts away from the SS officer and focussed on Owens. Making friends with the athlete was going to be a real challenge. He walked on, past the track and the swimming pool building, on one occasion drawing the attention of a patrolling Hitler youth, on another being stopped momentarily by a well-armed soldier. The last time he'd seen a place this secure was when he visited FDR in the White House.

In one sense, Nathan told himself, if Owens had been in protective custody, he couldn't be safer. No way could any stranger get to him here. But in another sense, he was a sitting duck. Put an assassin in the right uniform, an SS uniform, perhaps, give him the right credentials, and the rest was child's play. So how the hell was he supposed to protect Owens if he couldn't get close to him?

He spotted one of the Nazi Boy Scouts and walked up to him. The boy *heil* Hitlered him and checked out his press badge. "How may I be of service?"

"I have a question young man," Nathan said.

The boy nodded eagerly. "Happy to answer it, if I can."

"Okay. I know the Olympic Village is set up for the athletes," Nathan said, "but is there any way a journalist can stay here as well?"

"Oh no, *mein Herr*, the residences are strictly limited. Only athletes and coaches."

"I see. Thank you." Well, so much for sleeping near his charge.

He smiled at the boy, who *heil*-Hitlered him again, and walked on.

Up ahead was the most impressive building in the Village, Hindenburg *Haus*. Nathan decided it needed checking out. Inside, he found a huge dining hall, a movie theater and rooms for card playing, reading and ping pong.

As Nathan left the building, he was flabbergasted to find himself face-to-face with Eleanor Holm, Dick Helms and, of all the people in the world, a well-dressed man in a white Panama hat, a sallow-skinned man. In fact, *the* sallow-skinned man.

"Hi," Eleanor said brightly. "We decided to come out and have a look-see."

Chapter Eight

For a moment, Nathan just stared. Then the power of speech returned. "What in the world are you doing here? How did you even get here?"

"I'm afraid it's my fault, old man," Richard Helms said. "Curiosity just got the best of me."

Nathan turned to Eleanor, who once again produced that bright, infuriating smile, "Me too."

"But the buses…"

"Now that we're actually in Germany, allow me to introduce myself," said the sallow-faced man standing nearby. He wore an elegant charcoal pin-stripe suit with a small gold Swastika pin in the lapel. "I am Karl Oldenburg, sports editor of the Berlin daily, the *Vossische Zeitung*."

"I think we saw each other on the boat," Nathan said. "I'm Mike Novak, *Cleveland Plain Dealer.*"

"Yes, your face is familiar."

They shook hands quite formally.

"On the boat, you didn't stay with the other journalists."

"No," Oldenburg said, "we Germans had separate quarters," Oldenburg said. "As representatives of the sponsoring country, and as part of our arrangement with the steamship company, we had certain privileges."

"They had first class cabins," Eleanor piped up, sounding helpful.

"Well, yes," Oldenburg admitted. "But now that we're home, we German journalists have other duties."

"Other duties?"

"Yes. Our office has asked us to help the foreign journalists with anything they might need while covering the Olympics."

He reached into a vest pocket and came up with a couple of business cards, giving one to Helms, the other to Nathan,

"Your newspaper office?" Helms asked, examining the card with curiosity.

"The Propaganda Ministry."

"Ah," said Helms. "Goebbels' outfit." He stuffed Oldenburg's card in a pocket.

"That's right. He is very concerned about the foreign journalists and their comforts."

Nathan was intrigued. "Help in what way?"

"With transportation, sightseeing, restaurants, shopping—whatever you need. Just call the number on the card and they'll summon me promptly."

Nathan had another question. "You were assigned to particular people?"

"Yes," Oldenburg said, "Well, yes. I was assigned to you and Mr. Helms."

"Not me?" Eleanor asked, playfully pretending to be insulted.

"You are not a journalist," Oldenburg said.

"She wasn't," Helms said, "but she is now."

"You should see Karl's car, Mike," Eleanor said. "It's gorgeous. What is it again, Karl, a Torch?"

Oldenburg regarded her with a tolerant smile. "*Einer Horch, Fraulein* Holm. A type 850 convertible. A very fine machine, no?"

"Yes. And please call me Eleanor."

"Eleanor. Of course, *meine liebe*."

"And brand-new, too, Mike," she said.

"Alas no, *Frau*—Eleanor. Last year's model."

Helms was gazing at the Hindenburg *Haus*. "I assume you've been looking around, old man."

"Yep," said Nathan. "Nice place. Pretty buttoned up, though."

"I was here during construction," Oldenburg said. "I think it's absolutely beautiful. They spared no expense—Hitler's orders."

"You know about *Herr* Hitler's orders, Karl?" Helms asked.

"Well, as you might guess, I have very good government contacts," Oldenburg said. "Before I became an editor at the paper, I helped Goebbels set up his ministry."

Nathan considered this. "So you were reporting from Berlin even before *Herr* Hitler took over? I imagine things have changed quite a bit since then."

"It's practically a different country," Oldenburg said. "We are revived. We have purpose. People are working, building. It's been an amazing transformation. Like our brother fascist in Italy, *Herr* Hitler has made the trains run on time."

"Everyone is happy now?" Helms asked.

Oldenburg shrugged and grinned at the same time. "Almost everybody."

"I want to see the Olympic Village," Eleanor said. She reached into her purse, found a pack of Luckies and extracted a cigarette.

Oldenburg lit it for her with a swastika-engraved steel lighter. Then he held the lighter up for the rest of them to see. "A present from *Herr Reichsminister* Goebbels himself. I think he's trying to keep on my good side." He laughed and the others joined him, politely.

"Let's take a look around," Helms suggested.

They walked past the public buildings, toward the athletes' residences, Oldenburg playing tour guide. "The *Reich* has made every effort to make the athletes feel at home regardless of nationality," he said. "The Japanese get *tatamis* for sleeping, the Swiss and Austrians get feather comforters, and the Americans get Beauty Rest mattresses."

"I didn't realize Hitler was so considerate," Helms said.

"Oh, that's just the beginning," Oldenburg said. "They have different menus for every nationality—grilled meat "medium" for the British, fried chicken for the Americans, sausage for the Germans, sushi for the Japanese, vegetarian meals for, well, vegetarians."

"Impressive," Nathan admitted. He remembered that he was posing as a journalist pulled a slender notebook from a jacket pocket and made a couple of quick notes.

"And they vary the meals depending on the event," Oldenburg went on. "Beef tarter and raw chopped liver for the weightlifters, orange juice for the sprinters, fresh and stewed fruits for the rowers."

"Must have a lot of hotels and restaurants cooperating," Eleanor said.

"Not exactly," said Oldenburg. "They hired the stewards' department of the North German Lloyd line. They have one of the world's largest fleets of passenger liners, you know."

While Oldenburg rhapsodized, they all walked, Nathan looking for possible threats to his ward. He took note of the perimeter fencing—unbroken and protected by roving uniformed guards, he checked out the fire alarms—new and plentiful, and inspected the newly built clinic.

"Would you believe it?" Oldenburg said, noticing his interest, "We have provided doctors and dentists, not to mention masseuses and barbers."

"How about hairdressers?" Eleanor asked.

"Not here, but I believe there's a beauty salon in the women's quarters, near the stadium," Oldenburg said. "But you'd probably prefer the one at the Adlon." He smiled, displaying a mouthful of brilliant white teeth.

"Might be crowded with athletes," Eleanor said. "No, no," Oldenburg assured her. "The athletes are not allowed out of the village, except for the Olympic events. Buses will take them back and forth to their venues."

"They sound like prisoners," Nathan said.

"Well, the Olympic Committee wanted it that way," Oldenburg told him, "and the countries agreed—they didn't want their athletes roaming around Berlin getting into trouble. A lot of them are farm lads. But they will have one day of sightseeing in Berlin, chaperoned and on a strict schedule."

"Speaking of Berlin," Eleanor said, "I think I've seen enough of the Village, at least for today. I'd like to see a little of the real Berlin. Could you give me a ride back to the Adlon, Karl?" She gave him a smile that could have illuminated a coal mine.

"I'd be happy to," Oldenburg said. "There's plenty of room for the gentlemen too. The Horch has four doors."

Nathan realized there was nothing more he could do here—and Owens was as safe as he'd ever be. "Count me in, Karl."

"Me too," Helms said.

They headed for the parking lot, just inside the main gate. Oldenburg's car, the Horch, was in the first row, black, enormous, bristling with bulbous, chrome-rimmed headlights, foglights and mirrors. The top was rolled back. Oldenburg gallantly opened a front door for Eleanor, but she and Nathan took the back seat, with Helms sitting shotgun.

For the three Americans, the trip to Berlin was the reverse of their arrival, until they came out of the east end of the Tiergarten. Oldenburg stopped the car at a traffic light and there, spread out in front of them was Berlin's most recognizable landmark, the *Brandenburger Tor*.

As they waited at the stoplight, Oldenburg continued to play tour guide. "At the time of Napoleon," he said, "Berlin had thirteen gates. This is the sole survivor. It's two hundred feet side to side, if you include the pair of added structures."

"Reminds me of the Parthenon's entrance," Helms put in.

"You have a keen eye, young man," Oldenburg said. "The whole design is based on the gate to the Acropolis, in Athens."

"Except for the sculpture on top, Karl, no?" Helms said. "The four horses, drawing the chariot and the Goddess Victoria—I'm sure that's in the Roman style."

Oldenburg reacted dismissively. "Yes, of course. The Quadriga. It's a common theme from the ancient world." The light changed and he drove through the right-most of the five traffic lines that ran between the Brandenburg's Doric columns and onto the most famous boulevard in Berlin, *Unter den Linden*, with its grassy pedestrian promenade and its dual carriageways, its usual linden trees now replaced by four rows of tall white pillars each topped by a Nazi eagle or a swastika.

They drove into *Pariser Platz*, the big paved plaza at the top of the boulevard. Just ahead on the right was the prestigious Adlon hotel, an enormous block of yellow stone five stories tall, with a mansard roof of green copper. "Your palace, milady," Oldenburg said, turning into the entrance concourse.

Eleanor caught Nathan's eye. "Go check in at your hotel and come back for me," she whispered. "I want to take a little stroll down *Unter den Linden* and I need a gentleman to accompany me. You are an *entlemangay*, aren't you?"

The invitation caught Nathan off guard. Once more, he yielded to temptation. Better he keep an eye on her than wonder what she was up to. "Okay," he said. "In the lobby? Half hour or so?"

She nodded and slipped out of the car. "Thanks for the ride, Karl," she said, leaning over and giving him a kiss on the cheek, which seemed to please him enormously.

"Hey," Helms said, "could I have one of those?"

She laughed and obliged. Then, to Nathan, "I'll get to you later." And she winked.

They watched her disappear into the hotel. "Where now?" Oldenburg asked.

"The *Furstenhof,* on *Potsdamer Platz,*" Nathan and Helms said simultaneously. "Wherever the Hell that is," Nathan added.

"It's five blocks south," Oldenburg said with a laugh.

Oldenburg dropped them off at the *Furstenhof,* a vast commercial enterprise, the architecture a mixture of Art Nouveau, Modernism and neo-Baroque. Nathan and Helms hopped out of the flashy motor car and went in to register. Harried businessmen crowded the lobby, coming and going, as a three-piece band played an anemic version of "In the Mood."

"How did Oldenburg find you?" Nathan asked Helms.

"Picked us out of a crowd. Offered to show us the sights. But going to the Olympic Village was Eleanor's idea."

"I don't trust him," Nathan said. "Haven't trusted him since I first saw him on the boat. There's a furtive quality to him."

"Oh, I don't know, old man," Helms said. "He's a little full of himself, but I think he's harmless. And probably useful."

"I think we've picked up a minder," Nathan said. "Someone to make sure we see what the Nazis want us to see and nothing else. Someone to keep a close eye on us."

Helms took a long look at his companion. "You know, you're a pretty suspicious guy, Mike."

"My dad was a cop," Nathan offered. "I come by it naturally."

"I think Oldenburg is just what he says he is—a tour guide for us foreign newspapermen. It's a courtesy. Besides, there's no reason to think he's spying on us or anything. We're just journalists, here to cover the games. We're not looking for military secrets."

"That's true," Nathan said, glad that was Helms' assumption.

Nathan found a message waiting for him at the front desk. The American Ambassador Bill Dodd, had sent a dinner invitation.

"Secret lover?" Helms said, watching him read the note.

"I wish," Nathan said. "No, just a family friend. An obligation."

"My sympathies, old man," Helms said. He gave a little wave and trotted off to the elevator.

Nathan signed the register then sat down in one of the lobby's plush, Bauhaus-styled chrome-and-leather lounge chairs. He read Dodd's invitation again. It would be good to tell him how things stood with Jesse Owens, maybe ask for help. He could certainly use more manpower.

Or womanpower. Flighty and impulsive though she was, Nathan thought, his first instincts could still be right. Eleanor might be useful. For instance, he couldn't be two places at once—except if he had a confederate.

Nathan picked up a house phone and called Dodd. Would it be all right if he brought someone to dinner, someone who knows what's going on? Of course, Dodd said. Now all Nathan had to do is convince Eleanor, which should be easy enough.

Nathan walked out of the *Furstenhof* and got his first good look at central Berlin. One thing was for sure: this wasn't New York. He craned his head in every direction—not a single skyscraper. This was a flat city, And an old city, too—mostly big, 19th-century stone structures four or five stories tall, many crowned with mansard roofs and topped with arrays of chimneys, belfries, turrets and domes. The oddball was a large, curving office building a couple of blocks west, its façade faced with swathes of steel-and-glass—*Columbushaus*.

Almost all the buildings were festooned with an eye-watering array of signs large and small, many lighted, some in neon. As if all this weren't enough, brightly-colored flags, banners and pennants hung from every available spot—great red, black and white banners adorned with swastikas, German flags, Olympic banners and pennants, retail sales streamers and the like. It looked like twelve circuses and a bunch of carnivals had just come to town.

At the street level, of course, all of these big-shouldered grey stone buildings turned into a profusion of shops, hotels, cafes, restaurants, bars, cinemas, theaters, travel agencies, churches, and train stations. Just down the street was a building bigger than the others: Wertheim's *Kaufhaus*, Berlin's answer to Macy's, Nathan guessed.

From what he could see, this intersection—*Potsdamer Platz,* the sign said—made Times Square seem like the crossing of a couple of country cow paths. He counted five streets—major streets—all coming together in front of him in a star-shaped convergence.

The streets bustled with a rowdy mix of cream-colored electrified trolleys, whose catenaries fired off brilliant blue sparks, and red open-topped double-decker omnibuses rumbling past in every direction, plus trucks and automobiles, some of them chauffeured Grosser Mercedes, bearing aloof-looking Nazi officials, not to mention horse-drawn buggies and wagons and dog-drawn carts and their rag-clad hacks, and a sprinkling of motorcycles and wobbly bicycles manned by reckless young men.

It was a great cacophony. The streetcars' continual bell-ringing and the beeping and honking of the cars and trucks mingled with tolling church bells, in a barely tolerable mixture. On top of that was the rattle and clatter of the trolleys. And Nathan could make out band music off in the distance.

A tidal flow of people washed over the sidewalks—plump housewives carrying stuffed shopping bags; respectable burghers, some equipped with umbrellas or bulging leather portfolios, hurrying to meetings or assignations; pretty young secretaries back from lunch, walking arm-in-arm, gossiping and giggling and immigrant peddlers, pushing carts full of flowers or pretzels or cold drinks.

Nathan stood in front of the hotel for a minute, letting it all sink in. The problem was, if he wanted to walk to the Adlon and pick up Eleanor, he'd have to pick his way through this frenetic madhouse. How was it, he wondered, that none of these vehicles crashed into each other, that people could walk through this chaos and survive?

Then Nathan saw how. *Potsdamer Platz* was controlled—to the degree it could be controlled—by a cluster of traffic lights mounted on a spindly five-sided metal tower nearly thirty feet tall. The upper part was a little windowed cabin, through which he could make out a policeman surveying his jurisdiction—the master puppeteer of the whole unruly swarm.

This was a warm, lively, bustling big city not so different from New York, he decided. Commerce, society, culture—all were in full view here. If there were any repression, duress or coercion going on, it wasn't visible, and the German traffic police, in their white jackets, black pants and leather-covered Shako helmets, certainly didn't look like anyone's overlord.

So why was he in Berlin, charged with protecting an American Negro Olympic sprinter? Standing here, looking at *Potsdamer Platz*, it felt an awful lot like a fool's errand. But neither he nor Roosevelt were fools.

Now it was time to get across the intersection, which, Nathan thought, shouldn't be much of a problem for a cop who'd chased after criminals on the streets of New York and grown up playing stickball and riding bikes in Manhattan's Lower East Side.

Nathan waited until the light had turned green, then cautiously walked into *Potsdamer Platz,* his eye on one of the intersection's three traffic islands. He was three steps away from the first one when, out of the corner of his eye, he caught the approach of an electrified tram coming from the far left, its bell clanging frantically. He hopped on the traffic island just in time, the tram grazing the back of his jacket.

The problem was the traffic light. It had been green when he started, but red before he arrived. He stood on the island watching the light for awhile—the damn thing changed every thirty seconds. It turned green again and he darted across the rest of the intersection, barely avoiding a big green truck, on whose side were painted the words *"Aronofsky und Söhne. FEINE MÖBEL ZU GÜNSTIGEN PREISEN."* Möbel—he knew that word from an uncle. He'd just missed getting squashed by a furniture truck.

Safe now on the other side of Potsdamer Platz, Nathan walked north along Hermann Göring Straße, the Tiergarten on his left, shops and stores on his right. As the traffic noise fell off, he heard two birds in the Tiergarten, species unknown, giving an impromptu concert. It reminded him a bit of walking up Fifth Ave., alongside Central Park. But this walk, unlike that one, had a distinct undertone of menace.

Chapter Nine

Fifteen minutes later, Nathan walked into the Adlon's main entrance, past a stout, liveried red-cheeked doorman who bowed as he approached. He found himself besieged by luxury that made the Waldorf-Astoria's lobby seem shabby and cramped—floors of black and white marble, walls of silk and mahogany, crystal chandeliers hanging from vaulted ceilings, polished brass hardware, luxuriant greenery in spectacular ceramic pots, rugs so thick they could swallow small dogs, and, surrounding a burbling fountain, a group of brocade-covered chairs and couches from a more opulent era. A tuxedo-clad piano player, bent over a Beckstein baby grand in a corner, quietly played "My Heart Stood Still," the Rodgers and Hart number Jessie Matthews had turned into a hit.

The hotel lobby bustled with imperious women in the latest Parisian fashions, and distinguished men carrying silver-handled canes, as well as scurrying bellhops. messengers and elevator boys, all wearing funny little hats with chinstraps and red jackets with vertical rows of gold buttons. Nathan wouldn't have been surprised, he thought, to see Greta Garbo emerge from an elevator in a slinky black gown, leading a pair of snow-white Russian wolfhounds and smoking a long Turkish cigarette in an ebony holder.

Nathan stopped one of the porters, a grey-haired attendant in his mid-60s. "Telephones?"

"Yes, *Mein Herr*, of course. In the booths to the left." He pointed.

There were five of them, but only the middle booth was empty. Nathan picked up the phone.

"Call?" asked the operator, sounding bored beyond endurance.

He used her married name. "Jarrett," he said, "Eleanor Jarrett."

"One moment. I will connect you."

The phone rang four times. "Hiya," Eleanor said at last. "Who's this?"

"David Nathan," he said.

"You're my gentleman escort? I was expecting Mike Novak."

He ignored the teasing. "Listen, Eleanor, I have a surprise for you—a dinner invitation, if you're interested."

"Of course," she said. "I love surprises. I'll be down in a minute. Hope you have your walking shoes on."

One minute turned into twenty, but when she finally showed up, she was wearing something bright and flowerey and she'd arranged her golden blonde hair in a wonderous casdade. Nathan wished he'd changed into his other suit, the less wrinkled one.

She got to the point immediately. "So, we have a dinner invitation? Who from?"

"From none other than the American US Ambassador to Germany, William Dodd. We're going to talk about the Jesse Owens situation—and how you may be able to help."

"Oooh, that sounds absolutely wonderful!"

"We could walk over now," Nathan said. "We'd just be a little early."

The delight turned into a pout. "I want to see some of the city first."

Nathan checked his watch. "I suppose we could, for a little while. Have any particular destination in mind?"

Eleanor showed him a pocket-sized guide to Berlin she'd evidently picked up at the front desk. "Yes," she said. "I want to take a walk down *Unter Den Linden.*"

"The street at the corner, the one with all the flagpoles? We can see that from here."

"Not enough of it," Eleanor said. "I want to see it all. They say it's the Champs Elysee of Berlin."

"Sounds wonderful," Nathan lied. "How long will this take?"

Eleanor was piqued. "Oh, I don't know," she said. "You have something else to do before dinner? Going out to the Olympic Village to check on Jesse Owens?"

"Nothing much I can do there," Nathan admitted.

"So? Let's walk, all the way to the palace at the end of the street."

"Why there?"

"Well, a pair of stone lions stand in front of it. I understand that one of them roars when a virgin walks by."

"Wait just a minute," Nathan said, feigning shock, "don't tell me you anticipate a…"

Eleanor laughed. "Well, we'll just have to see, won't we? Walk."

There was no appeal. They walked, out of the Adlon onto the broad expanse of *Pariser Platz.* Waiting at the hotel's main entrance was

Karl Oldenburg's snazzy Horch. The man himself was standing at the passenger door, wearing an inviting smile.

"*Herr* Oldenburg," Nathan said, tempering his surprise with a smile. "What are you doing here?"

"I'm at your service, *Herr* Novak, And yours too, of course, *Fraulein...*"

"Eleanor," she reminded him.

"Ah, yes. Eleanor."

"How did you know we were here?" Nathan asked. He tried to make it sound like an innocent inquiry.

"I called the hotel," Oldenburg said. "They told me the *Fraulein* was still in her room. I guessed that either you or *Herr* Helms would be along shortly."

"You guessed right," Eleanor said.

"Will *Herr* Helms be joining you?"

Nathan shook his head. "No. Doing interviews today."

"Then it's just the three of us," Oldenburg said. "That's fine."

"Why are you here?" Nathan asked.

"I'm just doing my job as a welcoming German journalist. I'm ready to take you wherever you might want to go, or make some sightseeing suggestions."

"Hmm," Nathan grunted.

"You know, *Herr* Oldenburg," Eleanor said, "I think *Herr* Novak and I are in the mood for a stroll this morning. Get a little taste of the city." She produced a winning smile.

"Shall I meet you at the end of your constitutional?" Oldenburg asked hopefully.

"Won't be necessary, *Herr* Oldenburg," Nathan told him. "We have a meeting later today. Within walking distance."

Oldenburg nodded, looking disappointed. "Well, maybe after dinner. There's a fine band concert in The *Waldbühne*. It's a brand new outdoor theater at Olympia Park. Just off *Friedrich-Friesen-Allee*. Walking distance from the hotel, if you insist."

"We're probably going to be too late for that," Nathan said.

"But maybe another night?" Eleanor suggested.

"Of course. Give me a call."

"We will," Nathan said, meaning exactly the opposite.

Oldenburg nodded, hopped into his Horch and drove off.

"Is Richard really doing interviews today?" Eleanor asked.

"Damned if I know," Nathan said. "I checked his room before I left the hotel. He was snoring like a freight train."

Eleanor laughed.

She and Nathan watched Oldenburg's automobile pass through the *Brandenburger Tor* and disappear into traffic.

"Persistent little man," Eleanor observed.

"Too persistent for my taste," Nathan said.

Eleanor was surprised. "Do you think…?"

"I don't know what to think," Nathan said. "And that worries me."

"Well, he's gone now and we're on our own in the middle of Berlin. Let's look around."

And this they did, finding themselves facing a ghostly neo-Baroque hulk of a building on the far side of *Pariser Platz.*

Then the narration began, Eleanor reading from her little guidebook. "That," she read and pointed, "is the Reichstag, Germany's parliamentary house, mysteriously burned out not long after Hitler assumed power."

"Mysteriously, eh? Does the guidebook explain how?"

"Nope. Just 'mysteriously'. It's the 1933 edition, you know."

Eleanor took his arm, a gesture more possessive than affectionate, and they headed down *Unter den Linden*, taking the grassy promenade in the middle of the boulevard, joining a stream of pedestrians, everyone sauntering much too languidly for Nathan's taste.

"Okay," Nathan said, pointing at another large building, "what's that?"

She consulted her guidebook. "The Soviet Embassy."

"And that?" He pointed to a building on the other side of the street.

"The National Library," Eleanor told him.

They kept walking. For Nathan, *Unter den Linden* was a beautiful but bland succession of neo-classical buildings of various types and sizes. If you ignored the restaurants, the shoe stores and jewelry shops squeezed between them, he told himself, you might think you were strolling in Caesar's Rome.

The walking continued, Nathan trying to up the pace, Eleanor playing millstone.

"And that building," he said, pointing at another classic structure. "What's that?"

"Assuming you really want to know," she said, consulting her guide, "That is the *State* Library. Conveniently located next to the National one."

"No, the one in front of that."

"You mean the Kranzler Café?"

"Yes," Nathan said. "Let's sit down and have a cup of something."

"In a moment," Eleanor said. "I see a shoe store just around the corner."

Nathan knew better than to interfere with her. While she studied the shoe store display windows, he gazed at the building next door, a barber shop. Some kind of red label was pasted in the middle of the front window. He took a closer look. Prominent black letters on the label said, *Wir servieren keine Juden.* Nathan didn't know German, but the sign's meaning was clear enough, if you happened to be *ein Jude*. Evidently, the clean-up crew had missed this one.

When Eleanor finally lost interest in the shoes, they took seats in the cafe's sidewalk section. They sat, drank tea, listened to the café's radio playing Franz Lehar's cheery and innocent "Merry Widow Waltz," and watched the people passing by, a parade that composed of an entertaining mixture of gawking tourists of every imaginable ethnicity and, of course, military men in uniforms in a bewildering variety of colors.

There was something almost ceremonial about the scene, as if at any moment, a marching band might come around the corner, leading a glorious parade. What came around the corner, however, was something else—a small knot of swaggering teenaged Hitler youth in brown shirts with badges and epaulets, grey shorts and white knee-socks, and the requisite swastika arm bands.

They were performing a duty. Each time anyone approached—tourist or local, man, woman or family—they *Heil* Hitlered, coming to attention with right hand extended arrow-straight. It was not just a greeting. It was a demand, that the greeting be returned forthwith. And it was, sometimes immediately and with enthusiasm, sometimes hesitantly and with fear.

Nathan and Eleanor watched, fascinated, as the boys came toward them, silently trying to guess how each approaching stroller would respond. One man in particular caught their eye, a shrunken old peddler swathed in rags, pushing his cart, a small four-wheel wooden wagon displaying pots and pans, brooms, knives and other household items.

The little man, bent over with the effort of making his way down the street, had fixed his eyes on the cart ahead of him, avoiding collisions thanks to brief glimpses of approaching footwear and the alertness and courtesy of those coming his way.

He did not see the Hitler youth group. They saw *him*, however. "*Heil* Hitler," proclaimed the leader, arm snapping into position. He was a perfect specimen of Aryan physiognomy, tall for his age, hair blond and parted on the right, eyes blue and open wide, calf muscles bulging. The peddler did not look up.

"I said," the Hitler Youth leader repeated, as if he expected his patience to be appreciated, "*Heil* Hitler!"

The peddler looked up now, dimly aware now that he was being addressed, but having no idea how to respond. He was confused, blinded by the sunlight.

"*Heil* Hitler!" Shouted the Hitler Youth second-in-command, raising his arm to salute—and demand a response. This one was no model of Aryan perfection. He was a dark-haired shrimp with a nose like a coffee cup handle. "*Heil* Hitler, scum!"

The peddler stared at the Hitler Youth, terrified. "*Mit akar velem*?"

The Hitler Youths looked at each other, confused and angry.

"What did he say?" Eleanor asked. "Was he speaking Jewish?"

"I don't know," Nathan said, "but he sure wasn't speaking German. Something Eastern European maybe."

Once more, and for what he made clear was for the very last time, the group's leader *Heiled* the peddler, and stood impatiently waiting for a reply.

"*Mit akar velem*?"

The Hitler Youth Group did not find this satisfactory. It was the second-in-command who struck the first blow, actually a kick in the peddler's shins. When the old man somehow managed to remain standing, the others joined in, kicking and punching.

The leader had another target: the peddler's cart. He wrenched it out of the old man's grasp and twisted it violently, finally overturning it and spilling the pots and pans and knives and sieves clanging out onto the street. The peddler shortly joined his goods in the gutter, where the Hitler Youth kept kicking him until he stopped moving.

Then they formed up again and marched on, without looking back.

Nathan and Eleanor hurried to help the old man, lifting him to his feet and trying to dust him off. He seemed shaken, but not badly injured. Kranzler's other patrons, most of them, simply sat where they were and continued their conversations.

Finally, when the Hitler Youth were no longer in sight, an older man and his wife, and helped by one of the waiters, righted the cart and started picking up the peddler's stock, the peddler offering words of gratitude in a language no one understood.

"My God," Nathan said.

"Thugs!" Eleanor said. "Where are the cops when you need them?"

"Good question," Nathan said. His mind was back on Jesse Owens. What would happen if he were confronted by a group of young thugs, demanding that he say *heil* Hitler? It was not a pleasant thought.

They decided to skip the stone lions and flagged down a cab.

Chapter Ten

Ambassador William E. Dodd, a former history professor at the University of Chicago and long a committed liberal, lived with his wife and daughter Martha at 27 A *Tiergartenstrasse*, across the street from the north side of the park.

His home, which was much more pretentious than the man himself, was a four-story stone building rented to the US government by its owner, the German-Jewish financier, Frederick Warburg. The yard was filled with trees and flowers and surrounded by an iron fence.

Nathan and Eleanor's taxi drove through the elaborate ironwork arch at the front of the house and let them out under the story-and-a-half *porte-cochere*. Music was drifting out of the mansion's windows and Nathan recognized it—it was a Strauss waltz.

At Nathan's knock—he used the elaborate brass bear's-head knocker—the door was opened by a small, delicate-looking girl in her late 20s, a little blue-eyed Dresden doll, with a pink-and-white complexion.

She greeted them with a pretty smile. "Hi. I'm Martha Dodd. You must be David Nathan." She looked at Eleanor, slightly perplexed. "And this would be…"

"Eleanor Holm," said Eleanor, extending a hand. "I'm a friend of Mr. Nathan's."

"Please come in." She said. "And let me turn down the music."

After she switched off a phonograph, Martha Dodd led them up an elaborate staircase to the main floor, past a ballroom, a formal dining room, a *Wintergarten*, a glassed-in porch that overlooked the outdoor garden and into a library paneled with dark wood and red damask. Standing beside a great old fireplace whose black-enameled mantle was carved with forests and human figures, was a stern-looking man in his mid-fifties, with deep-set eyes and grey hair parted almost in the middle.

"Hello," he said, with an engaging smile and an extended hand, "Bill Dodd."

"David Nathan," Nathan said, shaking the hand. "And this is Eleanor Holm Jarrett."

Dodd took Eleanor's hand and kissed it, much to her surprise. "When in Europe..." he explained, with a twinkle in his eye. "Come, sit."

They all took seats on the library's brown leather chairs and couches, Martha Dodd included.

"So, are you enjoying Berlin, Mr. Nathan?" Dodd asked.

"It's *David*," Nathan said. "And Berlin certainly isn't New York. There's a very different feeling to the place."

"Yes," Dodd agreed. "Takes some getting used to." "The police are very lax here," Eleanor said.

Dodd was taken aback. "Lax? That's the first time I've heard them described that way."

"We saw it with our own eyes," Eleanor said. "A poor old peddler beat up by some teenage boys in uniform. No police in sight. No one even came to help the man. And this happened right on *Unter den Linden*! In broad daylight!"

"Hmmm," said Ambassador Dodd. "Yes, such things do happen. Very upsetting."

"Mostly Berlin is just wonderful," said Martha Dodd. "But it's a big city. And bad things can happen in big cities—New York, even Chicago."

"They attacked him because he didn't say *heil* Hitler," Eleanor said.

"There have been incidents like that," Dodd allowed. "Some of the Nazis are over-zealous, especially in groups—and particularly the young ones."

"Must Germans greet each other with a *heil* Hitler?"

"Actually, no," Dodd said. "The government recently put out a directive. Foreigners are not required to say *heil* Hitler. But some of the young Nazis may not have gotten the word."

"There are some rowdies among them," Martha said. "But mostly they're just boisterous."

Nathan watched Dodd's reaction. Clearly, he and his daughter had their differences. "Maybe this is the time to bring up my reason for being here," he said.

"Yes," Dodd said. "The young Negro sprinter. The President is concerned about his safety, but of course he's viewing Germany from a distance. If he were here, I think, he wouldn't be as worried."

"The whole thing is ridiculous," Martha said. "Jesse Owens is as safe here as he would be in New York or anywhere else in America. Especially now, with the Olympics. Germany is *very* respectful to foreigners."

"Well, a few Americans have encountered trouble," Dodd said. "But not since I got here."

Martha Dodd leaned forward, fixing her gaze on Nathan. "It's really remarkable, David. I mean what the German government has accomplished in the three years it's been in power. No one's out of work anymore. The economy is booming. The streets are safe."

"Fairly safe," Eleanor corrected.

Martha couldn't be stopped. "Do you know what Germany was like before the Nazis took over? It was a disaster. There was fighting in the streets. The country was falling apart. Now…well, it's just about a miracle." She was nearly breathless.

Eleanor was skeptical." How do you know all this?"

"Well, I *live* here," Martha responded. "And I have German friends. *Good* German friends, some in very high places who tell me what it's really like." She looked at her father, as if daring him to contradict her. He didn't meet her gaze.

Nathan took a closer look at Martha. For a moment, he wondered about her. But he dismissed the thought. After all, this was Dodd's daughter. She might be a rebel, but she certainly wasn't a traitor. And he had more important things to think about. "I have to assume Jesse Owens is at risk," Nathan said. "It's my job and I intend to do it."

"I understand," Dodd said. "Roosevelt asked me to look after you and help in any way, unofficially of course…"

Nathan thought a moment. "I could use a little more manpower—a few more pairs of eyes. Eleanor's going to help me, but even with two of us—the Olympic Village, the stadium, the bus trips, I don't know how we can cover it all."

The Ambassador listened, but it was obvious from his expression that he couldn't help. "I can give you money," he said. "New credentials if you need them. I might be able to help if you run into the police, although I can't guarantee it."

"And if, for some reason, I have to run…?"

Dodd grimaced. "Could I provide refuge here at the embassy? Maybe. But, by God, let's hope it doesn't come to that."

"This is all pretty silly if you ask me," Martha put in.

"Just one thing," Dodd said. "You're Jewish, aren't you David?"

"Guilty as charged. But my passport says I'm Michael Novak—could have had parents who were Czech or Polish or almost anything else."

"I'm a little surprised Roosevelt assigned this particular job to a Jew," Dodd said. "I mean, I'm sure you're a capable man. But Jews aren't so popular here these days. Could complicate things if you get into trouble."

"I'll do my best to stay out of trouble."

"Oh, Daddy, you're being silly," Martha said. "That anti-Semitic stuff is *really* all talk. At its heart, Germany is a highly civilized country. Everyone knows that. The home of Beethoven, Goethe and Leibniz."

"And Hitler," Eleanor said with a smile.

A round-faced older woman appeared at the door. She was wearing an apron and her grey hair sat on top of her head, in a perfect bun. "Meester Dodd," she said. "Dinner iz sherved. Alzo, zomeone iz at ze front door."

Martha was up in an instant. "I know who it is," she said. "I'll get it."

"David, she invited another guest for dinner," Dodd said. "Couldn't stop her. So if we have any more Owens business to discuss, maybe it should wait until he's gone."

"I think we've pretty much said what we had to say," Nathan said. "Just be sure to introduce me as Mike Novak."

"Who's the other guest," Eleanor chimed in.

"It's that writer from North Carolina," Dodd said, "Thomas Wolfe."

"Oh, I know who he is," Eleanor said. "He wrote *Look Homeward, Angel*. I read it, well, some of it. It was a best seller."

"He's very popular in Germany," said the Ambassador. "Spent some time here when he was younger, I think."

They headed for the dining room, Dodd leading. Eleanor dawdled and Nathan waited for her. "I didn't know you were an *ew-jay*," she whispered with a mischievous grin.

"Do you think I tell you all my secrets?"

Martha and Thomas Wolfe were waiting in the hallway. Wolfe was a tall, handsome, dark-haired man in his mid-thirties, with one of those smiles that turn down instead of up.

Introductions were made, hands were shaken, and seats were taken, with Wolfe making it a point to sit next to Eleanor. The cook served the meal—steak and potatoes, Dodd's preference.

"I think I've heard your name somewhere," Wolfe said to Eleanor.

"Well, I certainly know your name, Mr. Wolfe," Eleanor said, giving him a dose of her baby blues. "I read your book, the bestseller."

"*Look Homeward, Angel*?" Wolfe asked, "all of it?"

"Still in the middle," she smiled and the immediate vicinity lit up.

"I hope when you finish you'll tell me how you liked it," Wolfe said, smitten.

"I've read it too," Martha called from across the table. She tried to match Eleanor's smile. "It was perfectly marvelous."

"Why thank you," Wolfe said, glancing in her direction.

"I understand this isn't your first visit to Germany," Nathan said.

"I've been here several times, actually," Wolfe said. "The first time was in 1926, when I started to write *Look Homeward, Angel*."

The Ambassador joined the conversation. "Mr. Wolfe is very popular in Germany. His books are best sellers here."

"Escaped the bonfires, have they?" Eleanor asked innocently..

"The Germans seem to like me," Wolfe said, taking a bite of steak. "And I return the affection. It's really a wonderful country. It has an incredible spirit."

"I couldn't agree more," Martha put in, gazing at Wolfe.

"But I understand not everyone is happy here," Eleanor said. She smiled at Nathan, ignoring his dirty look, and took a drink of wine.

"Ah yes," Wolfe said, leaning back, turning philosophical. "The Jews. Well, in Germany, there are two kinds of Jews. The first group clannishly clings to its ancient ways. These people are outsiders. They will never be part of Germany, but always a drain on her resources, a carbuncle if you will. The second group obsequiously tries to assimilate, but all the fine clothing, all the fine manners, all the money in the world will never straighten their noses or make them Germans. They will always be trespassers, diluting what is truly German."

"But they are human beings too, are they not?" Dodd asked. "And do they not deserve all the rights enjoyed by other human beings?" He meant it to sound like a simple inquiry.

"Well, of course, Ambassador Dodd, there are always humanitarian considerations. And I have no personal animus toward

Jews, although you must admit they are generally not an appealing race."

Eleanor exchanged glances with Nathan, who almost imperceptibly shook his head 'no'.

"I guess that sort of thing is in the eye of the beholder," Dodd said. "As for me, I never notice, one way or another. For all I know, Mr. Wolfe, *you* might be Jewish."

Wolfe laughed. "Ah, but I am not." He winked at Eleanor.

"I don't know why we talk about such things," Martha said. "I would much rather talk about Mr. Wolfe's books. Are you writing a new one, Mr. Wolfe?"

"Please, it's Tom. When someone says 'Mr. Wolfe,' I always look around to see if my father is standing nearby."

"Are you writing a new book, Tom?"

"Yes I am. Something short this time, a novella."

"When do we get to read it?" Martha asked..

"When I finish with it," Wolfe said. But he was looking at Eleanor.

The cook appeared again, this time with dessert.

"Looks delicious," Nathan said, happy for the interruption. "What is it?"

"*Schwarzwalder Kirschtorte*," the cook said, holding out the platter for all to see. "Black Vorest Cheery Cake."

They ate cake and chatted about trivia.

"Are you here for the Olympics?" Wolfe asked Eleanor.

She paused. "Yes, I'm covering it for the INS."

"Ah, another writer." Wolfe said.

"Him too," Eleanor said, pointing at Nathan. "Mike is a correspondent for the *Cleveland Plain Dealer*. Right, Mike?"

"What she said."

Wolfe looked Nathan, then at Eleanor. "Are you two…"

"Just friends," Eleanor said. "We met on the boat."

Wolfe smiled. "Aha," he said. "And where are you staying in Berlin, Eleanor?"

"The Adlon."

"Well, that's a coincidence," he said. "So am I. Would you like a ride back?"

She looked at Nathan, and Wolfe spotted the gesture. "Happy to drop you off too, Novak. Are you at the Adlon too?"

"*Furstenhof*," Nathan said.

"Right on the way," said Wolfe.

Chapter Eleven

David Nathan woke up early and dressed quickly, troubled by the notion that he'd been neglecting his duties. He'd wasted a lot of time on attractive distractions while Jesse Owens, the man he'd pledged to protect was at the Olympic Village, accompanied only by his coach and his teammates—and the dozens of uniformed German youths who made up the colony's security corps.

Owens was probably safe enough in this environment, Nathan told himself again, but that was a gamble—a convenient rationalization that didn't bear much scrutiny. What he should have been doing was keeping a close eye on Owens at all times, not running around with Eleanor. What kind of a cop was he?

Nathan checked the schedule again. The games' opening ceremonies were set for the next day, with the competition to follow during the rest of the week. Today, he assumed, the athletes would be at the Village, working out, stretching and practicing their skills.

He left the room and headed downstairs, expecting to find a group of foreign journalists in the hotel lobby. With luck, one of them would have a car and he could wheedle himself a ride to the Village.

When Nathan entered the Furstenhof's dining room, he found many more of his fellow scriveners—among them Red Knickerbocker, Quentin Reynolds, Louis Lochner and, of course, Dick Helms. This group sat at a large round table, drinking coffee and wolfing down platters of pancakes and sausages.

"G'morning, gents," he said, "room for one more?"

"Morning, Mike," said Helms. He scooched his chair toward Lochner's, and Nathan managed to squeeze another seat into the vacancy.

"So who's going out to the Olympic Village today?" Nathan asked. "I could use a ride." He was greeted by silence and puzzled looks. Would he have to go looking for Oldenburg and his Horch?

"Um, Mike," Helms said. "No one is going out to the village today. We're all headed to Tempelhof Aerodrome. The famous American pilot, Lindbergh, is flying in this morning and Göring is going to greet him. There's going to be a formal luncheon and a press conference."

"Lindbergh?" Nathan said, surprised. "I didn't know that."

"Well," said Helms, "while you were traipsing around Berlin with Mrs. Jarrett, the rest of us were at the Berlin Press Club. The Lindbergh press release came in about 3 p.m."

"I see," Nathan said. "Well, no matter. I'm going out to the Olympic Village. You can tell me if anything interesting happens with Lindbergh and Göring."

"What?" said Louis Lochner. "Did I just hear you say you're giving up the opportunity to meet Lindbergh so you can check out the Olympic Village?"

"Yes," Nathan said. "I want to stick as close to the athletes as possible. That's what my editor told me to do."

"By God, man," Red Knickerbocker, "you're going to skip a press conference with Charles Lindbergh and Hermann Göring for a chance to watch the athletes exercise? What kind of a newsman are you anyhow?"

"Just doing my job," Nathan insisted. This is getting awkward, he thought.

"Young man," said Quentin Reynolds, "I realize you are new at this game, so I hope you won't be offended if I share a little information with you."

"Go ahead," Nathan said, dreading what was coming.

Reynolds cleared his throat. "Well, it just happens that Charles Lindbergh is probably the most famous person in the world and since his baby was kidnapped and killed four years ago, he's rarely held a press conference—much less one with Hermann Göring, who is famous in his own right."

"If you miss this one, Mike," said Red Knickerbocker, "you'd better go back to selling children's shoes in your father's department store. The only way you'll see the *Plain Dealer* again is if you give a dime to a newsboy."

"The entire foreign press corps will be there," Lochner added. "If you don't file a story, you'll be the only reporter who doesn't."

Nathan realized he was faced with a bad choice. If he didn't go to Tempelhof, he could end up blowing his cover. But if he didn't go to the Olympic Village, he couldn't protect Owens. In the end, he once more convinced himself that Owens would be safe at the village, at least for a little longer. He knew he was kidding himself, but he was stuck with his cover story and had to take the risk.

"Okay, okay," he said. "I give up. Which of you guys is driving to Tempelhof and has room for me?"

Knickerbocker had the car and he was taking everyone, and "there's room for you, too, Novak, if you're willing to take the rumble seat." Sitting on the automobile's poorly padded and folded back trunk lid, exposed to the cold wind wasn't Nathan's favorite method of car travel, but he had no choice.

"Sure," he said, smiling. "That would be fine. Perfect spot for a greenhorn like me."

Tempelhof Aerodrome turned out to be just a fifteen minute drive from the Furstenhof in Knickerbocker's impressive 1935 blue Pierce-Arrow, a *New York Post* company car, he explained, which the paper, hoping to impress, had shipped directly to Berlin from New York.

What Nathan saw ahead of him, as Knickerbocker parked the car, was nothing like the only other airfield he'd ever seen, the primitive, ramshackle facilities of the tiny North Beach Aerodrome on Long Island Sound in Queens. He stared. The Tempelhof terminal was an enormous, but unfinished gray concrete quadrant, a quarter of a circle thirty feet high, at least sixty feet wide and nearly a mile long.

A dozen or so aeroplanes were parked on the tarmac in front of the terminal and the hangers, some single-engined, some with a pair of engines, and one giant with four engines. Most were painted in Lufthansa colors, but Nathan also spotted planes from KLM, Swissair, Sabena and Aeroflot.

Lochner walked up behind him. "Impressive, no?"

"Amazing."

A reception party waited in front of the terminal—a couple hundred uniformed Luftwaffe officers, many with wives, plus a sprinkling of civilian VIPs and all the reporters Nathan had seen on the *SS Manhattan.* And there, by God, was Eleanor Holm, wearing something yellow, casually smoking a cigarette, looking like a sunbeam. How the Hell had she gotten here before he did? How had she even heard about the event? The girl continued to confound him. He walked over to her.

"Oh, hello," she said. "He's not here yet."

"He?"

"*Indbergh-lay.* He's flying in."

"Yes," Nathan said. "I must say, I'm a little surprised to see you here, Eleanor. I thought you might be with Tom Wolfe."

"You did?"

"There seemed to be a mutual attraction."

"We ran into some inclement weather."

Nathan gave Eleanor a skeptical look. "What? It rained last night?"

"We had a political kerfuffle."

"I see," Nathan said. "How did it end?"

"Not well. He sauntered off, muttering something about arguing with a woman, saying he planned to drink away his time in Berlin until the competitions began."

"Hmm."

"I let him go. There was no way I was going to miss a chance to meet Charles Lindbergh."

"I understand," Nathan said. "But how did you know…"

"All the members of the press were invited, David. You didn't get your invitation?"

"I probably should have checked with the desk clerk."

"Some journalist you are."

He gave her a dirty look. "Just how did you get here? Oldenburg ferry you out in that land yacht of his?"

"I rented a car, of course."

"Really? What kind?" He supposed she knew nothing about cars, like most women, and guessed the rental agency had stuck her with a little Italian rattletrap, or worse, a flimsy Citroen.

"Oh, it's right over there." She pointed at a sparkling two-seat convertible, a greyhound in racing green. "It's an Auto Union W 25 K Wanderer roadster with a six-cylinder supercharged engine."

"Looks fast," Nathan said, confounded again. *This one knows about cars?*

"It is. Top speed is 90 miles an hour, they told me. What do you think of the wire wheels?"

"Very stylish," Nathan conceded.

Dick Helms came walking up. "Well, I see you made it out here, Eleanor."

"You never can tell about me."

"Can't argue with that—can we, old man?" He chuckled and jabbed an elbow into Nathan's ribs, but Nathan barely noticed. He was gazing into the sky.

"I think I hear something," Nathan said. "Actually, I think I see something." He buttoned his tweed sport coat—wouldn't do for

Lindbergh to see he was armed. Then he suddenly realized he'd left his shoulder holster in the hotel. God damn it, he thought. Had he forgotten that he was a cop, on a critical assignment? Fortunately, he thought, He wouldn't be needing it out here at Templehoff. He'd go back to the hotel later and pick it up. But this carelessness had to stop.

By now, Eleanor, Helms and other spectators had followed Nathan's gaze skyward. "Looks like a maple seed," Eleanor said.

"It's a tiny little airplane," Helms said. "Could Lindbergh be coming in *that*?"

A wave of excitement surged through the welcoming delegation and Hermann Göring stepped forward, attired now in a grey cashmere jacket emblazoned with medals and gold braid. He was smiling broadly and rubbing his hands together, evidently elated with anticipation.

"That's Göring," Helms told Eleanor, to Nathan's annoyance.

The little plane was clearly visible now, high in a cloudless sky, and the buzz of its engines sounded like a box full of house flies. Everyone shaded their eyes and stared into the sky.

Far above, coming out of the sun, was a toylike single-engine biplane, green with white wings, floating closer. It circled the field once, waggled hello with its wings, then set down—a little abruptly— at the far end of the field, bounced twice, and taxied toward the welcoming delegation.

"It's a de Havilland Hornet Moth," Helms said. "Not very fast, but highly reliable."

Nathan was a little surprised. "You know about British aircraft, too?"

"You forget I was stationed in London for six months before they gave me this little assignment, old man," Helms said.

"He knows about everything, Mike," Eleanor teased.

Lindbergh's plane taxied toward the crowd, stopping less than twenty feet from *Reichsminister* Hermann Göring. The engine died, the wooden propeller stopped spinning, a little door opened and out stepped a tall, slender man wearing a flight jacket, a leather cap and goggles. Off came the cap and the goggles, revealing the strong, handsome, all-American face of Charles Lindbergh, conqueror of the Atlantic. He was squinting in the sun and smiling uncertainly. His wife, Anne Morrow Lindbergh, a slender, dark-haired woman, followed him out of the plane, removing her cap and goggles.

Göring, magnetic, genial and a trifle grotesque, rushed to greet the famous pilot, throwing open his arms and smothering the American aviator in an enthusiastic bear hug. He elaborated the hug with passionate kisses on both cheeks, leaving Lindbergh a little overwhelmed and, to judge by his body language, a bit flustered. Then he turned to Lindbergh's wife and repeated all of his gestures.

Göring disengaged, hopped up on a little wooden podium no doubt built for the occasion and welcomed to the glories of the Third Reich, "my fellow pilot," and "one of aviation's greatest heroes." He promised to show Lindbergh "all the secrets of Germany's great aeronautics advances" while he was here for the Olympics. The applause was polite, although brief.

Finally, Lindbergh mounted the podium, thanked Göring and told the crowd how honored he was to be here, on his first trip to Germany, and how eager he was to see Germany's aviation progress with his own eyes. He said he'd heard wonderful things about German airplanes and about Germany itself. This time, the applause was generous.

Afterward, at the luncheon in one of the terminal's large public rooms, Nathan and his friends managed to find places within earshot of Göring and the Lindberghs. And during lunch, they eavesdropped and feasted on crust-free chopped liver sandwiches, held together with toothpicks, brought on silver platters by uniformed young men with uniformly excellent postures.

"Tomorrow, after opening ceremonies," Göring told Lindbergh, "I will take you to the Richthofen *Geschwader*, the Luftwaffe's elite fighter group. You can confer with the pilots."

"I would enjoy that very much, *Reichsmarshall*," Lindbergh said.

"And the day after that," Göring continued, "Generalfeldmarschall Milch will take you and your wife to two of our Heinkel factories, and show you our latest bombers and fighters."

Generalfeldmarschall Milch, sitting at Göring's elbow, reached over and extended a hand, which Lindbergh shook. "Erhard Milch," he said.

"Pleased to meet you."

Göring, who was the unchallenged ringmaster of this circus, proceeded to tell the American aviator how he would spend the rest of his visit. "And the day after that, *ehrte gaste* Lindbergh, *Oberst* Udet will take you both to the German Air Research Institute and acquaint you with our latest aeronautical experiments. Ernest?"

"I look forward to being your host at the state laboratories," said Udet, a handsome, open-faced man with a lively smile.

"Honored to meet you," Lindbergh said. "I've read of your exploits in the Great War. You shot down more enemy planes than anyone…"

"Except the Red Baron," Udet said, completing the sentence. "Yes, that's true. But today I am more interested in manufacture and development."

Generalfeldmarschall Milch bent toward Lindbergh. "He's being modest, *Herr* Lindbergh. He taught me to fly, which had been thought impossible."

They laughed, these comrades of the sky.

"What I'd really like to do," Lindbergh said, "Is to *fly* one of your marvelous airplanes."

Göring and Milch exchanged glances. "You had but to ask," said the *Reichsmarshall*. "Milch, make sure we have a fully-fueled JU-52 out there. And Ernest, would you care to be *Herr* Lindbergh's co-pilot?"

Shortly afterward, Göring headed out to the tarmac, Lindbergh in tow, the press scrambling after them. Helms was leading the pack, Nathan and Eleanor close behind. They were proceeding directly toward a big, three-engine aircraft with a corrugated aluminum skin sitting at the near end of one of the runways, where the grass ended. Anne Morrow Lindbergh hung back, content to see her husband honored.

"*Herr* Lindbergh," Göring said, "this is our largest landplane, the Junkers JU-52. Hitler uses one for his personal transportation. As do I."

"Impressive," Lindbergh said, "But please call me Charles, *Reichsmarshall* Göring."

"Only if you will call me Hermann," Göring said expansively. He opened the airplane's door, just aft of the wing. The American airman clambered aboard, followed by Udet. Göring looked out at the eager newsmen nearby. "Come on," he said, waving them in, "A dozen of you are going for a ride with Charles Lindbergh."

Helms was the first journalist on the airplane and he blocked out some of his colleagues so Nathan and Eleanor could get seats up front as well.

"Enough," Göring said. "All full now." He closed the door and went up front with Lindbergh and Udet. Udet quickly briefed Lindbergh on the controls, got takeoff clearance, then, in short order, the engines rumbled into life and the plane taxied down the runway, which proved to be a little bumpy. Sooner than Nathan had expected, the aeroplane leaped into the air and began to climb into the sky.

"What's the top speed?" Lindbergh asked, raising his voice.

"One hundred and sixty-eight miles an hour, at about 3,000 feet," Udet replied.

"Impressive," Lindberg repeated. "Well, let's give it a try."

Still climbing, he ratcheted the throttles forward as far as they could go. The engine growl turned into roar and the roar into a scream. After the plane climbed for several minutes, Lindbergh pushed the yoke forward and the plane suddenly began to fall out of the sky.

In the passenger compartment, Nathan and Eleanor looked at each other in surprise and concern. "Don't worry," Helms said, sounding a bit worried himself. "It's Lindbergh at the controls."

Nathan glanced back at the other journalists, who were all were gripping their armrests as though they feared being flung out of their seats. Then he realized he was doing the same thing. He made a conscious effort to relax, without success.

"One-Seventy, one-eighty, one-ninety," Lindbergh called out to Udet and Goering, reading the speedometer. "Two-hundred, two-ten, two-twenty!" And the plane tumbled out of the heights.

"Better level it off, *Herr* Lindbergh," Udet suggested. "This isn't *The Spirit of St. Louis*."

Lindbergh chuckled and pulled back on the yoke. The airplane leveled out and its speed dropped. "Sturdy beast," he observed.

Nathan gulped and turned to Eleanor, who seemed delighted by the flight. "Having a good time?" he asked.

"I've flown before," she said, "but it's never been this exciting."

In the cockpit, Göring turned to Lindbergh. "Yes, the JU-52 is a fine aircraft," he said. "It's built to withstand the rigors of combat."

Lindbergh peered out the side window. "The wings are interesting," he said. "Cantilevered."

"Yes," said Udet, "and you'll notice that it employs a *doppelflugel*. The trailing section of the wing is divided in two, along its entire length. The inner rear section functions as a flap, while the outer section acts as the aileron."

"Ah. Well, let's test that out." Lindbergh racked the yoke far to the left and the airplane suddenly—precipitously—banked in that direction, inspiring cries of surprise and dismay from the passengers.

So this is the way it ends, Nathan thought. The President sends him on an important mission. Not only does he ignore it, but in his pride and for his pleasure, he allows himself to be lured onto this aircraft. And now, he was going to pay the price, the price for Lindbergh's arrogance. He braced himself. They were going down. And Jesse…he was on his own.

But they weren't going down. A bare instant before the airplane was about to flop over on its back, with who knew what consequences, Lindbergh abruptly wrenched the yoke in the opposite direction. The Junkers slowly righted herself, then banked sharply to the right.

They were throwing up in the passenger compartment now, Helms being the first, apparently inspiring the others. Even Lochner was vomiting. But Nathan was fine and so was Eleanor. She acted like Lindbergh's aerial acrobatics were just a noisier variation on a Coney Island roller-coaster ride.

Ten minutes later, Lindbergh brought the Junkers in for a relatively smooth landing and taxied up to the terminal to free his captives. They stumbled out of the plane, definitely the worse for wear, Helms, Eleanor and finally Nathan exiting last.

"*Fraulein* enjoyed the flight?" asked *Reichsmarshall* Göring, taking Eleanor's elbow and helping her down the little ladder.

"Immensely," she said. "Lindbergh is a great pilot."

Lindbergh's wife, who'd been standing next to Göring, smiled broadly.

"Yes indeed," said Göring. "I'm sorry, *Fraulein*, I didn't catch your name."

"It's Holm," said Eleanor. "Eleanor Holm. I work for the International News Service."

"*Reichsmarshall* Hermann Göring, at your service," he said, making his eyes twinkle.

Eleanor gave him a radiant smile. "Very pleased to meet you, *Reichsmarshall*."

"I assure you, *Fraulein*, the pleasure is mine."

Udet and Lindbergh found their way out of the plane and the reporters crowded around them, eager to hear the conversation.

Göring eased into the group. "You approve of our airplane, *Herr* Lindbergh?" he asked.

"I admire it, *Reichsmarshall*. In fact, I envy it. German aviation is second to none and Germany is a great nation."

Out of the corner of his eye, Nathan saw movement in the press corps. It was one of the older reporters, William Shirer, a small, balding man with a natty black mustache and wire-framed glasses. He was shaking his head sadly.

Göring checked his watch. "Almost time for your press conference, *Herr* Lindbergh." Göring turned back toward Eleanor and Lindbergh headed for the terminal, surrounded by several reporters. Nathan left Eleanor to the *Reichsmarshall* for the moment and tagged along with Lindbergh. So did Shirer.

"Mr. Lindbergh, I know you were impressed by the airplane," Shirer said, "And at first glance, everything looks great in Germany. But I urge you to withhold your judgment. The Third Reich is not a normal government and Hitler isn't a normal head of state. There is evil here, profound evil. Nazi Germany is a terrible threat to Europe, and not just Europe."

"Well put, Bill," said Quentin Reynolds. He turned toward Lindbergh. "Look, Slim, you and I have known each other for almost a decade now. Take it from me, Shirer knows what he's talking about, Don't be so quick to praise Germany. Don't let yourself be taken in by Göring and his buddies."

"Count me in on this too, Mr. Lindbergh," said Red Knickerbocker. "Berlin has been cleaned up for the Olympics, but as soon as the games are over, the rats will come out from under the rocks."

Lindbergh was shaking his head, looking at the floor. When he looked up, he chose to speak to Quentin Reynolds. "Quent," he said, smiling, "you and I have known each other for a long time and I know you believe what you're telling me. That goes for the rest of you, too...."

"But..." Reynolds said, having heard it coming.

"But you're asking me to deny what I've seen with my own eyes. You're asking me to ignore my own instincts and my own impressions. I just don't see the world the way you do. Germany was down and out. Hopeless. Hitler has raised it up like Lazarus. He made it into a great nation again...."

"At a very great price…" Shirer said.

Lindbergh held up a hand. "Destruction always comes first, gentlemen. Then comes the rebuilding. That's the way life works. I've seen it for myself."

Hermann Göring and Eleanor Holm came walking up to the group. "I hope I am not interrupting something," said the *Reichsmarshall*.

"No, not at all," Lindbergh said with a smile. "Just nosey newspapermen trying to get me to say something controversial. As usual."

Göring led the crowd into a nearby room, where a podium and several rows of chairs had been set up.

"Now I ask you, Mike, old man," Helms said, "isn't this more interesting than going sightseeing with the athletes?"

"Yes, I…" Nathan said, then came to a dead stop. "Sightseeing with the athletes?"

"Yes. Today is sightseeing day for the athletes, their chance to see Berlin, Mike," Helms said. "You didn't know?"

"Forgot to check my mail," Nathan said. Damn it! He thought. Another rookie error.

Helms pulled a press release from a jacket pocket. "Here's the schedule, old man."

It came to Nathan in a flash—Jesse Owens wasn't confined to the Olympic Village at all. Not today. He was someplace in Berlin, far from the platoons of guards and soldiers, out in public, totally vulnerable. And *he* was guilty of dereliction of duty.

Nathan grabbed the paper out of Helms' hand and slid a finger down the sightseeing schedule, looking for where the US team was supposed to be. "Oh shit," he said. "Oh shit."

"What?" Eleanor asked, surprised at the outburst.

"He's at the zoo—or he'll be there in a few minutes."

"He who?"

"Owens."

Helms looked at them in confusion. "Owens? You mean *Jesse* Owens?"

"Yes, I had an appointment with…oh, it's a long story, Dick, complicated. But I have to go. Now."

"Well, whatever you say, old man."

"I have to go too," Eleanor said, grabbing hold of Nathan. "I'm driving."

"You are?" Nathan said.

"I'm the one with the automobile," she pointed out.

They hurried off to Eleanor's rented convertible.

The moment they got there, Nathan started rifling through the glove box.

"What in the world are you looking for?" Eleanor asked.

"A map. A map of Berlin. We have to figure out how to get to the Zoo."

Eleanor slipped into the driver's seat and switched on the ignition. "I already know where the Zoo is. I passed it coming out to the aerodrome this morning."

"Good," Nathan said. "Now let's see how fast you can get there."

Moments later, they were barreling down the street, cutting through sluggish traffic, racing toward the city center.

"Hey!" Nathan said, as the little convertible squeezed between a limousine and an ancient taxicab.

"You wanted fast, remember—although I don't know why we're hurrying."

"We're hurrying because Jesse Owens is out in public and in danger."

"You really think so?"

"Imagine what will happen if he runs into a group of Hitler Youth, demanding *Heils.*"

"That would be quite a coincidence," Eleanor said.

"Are you sure it would be a coincidence?"

Eleanor considered the remark. "You may have a point."

"Watch out for the moving van," Nathan yelled out, pointing frantically.

Eleanor cooly evaded the truck, slipping her car between a long black Mercedes and a Horch.

"I think that was Oldenburg," Nathan observed. "A little late to the party."

"Did he see us?"

"I hope not."

They took a left turn and found themselves facing the Zoo's main gate. "Park here," Nathan instructed, but Eleanor was already spinning the wheel, expertly maneuvering the car into a parallel parking spot.

Then they were out of the car, sprinting through the Zoo's wrought iron gates and into the Zoo.

Chapter Twelve

It was not a statue. It moved. It swung its trunk and snatched a thrown peanut right out of the air. But a moment before, it had looked like a statue, a giant elephant standing on a high, drum-like concrete pedestal about twenty-five feet in diameter, nothing between the animal and the public but a moat and a low fence to keep people from falling into it.

Even though he was desperate to find Jesse Owens and protect him from any threat, the sight was so surprising that Nathan paused to look at it. For a moment, he thought the great beast was simply going to step off its pedestal, hop over the moat and stroll into the crowd, with who could guess what consequences.

But no. The outer edge of the pachyderm's pedestal had been rendered impassible, at least for elephants, by six closely spaced rows of nearly invisible metal spikes around the edge of the pedestal, each sticking up about two inches above the concrete surface. This, apparently, was enough to trap the creature, which had learned that stepping on the spikes would hurt its feet.

By the time Nathan figured this out, a large, boisterous group of young men, obviously Americans, came into view, sauntering past the hyena pens and the monkey cages and planting themselves in front of the elephant, not far from Nathan and Eleanor. A herd of young boys, autograph hunters, came trailing after them, begging for signatures.

"See, I got you here right on time," Eleanor said, pointing to the Americans.

"You almost killed us," Nathan said. But she was right. There was Owens, to Nathan's great relief, right in the midst of this lively group, accompanied by other sprinters and by coach Snyder. Owens and the others were entranced with the elephant and happily signing autographs for the pesky children tugging on their pants legs.

"But he's perfectly safe, just like I said," Eleanor taunted.

"Yes. We were lucky."

She poked him, then pointed at the elephant keeper, a little old man in a dirty white uniform, looking bored, sitting next to a wooden box full of bagged peanuts. "Buy me one," she instructed.

Nathan smiled. "For you or the *elephanthey*?"

She gave him a nasty look. He shrugged, then dropped a few coins in the elephant keeper's hand. He gave Nathan a bag of peanuts, which he passed on to Eleanor—all the while keeping a close eye on Owens and the people around him.

Eleanor started tossing peanuts at the elephant, who caught them with his trunk as gracefully as Babe Ruth. "Here," she said, grabbing Nathan's hand and dumping a pile of peanuts in his palm. "You try it."

He threw a few, poorly, simultaneously trying to focus on Owens and those around him, while scanning the zoo pathways, looking for something suspicious, wandering Hitler youths, something out-of-kilter. Most people come to the zoo on only three occasions—first, when they are toddlers, second, when they are parents of toddlers and finally, when they are grandparents of toddlers. The zoo was crowded with representatives from each group, especially the toddlers.

And then he noticed a big brute of a man on a bicycle, wearing a floppy grey cap and work clothes, quickly pedaling down a pathway. The man was carrying a long, well-wrapped baguette of French bread in one hand, and heading toward the elephant exhibit, looking a little ridiculous on his spindly contraption.

Nathan regarded the fellow with interest, trying--but failing—to fit him into one of the three zoo visitor categories. He was particularly puzzled by the French bread. He couldn't figure out why a man would be bicycling through the zoo carrying a loaf of bread in a paper bag. Unless it wasn't a loaf of bread. And then, he realized he'd seen the man before—but where?

The bicyclist was picking up speed now, coming on strong, too strong—he couldn't possibly stop before smashing into the athletes at the elephant exhibit. Nathan was about to shout a warning when he suddenly saw what the French bread actually was: a long billy club, a nightstick, a truncheon designed to break bones.

At the same instant, he understood man's intent. He was heading directly for Jesse Owens, pounding the pedals, eyes pale and cold, raising his arm now, the one with the French bread—or, rather, the truncheon—aiming for Owens' legs and preparing to strike a crippling blow. Nathan imagined the sickening crunch, the shattered bones.

He took two steps forward, quick time, hoping to deflect the bicyclist before he could strike. And as he moved, he spotted a bewhiskered grandfather leaning on a walking stick. Functioning on pure instinct, Nathan quickly grabbed the thing—to the grandfather's outraged astonishment—and rammed it into the spokes of the bike's front wheel.

The bike's revolving front wheel wrenched the cane out of Nathan's hands, cracking it in half and sending Nathan sprawling. At the same time, the bike came to an instant stop, as if it had hit a brick wall, the front wheel disintegrating into a jumble of broken spokes and twisted rubber. Simultaneously, the rear wheel shot up into the air, flinging the rider out of the saddle and onto the tarmac, just short of the athletes—and Jesse Owens. The bike fell to the pavement, pole-axed.

The rider, a husky, square-jawed, man rose unsteadily. His floppy cap was gone, revealing his hair—a dull, rusty red. One pant leg had been torn at the knee and his left elbow was scraped and bleeding. He took a moment—nothing more than that—to re-orient himself, then started searching for the truncheon, which had slipped out of his hands.

Nathan also scrambled to his feet. A patch of soft grass had broken his fall. He saw the bike rider hunting for the billy club and he pounced on him, determined to keep the man from attacking Owens. He remembered the red hair. This was the SS officer he'd seen taking notes at the Olympic Village. And there was no question now that he still meant to do serious harm to the young American athlete.

Nathan swung on him, getting in one stiff punch to the jaw, but his assailant struck back, hard, knocking Nathan to the ground.

Meanwhile, the other zoo visitors were beginning to realize something strange had happened here and it wasn't over yet. Nathan struggled to get up again, but this time, a few bystanders, figuring this was just a common fistfight, decided to be good Samaritans. They grabbed Nathan and prevented him from striking the bike rider again.

"Ich denke, Ihr Fahrrad kaputt ist," said one of the good Samaritans, in fact the very patriarch from whom Nathan had grabbed the walking stick. He put a sympathetic hand on the bike rider's back, pointed at the wrecked bicycle, and shook his head sadly.

The bike rider brushed off the sympathies. Seeing Nathan back on his feet, he bolted down a zoo pathway, shoving his way through the crowd of parents, grandparents and children, knocking one little five-year-old boy into the bushes, provoking indignant shouts from the boy's mother and father, which he ignored.

Without a word to Eleanor or anyone else, Nathan took off after the red-haired brawler, thinking of what a fool he'd been. Roosevelt had been right. The man on the bike had been sizing up Owens for days. And now he meant to disable Owens or even kill him. And he might very well try again. He had to be stopped.

At least this was familiar territory—not Berlin, of course, but chasing some miscreant down the street. He felt like he was in uniform again, racing after a purse snatcher or hold-up man.

But the red-headed brute a hundred yards ahead of him was no purse-snatching Lower East Side juvenile delinquent. This was a strong, athletic man—a would-be assassin—who was evidently in better shape than Nathan , pulling away, loping down the street with the speed and grace of a triathlete.

They were out of the Zoo now, and heading out of the Tiergarten altogether. Nathan wasn't losing ground, but he wasn't gaining either. Up ahead, the man shot him a glance over his shoulder, and it was chilling—diabolically arched eyebrows over wolfhound eyes, face rigid with fury and purpose.

They sprinted past a big, well-appointed stable, with a dozen stalls, half of them filled with horses, surprising a few riders coming and going, then they were out in the street, both of them. Nathan's quarry gave him another quick look, without breaking stride. They were on a major road now, thick with traffic, the park on one side, a row of handsome stone mansions on the other.

They ran on for several blocks, Nathan beginning to close the gap, thanking God for all the hours he'd spent in the gym, boxing, and wondering where this gorilla had gotten his amazing endurance—he looked almost the size of that gigantic Italian heavyweight, Primo Carnera. And that brought up another problem. What, Nathan wondered, would he do with the guy when and if he caught him?

Pedestrians had been few and far between on *TiergartenStrasse*, since it was mostly residential, but now, here on *Bellevue* the pursuer and the pursued found themselves weaving their way through a growing number of strollers, most of them shoppers or business folk. And the chase was not going unnoticed, especially by those the fleeing assassin recklessly ran over. How long would it be, Nathan wondered, until the police took notice and arrested someone, probably him since he couldn't explain himself.

Evidently, the would-be assassin had the same fear. He suddenly slowed to a quick walk, tried to avoid crashing into pedestrians and he shot a quick look back at Nathan. The chase continued in a kind of desperate slow motion, to which the throngs on the sidewalk were oblivious.

First Nathan's quarry, then Nathan himself, strode past by a huge brick and stone building on the left, this one festooned with enough red swastika banners to carpet a football field. The attacker moved on, making for an enormous, stucco-covered structure next to the train station, an oval building standing out among central Berlin's prevailing rectangular Neoclassical stone buildings.

He sprinted toward the main entrance, just behind a movie house-like marquee, emblazoned with *Haus Vaterland* on all three sides. Just above the marquee hung a huge, colored version of the Olympic symbol—five interlocked rings. What kind of place was this? Nathan wondered.

Elbowing his through a group of lackadaisical tourists, Nathan rushed ran past a series of wall posters, evidently promoting whatever was going on here, and entered the building. He immediately found himself confronted by a turnstile, which was operated by a smiling brunette of about nineteen, hair in twin braids, dressed like a little Bavarian doll, her Dirndl ending significantly above mid-thigh.

She smiled and held out her hand. *"Das wird ein Zeichen sein,"* she said.

Money, Nathan thought. She wants money. But how much? It would have been a lot better if he spoke German. He pulled a few bills out of his wallet and showed them to the girl.

"Ein Zeichen," she said, delicately removing a single bill from his hand and beckoning him to go through the turnstile.

"Danke," Nathan said. He pushed through it and tried to find his red-haired foe. No luck. Instead, he was confronted by a modernistic flight of stairs, plus a pair of elevators with art deco doors and, perched on a thick carpet with a colorful geometric pattern, four flat-topped parquet-covered obelisks, one in each corner of the lobby.

Nathan took inventory—one flight of stairs, two elevators. According to the indicator, one elevator was at the top floor and the other was just coming down to the lobby. If the guy had taken the stairs, Nathan thought he still had a pretty good chance.

He was at the elevator door when it opened. The attendant inside—another one of the girls in an alarmingly short Drindl—smiled and bade him enter. Nathan didn't need a second invitation. "Up! Now! Fast!" He said. *"Schnell!"*

"Was hast du gesagt?"

"Up! Up! Up!" Nathan said, jabbing his finger toward the roof again and again.

Nathan still didn't know what this place was or where he was going, but attached to one wall, he found a framed directory—in German, French, Spanish, Italian and English. As the elevator rose, he studied it. And he began to realize he had stumbled into a truly remarkable building.

Haus Vaterland was a kind of department store of international restaurants and entertainment venues. On the first floor was a student beer hall. On the second was something called the Café *Vaterland*. On the fourth floor were the Viennese restaurant and the Rheinland Terrace. The fifth floor consisted of a Turkish Café, a Spanish Bodega, a Japanese Tea House and the Lowenbrau Beer Garden. And on the sixth, not only a Wild West bar and a Hungarian restaurant but the Palm Court Ballroom.

Nathan tapped on the sign to get the operator's attention. She saw where he was pointing and nodded. Finally, the elevator glided to a stop at the top floor, the girl pulled the door open and Nathan practically sprang into the Palm Court foyer. A small man in evening clothes, with very neatly combed hair and a supercilious smile approached him.

"Ein zum Abendessen?" He purred, offering Nathan a menu.

"Just looking for someone," Nathan said, pushing past him and hurrying into the dining room. He was hit with a wall of German dance music. At the far end of the room, framed by a profusion of silvered palm fronds, a dozen scantily-clad chorus girls were dancing and singing energetically.

The room was gigantic—two stories for most of its length, and then the dome at the far end, plus hundreds of tables, most of them occupied by well-dressed and obviously well-to-do Berliners, as well as Nazi officers in tailored uniforms, and enough potted palms to landscape Tahiti.

Nathan turned a practiced cop's eye on the room, scanning not only for his adversary, but for any kind of disturbance, any sign that the man might be hiding under a table or among the palm fronds. Nothing. He abandoned the Palm Court, leaving the Maitre'd thoroughly confused, and he raced across the hall.

Now Nathan found himself facing a pair of wooden swinging doors. He pushed through them and entered yet another restaurant, well, actually a Wild West saloon, complete with pine walls and a heavily timbered ceiling, from which hung clusters of antlers and something that looked like buffalo horns.

Waiters in ten-gallon hats circulated among the diners at the rough-hewn tables, stopping from time to time to perform some lariat tricks. On a small stage at the center of the room, a black-faced minstrel show was in progress, backed by the Sidney Bechet band, according to the sign. They were performing a melody Nathan recognized, *Streets of Laredo.*

"Howdy," said the hostess, a boot-clad cowgirl with blond braids. Evidently, she played two roles. *"Ein zum Abendessen?"*

"No thanks," Nathan said, scanning the room. No thug here, either. He hoped the man hadn't been smart enough to double back and leave the building. If he had, there'd be no finding him.

"Stairs?" He asked the braided cowgirl. She shrugged, not understanding. He offered a bit of sign language. She got it, and pointed to a door, and Nathan was off again. Pushing through the door, he found a set of wide, poorly-lit concrete stairs with steel pipe railings.

He hesitated a moment, listening for footsteps. And he heard them—heavy, thumping footfalls, a big man's footsteps, lumbering up toward him, accompanied by loud, harsh, raspy breathing. Was this his quarry?

Nathan held his position, trying not to breathe, trying to let the assailant come to him. But at that moment, the footsteps also stopped. Where was the guy—one flight down, two flights down? Was he listening for his pursuer?

Keeping his movements to a minimum, Nathan leaned toward the railing until he could see the stairs below. And there was the red-haired man, all right, looking down the stairwell, in hopes of spotting his pursuer. Nathan pulled back swiftly, before the man had the impulse to look upward. Two flights of steps separated them now, sixteen steps.

Keep coming, Nathan thought. Come to me.

The footsteps began again, more slowly, more cautiously. Nathan prepared himself. He intended to jump his opponent as he turned onto this flight of stairs, and kick him. The guy was big—he'd have to go for his head, knock him unconscious if he could.

Then what? Call the cops? Report the attack to Olympic authorities? No—those didn't sound like good ideas. So what could he do if he managed to catch the thug? Two things, he thought: First, assuming the man spoke English, get as much information out of him as possible—especially who put him up to the attack and if there's more on the way; Second, disable him—break an arm, or better yet, a leg. That, at least, would take one player out of the game, maybe the key one.

The footsteps stopped one flight of stairs below him. Then they resumed, without getting closer. A door opened and music flooded out into the stairwell—oompa, oompa music. Then door closed and the music disappeared, along with the footsteps. Nathan's quarry had decided to take his chances on the fourth floor.

Down the stairs Nathan came, two at a time, and found two doors at the landing, one to the right, marked *'Bodega,'* one to the left, which bore the sign *'Muchener Loenbrau Saal.'* Nathan recalled the music— the oompa oompa. Nothing Spanish about that.

He opened the door cautiously, and found himself in yet another large restaurant, this one two stories tall, with tables on both the main floor and a mezzanine, all of them covered with broad white table cloths and set with four elaborately carved and painted chairs.

The place was nearly full of carousing beer drinkers, hoisting steins, making toasts and singing Bavarian melodies along with a promenading brass band. Buxom barmaids in traditional costumes carried trays full of overflowing beer mugs, trying to keep the patrons supplied with suds.

His red-haired antagonist was hurrying down a broad, middle aisle between the rows of tables, past the carousing beer-drinkers. And coming up the very same aisle was one of the room's most buxom barmaids, who was, with remarkable skill, levitating two huge wooden trays of full beer steins and a few dishes of *bratwurst* and *wiener schnitzel* .

The red-haired man, concentrating on his pursuer rather than on where he was going, looked back over his shoulder at exactly the wrong moment. Though the barmaid tried gallantly to swerve, preventing the collision was impossible. And when they smashed into each other, the trays, the *wiener schnitzel* and the screaming barmaid flew into the air and showered the diners at the nearby tables with food and drink.

Nathan held back, waiting to see what would come of this, hoping that the beer-soaked diners would grab the red-haired brute, the agent of their dishabille. But they chose to view the spectacular mishap as a cause for renewed cavorting and carousing, and further drenched each other with the dregs left in their own mugs. No help here, Nathan realized.

The attacker somehow disentangled himself from the mess and continued down the aisle, brushing aside the few who tried to hold him responsible. Nathan followed, finding his way through the shattered steins and bratwurst scattered over the parquet floor. And he cursed himself for leaving his gun at the hotel. This whole thing could have been over a long time ago.

Nathan's opponent shot another look over his shoulder and strode around the tables at the far end of the room, doubling back toward the door. Nathan couldn't cut him off. He had to follow. Only a couple of hundred feet separated them now—he would be catching up soon and the fight would be on.

Nathan had been raised on New York's Lower East Side and he'd always been handy with his fists, a talent that had proved very useful when he was a uniformed cop. He knew how to deal with thugs—he'd spent ten years of his life doing just that. He'd often taken on men bigger than himself, and occasionally two or even three punks at a time, usually holding his own, usually the last man standing. He had a technique that almost always worked: Left to the gut, to stop the man in his tracks, then right to the jaw, to put him down. Repeat as needed.

Up ahead, Nathan saw the would-be assassin fling open the door and bolt through it. The door automatically closed behind him. Three steps more and Nathan put his hand to that very same door. And he hesitated. If he were this man, he would have stopped running. He'd be waiting on the other side, ready to bash his pursuer.

But there are ways to deal with surprise ambushes, chief among them—give the ambusher a taste of his own medicine. Present him with a surprise of your own. Nathan took a step backward, banged the door open with a single kick and burst through it, fists up and ready.

The blow, shooting out from behind a waste can, caught him on the side of his head and if he hadn't been able to hang onto the door frame, he would have gone down. He struck back weakly, blindly, a glancing blow off the mug's shoulder, a blow that was immediately returned, smartly, to his chest.

Nathan swung again, right hand, and missed entirely. He went into a defensive crouch, both hands up, but his rival popped him again, this time in the nose. Finally, Nathan got in a serious blow—a deep thrust to his opponent's breadbasket, producing a very satisfying "woof."

They circled each other, both wary now, missing haymakers, exchanging jabs, most of which landed ineffectively on each other's forearms. "Who are you?" Nathan demanded. "Who put you up to this?" It was what he'd ask a criminal.

"Ach," said the brawler, unleashing a stinging jab that caught Nathan in the cheek, "an American. I suspected as much. You are his bodyguard?" He grinned, entirely without humor and lashed out again, this time with a long left. Nathan knocked it aside.

"Who sent you?" Nathan was using his most intimidating voice, to no effect.

"Take a guess," the Nazi *mamser* suggested, slyly. He let loose a fast combination that pushed Nathan to the wall.

"Hitler?" Nathan asked, advancing again, keeping his right high, to protect his face, punching with his left, trying to find an opening and failing. The man was experienced—and very fast, considering his size.

Nathan shot a ferocious punch to the man's liver. It triggered a momentary wince, too swiftly followed by a contemptuous smile. "It doesn't matter who sent me," the hoodlum said, "you've only delayed the inevitable."

Nathan popped the man in the face with a jab and reared back for a knockout blow, but the assailant batted it away. "What do you mean, 'the inevitable'?" Nathan asked, grunting.

"I mean, next time we will finish him off—and you as well," said his adversary. He followed his words with a sharp right cross that caught Nathan in the jaw, and a left hook that put him down, although not out. "But for now," he said, standing over Nathan, "I must leave you."

The red-haired perp turned away from his fallen opponent and started down the concrete stairs. But he slipped—maybe it was the beer he'd walked through after the collision, maybe the fight had shaken him. At any rate, he lost his footing on the first step and his hands sprang out, trying—but failing—to grab the steel pipe railing. He stabbed at the stair with his other foot and missed. He began to fall.

By now, Nathan was sitting up again, but there was nothing he could do, even if he'd been inclined to do something. The assailant's head bounced off a wall. Somehow, he caught a foot underneath a railing, but continued to fall. His ankle broke with a resounding crack, then he tumbled again, bouncing, crashing, appendages thudding into walls and stairs.

Nathan watched it all, fascinated. People didn't walk away from falls like this, unrestrained tumbles down a dozen concrete steps. Sometimes, they didn't walk again for months. Sometimes, they never walked again—or did anything else.

The body lay on the landing below, crumpled awkwardly, bleeding from a number of places, mostly the head. The eyes were blank now, the mouth contorted with a mixture of fear and anger. Nathan walked down the stairs—carefully—to take a closer look.

His adversary was a big man, red hair, clean-shaven, muscular, wearing clean gray work clothes, probably new, and—to Nathan's surprise—custom-made shoes. He checked the man's left wrist and found a gold Hanhart chronograph with a calfskin band. Now that's interesting, Nathan thought.

He went through the assailant's pockets. A little cloth bag of Bosco *Superieur Cigaretten* was tucked into his left shirt pocket. His side pockets contained a carefully-folded clean white handkerchief, some keys and a few coins. And, lo and behold, in the man's left rear pocket, Nathan found a black, crocodile-skin wallet.

Nathan pocketed the wallet and the watch, brushed himself off, straightened his jacket and tried to finger-comb his hair back in place. Then, he cautiously opened the door to the left and slipped through it, finding himself in yet another one of the *Haus Vaterland*'s gastronomic wonderlands, the *Rheinterrasse*, according to the sign.

The vast dining room was surrounded on all four sides by a huge and highly realistic diorama of what Nathan assumed was the Rheinish countryside. It gave the impression that the entire restaurant was outside, overlooking a river. And the river? Nathan did a double-take. The river was real. At least, it was real water, burbling around the edges of the dining room.

Something was happening. The room was getting darker. God help us all, he thought, storm clouds are gathering in the diorama and the sunlight is fading. Then, thunder—and lightning—and damned if he didn't feel a little sprinkling of rain, which set off outbursts of giggling and cries of delight among the diners. It was a pretty convincing illusion, especially for the well-lubricated beer drinkers in the crowd, which included almost everyone.

Not surprisingly, none of the diners were paying much attention to him, even though he looked like the loser in a knock-down, drag-out fight. He cut through the tables, walking swiftly, and headed for the door on the far side of the room. He had to get out of here. He'd been a fool. The danger to Owens was very real. Roosevelt had been absolutely right to worry. He'd thwarted one attack on Jesse Owens, but that didn't mean anything. More would be coming.

Nathan took the elevator down to the lobby. Where now? It had been a good half-hour since he'd run out of the zoo. Owens and the athletes must be long gone by now. And, damn, he'd forgotten about Eleanor. She must be frantic, not knowing if he was dead or alive. He had to get back to the zoo.

Nathan flagged down a taxi, got in and sat down. It felt so good to be sitting.

"*Wo willst do hin*?" asked the taxi driver in a gravely voice. He was a little grey-haired old man, barely able to see over the steering wheel.

Nathan didn't have to know German to answer, and the taxi driver didn't have to know English to understand what he said. "The Zoo."

As the taxi joined the traffic stream, Nathan remembered that he had some unfinished business. He pulled out the hoodlum's crocodile wallet and began going through it—more than two thousand *reichsmarks*—this was no low-level *schlepper,* Nathan thought; a well-worn photo of a saintly-looking grey-haired woman with her arms folded across her chest, the guy's mother, he figured; a Berlin driver's license, a *Luftwaffe* identification card and a dog-eared Nazi Party Membership card dated Sept. 1921—all in the name of Alfred von Falkenhorst.

The name meant nothing to him, but the date did—von Falkenhorst had been a party member for fifteen years, an early joiner, probably well-known to party leaders, which meant his orders no doubt came from the top or somewhere near it. Someone in the Nazi hierarchy was determined to injure or even kill Jesse Owens. And when he discovered his man was dead, he might guess Owens had a baby sitter.

The taxi pulled to a stop. *"Wir sind hier,"* said the driver.

Nathan peeled off a few of von Falkenhorst's banknotes and handed them to the driver. The Zoo gate was directly ahead, but Eleanor's dark blue Auto Union Wanderer, which had been parked right beside it, was missing. He fervently hoped she had not gone looking for him.

Nathan walked back into the Zoo, for no good reason. He knew Owens and the athletes were gone, back at the Olympic Village according to the schedule, and not going anywhere until tomorrow morning, when everyone will head for Opening Day Ceremonies at the Olympic Stadium. And Eleanor wasn't there either. Could she have been snatched? He had to break himself of this habit—asking himself terrifying questions. They never helped.

Just inside the gate, the elephant was up to its usual tricks, plucking thrown peanuts out of the air to the great delight of its latest audience and to the profound boredom of its keeper, who had seen enough of this to last a lifetime.

Nathan approached him. "Do you remember? I was with a blonde *Fraulein"*

The elephant keeper studied Nathan's appearance with obvious disapproval, then sighed. *"Ach, die Fraulein."* He reached into a pocket of his dirty white uniform and handed Nathan a scrap of paper.

Nathan unfolded the note, which was scrawled in pencil: "David-- stayed as long as I could. Going back to the Adlon. Probably see you later. EH."

Hmm, Nathan thought, *probably see you later.* So much for frantic Eleanor, oh so concerned about his health. Still, he wanted to tell her what had happened. He needed her help more than ever.

Nathan flagged down another taxi and headed for the Adlon. As the cab was dropping him off, he saw Eleanor parking her car on *Pariser Platz*, in front of the hotel. Did she ever look any less than gorgeous, he asked himself.

"Aha," she said, "the missing David Nathan, and somewhat the worse for wear, I see. You caught the man?"

"We caught each other, you might say. But I was the one who walked away."

"You had him arrested?"

"Ah, no," Nathan admitted. "But he isn't a threat to Jesse Owens anymore."

Her eyes widened. "You didn't—um—kill him, did you?"

He couldn't think of a good reason not to trust her. "No, I didn't kill him. But he died, accidentally."

"Accidently? How?"

"You won't believe it if I tell you. He fell down a flight of stairs, concrete stairs."

She considered this. "So…that's it? It's all over?"

"That's the bad part. Before he died, he made it clear that Owens would be attacked again."

"But not by him," she said.

"No, not by him. But whoever sent him after Owens will just send someone else. Even worse, when the original hachetman doesn't report back, his boss may realize Owens has a bodyguard."

"Did you discover who he was?"

"Yes," Nathan said. "A man named von Falkenhorst, according to the Nazi Party membership card in his wallet. It was dated 1921, which means he was a very early party member."

"And given the 'von' part of his name, probably a high ranking one, although Falkenhorst doesn't ring any bells for me."

"He was also a superb athlete, possibly an Olympic competitor." Nathan said.

"You still won the fight," Eleanor said.

Nathan snorted. "I was extremely lucky. But I'm afraid his death might result in a search for me. And maybe you too."

"I think you're a little too worried," Eleanor said. "No one knows who you are—unless you left clues. Did you?"

Nathan was insulted. "What do you think?" he said.

"No. I'm sure you didn't. Anyhow, no one will be looking for me. No one knows we're together."

"Not even the elephant keeper?" Nathan asked.

"Well," she said, and let it hang.

"So," said Nathan. He checked his watch. The evening was here. Maybe they would spend it together if he could think of the right way to suggest it. "Maybe we…"

"You know," she said, "I'm exhausted. I'm going to go upstairs and turn in."

Nathan successfully resisted the urge to finish his sentence. It was just as well, he thought. He had serious thinking to do. "Yeah, me too. We'll probably run into each other tomorrow or the next day."

"No doubt," she said, and smiled. It was a little like looking at a sparkler.

Chapter Thirteen

Nathan was up early the next morning. He had to get to the Olympic Village as fast as possible. He mustn't wait until Owens got to the stadium. Another attack would be coming soon and he had to be there to protect his man—if he could.

Except for a few early-rising tourists and uniformed waiters, the *Furstenhof*'s breakfast room was empty. The other journalists were sleeping in, since the game's opening ceremonies didn't begin until mid-afternoon. Nathan wolfed down some scrambled eggs and toast and headed out the door.

Eleanor's little blue convertible was parked directly in front of the hotel. "Hi," she said. She was in blue this morning, a perfect match to the car.

"Hello," Nathan said, surprised. "What are you doing here?"

"I have decided, that you can't be left to wander around unsupervised anymore. Get in."

"Get in? I have to go to the Olympic Village to protect Owens."

"I figured that. Let's go."

Nathan felt a few drops of rain and looked up. The sky was full of dark clouds. "Maybe we should put up the top," he suggested.

Eleanor looked skyward and frowned. "I'll drive between the drops," she said. "Get in."

He shrugged and took the passenger seat. "No crazy driving like yesterday, okay?"

"What are you gonna do? Arrest me?"

****

It was breakfast time at the Olympic Village. Thousands of athletes filled the vast dining hall in *Hindenburg Haus*, all dressed in jackets and ties, ready for the opening ceremonies later that day. They were seated by nationality to make it easier for the wait staff to deliver the appropriate national dishes. David and Eleanor quickly spotted the Americans, seated at a far corner of the room.

"You see him?" Nathan asked.

"There," she said, pointing.

Owens was seated at a nearby breakfast table, looking elegant in his jacket and tie, but he wasn't eating. Something was wrong. A few of his fellow athletes had left their chairs to talk to him and Snyder was patting his back, trying to reassure him. Owens seemed distraught.

Nathan and Eleanor found their way to his table.

"What's wrong, Jesse," she asked him, genuinely concerned.

He looked up at her, eyes filled with tears. "I just got this telegram." He handed it to her.

At the same moment, Snyder noticed Nathan and shook his head, as if to say *Not now.*

Eleanor read the telegram and handed it to Nathan, her expression grim.

Nathan read it Hout loud: "*Jesse Owens. Wife deathly ill. Come home soonest. Love. Mother.*" Well, he thought, looks like this assignment is going to be shorter than advertised.

Hearing the message spoken, Owens drew a sharp intake of breath, then choked back a sob. Eleanor and Snyder tried to comfort him.

Nathan continued to study the telegram, looking closely at the transmission codes printed on yellow paper tape above the ten-word message. He took Eleanor aside. "Something's wrong here," he told her.

"You're not kidding," Eleanor said, evidently thinking he was referring to Owens. "But it looks like he'll be out of your hair soon."

"I mean with the telegram."

Her reply was quick and sarcastic. "We all know that."

"I'm not talking about the message."

That stopped her. "What do you mean?"

"The transmission codes aren't right."

Eleanor didn't seem to understand. "That means what?"

"It means the telegram is a phony."

She looked at him, dubious. "You're sure?"

He showed her the codes. "These numbers indicate the telegram originated domestically, here in Berlin, in a government office. It was sent by way of the German Telegraph Union."

"I don't understand."

Nathan showed her the code again. "Look, if this had come from America, the codes would show it originated in Cleveland, Ohio, with Western Union, transmitted via the German-*American* Telegraph Union."

Owens, openly crying now, asked Snyder to get him a ticket home. He wanted to leave as soon as possible, immediately.

Eleanor looked at Nathan with undisguised suspicion. "You're sure about this code stuff? How do you know?"

Nathan pulled her aside. "I know because I once worked on a criminal investigation that involved Western Union. The codes broke the case."

She nodded. "You gonna tell all that to Jesse?"

"I can't. You know that."

"So?"

"So I'll tell him I was a Western Union courier before I was a reporter."

She smiled. "I may have underestimated you, David Nathan."

"Thanks, and it's Mike Novak."

"Right."

Nathan got Snyder's attention. "Something's wrong with this telegram."

"Yeah, sure," Snyder said, clearly annoyed, as though Nathan was butting in. "What's that?"

"The codes are all wrong," Nathan said. "This didn't come from America. It came from Germany."

"Meaning?"

"Meaning it's a fake."

"Why would someone send Jesse a fake telegram?"

Nathan shrugged. "Who knows? A prank? A gag? Someone trying to spook him? Your guess is as good as mine." Of course, Nathan knew exactly what this was about. And despite his better instincts, he admired the gambit. It should have worked. It damn well *would* have worked if he hadn't been there. The question now was what would they do next? Would it be another clever ploy—or another physical attack?

"Are you absolutely sure about this, Novak?" Snyder asked.

"I'm dead certain," Nathan said. "I was a Western Union delivery boy when I was in high school. Tell Jesse."

Snyder bent over Owens and whispered in his ear. It took a while before Owens paid any attention to him, but suddenly the sprinter raised his head and looked his coach in the eye. "You telling me the truth, Coach?"

"Damn straight I am, Jesse."

"But why would anybody do that?" Owens said, shaking his head. "It's stupid and it's cruel."

"Yeah, I agree," Snyder said. "Novak here thinks someone's trying to spook you, throw you off your game."

Owens was sitting up straight now, defiant. "Well, that's not gonna happen. I came here to run—and to win. And that's what I'm gonna do. But I'd sure feel better if I knew Ruth was okay."

"I think I can take care of that," Eleanor chimed in. "I'll cable the US and have your wife send a return message."

Owens wasn't convinced. "What will you say?"

Eleanor thought a moment. "How about this: *To Ruth Owens. Having great time. Will run tomorrow. Wish me luck. All well with you and mom? Love, Jesse.*"

"That's more than ten words, m'am, leastways I think it is."

"Don't worry about it," Eleanor told Jesse. "I'll cover the cost—and arrange for a pre-paid return."

"Will she reply, Jesse?" Nathan asked.

"To the telegram?" Owens asked, taken aback. "Oh, yes sir, we don't get many telegrams at my house. We take them very serious."

Eleanor went off to send the cable.

"Now listen, Novak," Coach Snyder said, "I don't want any of this showing up in the papers. You got that?"

"I have no intention of reporting any of this," Nathan said. "I'm 100% on Jesse's side. We all are, all the reporters."

"What are you doing here, anyhow?" Snyder asked. "We didn't expect to see news people until we got to the stadium."

"Sorry about that," Nathan said. "But Eleanor…well, she wanted to come out here this morning, and she's kinda hard to refuse. Women, you know?" He offered a sheepish smile.

Snyder nodded, knowingly. "Yeah. Women. And that one in particular."

Nathan gave him the *well-what-can-you-do* shrug, a gesture all men understood.

Snyder remembered his protégé. "So, Jesse, feeling a little better now?"

Owens looked up from his plate and broke into a big smile. "Much better, Coach. And soon as I hear from Ruth, everything will be fine."

"Well, eat up," Snyder urged, "I want you to get all the nourishment you need. Want another helping of eggs or bacon?"

"Coach, I'm pretty much stuffed now."

"Got time for a little interview now?" Nathan asked the young sprinter. "You know, while we wait for your wife's return telegram."

Owens glanced at Snyder, who gave an affirmative nod, apparently having warmed to Nathan a bit. "Sure, I don't think it would hurt none. What would you like to know?"

While the dining room emptied out, Nathan kept Owens talking for nearly a half hour, talking to him about his younger days, his remarkable triumphs, his chief competitors, his parents, his wife. It was a friendly, no-stress conversation and before long, Owens was relaxing, smiling, even laughing—the morning's scare fading away.

Eleanor was back in an hour with another telegram. She handed it to Owens, but he waved it away. "Read it to me," he asked, his voice quavering slightly.

"Sure, Jesse," Eleanor said. "*Jesse Owens. Everything fine here. Sure you'll win. Our prayers are with you. Love, Ruthie and Momma.*"

"Show it to him," Owens pointed to Nathan.

Nathan examined the telegram. "This one's genuine," he decided. "Originated in Cleveland, Ohio, about twenty minutes ago."

Owens flashed his most endearing smile. "Thanks. Thanks for everything, both of you."

"Happy to help," Nathan said. "Thanks for the interview."

The dining hall's loudspeaker crackled into life: "All athletes and coaches report to the main entrance for transport to opening ceremonies at the stadium." The message was repeated in half a dozen more languages.

Owens got up. "Better get goin', Coach." He walked toward the main entrance, and Eleanor went along with him.

Snyder got up to follow, but Nathan put a hand on his arm. "Keep an eye on him. They may come at him some other way."

"What do you think I've been doing for the last three years?" Snyder reacted. his eyes narrowing. "And what do you mean *they*?"

"I don't know. Whoever sent that wire. Pretty nasty."

Now Snyder was suspicious. "You know something I don't?"

Nathan laughed. "Know something? I'm a journalist. All I know is what I read in the newspapers."

They walked out of the dining hall together, joining thousands of athletes from every country, all wearing their finest, waiting for the buses that would take them to the Olympic Stadium. And at precisely

1:15 p.m., they began to pull into the driveway, maybe two hundred of them.

Nathan and Eleanor said their goodbyes and headed for the little blue convertible. "Nothing more to do here," he said. "We should head for the stadium."

"I agree."

Nathan nodded. "I'll drive this time," he told her. "You navigate."

She wiggled the key in his face and smiled. "Not bloody likely." she hopped into the driver's seat.

"Well, color me impressed," Eleanor said.

"What? Why?"

"Unless I've misunderstood what just happened, you've proven yourself to be fairly good at your job."

Nathan raised an eyebrow. "You think so?"

"I do, actually. First of all, you thwarted a vicious attack on Jesse by that Nazi bicycle rider."

"Mostly luck," Nathan touched his bruised chin.

"Maybe so, but for an encore, you uncovered a clever fraud that would have sent your charge hurrying home on the first boat that would take him."

"Also luck," Nathan replied.

"Don't be so modest," Eleanor told him. "You saved Owens— twice, once from a brutal physical attack, the second time from an insidious psychological hoax."

Nathan regarded the pretty woman and sighed. "You don't get it, do you?"

"Get what? That you know your job? That's more obvious than I thought."

Nathan shook his head. "Here's what you don't get, Eleanor. Those two attempts are just the beginning. The people who planned the bicycle attack are sure to strike again, somewhere, somehow. Same with the people who devised the false telegram."

"Wait. You think Jesse's being targeted by multiple people?"

Nathan nodded. "Yes. I think the attacks were conceived by two different people, one inclined to violence, the other a far more cunning enemy, someone who relies on guile. Maybe they're both trying to please Hitler. But both are very dangerous. Each could easily have succeeded."

"But they didn't."

"Not this time. But I am sure they'll try again. And you can't count on luck."

"So, what do we do?"

"We stick as close as we can to Jesse and keep our eyes wide open."

Eleanor saluted. "Aye, aye, sir."

Nathan frowned. "That wasn't a joke."

"I know," Eleanor said. "I promise to stay alert."

"If you see anything suspicious…"

"I'll tell you immediately, sir."

"Good." He quit while he was ahead.

****

It was about a twenty-minute drive from the Olympic Village through Berlin's outlying districts to the sports complex, of which the stadium was only a part. Even though the ceremonies weren't due to start for a couple of hours, the parking lot was already filling up and milling throngs were headed into the stadium. They parked and joined the crowds, who were not only hoping to catch a glimpse of the star athletes, but even more, of the glorious leader of the unquestionably glorious Third Reich.

"I thought it would be bigger," Eleanor pointed ahead, to the stadium, a low, grey limestone, granite and marble structure with simple lines festooned with flowing red swastika banners and billowing Olympic flags.

"It *is* bigger," Nathan said. "You just can't see it all—half is below ground level. They say it can seat one hundred and ten thousand people."

"Looks like it's going to be full."

Nathan stopped and tilted his head attentively. "Listen. Do you hear music?"

Eleanor imitated Nathan. "Franz Liszt," she announced after a moment. *"Les Preludes.* Must be a symphony orchestra in there. Wonder what they'll do if it rains."

Nathan held out a hand. "I think it's already starting to drizzle, and it looks like worse is on the way. Wouldn't that be a fine thing, Hitler and all his minions showing up for all the merriment, then having the whole thing rained out?"

At the gate, Nathan and Eleanor showed their press badges to the ticket takers and soldiers directed them to the well-guarded VIP stairway, which led not only to Hitler's private loge, but also to the press box only a few feet above. Both were cantilevered out toward the sports field.

Nathan and Eleanor stopped at the top of the stairs to gaze at the interior of the vast building. For the first time, they could see how truly enormous it was. Spectators already filled a third of the concrete benches that circled the stadium. It was the Third Reich's version of the Roman coliseum, minus gladiators. But they'd be here soon.

A full symphony orchestra was seated on the sports field, some sixty feet below, playing "Entry of the Gods into Valhalla," by Wagner. The rest of the field was covered with close-cropped grass, startlingly green, and filled with athletic apparatus—a pole-vaulting station, a long-jump pit, a hammer-throw setup and, most prominently, a red cinder race track, divided into lanes. Workmen were making final adjustments on the timing devices and camera crews were setting up in multiple locations.

A faint cigar-shaped shadow slowly made its way across the field heralded by a murmur of awe and Nathan looked up to see what might have caused it. It was the giant dirigible *Hindenburg*, about 500 feet above, floating just below the broken clouds, dangling a five-ringed Olympic banner from its gondola. It was bragging, masquerading as decoration, Nathan thought.

A score of journalists, mostly Americans, were already in the press box, smoking cigarettes, typing on the machines provided for them, sifting through German press agency photographs, and taking notes about the stadium.

"Hey, Eleanor," Helms said, waving, "over here. I saved you a seat."

"Got room for me?" Nathan asked.

Helms laughed. "Why don't you sit at the other end of the row? Plenty of room there, old man."

Nathan squeezed in, managing to sit between Helms and Eleanor, drawing a frown from Helms.

"Where've you two been?" Helms asked. "You missed all the fun."

"All what fun?" Eleanor said.

"We've been at the Olympic Village, interviewing athletes," Nathan explained, trying to stick it to him.

"I didn't realize you were so industrious." Helms replied.

"I was showing Eleanor the ropes," Nathan explained.

Helms glanced at Eleanor, who rolled her eyes.

"Well, you missed some amazing stuff," Helms said.

"Do tell," said Eleanor, sounding fascinated.

Helms leaned back in his chair and assumed a story-teller position. "It all began at *Pariser Platz* at 8 a.m., although I admit I got there a little late. The Berlin Guards Regiment band was playing *Grosses Wenken*—that's German for Grand Reveille, Mike."

"Keep talking," Eleanor prompted.

"Okay, well, all this was happening in front of the Adlon Hotel, where all the International Olympic big shots were staying," Helms continued. "Then, came the limousines, to take said big shots to church."

"But this is *Saturday* morning," Nathan put in.

Helms shrugged. "Anyhow, after the band concert, everyone headed down *Unter den Linden* to the *Lustgarten*—the big field at the end of the street. A few thousand school children showed up and started doing gymnastics."

"Rather bizarre, I'd say," Eleanor opined.

"Yes, I thought so too," said Helms. "Anyhow, they held a big ceremony to honor the Great War dead, and right in the middle of that, thousands of uniformed Hitler Youth and SA men showed up in the *Lustgarten*, all in formation—we had no idea why."

"Part of the ceremony, no doubt," Nathan theorized.

"Obviously," Helms said. "Anyhow, that's when we started hearing the cheering, coming from a few blocks down the avenue. Turns out, they were cheering the runner bringing the Olympic Torch. He jogged into the *Lustgarten*, lit a flame at the Old Museum, ran across the street and lit another at the Royal Palace."

"Is he going to light one here at the stadium too?" Eleanor asked.

"Dunno," Helms said. "Don't think so. Anyhow, after the fires were lit, the soldiers appeared, marching—hundreds of them, maybe thousands. It was all just grand fun—sorry you weren't there to see it."

Beside him, Grantland Rice, America's most famous sportswriter, had stopped typing. He'd evidently been eavesdropping. "Oh yes, it was all grand fun," he said, with more than a touch of irony in his rough, Tennessee accent. "Here, I've just been writing about it. I'll read you the lead to my story."

He rolled a piece of paper out of his typewriter and cleared his throat. "Just twenty-two years ago, this day the world went to war," he read. "On the twenty-second anniversary of the outbreak of that great conflict, I passed through more than seven hundred thousand uniforms on my way to the Olympic Stadium—brown shirts, black guards, grey and green waves of regular army men and marines—seven massed military miles rivaling the mobilization of August 1, 1914. And so the opening ceremonies of the Eleventh Olympiad looked more like the start of a world war than the beginning of the Olympic Games."

He looked up at Nathan, Eleanor and Helms. "Great fun," he repeated, an ironic smile on his big American face.

Helms wasn't ready to let it go. "What point were you trying to make?"

"Point?" said Rice, feigning offense, "I wasn't making a point. I was just describing what I saw." He rolled the paper back into the typewriter, paused for a moment of thought, then started typing again.

"Hey," Eleanor said brightly, "these are the Olympic *games*. And games are supposed to be fun. Aren't they?"

"Of course they are, Eleanor," said Helms. He turned toward Nathan. "Don't you agree, old man?"

"I'm not going to argue," Nathan said. He'd noticed a pair of binoculars sitting on Grantland Rice's table. "Mind if I borrow these, Mr. Rice?"

"Not at all, young man, and people call me Grannie. Can't say as I like it."

He handed the binoculars to Nathan, who pointed them at the grandstands and peered through them for a while. "I'm going to study the spectators," he told Eleanor, keeping his voice low. "Could you check out the sports field and let me know if you see anything, well, odd or suspicious?"

"Yes, boss," she replied. She lit a Lucky Strike and started scrutinizing the field.

After a few moments, Helms apparently became aware of Nathan's intense concentration. "What are you looking for, old man. Aren't there enough pretty girls close at hand? Eleanor, for instance." He looked at her and winked. She laughed and turned her attention to the sports field.

Nathan had scanned about a quarter of the stadium's top rows when Eleanor inhaled abruptly, turned to him, stone-faced and tugged at his sleeve urgently.

"What?"

"Take a look at the man beside the pole-vaulting set up," she whispered, "the one digging in the dirt with a trowel."

Nathan did as he was told. Something was odd about the man's movements. He seemed extremely watchful, almost furtive, as though he were afraid someone might be observing him.

"Use the binoculars," Eleanor prodded.

"Don't push," Nathan murmured, lifting the binoculars to his eyes. He watched for quite awhile. "Man's drunk," he finally decided. "No threat. But you were right to point him out

Overhead, the *Hindenburg* drifted past again, engines buzzing softly, t made a slow, wide circle and came back over the stadium once more, prominently displaying the red, white and black swastika emblem on its tail fins. Eleanor surveyed the packed stands, now full to the highest row. "Seems like everybody's here," she said. "So when does this shindig begin?"

Richard Helms checked his watch. "Almost four o'clock," he said. "As soon as *der Führer* shows up, I guess. Shouldn't be long now."

Chapter Fourteen

The blond, chisel-featured, broad shouldered adjutant knocked on Hitler's office door.

"Come," Hitler barked, almost immediately.

He entered the wood-paneled office and saluted. "*Reichsmarshal* Göring is here, with *Generalfeldmarshal* Sperrie and *Oberstleutnant* von Thoma. Also *Reichsminister* Göbbels ."

"Yes, yes," Hitler said without looking up. "Send them in."

The four men marched into the office, all resplendently uniformed and perfectly manicured, their gleaming boots soundlessly passing over the thick beige carpeting. They halted in front of *der Führer's* massive mahogany desk and simultaneously performed a brisk "*Heil Hitler,*" clicking their heels together smartly. Hitler gave his usual perfunctory response.

"Have a seat, gentlemen," he instructed. They obeyed. "So—the deployment of the Condor Legion—it is proceeding as scheduled?"

"*Ja, mein Führer,*" said the corpulent *Reichsmarshal*, still wearing the powder blue uniform in which he'd worn at the memorial ceremony earlier that day. "The first contingent of eighty-six men leaves today, along with six fighter planes, a dozen anti-aircraft guns and a ton of supplies. They will be stationed near Seville."

"Do they themselves have any idea where they're going?" Hitler asked.

"None at all, *mein Führer,* as you directed."

"And our transport of Franco's army from Spanish Morocco to Spain itself? How does that proceed?" Hitler asked.

"I believe *Generalfeldmarshal* Sperrie is best able to answer that question, *mein Führer,*" Göring replied.

Generalfeldmarshal Sperrie sat upright in his chair. He was a stocky, fat-faced, scowling man with a monocle in his right eye. "*Mein Führer,*" he said, his body rigid, "At first, we believed that ten JU-52s would be adequate to ferry Franco's army to Spain, but further calculations by the air transport office show that we will need twice that number."

"And when will Franco's troops begin arriving?" Hitler persisted.

"We are beginning transport today," Sperrie said. "Within two weeks, we expect to deliver twenty-five hundred troops of the Army of Africa to Spain. The entire force—Thirteen thousand five hundred soldiers, one hundred and twenty-seven machine guns, and thirty-six field guns—will be in Spain by October 11th."

Hitler nodded, pleased. "It will be interesting to see what happens when Franco's troops encounter the untrained militia of the so-called Republican regime. And when will we send more men and munitions, *Reichschmarshal* Göring?"

Göring consulted a small notebook. "Next month, we will deliver eight-six tons of bombs, forty Panzer tanks, and one hundred twenty-two tank officers to man them, plus support staff. At the same time, we will ship one hundred and eight aircraft to Spain to support General Franco's attacks on the Republican forces."

"Al manned by German pilots, of course," Hitler remarked.

"Half manned by our volunteers, the other half by Nationalist airmen, *mein Führer*."

"Good, good," Hitler said. "We want to give Franco just enough help to defeat the Republicans, but not enough to drag us into a European war. We're not ready for that. Not yet."

"We have calculated our numbers with great care," Göring assured him.

"And if the Soviets decide to send help to the Republicans?"

"I am confident we can out-supply them two-to-one," Göring said.

"This operation must be kept a strict secret for now, *Reichsminister*," Hitler insisted. "I want no notice in our newspapers and not a whisper in the foreign press."

"Our participation inevitably will become known once we engage Republican forces, said

Reichsminister Göring. "But I will make sure nothing appears in our newspapers or radio stations prematurely."

"Good," said Hitler. "I trust by the time the news comes out, we will have accomplished our aim."

"I can guarantee that," Göring offered.

Hitler smiled briefly, which Göring considered a reward. He spent a lot of time figuring how to earn those rewards. That was why he had decided to sabotage Jesse Owens. It was a quick way to earn Hitler's approval.

An unwelcome thought slithered into Göring's mind. He had heard nothing from Falkenhorst. No news about Jesse Owens suffering from a mishap had crossed his desk. This was annoying, even disturbing. By now the deed should have been done. He made a mental note to check up on his henchman.

"Excuse me, *mein Führer*," said *Oberstleutnant* von Thoma, a beanpole of a man, with a face like an ax blade and Mickey Mouse ears, "but may I be permitted a question?"

Hitler turned a cold eye on the man. "I do not believe we have met."

"I am *Oberstleutnant* Wilhelm Ritter von Thoma, *mein Führer*," he responded said. "I wil be commanding our Panzer division in Spain."

"You may proceed, *Obersleutnant* von Thoma," Hitler said, with a dismissive wave.

"Wel, *mein Führer*, I believe it would help me do my job better if I understood your reason for supporting Franco."

Generalfeldmarshal Sperrie gasped and *Reichsmarshal* Göring stared at von Thoma as if the *Obersleutnant* had lost his mind. "Von Thoma, how dare you…"

Hitler held up a hand. "I think the *Obersleutnant* has a good point about doing his job better if he understands why he is doing it."

"*Danke, mein Führer*," von Thoma said, breathing again.

"I have several reasons for helping Franco," Hitler began. "First, a civil war in Spain wil distract the world from our remilitarization. Second, it will create an ally, a counterweight to Britain and France. Third, it will give us the opportunity to test our new weapons and military theories in actual combat. And finally, it will keep Mussolini guessing about what I plan to do with Austria."

"Brilliant," Göring announced, "absolutely brilliant! You are a living genius, *mein Führer*."

"Makes perfect sense when you explain it, *mein Führer*," von Thoma agreed.

Hitler ignored the flattery, which was a way of life for him. "And if these measures fail to defeat the Republicans, *Reichsmarshal*? What then?"

"We will bomb the cities," Göring told him. "We will start by obliterating a small town."

"One small town?" Hitler asked.

"Yes," said Göring. "as a demonstration. I've already found the perfect target—a Basque town in the North, near Bilbao. It's called Guernica."

Hitler nodded. "Good, good."

The adjutant knocked on the door again and Hitler bade him enter. "*Mein Führer*, it is nearly three o'clock, time to go to the stadium."

"The streets are prepared?" Hitler asked his adjutant.

"Yes, *mein Führer*. Forty thousand SA men guard *Unter den Linden* and the *Via Trimumphalis*, all the way through the Tiergarten, holding back crowds twenty to thirty people deep. The people of the Third Reich are eager to get even a glimpse of you."

Ah yes, Göbbels thought. The games are about to begin. And soon, thanks to me, Hitler will have a surprise, a very pleasant one. He will hear that his greatest annoyance with the Olympics—that American *schwartze* runner who aroused his intense distaste--will be absent, that he has fled back to America for some inexplicable reason and will not be able to challenge Aryan supremacy. And this without the slightest hint of violence, without even the faintest stain on Germany's Olympic Glory. Only the subtlest mind in Nazi hierarchy was capable of such a thing, he told himself.

Gobbels imagined Hitler's reaction—the smile, the handshake, the admiration. And that left Göbbels with only one problem: How could he modestly take credit for this achievement? How could he use it to tighten his bond with *der Führer* and further extend his powers?

Hitler stood, checked the buttons on his brown military uniform, adjusted the red swastika band on his right arm, put on his peaked army hat and left his office, Göring, Gobbels, and the others following.

****

The long motorcade of four-door open-topped *typ 770 Grosser* Mercedes left the Chancelery on *Wilhelmstrasse* and turned onto *Unter den Linden* just after three o'clock, proceeding through the rapturous crowds at a walking pace, Hitler in the lead vehicle. He stood in the front passenger footwell, smiling, right arm cocked and rigidly raised, palm outward in acknowledgment of the crowd's ecstatic cheering and the incessant roars of *"Heil"*, his left hand resting on top of the windscreen. His crude but prominent mustache, cut short to fit with the muzzle of a gas mask, memorialized his heroism and suffering as a courier during the Great War.

Every window along the ten-mile route to the stadium was filled with elated onlookers Olympic flags, and swastika banners flew from every building, every lamppost, every flagpole. The entire convoy was reflected in the glistening streets, wet with rain—which had honored the procession by letting up for the moment. A relay of white-clad runners brought up the rear, carrying the Olympic torch to the stadium.

At exactly two minutes to four, Hitler's car pulled up to one of Berlin's new Olympic landmarks, a short, squat tower on the edge of the sports field, which contained a gigantic bel, cast for just this occasion. A guard of honor drawn from all three military services met him as he set foot on the turf, as well as IOC VIPs and all fifty-two national athletic teams stood neatly arrayed on the vast grassy field.

Surrounded by uniformed and plainclothes bodyguards, Hitler walked purposefully through the national team formations. He was accompanied by the two highest officials of the IOC, both dressed like 19th century diplomats in top hats, starched collars and tails.

They were followed by representatives of several of Europe's crowned heads, then by *Reichsmarshal* Göring, Joseph Göbbels , now dressed in a white business suit, and finally a variety of other Nazi VIPs, including some soldiers in gleaming black boots and steel helmets. All were silent.

The procession entered a wide tunnel at the western end of the stadium, the Marathon Gate. As Hitler came into the stadium itself, thirty trumpets sounded an electrically-amplified fanfare, and soldiers hoisted the *Führerstandarte*, a red swastika on a purple background indicating that the leader of the Third Reich was on the scene.

Inside the stadium, the foreign press corps watched in fascination, and perhaps a little fear, as one hundred and ten thousand people, men, women and children—the vast majority of the crowd was German—rose as one, cheering in adulation, on the edge of hysteria.

After a few moments, Germany's most renowned musician, Richard Strauss, tapped his baton on the podium and led his huge orchestra, augmented by a chorus of three thousand, in Wagner's "March of Allegiance."

Marching toward his box, entourage in tow, Hitler was interrupted in mid-field by a five-year-old flower girl in a white dress with posies in her hair. When she curtsied, Hitler stopped to greet her, smiled warmly and bent to take the bouquet she had offered.

"So that's Hitler," Eleanor said to Nathan. She was gazing at the man, momentarily spellbound.

He had Nathan's attention as well. "The very same," he whispered.

"You know," Eleanor said, biting her lower lip, "when you see him up close, he's nothing much. Short and a little pudgy. The Charlie Chaplin moustache looks pasted on. And he seems a little ridiculous in that army uniform."

"I agree," Nathan said. "But apparently we are in the minority."

Bouquet in hand, Hitler continued his slow procession across the sports field, heading toward the Honor Loge, his personal box while the orchestra played "*Deutschland Uber Ales*," and the "*Horst Wessel Lied.*" Many of the spectators sang along. Far above, the *Hindenburg* took another turn around the stadium.

The music continued as Hitler and the IOC big-shots climbed the stairs to Honor Loge on the south side of the stadium. As he sat, the bell tower's huge bell began to peal, once every thirty seconds. The true protagonist of the Olympic Games had finally taken his place.

"Well now," Eleanor observed. "That was pretty amazing."

"Look at him sitting there, just below us, behind the bulletproof glass and concrete shield," Nathan said. "Imagine him watching Jesse Owens beating all the German runners, not just once but again and again and again."

"He might not be pleased," Eleanor said.

"No. Probably not."

The bells finally ceased, and, at the instant they did, two sailors manning each of the fifty-two flag poles around the rim of the stadium, began hoisting the flags of all nations participating. At this signal, the athletes began to enter the stadium, country by country, alphabetically by their German names, in the traditional opening ceremony parade, the orchestra providing march music.

Grantland Rice leaned toward Nathan. "This ought to be interesting."

"How so?"

"Wel, as each team passes Hitler's box, the athletes will acknowledge him and the IOC bigwigs somehow."

"With a *heil* Hitler and a Nazi salute?"

"I guess we'll have to see, won't we?" Rice said.

"It's even more complicated than that, old man," Helms told Nathan. "Seems that there are *two* kinds of salutes—the good old *heil*

Hitler, with the arm straight forward, palm down—and something called the 'Olympic' salute, arm stretched out to the right. They look pretty similar, but the meaning is very different."

"Interesting," Nathan said.

"Here come the Greeks," Eleanor sang out.

As the Greek team marched past Hitler's box, it executed what was clearly an Olympic salute, which Hitler returned in kind. Eleanor and Nathan exchanged glances.

The first team to use the Nazi salute were the Austrians, who performed a snappy *heil* Hitler as they went by the Honor loge. Hitler returned that one too, and the thousands of spectators, all of whom were paying close attention to the gestures, erupted in applause and cheering. Another glance passed between Nathan and Eleanor.

But it was the French who caused the greatest excitement. As the two hundred fifty team members marched past Hitler, looking sharp in their blue jackets, blue berets and white trousers, they gave what the spectators interpreted as another Nazi salute.

The huge crowd went crazy—here was *France*, their traditional enemy, making obeisance to Hitler. The Great War was behind them at last. Hitler's illegal seizure of the Rhineland was forgiven. Peace was at hand! Their dreams had come true.

Nathan peered down toward Hitler's box, hoping to catch *der Führer's* expression—and he did. To his surprise, Hitler was not pleased with this spontaneous reconciliation.

Grannie Rice leaned over toward Nathan and Eleanor. "The crowd got it wrong," he said. "That was definitely not a *heil* Hitler. It was an Olympic salute. And Adolf knows it."

"Here come the British," Helms announced. "You can be sure they won't be giving any *heil* Hitler." And they didn't. They acknowledged Hitler and the IOC VIPs with nothing more than a sharp eyes-right. In the stands, the spectators were conspicuously silent, except for the few Britons in attendance.

But other teams gave Hitler exactly what he wanted. The Afghans, the Bermudans, Bolivians, the Icelanders, the Turks and of course the Italians performed *heil* Hitlers that would have made a storm trooper proud.

Then came the US athletes, the last team before the final entry, the Germans. The crowd was conspicuously quiet as the Americans approached. Unlike the others, the Americans were not marching—they were walking, almost strolling.

Nathan and Eleanor tried to simultaneously keep their eyes on the Americans and on Hitler, no easy task.

"This oughta be interesting," said Grannie Rice.

"Because…" Nathan prodded.

"Because America is a very proud nation," Rice said. "No flag dipping for us. No saluting. No paying homage. See for yourselves."

And the Americans came on, dressed in white flannels, blue blazers and straw boaters, led by Avery Brundage and a flag bearer, a gymnast with two silver medals hanging from his neck, evidently from previous Olympic games.

Nathan put the binoculars to his eyes again and slowly surveyed the US team, looking for Jesse Owens and Coach Snyder. For a few scary moments, he couldn't find them. Then, there they were, in the midst of the team, gazing at the stadium that surrounded them, open-mouthed, laughing and talking. He scanned the immediate area. No threats. Nothing out of the ordinary.

Eleanor whispered in his ear. "Everything okay?"

"Best I can tell," Nathan told her.

As the Americans passed Hitler, they removed their boaters and clasped them to their hearts, resolutely gazing at the undipped stars and stripes. The crowd reacted with almost total silence. Hitler's expression was unreadable.

"They don't seem to like us," Eleanor observed.

"Yes. Well, we weren't particularly deferential," Nathan said.

"That's part of it," Grannie Rice agreed, "the other part is that everyone's picking us to beat them pretty badly. And then some may remember that nasty little war—who won, I mean."

At that moment, the German team came through the entrance in perfect rows, eight across, dressed completely in white, wearing yachting caps. Richard Strauss and the orchestra launched once more into *Deutschland Uber Ales* and the *Horst Wesselied*.

With a great roar, all the Germans in the packed stadium suddenly rose, one hundred and ten thousand arms outstretched in a vast, simultaneous *heil* Hitler salute, repeated by the entire German team as it marched past Hitler's box and joined the other five thousand Olympic athletes, officials and coaches on the stadium's grassy infield.

Now, the music ended and the stadium's loudspeakers crackled on. A phonograph record began playing, filling the air with the voice of the modern Olympics' frail founder, Baron de Coubertin, who hadn't been strong enough to come to Berlin, He spoke briefly and haltingly, offering words of welcome and consecration. This was followed by an agonizingly long speech by the chief German Olympic official.

Then, finally, it was Hitler's turn. He stood and spoke into a microphone. "I now announce as opened the Games of Berlin celebrating the Eleventh Olympiad of the modern era." Once more, the spectators roared their approval.

At that instant, a handsome young runner with platinum blond hair, wearing a white track suit emblazoned with an eagle, appeared at the stadium's east portal, carrying the Olympic torch, a hollow stainless-steel rod with a magnesium wick, lit by the fire that had come al the way from Greece. He trotted around the track, holding his torch aloft, climbed a set of steps and dipped the torch into the Olympic chalice, which was guarded by twelve Greek girls in scanty costumes. It burst into flame, to the wild cheers of the crowd.

This was followed by the raising of more flags, the unfurling national banners and, most spectacularly, the sudden release of twenty thousand doves or pigeons, their species dependent on the person referring to them. For some reason, someone had scheduled the simultaneous firing of a twenty-one-gun salute for just this moment.

The startled birds wheeled and turned back over the stadium, and in their fear and confusion released great gobs of guano. Thus lightened, they turned again, flying out toward the far horizon.

"Naughty *ovesday*," Eleanor said, grinning.

"They're not doves," Nathan said. "They're pigeons. I oughta know. In New York, we call 'em flying rats."

"Pigeons, doves, doesn't matter," Helms interrupted. "Different name, same bird, old man."

Al Laney, a writer for the International Herald Tribune began to type. Grannie Rice stopped him after he'd written a few lines. "Mind sharing?"

"Not at all," Laney said. He pulled the sheet of paper out of his typewriter have just watched the opening of the Berlin Olympic games," he read. "And it was a magnificent success, a remarkable demonstration of Nazi organizing efficiency, a personal tribute to

Adolf Hitler and a pageant such as the modern world seldom has witnessed. Germany has regained its place among the great nations."

"Yes," Grannie Rice said, "and there's nothing we can do about it."

****

Author's note: If you are of faint heart or easily offended, you need not read this next chapter. The story hangs together without it. However, if you want to know how Eleanor and Nathan, giving in to their curiosity, almost wrecked their mission, feel free to read on.

Chapter Fifteen

If they'd wanted to, Eleanor and Nathan could have lingered after the Opening Ceremonies ended, subjecting themselves to more hours of marching and band music, but enough was enough.

As soon as Hitler and his troupe departed, Eleanor and Nathan left the stadium and walked out to the nearby sports field, where they watched Owens and the other athletes board their buses.

"Notice anything odd?" Nathan asked Eleanor.

Eleanor surveyed the scene. "Not really," she said. "You see something?"

"Yes. The American athletes seem to be making a point of surrounding Owens. I wonder if that's on purpose." He spotted Coach Snyder and waved him over.

"What's up, Novak?"

"Our team seems almost to be guarding Jesse," Nathan said.

"There's no 'almost' about it," Snyder admitted. "I asked them to watch out for Owens. That telegram business really bothered me. Someone is trying to tamper with him."

"I agree," Nathan said.

"So, I asked the rest of our boys to keep a close eye on him."

"Good idea," Eleanor put in.

She and Nathan waited until the US athletes boarded the buses and left for the safety of the Olympic Village. Then, the two of them hopped into the little blue convertible and drove back into the city, the lady at the wheel.

What now, Nathan wondered. They could go back to their respective hotels and get a good night's sleep, which would be good. They had to be up early the next morning, to check in with Owens at the Olympic Village and make sure he was safe.

On the other hand, Nathan thought, he was with this beautiful, and for that matter, very flirtatious girl and neither of them had anything pressing to do that evening. She'd brushed him off before, but there might never be a better opportunity to try again.

He tried to imagine his next line of dialogue before he uttered it and came out with this: "So, it looks like we have a free evening…"

"You want me to drop you off at your hotel?" She asked.

"Not necessarily," he said, improvising now, "we could have dinner and…" He couldn't think how to end the sentence.

"You know what I've been dying to do?" Eleanor asked, evidently missing the point entirely.

He sure knew what she hadn't been dying to do. "No idea," he said.

They were driving through the Tiergarten now, through the Brandenburg Gate, heading for the Adlon Hotel and the *Unter den Linden.*

"Go to a cabaret," she said. "Berlin is absolutely famous for them."

"Notorious might be a better word."

"My Aunt Pauline from Muncie, Indiana—she's the Bohemian one—she visited Berlin twice in the late 1920s and she gave me a list."

"Of cabarets? Will they still be open?"

"The best ones, wildest ones, the ones with homosexuals and naked women, the political ones that make naughty fun of Hitler."

This was not what Nathan had in mind. "Couldn't we just spend a quiet evening at the Hotel—dinner in the restaurant and maybe…"

She interrupted. "You don't want to take me to a cabaret?"

"Are you really sure you want to go? I have to be at the Olympic Village first thing tomorrow, you know. Don't you…"

They stopped at the traffic light just in front of the Brandenburg Gate. "Hmmm," Eleanor mused. "Maybe Dickie will take me."

"Dickie?

"Dickie Helms, silly. Or maybe Tommy would be up for it."

"I assume you're referring to Tom Wolfe."

She gave him a bright, innocent smile. The light changed and she drove into *Pariser Platz.*

Nathan sighed. He knew when it was time to give up. "Okay. A cabaret. But let's talk to the Adlon concierge. He'll know the best one. Dinner afterward. Deal?"

"Deal," she said, pulling up to the hotel.

Inside, they found a slim, blue-eyed, immaculately uniformed and perfectly manicured young man seated at the concierge desk. He looked up at them with the polished, totally artificial smile of a man whose entire job it was to seem eager to help. "Yes?" he said. "How can I be of service?"

Nathan cleared his throat. "The lady wants to go to a cabaret tonight…"

"Something debauched or hedonistic," Eleanor interrupted, beaming angelically. "You know, with naked women or men kissing men and women kissing women. Or maybe some political satire."

Nathan opened his mouth, hoping to say something to tone down Eleanor's request, but nothing came to him.

The concierge shook his head sadly, apparently having heard the request all too often, and from people even less likely than this blonde young lady. "Those days are over, I'm afraid. The Third Reich doesn't approve of such places. The few cabarets still open feature acrobats, jugglers, harmonica players, that sort of thing. *Very* tame, nothing shocking. The rest have been shuttered."

"Oh well," Nathan said, taking her elbow. This was exactly the response he'd hoped for.

"Come on now," Eleanor said, with a little wheedling smile, "one of the old cabarets must still be open, the Nazis couldn't have closed them *all*. You must know of some little-known out-of-the-way spot where we could still get a glimpse of, well, what it used to be like."

"No, I'm sorry," says the concierge. "I don't know of anything…"
Her face fell.

"If I may make a suggestion," the concierge said, "You could go to the Eden Roof Garden. Some of the best people go there. Or, since you prefer something racier, you might try the Rio Rita nightclub. All the tables have telephones. You can call any of the other guests—strangers even—and indulge in a little harmless flirting."

"Perhaps I can be of assistance," said a voice behind them.

Eleanor and Nathan turned simultaneously, both absolutely astonished by whom they found addressing them. It was none other than Carl Oldenburg, their self-proclaimed tour guide, the man with the Horch roadster, dressed quite formally. He was studying some tourist pamphlets in a wire rack.

"*Herr* Oldenburg?" Nathan said, trying to suppress his surprise. "What are you doing here?"

"I just came into the hotel to visit the tobacco shop. I'm headed to the opera," he explained. "They're doing *The Magic Flute* tonight. And by sheer coincidence, I happened to see the two of you talking to the concierge and I accidentally overheard your question." He looked at Eleanor with a smile.

"That is quite a coincidence," Eleanor observed.

"Oh, I am a peripatetic sort," Oldenburg said, "you never know when you might run into me."

"That's for sure," Nathan agreed. He was dubious.

"At any rate," Oldenburg went on, "it just so happens that I might be able to help the two of you. There just may be one place…"

Eleanor immediately perked up. "Oh goodie! What's it called? Where is it?"

The concierge gave Oldenburg the evil eye, but he went on, undeterred. "It wasn't very well known, except to the connoisseurs….but I've heard some whispers…it's just barely possible…"

The concierge stood up and confronted Oldenburg. "We can't recommend anything that isn't on the list, sir," the young man said.

"I'm not recommending it," Oldenburg said. "In fact, it may be too disreputable for you two innocent Americans."

The concierge nodded eagerly, crossed his arms over his chest and sat back down, pleased.

But Eleanor wasn't ready to drop the subject. "Is it very debauched?" She asked, ever hopeful.

"Well, no guarantees, young lady, but as I recall, it had quite a reputation. Among the aficionados of such things. Of course, I've never been."

"And yet you're willing to recommend the place," said the concierge.

"Not recommending, young man. Just acknowledging its existence. It is our duty, is it not, to answer all of our visitor's questions."

Eleanor regarded the concierge. "He seems to be doing your job, young man?" Eleanor said." Then she turned to Oldenburg and smiled. "So. Are you going to tell us the name and whereabouts of this place?"

Oldenburg glanced around the lobby, as though he were afraid of being overheard. "It's called Pandora's Box," he said in a stage whisper. He purloined a pencil and a little notebook from the concierge's desk, jotted down an address and handed the page to Nathan. "Taxi driver shouldn't have any problem finding it. But don't say the name. Just give him the address."

"Thank the man," Eleanor told Nathan.

Nathan obeyed. "Thank you *Herr* Oldenburg."

"Happy to be of service."

Eleanor put her arm through Nathan's and walked him out of the lobby, leaving the argument to the concierge and *Herr* Oldenburg. "Couldn't be any harm in a little sightseeing," she said. Nathan surrendered and they slid into the first taxi in a line of five, all with checkerboard stripes painted on their sides.

"I wonder how Oldenburg found us," Eleanor said.

"Yes," Nathan agreed. "Very odd." He shrugged and read from the slip of paper Oldenburg had given him. "Twenty-eight *Martin Luther strasse*," he told the cabbie, an unkempt man in his forties who looked to be made of matchsticks.

"Off the *Ku-damm*?" he asked. He put the vehicle in gear and pulled away from the hotel.

Nathan shrugged. "If you say so."

"You know the place?" Eleanor asked.

"I know where twenty-eight *Martin Luther strass* is," said the cabbie, in almost unaccented English.

Nathan turned to Eleanor. "I guess we might as well take a look at whatever it is that Oldenburg wants us to see."

"Might as well."

They drove down the *Ku-Damm*, the Broadway of Berlin, then turned off at a small street and drove another couple of blocks, past warehouses and industrial buildings. The driver let them off in front of a gray and weathered two-storey wooden building.

The street was devoid of parked cars and pedestrians. The nearest street light was at least a hundred meters away. The building had no sign. If it weren't for a single sliver of yellow light shining through a shade in a second-story window, it would have looked totally abandoned.

Eleanor and Nathan glanced at each other, confused and doubtful. "Does this look like a cabaret to you?" he asked.

"Well, let's see," Eleanor said. She tried the door, which fell open. "Shall we?"

They entered the building and the door closed behind them with a creak. It was all one large mostly empty room, two stories high, with what seemed to be a cloakroom on one side and, in a corner, a pair of bathrooms. It was set up—to the extent it was arranged at all—like a theater, with a small stage at the far end and a few rows of folding wooden chairs in front of it, scattered haphazardly.

A single bare bulb hung over the stage, which was also bare, except for a few half-painted flats leaning against a back wall, an old set of drums, a big brass horn with a squeezable bulb, two ancient saw-horses and maybe a dozen ratty-looking costumes hanging from a badly bent metal clothes rack.

Eleanor took a few cautious steps, Nathan following and they surveyed the room. The ceiling was black and invisible. The walls were covered with fading anti-Nazi posters by Otto Dix and George Groz and the floor was unswept and deep in debris—discarded programs, here and there a soda bottle, a dusty, battered fedora, a glove. They slowly walked into the center of the room.

"Looks like the whispers were out of date," Nathan said. "This isn't a cabaret. This is the corpse of a cabaret."

Suddenly, the house lights went on, sending them into startled retreat. "I think there may be *Osts-ghay ere-hay*," Eleanor said, eyes wide and stifling a nervous laugh.

"Maybe we stepped on a switch," Nathan said, as if to convince himself.

Then they saw a flicker of movement at the left side of the stage. Someone—or something—was entering from the wings. It was a strange little man—or woman, it was impossible to tell—a dwarf perhaps or some kind of circus freak, with raccoon eyes from too much eye-shadow, attired in a gold silk kimono top, heavily embroidered, and a ruffled tutu bottom, with pink tights and toe shoes, topped off by a wizard's cap festooned with glittering stars, moons and planets. He was carrying a long, braided leather whip.

The dwarf sized up his visitors. "Ah," he said, with great good cheer, in a high, crackling voice, "I see you are Americans. Good evening, good evening. You are just in time. The performance is about to begin. I believe there are two empty seats in the front row. Please feel free to take them, as my guests. Refreshments will be served after the show." He cracked his whip against the stage floor and laughed.

Eleanor and Nathan stared at the little figure, totally amazed. "D-do you see what I see?" Eleanor asked.

"I think so," Nathan said, "if you're seeing a weirdly-dressed dwarf."

"Please make yourself comfortable," said the dwarf, offering a gleefully evil smile. "Welcome to Pandora's Box, the last real cabaret in Berlin. The others are nothing more than vaudeville. Tingle Tangel?

Gone. The Weiss Maus? Closed. The Blue Stocking? Burned to the ground, by accident of course. The Stork's Nest? Shuttered. The Catacombs? Razed. The Eldorado? Now it's a Nazi office."

"And I am the last of my kind. Kurt Gerron? Willy Rosen? Fritz Grunbaum? Werner Finck? Dead, in Dachau, committed suicide (they tell us), led away by the SS never to be seen again, fled to Belgium or Switzerland with nothing more than the clothes on their backs. But I'm still here, the last of the last."

"How much is the show?" Eleanor asked.

"How much do you have?" asked the dwarf, grinning mischievously

Eleanor dug in her purse and pulled out a wad of *reichsmarks*, which the dwarf snatched in one quick movement.

"Wait a minute," Nathan objected.

"I have to pay the performers," said the dwarf. "We're all here, you know, the whole troop—the mimes and the ventriloquists, the acrobats, the jugglers, the animal trainers, the chanteuses and of course the chorus girls, every last one simply dying to perform for you. But please be patient, our pretty ladies are still getting undressed, and the less they wear, the prettier they are. Sometimes they are quite bea-u-tiful." He cackled crazily. "Besides, the show would be cheap at half the price."

"What?" Nathan asked. "There are other performers?"

The dwarf waved a hand dismissively, counted the money and stuffed it into a pocket, obviously pleased with himself. "Okay," he said, "now make yourselves comfortable. You are about to witness what might be the final performance of the last surviving cabaret in Berlin. Tonight, you will see the naughty songs, the dances and the satire you seek as well as our uniquely twisted world view."

He gestured toward the front row seats, obviously trying to make them feel welcome, but Eleanor and Nathan were still too stunned to move.

"And I'll tell you a secret, don't tell Goebbels, don't tell Göring— but it's been a long time since we've had a house this full," the dwarf continued. "Yes, today we are open…Yesterday we were closed…If we are *too* open today…We will be closed tomorrow."

He paused to see if they were paying attention, then resumed, loudly and grandly. "And I will present the entire show to you, in English, since I see that you are both Americans. I'm Norbert Mann and I am the *conferencier* at Pandora's Box, or, as they say in America, the Master of Ceremonies."

The dwarf took two prancing steps toward the wings, then stopped, ogled his guests and produced a kind and tolerant smile. "I know why you're hesitating to sit down," he said, winking. "You're a little afraid. You think I just might be Jewish. Understandable, I suppose. But you needn't worry. I'm not Jewish. I only *look* intelligent." Again, the cackle.

This time, the dwarf sashayed away. Almost immediately, a pair of faded red velvet drapes fluttered out of the wings and fitfully proceeded across the stage, meeting at the center but leaving a three-inch gap, through which all kinds of movement was visible. Then house lights blinked out and a Victrola started playing jazzy guitar music.

Eleanor listened a moment. *The Sheik of Araby*, she said. "Django Reinhart."

"If you say so," Nathan replied. "I say let's get out of here. This is too weird for me. And I don't think it's going to end well."

"Nonsense," she said. "This is exactly what I was looking for. Sit. It won't kill you."

"Why are we here again?"

"For the sake of culture, German *kulture*."

He sighed. They sat. A moment later, the music died and the dwarf's head poked through the curtains, one eye looking directly at them, the other slightly to the side. "And now, Pandora's Box is proud to present our first attraction of the evening, the great—and quite notorious--Bergburg, ventriloquist extraordinaire. You will love him, money back," he said, and snickered.

"And don't worry," he went on, assuming a naughty leer, "soon enough, you'll see the *Nackttanz* –the nude dancing, which we all know is the real reason you're here. But you'll have to sit through this first. Can we have some applause for the famous ventriloquist, *Generaloberst* Bergburg and his remarkable nephew Otto?" He grinned at Eleanor and Nathan, who shared a *well-we've-gone-this-far-we-might-as-well-keep-going* look and broke into modest applause—apparently enough for the dwarf, who again disappeared behind the curtains.

A moment later, the moth-eaten red velvet drapes swung open again, revealing two figures, a man—the dwarf—in what appeared to be a comic General's uniform, complete with peaked military hat, a chest covered with medals, enough gold braid to outfit Lord Nelson, a revolver strapped to his waist, a monocle in his left eye. A much smaller figure was seated on his lap, a dummy, a little golden-haired boy in a Hitler Youth uniform, with apple-red cheeks, big eyes, bare knees and a malevolent smile.

"Good evening, ladies and gentlemen," the General said, "that is, lady and gentleman." He looked at the little boy. "Say hello to our guests, Otto."

"Hiya," the boy dummy said in a fair approximation of an adolescent squeak. "Hey, you're pretty cute, lady. What are you doing with that dog?"

"Stop that, Otto. Be respectful," the General scolded. He smiled at Eleanor and Nathan. "He's just a little boy, full of mischief. Don't mind him. We've been rehearsing Otto's lessons backstage and now he's ready for his examination. Aren't you Otto?"

"I'm ready for a nap," Otto said.

"Come now, Otto, we've gone over the answers again and again and I know you're ready for the test. Shall we proceed?"

"I wanna proceed to the bathroom," Otto said.

"No, no, Otto. You just went to the bathroom. It's time for your test now."

The boy folded his arms over his chest defiantly. "I'm not gonna answer."

"If you don't, I'll have to spank you."

The boy gave the General a nasty look. "You promise?"

"You'd better be a good boy, Otto," the General warned. "Now let's see if you can answer this question. How many kinds of Aryans are there?"

"Two," Otto said, turning his grinning face toward the General. "Non-Aryans and Barb-Aryans."

"No, no, Otto," the General said in dismay. "You can't talk like that. I warned you. If you keep it up, I'll tell your mother."

"When? While you're *schtupping* her?"

"Otto! Don't say things like that. Your mother and I are just friends."

"That's not what Daddy says," Otto said.

"Otto, you're just trying to avoid the test. Let's go on. Here's the next question: What does Hitler mean when he says he wants peace?"

"He means he wants a piece of Czechoslovakia, a piece of Poland and a piece of France."

"Now, now, Otto. You can't say things like that. You'll get us all in trouble." He caught Nathan's eye. "Even you and your pretty friend."

Nathan and Eleanor exchanged uncertain glances.

The General looked around in a panic to see if anyone—other than Eleanor and Nathan—had heard. "I hope the *Gestapo* isn't around," he said, looking thoroughly frightened.

"Don't worry, Pops. I'm just a little boy. What could the Gestapo do to me?"

"Well, they burned books, you know. Must I remind you that you are made of wood? But let's not get into that, Otto. Tell you what," he said, pulling a soda bottle out of a pocket. "Would you like a drink?"

"It's not whiskey is it?"

"No, no. I wouldn't give you whiskey. Even Hitler doesn't drink whiskey."

"Yeah, and I know why."

"Why, Otto?"

"'Cause he's a really *mean* drunk."

The General clapped a hand over Otto's mouth. "Don't say such things," he said. "*Der Führer* might get mad."

"You mean he isn't mad already?"

"Otto, Otto, what am I going to do with you? You should show reverence to Hitler, who is the savior of our nation. That's why in Germany today, the proper form of grace is 'Thank God and Hitler'."

"But suppose *der Führer* dies?" The boy asked.

The dwarf produced an evil grin. He looked left, into the wings, then right. Then he cupped his hands around his mouth. "You know what you say? You just say 'Thank God'," he said in a stage whisper. He winked lewdly and snickered again, then rose from his chair, bowed and pranced off the stage and the curtains closed once more.

Eleanor applauded and poked Nathan, who clapped a few times, halfheartedly.

"This is just what I was hoping to see," she said happily. "Isn't it just wonderful?" She pulled out a cigarette and handed the lighter to Nathan.

"I'm not so sure," Nathan said. He lit her cigarette and handed the lighter back. "I don't know that it was a good idea to come here. I have a feeling the Stormtroopers are going to arrive at any moment."

"I think you're being a little *aranoid-pay*, David."

"It's my job, you know."

The dwarf's head popped through the curtains again. "And now," he said sticking his tongue out and licking his lips lasciviously, "*la pièce de résistance*, the legendary chanteuse, Marlene, and her very special girlfriend, Martha. Some applause please."

Nathan and Eleanor complied, she more enthusiastically than he, although he found himself a shade less reluctant than before.

The Victrola started up again, beginning with a few clicks and scratches, which were soon replaced by tinny-sounding orchestra music. Then, the curtains stuttered open again, revealing two young women—a blonde and a redhead—standing in the middle of the stage, arms around each other's waists.

But only one of this duo was a living creature. And this was the bizarre little dwarf, the figure on the left, now a fantastical caricature of Marlene Dietrich, rouged, lipsticked and wearing a long blonde wig with hair that flowed over his shoulders and mostly covered what appeared to be a truly noteworthy pair of breasts. "She" ogled Eleanor and wiggled her eyebrows like Groucho Marx. "She" was wearing a bright red skirt so short and spreading her feet so wide that a gynecologist could have examined her as she stood.

The figure on the right was not a living being, but a life-sized female puppet, flesh-colored, a dummy, naked to the waist but for a gauzy, nearly transparent top, her long red wig purposely failing to cover her breasts, which stuck out like artillery shells. Each one was tipped with an enormous rosy red nipple, clearly visible under the gauze. She was dressed in black, patent leather shorts and thigh-high boots of the same material.

The dwarf and the puppet were connected by rods at their ankles, knees, elbows and hands, so that when the dwarf moved, the dummy moved with "her," creating a grotesque duo of coordinated songbirds, more a nightmare than a fantasy

As the music picked up, dwarf "Marlene' slowly swayed to and fro, bumping and grinding suggestively against her counterfeit companion, who returned the favor with echoed enthusiasm. "She" also flirtatiously batted her enormous false eyelashes at Eleanor and Nathan, who both reacted with obvious discomfort.

And then the singing began, the real Marlene Dietrich on the Victrola, her husky, suggestive, world-weary delivery unmistakable, and the phony 'Marlene' --the dwarf and "her" quavering falsetto—on stage, in a bizarre duet.

When the special *girlfriend*
Meets a special *girlfriend*
For a little shopping shop-the-shop hopping
Shopping without stopping

'Marlene' turned her head to the dummy and gave her companion a leering, yet chaste kiss on the cheek—evidently "shopping" meant something entirely different from shopping.

Nathan stole a glance at Eleanor, who reacted with theatrical shock for his benefit, gasping, then daintily putting a hand to her mouth and smiling slyly in his direction.

Nathan gave her a look. "Ready to leave?"

"Very funny."

On stage (and on the Victorola), the two 'Marlenes' resumed their song:

There's no greater pleasure
Than to shop *together*
And the special *girlfriend*
Tells the special *girlfriend*
'You're my special *girlfriend'*

As she and the real Marlene sang, the dwarf 'Marlene' caressed her girlfriend's hair, and looked at her with a tender, loving expression, tarnished only slightly when she licked her lips lewdly. By now, Nathan was making a point of not looking in Eleanor's direction. But if he had, he suspected, he would have seen a merry smirk.

The duet continued…

Oh you're my favorite girlfriend
My sweet and pretty girlfriend
I trust you, my girlfriend
To keep our secrets, *girlfriend*

Now 'Marlene' turned toward her imitation girlfriend, and the dummy turned toward 'Marlene' and the two of them kissed, briefly, on the lips—'Marlene's' tongue giving her girlfriend's lips a quick, mischievous little flick. The "secrets" between them were not exactly secret.

Eleanor produced another theatrical gasp. Then 'Marlene' resumed her duet with the actual Marlene's recorded voice....

So what does my special girlfriend say about that?
'Well I can I only tell you one thing
If I didn't have you we'd get on so well
'We'd get on so awfully well'
'Oh how well we get on together'

'It's almost unbearable *how well we get on together'* sang the tiny transvestite, slipping an arm around the waist of the grotesque redheaded female puppet on his left, clutching her close, then leaned over and planted a big wet kiss on the dummy, pretending to shove his tongue halfway down her throat. Then he hooted with laughter, turned back toward Nathan and Eleanor and sang in a suggestive stage whisper…

Just last week
Her boyfriend had her in a whirl
That romance is over
She's dropped him for a girl

'Marlene', the dwarf, snuck an arm around behind the redheaded dummy, then grabbed one of her pneumatic breasts and squeezed it like the lecher he was. The dummy's mouth turned up in a shy smile. Then dwarf ran one horny hand up the legs of the redheaded dummy, his fingers ending up in her crotch, which he fondled shamelessly, breaking into obscene cackling.

The duo ended the number with more shimmying and obscene gesturing, finally attempting and somehow succeeding in doing an impossible two-way split, the dwarf and the dummy girl, spreading their legs as widely as legs can be spread. In the dwarf's case, of course, the trick was both comic and pathetic.

Finally, the dwarf—and the attached dummy—pulled themselves up to a standing position and bowed deeply. "*Danke, viele dank*, said the dwarf, prompting his dazed audience to applaud, which they did, as much to get the pornographic pair off the stage as to show their appreciation. The dwarf and the dummy bowed again, and then glided across the stage, and the curtain closed.

As a cop on the beat in New York for nearly eight years, Nathan thought he had seen just about every depravity to which the human race was subject. But this kind of public decadence was new territory for him. He was actually shocked, an emotion to which he had believed he was immune. He was also embarrassed for Eleanor.

If Eleanor had been shocked, she had different way of showing it. "Isn't it scandalous?" She asked, giggling in delight.

"That's one word for it," Nathan granted. "But this is the kind of cabaret you wanted to see, isn't it, the kind your Aunt Pauline told you about?"

"It certainly is," she agreed. "Aren't you enjoying yourself?"

Before he could answer, the dwarf, sans rouge, lipstick and wig, stuck his head through the curtains again. "Lady and gentleman," he said, "I hope you found Marlene's performance to your taste. But in the event you are still unsatisfied with your visit to Pandora's Box, I am pleased to announce this evening's third act, the legendary comic stylings of one of Germany's greatest funnymen. I refer to myself, of course, Norbert Mann.

The drapes glided open again, spasmodically as usual. The dwarf was standing in mid-stage, next to a drum set, this time dressed in a tuxedo and a top hat. He was smoking a huge cigar. "Good day," he said to Eleanor and Nathan, "good afternoon, good evening, good morning, *gut yontif*."

He grinned broadly, took a deep puff on his cigar and blew a smoke ring as big as a frying pan. "Now, my audience, all two of you, I gather that you are merely visitors to our great city. So, before I begin my routine, I must teach you something, for your own safety. It is called *der Berliner blick* or, as people say in the hinterlands, *der deutch blick*. Watch me carefully…"

The dwarf stepped forward to the very edge of the stage and, very casually, turned his head toward the right just as far as it could go, looking over his shoulder. He held that position for just a fraction of a second, then turned his head just as far in the other direction and looked over the other shoulder. Finally, he looked down, to the right, then to the left.

"That, lady and gentleman, is the *der Berliner blick*," he said, "the Berlin Glance. You may have seen it on the street or in a restaurant. Men do it, women do it. Soldiers do it. Even policemen do it. Its purpose is to let you talk freely without fear of being overheard by the

Gestapo, or some nosy busybody who might tell the Gestapo. If you're going to be in Berlin for long and if you want to say what you think, you'd better master it."

He took another lung-filling puff of his cigar, and let loose another smoke ring, which quickly grew large enough for a poodle to jump through. Then, with an evil smirk, he performed an elaborate *Berliner blick* and sat down at the drum set. "Did you hear the Pope is visiting Warsaw?" he said in a stage whisper. "He came to give Poland Extreme Unction." He did a ta-dum with the drumsticks.

The dwarf looked at Eleanor and Nathan again, cackling. "A high-ranking Nazi visits Switzerland, points to a public building and asks what it is for," he said, grinning. " "That's our Navy ministry,' says his Swiss host. The Nazi laughs and says, 'Why does Switzerland need a Navy Ministry? You've only got two or three ships.' The Swiss answers, 'Why not? Germany has a Ministry of Justice." He did another ta-dum.

Eleanor laughed. It was a gentle tinkle.

"Think that's funny?" Nathan said.

"Shhhhh!"

The dwarf did another *Berliner blick,* then spoke in a stage whisper. "The Gestapo is about to shoot some Jews when the commanding officer walks up to one of them and growls, 'You almost look Aryan, so I'll give you a chance. I wear a glass eye but it's not easy to tell. If you can guess which eye it is, I'll let you go.'

The Jew answers immediately, 'the left one.'

The commander is amazed. 'How did you know?'

"Because it looks almost human."

The joke was followed by more of the dwarf's mordant cackling.

Once more, he walked to the edge of the stage for a *Berliner blick.* That accomplished, he continued. "One day," he said, "our esteemed Propaganda Minister Dr. Goebbels was touring German schools, to make sure the Nazi message was getting through. He asked one class to call out patriotic slogans. '*Heil* Hitler,' shouted one little girl. "Very good," said Goebbels. '*Deutschland über alles,*' another called out. 'Excellent,' said Dr. Goebbels. 'Now how about a strong slogan?' 'Our people shall live forever,' a little boy said. 'Wonderful!' Goebbels said, 'what is your name, young man?' 'Minister, my name is Israel Goldberg.' The dwarf did a ta-dum on the drum.

"Funny?" asked the dwarf. "To us, yes. But maybe not so much to Jews."

Nathan considered the little man, the ugly little man, the man with the obscene cackle, with the eyes that didn't quite point in the same direction, wearing a ridiculous and tawdry costume, a man, barely a man, on the final fringe of society. This man, he thought, has seen death. A lot of death. Including, without a doubt, his own. He is a bizarre little ghost, a wraith who had seen fit, for reasons known only to him, to materialize in front of them tonight.

Once again, this strange creature stepped forward, to the edge of the stage, and performed his customary *Berliner blick*. Finding no eavesdroppers, he continued.

"One fine summer day, a *Oberstleutnant* and his driver were whizzing along a country road in the officer's *grosser* Mercedes when a pig ran out of a farm and into the road right in front of them. They ran it over and killed it. 'Better tell the farmer,' said the *Oberstleutnant*. They stopped in front of the farm and the driver went in to tell the farmer what had happened.

After ten minutes, the driver came back to the Mercedes, arms loaded with sausages and wine. The officer was amazed. 'Why did they give you the food?' The driver said, "I do not know, *Oberstleutnant*. All I did was knock on the door, and when they answered, I said 'Heil Hitler! The pig is dead!'""

At that moment, the front door banged open, and two black-uniformed, obviously high-ranking Nazi officers entered, bristling with medals and malign curiosity. "What is going on here? What are you Americans doing here?" demanded the taller one, a handsome, long-faced man with eyes the color of polar ice. His voice was strangely high, but commanding nonetheless.

Nathan tore his eyes off the Nazi officers and peered at the stage. The dwarf had disappeared. The last vestiges of the cigar smoke had vanished.

"Do I have to repeat myself?" The officer asked. He sniffed the air as if he'd detected something and surveyed the room suspiciously but found nothing.

"We came to see the show," Nathan said.

"Show? What show?" the Nazi demanded to know. "There is no show here. This place is closed by order of the Gestapo."

"We only came in because of the lights," said the other Nazi, a little dumpling of a man with bulging eyes and a belly barely contained by his uniform.

"What are you doing here?" said the taller Nazi. He was talking to Nathan now and he sounded angry.

Nathan got to his feet, looking helpless and confused. "We're just American tourists here for the Olympics," he said.

"Someone told us there was a show here," Eleanor said.

"Who?"

Eleanor shrugged. "I don't know, someone at the hotel. The Adlon."

Nathan would have rathered she hadn't mentioned that, but there was no taking it back. He hoped she wouldn't say more.

"The Adlon, eh?" The officer nodded. "How did you get in here?"

"The door was unlocked," Nathan claimed.

"How long have you been here?"

"A couple of minutes," Eleanor said.

"See anyone else?"

Nathan shook his head, trying for exasperation. "That's just it—no one. No one to serve drinks, no one on stage."

"We were just about to leave," Eleanor added.

"It didn't look that way," said the Nazi officer. "You were sitting in the front row, as though you were watching something on stage."

Eleanor giggled and looped an arm over Nathan's shoulder. "Well, Mr. Officer, to tell you the truth, we were…it was a, um, private moment…"

The two Nazis looked at each other. "Passports, please," said the dumpling.

Nathan and Eleanor walked over to the Nazi officers and presented their passports. The dumpling examined them carefully, then handed them to his superior.

"Mike Novak," he said, reading. "And Eleanor Jarret."

"That's us," Eleanor said.

"I'm a reporter for the Cleveland Plain Dealer," Nathan said. "And she's working for the International News Service. We're covering the Olympics."

The Nazi officer compared the people with their passport pictures, then handed back the documents. "This is a disreputable place," he said. "You were lucky nothing happened to you."

Eleanor offered him one of her very best smiles. "I'm glad you got here when you did."

The Nazi officer gazed at them, smiling slightly. It was impossible to say whether he was being threatening or pleasant. Nathan thought it wise to assume the latter. "I guess we'd better be going," he said, "Do you know where we could find a taxi?"

The Nazi officers exchanged glances. The moment of decision was upon them. "When you come out of the door, turn left and walk three blocks," said the senior officer. That will bring you to the Ku-Damm. Plenty of taxis there."

"Thank you," Nathan said, taking Eleanor's hand.

"Try to limit yourselves to the main streets and the well-known tourist attractions," the taller officer said. "I don't want to have to rescue you again."

"Don't worry," Nathan said. "We'll stick to the Olympic stadium and the museums."

Eleanor smiled at the officer again. "Scout's honor."

"I'll hold you to your promise," said the tall Nazi officer, flashing his unreadable smile.

As they left, the two Nazi officers began ripping down the satirical posters on the walls.

Back on the street, Eleanor and Nathan looked for another cab.

"Do you know who that was?" Nathan asked her. "The taller one, I mean."

"Some Nazi bigwig. Looked like he had ice in his veins."

"He's not just your average Nazi bigwig," Nathan told her. "That was Reinhold Heydrich. I recognize him from photos I've seen. He's the head of both the *Gestapo,* the secret police and the SS, the *Schutzstaffel,* Hitler's elite bodyguard."

Eleanor frowned. "Bad guy?"

"According to his nickname."

"Which is?"

"They call him Hitler's hangman."

"Yikes. What was he doing here? Could he have been looking for us?"

"Good questions," Nathan said. "I wonder if Oldenburg had anything to do with it."

"Or the concierge?"

"Hmm," Nathan said, lifting an eyebrow.

"Do you think Heydrich may be one of the men trying to derail Owens?"

Nathan thought a moment. "Another good question," he said. "Have we done enough sightseeing?"

"For now," she replied.

Chapter Sixteen

They were up early, those who slept at all. It was the first day of competition. Yesterday's pomposities aside, today was the actual beginning of the Olympics. The athletes were overflowing with emotions: confidence real and feigned, carefree excitement—also real and feigned, very real fear of defeat and humiliation and, even among the most phlegmatic, the worst case of nerves they'd ever known.

Jesse Owens was naturally inclined to carefree excitement, the real thing. He knew his abilities. He'd accepted the adulation and the triumphs without being tainted by them. He was a natural man, who just happened to be the fastest human being ever to set foot on a track.

He was up this morning before his roommate and fellow sprinter, David Albritton. He stripped off his pajamas and reached for his running gear, which was still in his battered brown suitcase. Jockstrap, trunks, top, socks, running shoes. But there were no running shoes.

Owens felt around inside his suitcase, surprised his shoes weren't where he remembered packing them. He tried the other end of the suitcase. Nothing. He tried both sides. He dumped the suitcase out on the bed. No shoes. He thought a moment. Had he taken them out? Put them under the bed, maybe. He checked. Nothing.

Of course, they'd show up, he just didn't remember where he'd put them. But he remembered packing them all right, there was no doubt about that. He looked under Albritton's bed. No shoes there either. Strange. Disturbing even.

Albritton opened an eye, awakened by Owens' rummaging. "What's up?"

"Can't find my shoes," Owens said. He was puzzled.

"The ones you were wearing yesterday? They're over there by the closet."

"No, my track shoes."

"Must be around here somewhere."

"Yeah," Owens said, getting concerned, "but where?"

They scoured the room with increasing desperation. No shoes appeared. "Maybe Coach Snyder has them," Albritton suggested.

Owens grinned. "That must be it," he said. "Don't know why he'd take 'em though."

"For safekeepin' prob'ly," Albritton suggested.

"That's it," Owens said again. "Well, I gotta go git 'em. I be needin' em right now." He headed for the door.

"No," Albritton said. "You stay and rest up. I'll go for the coach."

He was back in ten minutes, accompanied by Coach Snyder. "What's this about your shoes, Jesse?" asked the coach.

"Can't find 'em anywhere," Owens said, really worried now. "You don't have them?"

"What would I be doing with your shoes?" Snyder asked.

"Dunno," Jesse said. "Just thought maybe."

"Your track shoes?"

"Yes. They're not in my suitcase."

"You packed them?"

"Not a doubt in my mind. Used them on the boat. Saw them in my suitcase yesterday."

Coach Snyder considered the situation. "Well," he said, "I just guess you'll have to use your emergency shoes."

"What 'mergency shoes?"

"You didn't pack an extra pair, Jesse? Everybody was supposed to pack an extra pair."

"I had a pair, Coach, but I lost them at the trials in New York. I guess some souvenir hunter swiped them."

"So you only brought one pair to Berlin?"

"Yes. They're my only pair, Coach. My lucky shoes. Coach Riley gave 'em to me in eighth grade. They're all I ever wear when I run, all I've ever worn. The hundred meter race is today. How can I run with no shoes?" It was the plaintive plea of a man who was confused and frightened, a man near tears.

"Well, we'll have to find you another pair," Coach Snyder reassured his star runner. "I'm sure one of your teammates has an extra pair and if not, one of the other teams surely will. What's your shoe size?"

"Size nine, Coach."

"Size nine it is," said Coach Snyder.

"My shoes are made of kangaroo leather, Coach. Don't know if I *can* run in anything else."

"Don't worry, Jesse," Snyder said. "We'll find shoes for you, good shoes. Why don't you and Albritton go to breakfast while I do some scouting around."

****

The little blue convertible pulled into the Olympic Village at 7:30 a.m., Nathan behind the wheel this time.

"Looks like they're already at breakfast," Eleanor said, observing the empty sidewalks and paths.

They entered the dining hall and headed for the corner the American athletes favored. Jesse Owens was sitting in front of a plateful of bacon and eggs, eating nothing, David Albritton sitting next to him, earnestly talking to his teammate.

"Hi," Eleanor said to Owens. "All ready for the race?"

Owens didn't look up, but Albritton glanced at her, shook his head and motioned for her to go away.

"What's wrong?" Nathan asked.

"We have a shoe problem," Albritton said, and he explained.

"They were a gift from my first coach," Owens said. "They're all I have left of him." He sounded devastated.

"What happened to them?" Nathan asked.

"They just disappeared," Owens told him. "They was in my luggage. Then they wasn't."

Nathan considered this. If the shoes have genuinely disappeared, he thought, the explanation was obvious. This was the second attempt to stop Owens in his tracks, literally. And he had to admire its simplicity and its subtlety. Owens will be out of the games and it won't seem like sabotage. It will seem like it's the runner's own fault. His carelessness. Very clever.

"Don't worry," Eleanor said. "It's just a problem to be solved. And we will solve it."

"You need the shoes to run today? You don't have any spares?" Nathan asked. He knew the answer before he asked the question.

Owens managed a feeble headshake.

Coach Snyder approached, arms full of old track shoes. "Hello Eleanor, Mike. You here again?"

"Can't stay away," Eleanor said, smiling.

"Jesse, let's go back to your room and check these out."

Nathan opened his mouth to speak, but Eleanor beat him to it. "Can we come, Coach Snyder?"

Snyder hesitated momentarily, then, remembering yesterday's business with the telegram, said, "Of course."

"Where did you get all these?" Nathan asked,

"Other sprinters. Other teams, too. They were very generous. They searched their quarters but this is all they could come up with."

"Sure to be something here," Nathan said. "Let me help you." He took some of the shoes and they all walked back to Owens' room, Eleanor chattering at the sprinter, trying to cheer him up.

The shoes Coach Snyder had collected fell into two distinct groups: the ones that didn't fit and the ones too worn out to use. None solved the problem, and each failure sent Owens deeper into depression. "What coulda happened to ma shoes?" He moaned.

"Probably some souvenir hunter, looking for a trophy," Snyder suggested.

"Could be," Nathan said. Not a chance, he thought. They'd been snatched in the middle of the night by some Nazi agent.

"Sporting goods shops?" Eleanor offered.

"Went through the phonebook with one of the German guides," Snyder said. "Only three shops carry track shoes and none have Jesse's size in stock. They offered to order up a pair. Take a week."

"We gotta have 'em this afternoon," said Albritton.

"Hmm," said Nathan, putting his chin in his hand, the pose Rodin had made famous. First, the telegram, now the shoes. Was it going to be this easy for the Nazis to get rid of Owens?

"We'll take care of it," Eleanor said brightly, looking at Nathan.

"How?" he asked. He wished he'd been sleeping outside of Owens' room and able to stop the shoe thief before he got away with his booty.

"I have an idea," she said with a twinkle.

"God help us," Nathan said, getting a smile out of Owens.

"Listen," Eleanor said. "Mike and I will find you some shoes. We'll meet you at the stadium before the first heat and give them to you."

"You will?" Owens said, disbelieving.

"We will?" Nathan asked. What did she have in mind?

"I guarantee it," she said.

"What are you going to do?" Coach Snyder asked.

"My secret," Eleanor said. "But you can count on me."

"Kangaroo leather?" Owens asked.

Eleanor nodded. "Yes. That or something close enough."

"European size forty-four," Snyder said. "Turns out they have different sizes here."

"Size forty-four in kangaroo," Eleanor said. She turned to Nathan. "You coming with?"

Nathan rose, feeling very dubious. Owens, he thought, seems safe enough here. Could Eleanor really pull this off? "Sure, if you think I can help," he said.

"Well, that remains to be seen," she said. "But let's give it a try."

"Okey dokey."

"Better hurry," Eleanor said, looking at her watch. "We have about six hours."

They said their goodbyes and walked briskly toward the blue convertible. "All right," Nathan said. "What's your brilliant idea? Do you know about a shoe store Snyder couldn't find?"

"Not exactly."

"What does that mean?"

They got to the car and Eleanor let Nathan take the driver's seat. "Well, my Aunt Pauline's list…"

Nathan started the car. "You're not going to tell me there's a secret sporting goods store on that list. And where are we going anyhow?"

"No. And we're going back to the Adlon. I left the list there."

"What good is the list?" He put the car in gear and drove out of the Olympic Village.

"My aunt is crazy about shoes. She wanted me to go to this fancy custom shoe store. It's a legend in Berlin, she says. I think the name is on the list."

"You think?" Nathan stopped at a red light and gave Eleanor a skeptical look. "You're going to tell me they sell men's track shoes, right?"

"No, silly. But I'm sure they know who does."

"And this is why you *guaranteed* Jesse Owens you could find shoes for him?"

"We had to raise his spirits somehow," Eleanor explained. "Anyhow, it's a chance, isn't it?"

The light changed and Nathan drove on, through the Tiergarten now, coming up on the Brandenburg Gate. "Just barely. If the name is there at all," he said.

They stopped at the Adlon and Nathan waited in the car while Eleanor hurried to her room to get Pauline's list. She returned in less than five minutes, choosing "triumphal grin" from her vast repertoire of smiles.

"The name was on the list?"

"Not only that, I have directions on how to get to the place. It's in Charlottenburg, less than fifteen minutes from here."

She navigated, he drove. Ten minutes later, they parked in front of Eleven *Goethestrass*, an elegant three-story brownstone with a small metal plaque on the door. A single word was embossed on it: *Schraeder*. There was a buzzer, but no knocker. Eleanor buzzed. No one came. She buzzed again and this time they heard movement inside.

The door opened to reveal a beautiful brunette woman just over six feet tall, obviously a model when she wasn't answering doors. "*Wir haben geschlossen*," she said, in a voice that was barely a whisper. Then, noting their lack of comprehension, "Sorry, we're closed." Not a trace of accent.

"My sister told me to come," Eleanor said. "She's a good customer, a *very* good customer."

The brunette looked them both up and down. "Name?"

"Um, Pauline Holm," Eleanor said. "I'm her sister, Eleanor."

"A moment," said the model. "I will speak to Schraeder." The door closed, leaving them standing on the stoop, wondering.

A long minute later, the door opened again. Standing there this time, evidently was Schraeder, a very tall, shaven-headed man with deep-set dark eyes, dressed entirely in black. If he'd been wearing a turned-around white collar, he would have looked exactly like a priest, the kind of priest often seen at funeral parlors. He held out a hand as if he expected it to be kissed, but Eleanor gave it a single shake and let go.

"You are not Pauline," Schraeder observed.

"I'm her niece." She tried a wheedling smile on him.

"You're younger," Schraeder said. "And prettier, if I may say so."

"It's been a long time since you've seen Pauline," Eleanor said. "I'm a little surprised you remember her."

"Who could forget Pauline?" he asked. "She bought thirty pairs of shoes from me on her last trip."

Eleanor laughed. "She always had trouble making decisions."

Schraeder stood aside, inviting them in. "So, Eleanor is it? What can I do for you today? You are shoe shopping, I hope."

Nathan considered answering—he hadn't said a word yet. But he thought better of it. This was better left to Eleanor, if there was any chance for success.

"Not today, Mr. Schraeder," Eleanor said. "I'm hoping for a favor."

The sepulchral proprietor raised one eyebrow and studied the two of them. "What can I do for you," he said finally.

Nathan couldn't resist any longer. "We have an urgent need for kangaroo track shoes, men's size 44," he said.

Schraeder looked at him for the first time. "And you are?"

"Mike Novak. I'm covering the Olympics for an American newspaper."

"Ah, a newspaper man. Who wants track shoes. You are planning to run in a race?"

"One of the American sprinters has lost his track shoes," Eleanor explain. "If we can't replace them in a few hours, he won't be able to run in the Olympics."

"So you've come to me?" Schraeder asked, incredulous.

"Well, I thought you might know…"

"You've called the sporting goods stores?" Schraeder asked.

"They don't have the right size or the right model in stock," Nathan said. "Take a week to get them."

"I thought you might know someone we haven't thought of, Mr. Schraeder," Eleanor said. "Pauline says you know everything about the German shoe industry." And there was the wheedling smile again.

Schraeder returned the smile. His was tolerant and perhaps a bit contemptuous, as though he were looking down on them. "I assume you have talked to the factory."

"The factory?" Eleanor said blankly.

"Yes, *Gebrüder Dassler Schuhfabrik*—the Dassler Brothers Shoe Factory," Schraeder said. "They make shoes such as you describe."

"We hadn't thought of the factory," Eleanor said.

Nathan was dumbfounded. "The *factory*. I am an idiot." He looked at Eleanor. "We are both idiots," he said, "and Snyder too. How could we not have thought of that?"

"Is it nearby?" Eleanor asked Schraeder.

Schraeder smiled again, this time a little sadistically. "Potsdam," he said and waited for a reaction. There was none. "Ten miles away, twenty minutes by car."

Nathan put a fist to his head. "Damn."

"Could you give us directions?" Eleanor asked, unembarrassed.

"Of course. But Adi Dassler does not sell to individuals, Only to stores. He is a very stubborn man."

"Could you talk to him?" Nathan asked.

"Dassler and I are not exactly friends," Schraeder said. "I can try, but don't be too hopeful." He pulled out a pad and started jotting on it.

Nathan glanced at the telephone on Schraeder's desk, then looked back at the man himself, making a point. Schraeder ignored him, tore off the sheet of note paper and handed it to Eleanor.

"Dassler's a talker," Schraeder explained. "It's going to be a long phone call. You're in a hurry, so go."

"Good idea," Nathan said. "Thanks, Mr. Schraeder."

Eleanor gave Schraeder one of her very best smiles, this one warm, even affectionate. "Pauline told me you are a remarkable man, *Herr* Schraeder. Thank you."

"Give my best to Pauline," Schraeder said. "Better yet, come back, buy shoes."

The brunette opened the door again and they left.

"I'll navigate," Eleanor told Nathan. "You drive."

"You know, that was a total waste of time," Nathan said, starting the car and driving off.

"Ridiculous," Eleanor said. "He helped in exactly the way I hoped he would."

"He just showed us how stupid we'd been. Factories. Why didn't *I* think of factories? If I'd been that dumb at the NYPD, Cardinal Conyingham would have ripped the stripes off my jacket."

"Cardinal Conyingham?"

"Nickname. Actually, it's Commander Conyingham. He's my boss."

"Really?" Eleanor said. "He sent you here? I thought it was Roosevelt."

"It *is* Roosevelt. I'm on detached duty, remember? I report to the President." And, he thought, the Schraeder detour was one part of the adventure he didn't plan to report to FDR—or Conyingham.

"Okay, the President, if you say so," Eleanor allowed. "Anyhow, I think seeing Schraeder was very clever."

"Waste of time," Nathan grumbled.

Twenty minutes later, they parked in front of *Gebrüder Dassler Schuhfabrik*, a neat, middle-sized two-story brick building in an industrial area. Before they got out, they exchanged glances. They both knew this was their last chance.

Inside the factory, Eleanor and Nathan were taken directly to Adi Dassler's office, the heart of the enterprise. To their surprise, he greeted them warmly. "Ach, Schraeder's Americans," he said. "I've been expecting you." Dassler was a handsome man in his mid-30s, with wavy dark blond hair. "Have a seat."

"I guess you know why we're here," Nathan said.

"Shraeder explained," Dassler said. "He said you were looking for a pair of these." He reached into a cardboard box, pulled out a pair of track shoes, and put them on his desk. "Kangaroo skin, size 44," he said, grinning. "Our most popular model."

"I'll be damned," said Nathan, genuinely amazed.

"That is *exactly* what we were looking for," Eleanor added.

"So I understand," Dassler said. He reached into the box and pulled out another pair. "Will two pairs be enough?"

Nathan and Eleanor were speechless.

Dassler reached into the box again and pulled out a third pair. "Just to be on the safe side," he said. "These are test models. They're all well broken-in."

"Mr. Dassler," Eleanor said with genuine gratitude, "You are a lifesaver."

"You're being very kind," Nathan said.

"Not at all," said Dassler. "I played soccer in my younger days. I know what it's like to lose your shoes." He put the shoes back in the box and put the box on his desk. "So these are yours—on one condition."

"What's that?" Nathan asked.

"First, tell me who will be using the shoes?"

"I guess there's no harm in telling you," Nathan said. "They're for an American sprinter named Jesse Owens. He misplaced his pair."

"*Mein Gott*, Jesse Owens!" Dassler said. "I think he's the greatest runner of our time. Okay, so here's my condition: after the Olympics, let me announce that Owens used our shoes."

Nathan considered this. "Anyone else make kangaroo-skin shoes?"

"No," said Dassler. "We're the first and so far the only. We chose kangaroo because it is uniquely flexible and tough—no other leather matches it."

Nathan nodded. "You probably made the lost pair as well," Nathan said. "Anyhow, I can't see any reason you shouldn't say Owens used your shoes."

"Me neither," Eleanor piped up.

A smile spread over Ari Dassler's face. "Then we have a deal."

Back in the car, heading toward Olympic stadium, plenty of time.

"Turns out Dassler wasn't difficult at all—just the opposite," Eleanor noted.

"Yes. Your Aunt Pauline's shoe supplier was the creepy one," Nathan said. "That tell you anything?"

****

By the time they got to the Olympic stadium, the place was already packed and the first heats of the 100--meter dash were already in progress. They found Owens in a dressing room, his track outfit covered by a blue sweatshirt with block letters spelling out USA, wearing his street shoes, waiting for his turn to run, but hopeless. Snyder was making every effort to comfort him, obviously without success.

"We're back," Eleanor said cheerfully, as soon as they saw Owens. "And we have shoes."

Owens looked up, surprised to see them. "You found shoes?"

"That we did," Nathan said, taking a pair out of the cardboard box. "Take a look." He handed the shoes to Owens,

The young Negro sprinter stared at them as though he were viewing a nothing less than a miracle, then he slipped them on, took a few steps and smiled broadly. "These are them," he said, gazing at them lovingly. You found my shoes," he said, astonished. "Where were they? Where did you find them?"

"They're just like your shoes, Jesse," Eleanor said. She looked at Nathan. Should they really explain?

"We went to the factory that made your original shoes, Jesse," Nathan said. "They're identical to the ones you lost. And if this pair disappears, we've got that covered too." He pulled out the other two pairs.

"You won't mind if I take charge of one of these," Coach Snyder said to Owens.

"No, coach. I want you to."

Snyder turned to Eleanor. "I can't thank you enough," he said. "You've saved the day—again. I'm grateful beyond words."

"You're welcome. But I did have a little help, you know." She tilted her head toward Nathan.

"Of course," said Coach Snyder, gripping Nathan's hand. "We owe you a lot."

"I owe you my life, Mrs. Jarret, Mr. Novak," Owens said.

Hope it doesn't come to that, Nathan thought. "Go run your race, Jesse. Go get your gold medal."

Owens took a few more steps, then stretched and headed for the door.

"One last thing, Jesse," said Coach Snyder. "When you run out on the field, remember that lot of Germans really believe in that Aryan racial superiority claptrap. So, don't get spooked if the crowd gives you a cool reception."

Owens was happily flexing his new shoes. "No reason to worry 'bout me, Coach."

But Nathan knew otherwise. There was good reason to be concerned—and not just about this race. So far, the attempts to derail Owens had been mostly benign. But the frustrated plotters may believe they have no choice anymore—they have to use violence to eliminate Jesse from the competition. He wondered—would it ever be possible to separate the Olympics from broader moral and political issues? Would they always pose risks? He followed Jesse out the door.

Chapter Seventeen

Joseph Goebbels leaned forward, holding a pair of binoculars to his eyes, as he surveyed the track-side benches where the Olympic sprinters sat. The phony telegram had failed, but he was confident his next gambit would work: stealing Jesse Owens' 'special' shoes. According to the newspapers, they were a gift from his first coach, now deceased, and an almost talismanic memento. And Owens himself would be blamed for their disappearance. How careless of him.

In a moment—once he was absolutely certain that Owens had lost the race--Goebbels intended to casually turn to Hitler, who was sitting next to him in the Box of Honor, and not only share the good news but take credit for it, with as much disarming modesty as he could muster.

Goebbels imagined Hitler's delight and the compliments *der Führer* would shower upon him. He also imagined the reaction of the man sitting on Hitler's other side, the fat and fatuous *Reichsmarshall* Goring, his frustration and dismay at being outwitted once again. Yes, Goebbels was all ready to be very pleased with himself.

At that moment, he spotted a Negro who looked very much like Owens taking his place on the bench. He spun the focus wheel on his binoculars, desperate for a clearer view, his heart pounding. Then there was no doubt, the perfect body, the broad smile. This was Owens. And, incredibly, wearing shoes the same color as those that had been stolen, shoes identical to those now sitting on his desk.

It was impossible, yet there he was. Somehow, the Americans had found a way to replace the missing footwear, even though had Goebbels had his men make sure that neither the other teams nor Owens' fellow sprinters had suitable extras to share, and no replacement could be found in any of Berlin's sporting goods shops. He didn't know where the Americans had found substitutes, but without a doubt, they had.

Goebbels put down the binoculars and Hitler casually reached out a hand, took them up and looked at something across the field. This was absolutely intolerable, Goebbels thought. He fought to control his rage. He had made two attempts to sideline Jesse Owens, two very well-conceived attempts, two beautifully subtle attempts and he had failed both times. Intolerable, absolutely intolerable!

What now? Was he ready to give up? No. He wasn't the sort of man to let failure derail him. If he had been, he would have lived his life as a cripple, depending on the kindness of others. But that was not in his character. In fact, he thrived on adversity. It inspired him.

Goebbels knew what to do now. He'd figured it out long ago, but he'd resisted the idea because it was just too…too crude…too obvious. Nonetheless, it had to be done, and the sooner the better. He rose and turned to Hitler. "Excuse me *mein Führer*," he said. "I have a little business to conduct."

"Don't be gone long, Goebbels," Hitler warned. "I know this next race is a preliminary, but the Gold Medal events are coming up soon."

"I will be back shortly, *mein Führer*," Goebbels said. He took the private stairway down to field level. That was Owens on the bench, all right, and as well-shod as a champion racehorse. And there, near the track, was the object of Goebbels' interest, the official starter, a portly man in a long white canvas coat that made him look like the town butcher.

Not wanting to attract attention by walking out onto the field, Goebbels stayed on the sidelines and waved the man over, but the starter either ignored him or didn't see him. He finally had to dragoon one of the ushers to go out and bring the starter back to him.

"Good afternoon, sir," Goebbels said. "I'm sure you know who I am.

The starter nodded, suddenly looking nervous.

"Could you tell me your name?"

The man straightened his back. "I am Franz Miller, official starter of the Olympic running and hurdling events."

Goebbels offered a hand and *Herr* Miller shook it once, briskly. "I would like you to do me a small favor, *Herr* Miller."

"Of course, *Reichsminister* Goebbels," Miller said. "What do you require?"

"Well, how do you start a race, *Herr* Miller? What is your exact procedure?"

"*Ach*. Well, I raise the starter's pistol, then I call out *Auf die Platze… fertig…* then, BANG!"

Goebbels had listened with great attention. "I note that you utter the words in perfect rhythm."

"Yes, *Reichsminister*. The timing is crucial. Too quickly—or especially too slowly, or out of rhythm—and you get false starts."

"If I am not mistaken, too many false starts disqualify a runner, even in a preliminary heat?" Goebbels asked.

"Yes. Any runner who makes three false starts in a single heat is disqualified from further competition in the event."

Goebbels seemed intrigued. "So you can actually *cause* false starts, if you say the words in a certain way."

"That is true. Of course, I would never do that. I take my job very seriously."

"I see. Now let's get back to this favor I'd like."

Herr Miller nodded. "Anything you want, I would be happy to comply."

"I know you would, *Herr* Miller. You are a true German. You love your country."

"I am a Bavarian," said *Herr* Miller, "And yes, of course, a German."

"A patriotic German?"

"Very much so, *Reichminister*."

"I was sure you were," Goebbels said. "Now this is what I'd like you to do. You know the American runner, Jesse Owens? Black fellow?"

"Oh yes. He's sitting over on the bench now. I look forward to his heat."

"I want you to cause him to false start. Three times."

Miller was genuinely surprised. "What? What do you mean?"

"I want you to disqualify Owens."

"I can't do that," Miller said, aghast. "That would be a dereliction of duty."

"On the contrary," Goebbels said. "It would be the highest form of duty. We must not let the world see inferior creatures like the Negro Owens triumph over our Aryan heroes. It would be a racial crime."

"I will not do it," Miller insisted. His mouth was set.

"Even if I *order* you to do it?" Goebbels inquired mildly.

"*Reichsminister* Goebbels, I am employed by the International Olympics Committee, not by the Propaganda Ministry of the Third Reich. I take my orders from them, not from you."

Goebbels kept his temper, although it took some effort. "That may be, *Herr* Miller, but you are living in the Third Reich, are you not?"

"I am."

"I assume you wish to keep living here."

"*Reichsminister*," Miller said, "Even I wanted to comply with your request, I could not do so."

"And why is that?"

Miller pointed to the camera operators setting up next to the red cinder track. "All of the races are being filmed, and any discrepancies would be noticed. I am not the only official starter working the Olympics. Our integrity is our proudest possession. I would be found out and your interference would become public knowledge."

"Nonetheless," Goebbels said, without expression, "you will do as I say. If you do not, there will be consequences, very, very unpleasant consequences. Do you understand what I am saying, *Herr* Miller?"

Miller sighed deeply and hung his head, and Goebbels recognized the signs of acquiescence. "I understand, *Reichsminister*," Miller said, almost whispering. "But I still cannot do it."

"Explain," Goebbels said.

"If I mangle the starting announcement, all four of the racers in this heat will be disqualified. Not just Owens and his teammate, but the two Germans racing with them."

Goebbels momentarily considered this. "There are Germans racing in other heats?"

"Yes, *mein Herr*. Two others in the third heat."

"Ah," said Goebbels. "Then one of them will win the Gold Medal."

"That's not fair," said the starter. "I won't do it."

"Yes you will," Goebels said. "Those are my orders and you will obey them."

Miller opened his mouth, as if he wasn't finished protesting. Then he nodded, surrendering.

Goebbels put a hand on the man's shoulder and smiled. "One more thing, *Herr* Miller," he said. "You will be well rewarded for your cooperation. *Der Führer* will hear of it." Goebbels walked away without another word. Miller forlornly watched him head for the stands.

Once again, Goebbels was pleased with himself. He didn't like involving an outsider, a third party, but there was beauty in this plan. Owens would disqualify *himself*, by his own actions. People would say it was nerves, the tension was just too great for him, the situation was at fault—how could you put a naïve, uneducated man, a boy, really—

a *Negro* boy—on the international stage, with a hundred thousand people watching and expect him to perform?

As for Miller's worries—the filmed record of the race—that would be easily dealt with. A brief conversation with Leni Reifenstahl would do it. All she needed for her movie was footage of the winner. No one would care about a disqualified loser, even a well-known one. That footage would disappear and no one would even notice.

Goebbels practically vaulted up the stairs, eager to watch his plan play out, imagining the smile on Hitler's face.

****

Their shoe errand accomplished, to everyone's surprise and gratitude, Eleanor and Nathan left Owens in the dressing room with his teammates and his coach, figuring he'd be safe enough there, and headed up to the press box.

"What have you two been up to?" Richard Helms asked.

"We were having a fascinating discussion with Heinrich Himmler," Eleanor said.

"No, really," said Helms. "You know you've missed a few of the race heats, not to mention some hammer throws and a couple of pole vaults."

"Anything important?" Nathan asked.

"Actually no," Helms said. "But fun to watch."

"Is it my imagination that the stadium is even more crowded than it was yesterday?" Eleanor asked. "I don't remember people sitting in the aisles or standing on the stairways."

Grantland Rice took a puff on his pipe and leaned over to join the conversation. "This is only the tip of the iceberg," he said. "People all over Germany and maybe everywhere else are following it all on the radio, in real time. And loudspeakers all over Berlin are blaring out the results. There's no way to avoid the Olympics, even if you try."

"Eleanor almost found a way," Nathan said. "She should be swimming today."

"This is more fun."

"Want to see something really impressive, old man?" Helms asked, teasing. "Look at those contraptions on the field, the grey, boxy things that look kind of like giant cameras."

Nathan peered toward the field. "I see them," he said, "what the hell are they?"

"Television," said Grannie Rice. "Can you believe it?"

"I didn't know the Germans had working television."

"Well, I've seen it," Rice said. "and I'm not sure 'working' is the right word. The pictures are very fuzzy at best. You can't always make out what you're seeing."

"Where did you see television?" Eleanor asked.

"There are twenty-five viewing rooms in Berlin, including one at press headquarters, which you would have known if you'd bothered to visit it," Helms said.

"We've been busy," Eleanor said.

"I know," said Helms. "But doing what?"

"Seeing the sights," Nathan said. He reached for Helms' binoculars and began scanning the stands, looking for suspicious characters. And there, in the third tier, almost directly across from him, he saw him—the sallow-faced man, Carl Oldenburg, well-dressed as usual, sitting by himself, holding his own set of binoculars.

While Nathan was looking, Oldenburg held up his binoculars and studied the men on the field. He didn't seem to be singling out Jesse Owens, but he certainly took in all the athletes on the benches. He must have seen the young sprinter.

Was Oldenburg's presence just another coincidence? Nathan didn't like coincidences, especially when he was on bodyguard duty. But how could this man threaten Jesse Owens, sitting up there in the stands. He was out of accurate pistol range and he certainly wasn't carrying a rifle.

Nathan had no answer to the puzzle, no answer but to keep an eye on the man and to be ready to stop him if need be.

At about noon, the stadium announcer read off the names of the men who would run the final heat of the 100--meter dash, the last heat before the Gold Medal round: Kichizo Sasaki, from Japan, Dieudonne Devrint, from Belgium, Jose de Almeida, from Brazil and several others, none of whom received more than mild applause, then "*Yaycee Ohvens, Ooh-Ess-Ah*," which triggered an enormous cheer from the crowd.

Nathan and Eleanor bent forward to observe Hitler, sitting nearby. *Der Führer* and the other Nazi bigwigs appeared to be studiously ignoring the crowd's warm reaction to the Negro sprinter, laughing and talking among themselves, as if Owens did not exist.

Up on a tower next to the Marathon gate, a twelve-foot stopwatch, the largest in the world, was turned back to zero. It, and the Siemens photo-electric mechanism that timed the runners, would be triggered by the sound of *Herr* Miller's .380 caliber starting pistol.

In the box of honor, Goebbels was bent forward, staring at the racetrack through his binoculars, focusing on Owens. Hitler reached over and took the binoculars for himself, but even that didn't disturb Goebbels' concentration.

The four runners kneeled. Standing slightly behind them, *Herr* Miller raised his right hand, pointing the starter's pistol toward the sky. The entire stadium went silent. Miller took a deep breath, then called out the starting sequence in perfectly-timed two-second pauses: *Auf die Platze...fertig...* BANG!!.

With the shot, they were off, all of them running with incredible grace and power. Thirty meters down the track Jesse Owens pulled away from the group, legs pumping in perfect rhythm, sweat glistening on his brown skin, running easily—loping, really—adding to his lead with every step. Twenty meters from the finish, Owens shifted into second gear, still gaining ground. He crossed the line seven full meters ahead of the pack.

The cheers started slowly, then built, one layer on top of another, until the entire stadium seemed to be going crazy—except in Hitler's box. *Der Führer* sat quietly, chatting with Goring, smiling grimly at the *Reichsmarshall's* witty attempts to dismiss Owens' performance. Goebbels fought to contain his rage, imagining the pain he would inflict on Franz Miller, the race starter who had defied his orders.

As the cheering died out, the stadium announcer's voice came over the loudspeaker. "Winner of the twelfth heat in the one-hundred-meter dash, Yaycee Ohvens, Ooh-Ess-Ah, with a time of 10.3 seconds, equaling his own world record."

Eleanor turned to Nathan. "That was pretty amazing."

"Yes, the man lived up to his billing," Nathan said. "Doesn't always happen."

"Now that he's won the race, maybe he's not in danger anymore."

"I wish that were true, Eleanor," Nathan said. "But this was only a heat. The Gold Medal event is tomorrow. And they're going to reduce the field with another set of heats later this afternoon. Besides that, Owens is competing in three other events. I think we have quite a ways to go yet."

"What are you two whispering about?" Helms asked.

"Mike said he thought Jesse Owens had perfectly shaped legs," Eleanor said.

"I did not," Nathan protested.

Eleanor shrugged. "I guess I misunderstood."

For the next three hours, the sports field was covered with javelin throwers, high jumpers, pole vaulters, and others of their ilk, most participating in event preliminaries. But two Gold medals were awarded, both to Germans: Tilly Fleischer, a javelin thrower and Hans Woellke, a hammer thrower. A delighted Hitler invited both of them to his box and congratulated them personally.

Meanwhile, Nathan spent more time scanning the stands than watching the events. Oldenburg had departed, which was reassuring. Eleanor might have a point. Maybe the danger to Owens had subsided, but Nathan wasn't going to take any chances. He was the lifeguard on duty and he took his job very seriously. However, he saw no sharks in the water.

"What's next, Grannie?" Eleanor asked.

Grannie Rice relit his pipe and leaned over toward her. "We have a Gold Medal event coming up next, the high jump," he said. "The result should be especially interesting."

"Why is that?" Helms asked.

"Well, the favorite is Cornelius Johnson," said Rice.

"Who's that?" Eleanor asked.

"He's another American athlete," Helms said. "Also Negro."

Nathan caught on. "So, if he wins, will Hitler invite him to the box of honor and shake his hand?"

"That, young man, is a very good question," Rice said. "We will wait and see."

"Wind doesn't matter this time," Helms pointed out. "All you gotta do is clear the bar. Black or white."

The athletic field was a busy place now, crowded with preliminaries in several events. But most spectators were focused on the high jump, which was surrounded by movie cameramen and judges, as well as the technicians who worked the bar and the pit.

Eleanor, Nathan and the other reporters, foreign and domestic, watched from the press box as athletes from several countries attacked the bar, one by one, and as the technicians raised it, notch by notch.

When they raised the bar to 2.03 meters—more than six feet--three competitors were left, a giant and thoroughly Nordic-looking Finn with tree-trunk legs, named Kalevi Kotkas, Owens' roommate. David Albritton, an American Negro, who had a bandaged left ankle, and Cornelius Johnson, a six-foot, five-inch brown beanpole. They jumped in that order, the Finn hitting the bar on the way up, and knocking it off its posts, Albritton, jumping straddle-style, hit it on the way down, with the same result, while Cornelius Johnson hurdled it with inches to spare.

"Well, well," said Rice. "It looks like our little drama is about to play out."

As they watched, the last three competitors mounted the three-tiered medal stage and the Gold Medal was hung around Cornelius Johnson's neck. Then Johnson mounted the stadium stairs and headed for Hitler's box, to get his congratulations.

"Keep an eye on *der Führer*," Grannie Rice suggested. They did. Seeing Johnson approaching, Hitler quickly got up and walked toward the box's back entrance, toward the private stairs. Goebbels, Goering and the other Nazi VIPs were close behind him.

Johnson watched, evidently nonplussed, as Hitler disappeared down the back stairs. Then he turned around and walked back down to the field.

"No handshake for Johnson," Eleanor said. "Very interesting. Do you think the other spectators noticed?"

"You bet they did," Helms said. "They watch Hitler's every little movement."

"I think I've got the lead for today's Olympics' piece," Rice said, rolling a piece of paper into his typewriter.

"You're going to write about the snub?" Nathan asked.

Rice shrugged. "Why not? News is news. Besides that, looks like everyone else has the same idea." He pointed down the press box, toward the row of reporters, some of whom were already starting to type up their stories.

"Why do you think he did it?" Helms asked Rice.

Rice thought a moment. "I would guess that *der Führer* didn't want to see photographs of himself shaking hands with a Negro on the front page of half the world's newspapers. Wouldn't do much for the Ayran superiority he'd been touting."

Looking down the line of newsmen, Nathan spotted Quentin Reynolds huddled over some of his friends, telling a brief story, then moving down the row to repeat it.

Rice saw it too. "Looks like our friend Quentin has some news he can't keep to himself."

"Should I go over there and see what it's all about?" Helms asked.

Rice sucked on his pipe. "Be patient, son. I expect he'll be here soon."

And a few minutes later, having told his story to all the other journalists, Reynolds arrived at the line's end, where Eleanor, Nathan, Helms and Rice sat waiting.

"Got a nice little story for you guys," Reynolds said, grinning.

"How much?" Rice joked.

"No, no, this one's too good to keep; to myself," Reynolds said. "I'm gonna share it with all of you, no charge."

Rice made a big show of getting a pad and pencil ready. "So, Quent, what's the big scoop?"

"Well, during this last event, I was sitting in the International Olympics Committee box, next to the organization's President, Count Henri de Baillet-La Tour. We saw Cornelius Johnson win the Gold and we also saw Hitler skedaddle immediately afterward, obviously to avoid shaking Johnson's hand."

"We saw that too," Helms said.

Reynolds gave him a *who-is-this-kid-and-why-is-he-interrupting* look, then went on. "Anyhow, the Count was not pleased with *Herr* Hitler. He was sufficiently displeased, in fact, that he sent *der Führer* a note."

He took a piece of paper from his pocket. "I made a copy. My dear *Führer*, it reads, please be advised that it is not customary for the head of state to congratulate event winners. If you decide to do so anyway, you must congratulate all or none."

"What do you know," Helms said. "The distinguished old man has guts."

"Surprised me too," Reynolds said.

"How do you think Hitler will react?" Nathan said.

"Well, the note was delivered to *der Führer's* office and the Count has already received a reply," Reynolds said. "Hitler has decided on option two."

"Option two?" Helms asked.

"Yes. He's decided not to do any more congratulating."

"Well in that case," said Grannie Rice, "he's not going to have any problem if Jesse Owens wins an event."

"Good choice," Nathan said.

The last event concluded, the thousands of spectators rose and began to file out of the stadium, their manner almost too orderly.

"Should we check on Jesse?" Eleanor whispered to Nathan.

"No need," Nathan said. "He's with Snyder and his teammates. They'll be getting on the bus and heading back to the Olympic Village about now. But I want to be there again tomorrow morning, for his trip back to the stadium."

Eleanor shrugged. "If you think we have to."

Helms interrupted the conversation. "Shall we go?" He asked. He stood and politely gestured to Eleanor to go ahead of him. She and Helms started down the stairs and Nathan got up to go after her. Maybe tonight, he thought.

"Novak, you're the fellow from Cleveland, right?" Grannie Rice asked.

"That's me," Nathan said, pausing.

"You catch that Indians' rookie pitcher—Bob Feller? The seventeen-year-old?"

"Haven't seen him yet," Nathan improvised. He wanted to get away.

"Well, you keep an eye on him," Rice said. "He's gonna be something special."

"I will," Nathan promised. He looked for Eleanor. She and Helms were halfway down the stairs, talking. He caught up with them. "Listen, Eleanor, I thought tonight…"

"Tonight, old man," Helms interrupted, "Eleanor is going to dinner with me."

"He could always come with us," Eleanor said, teasing.

"No, I think not," Helms said. "He's already taken up too much of your time."

Eleanor looked at Nathan with a smile and a shrug. It wasn't her fault.

"Can you find your way back to the hotel, old man?" Helms asked. "I don't think the three of us can fit into Eleanor's little automobile."

"Don't worry about me," Nathan said, contemplating murder. "If I can't get a ride, I'll take a taxi."

Nathan ended up cadging a ride back to his hotel with Grannie Rice, who had rented a black Opel Olympia two-door sedan, with a child-sized back seat. Quentin Reynolds and Red Knickerbocker joined them.

"File your story yet, Novak?" Knickerbocker asked when they started off.

Nathan came up with what he hoped would be a good answer. "I'm going to write it when I get back to the hotel."

"Gonna lead with Hitler's snub of Johnson?" Reynolds asked.

"Haven't decided yet," Nathan said. "I might just go with Owens equaling his world record. What about you?"

"I'm gonna lead with the snub," Reynolds said. "My editor probably won't print it, though."

"Not so sure about mine either," Rice said. "I got strict instructions: report on the games, stay out of politics."

"Frustrating time to be a journalist," Red Knickerbocker observed, a remark that was greeted with silent nods of agreement.

"So, gentlemen," Nathan said. "What are you guys going to do tonight?"

"Nothing good," Reynolds said with a laugh.

"Eat, drink and make Mary, if we can find her," Knickerbocker.

"No, I mean seriously," said Nathan.

"Well, young man, we're all on expense accounts," Rice said, "so we're going to eat very well and drink very much."

"And probably end up playing poker past midnight," Reynolds said.

"I guess you're footloose tonight," Rice said. "Young Helms grabbed off the girl. But you're welcome to join us, not that we're much fun. You're on an expense account too, aren't you?"

"Yeah, but I'm not really up for a night of drinking and card playing," Nathan said.

"Some journalist you are," Reynolds said. "Best way I know to learn your trade."

"Another night, maybe," Nathan said. "I think tonight, I'll take in a movie and turn in early. I haven't seen the new Chaplin film."

"*Modern Times*, you mean," Knickerbocker said. "It's excellent."

"If I were you," Reynolds said, "I'd see a German film. You're in Berlin, after all."

"Good idea, Quent," Rice said. "Why don't you see *Triumph of the Will*, Mike. I'm sure it's playing somewhere."

"That's a good idea," Knickerbocker said, "it'll give you some insights into Germany you might not see during the Olympics."

"*Triumph of the Will*," Nathan said. "I'll see if it's playing."

****

Back at the *Furstenhof*, Nathan grabbed a quick dinner, then asked the concierge if *Triumph of the Will* was playing anywhere nearby. Turns out, it was, at the Gloria-Palast movie theater on the Ku-damm, just a few blocks from his hotel. He decided to walk.

The Gloria-Palast, it turned out, was housed in a big, neo-baroque stone building with spires at each of its four corners and a restaurant on the ground floor. Half a dozen Hitler youth were standing in line, beautiful blond boys in short pants and knee socks, looking as serious as undertakers.

"Movie started yet?" Nathan asked the box office girl, hoping she understood English.

"*Nein*," she replied in a chirpy, girlish voice. "*Es beginnt in funf Minuten.*" She held up a hand showing him five minutes. He smiled, bought a ticket and entered the theater, coming into a large lobby plastered and painted to look like the inside of a medieval castle.

Nathan pulled open the heavy auditorium door and walked in. The house lights were still on. The theater, he guessed, had about five hundred cushy seats, of which about a third were occupied. The Hitler Jugend filled the first few rows, most sitting quietly, a few involved in teenage horseplay. Uniformed storm troopers and soldiers with faces like stone made up most of the rest of the audience, the few others being families and couples.

If there were any foreign tourists in the theater, Nathan didn't see them. He was probably the only American in the place, which made him a little uncomfortable. He took an inconspicuous seat toward the back, in the same row as a working class family with two teenage sons, neither wearing uniforms.

The house lights went down. The screen remained dark, but solemn Wagnerian music issued from the speakers. Then, slowly, the screen brightened and filled with the image of a Nazi eagle statue atop an immense stone pylon. Nathan tried to remember why he'd chosen this movie instead of *Modern Times*.

The main titles rolled against the Nazi eagle backdrop…"*Triumph des Willens*, Documentary of the Reich Party Day, 1934, Produced by order of the *Führer*, Created by Leni Riefenstahl...

"On September 5, 1934, twenty years after the outbreak of the World War…sixteen years after the beginning of our suffering…nineteen months after the beginning of Germany's rebirth…Adolf Hitler flew again to Nuremberg to review the columns of his faithful followers…"

The titles gave way to a view of a twin-engine aeroplane flying through mountainous clouds, over the medieval city of Nuremberg, a Nazi banner prominently fluttering from an ancient building, formations of brown-shirted stormtroopers marching through the streets.

There was a cut, to Hitler's motorcade driving through central Nuremburg, past cheering and *heiling* crowds many rows deep. Hitler stood in his open-top Mercedes, smiling indulgently, returning the countless tributes with his customary cocked-arm salute. Nathan sighed. He'd seen all this before.

Hitler's Mercedes Benz 770 pulled up at a hotel and he got out, exchanging more *heils* with the crowds, over more soaring Wagnerian music. He entered the hotel and disappeared. "We want our *Führer*!" The crowd shouted, "We want our *Führer*."

The camera panned up to a hotel window. A gracious Hitler stepped out, smiled and delivered a snappy Nazi salute to the crowds, who *heiled* him continuously and cheered again and again.

The scene shifted. It was early morning, dawn breaking, dawn with Wagnerian music, dawn with views of ancient Nuremberg from above, dawn over a city of tents, followed by close-ups of the men inside rising, shaving, joking around, wrestling, eating, getting ready for the Big Day.

After a bit, Hitler's car arrived. He inspected a large contingent of uniformed laborers, shook hands with a few pretty girls, and returned to his car, *heiled* the crowds, who *heiled* back again and again and cheered with great enthusiasm.

On screen, the scene changed once more, to the Congress Hall of the National Socialist German Workers Party, a room as long as three football fields. It looked as though an entire army were sitting inside.

Rudolph Hess, identified by a subtitle, stepped up to the microphone. "I am opening this, our Sixth Party Congress," the subtitles read, "in respectful public memory of Field Marshal, and President of the Reich Von Hindenburg, who has passed into eternity." He was a brutally handsome, dark-haired, beetle-browed man in his late 30s, tall and well-built. If it weren't for the vacant look in his eyes, he would have been frightening.

"My *Führer*," Hess said, according to the subtitles, "around you stand the flags and standards of this National Socialism...only when they are threadbare will humanity, in hindsight, be able to comprehend, the greatness of our time, because of what you, my *Führer*, mean to Germany. You *are* Germany! when you act, the nation acts, when you judge, the people judge! " He *heiled* Hitler and so did everyone else in the hall, in full voice.

The camera cut to Hitler, whose expression was one of the utmost appreciation and modesty. He *heiled* back with a cute little smile.

Nathan looked for Oldenburg among the speakers or the VIPs sitting on the stage. Instead, another familiar face leaped out at him— a thin, handsome, dark blond-haired man with ice blue eyes. It was the very same man who'd found Nathan and Eleanor at the cabaret. It was *ObergruppenFührer* Reinhard Heydrich, chief of the Gestapo, according to the subtitle that finally appeared over his picture,

Heydrich slowly turned and looked directly into the camera, straight into Nathan's eyes, as though he knew he were being observed. Nathan felt like ducking. Instead, he studied the man at length, something he hadn't dared do in the cabaret. He watched Heydrich's expressions, his bearing, the way his hooded eyes swept back and forth over his audience, missing nothing, judging everything.

To Nathan's relief, the camera cut back to Rudolph Hess, at the podium. Hess looked out the great mass of soldiers in front of him and spoke a single sentence: "Hitler will speak," the subtitle read. Hess yielded the podium to *der Führer.*

As Hitler began to speak, the emotions spilled out of him. He shouted, he whispered. He pointed and pounded his chest. He snarled and then became nostalgic, even affectionate. He was angry, then mild, commanding then supplicating. Sweat rolled off his forehead and his eyes gleamed almost manically.

After the usual cheers and *heiling*, Hitler stepped away from the podium and Hess returned. "The Party is Hitler! And Hitler is Germany just as Germany is Hitler! Hitler! *Sieg Heil*! *Sieg Heil*! *Sieg Heil*!"

All of the thousands of soldiers in the hall rose to their feet as one and returned the cheers and the *sieg heils*. The roar shook the entire movie theater—and it wasn't all coming from the movie. The Hitler Youth and the soldiers in the audience were also standing and shouting *"Sieg Heil! Sieg Heil!"*

How did Hitler intend to command the multitudes whose loyalty he'd won? Nathan wondered. What would he have them do? He played out the scenarios in his mind. Germany had a terrible defeat to revenge. Would displays of strength and unity be enough? Would it satisfy Hitler merely to dominate his country and its neighbors? Not very likely, Nathan thought.

And that was it. A little more music, another screen-filling swastika, more soldiers marching and, finally fade out, and the house lights came up. Nathan sat there, pulse-pounding, and waited for the SS men, the soldiers and, finally the Hitler Youth to file out.

No one paid him any attention, except the last of the Hitler Youth, the littlest member of the troop, a boy who should have been outside playing cowboys and Indians, or whatever little German boys played. He beamed at Nathan with the innocence of youth, straightened his cap, raised his arm and said, *"Heil* Hitler." Nathan couldn't bring himself to repeat the words. Instead, he smiled and nodded. The little boy hesitated, then decided that was good enough, and skipped on, to catch up with his companions.

Finally, Nathan got up and walked out of the theater. The night had cooled down considerably. And tomorrow, an American Negro named Jesse Owens would try to win a Gold Medal while Hitler watched.

Chapter Eighteen

Nathan's first question was answered the moment he walked out of the *Furstenhof.* The little blue convertible was waiting for him, Eleanor at the wheel. But he realized he might never know the answer to the second question—what had happened between her and "Dickey" Helms the previous night?

Oh well. He got into the automobile and looked at her. She was her usual sparkling self, dressed in something chic and flowered, and presenting him with one of her vast repertoire of smiles, this one of the genus *mischievous good morning.*

"*Olympic-way illage-vay?*" She asked.

"Yes," Nathan said. "I think Owens is still in danger, maybe greater danger than before—he hasn't won a Gold Medal yet and someone is trying to stop him."

"And you're going to make sure that doesn't happen," Eleanor said.

"If I can," Nathan said. "With your help."

When they got to the Olympic Village, the athletes were already at breakfast. Owens broke into a big grin when he saw them coming. He held up a shoe-clad foot. "See, I didn't lose 'em this time," he said. "Wore 'em while I slept. Right coach?"

Coach Snyder laughed. He was sitting next to Owens. "He said he didn't want to take any chances and I couldn't argue. Anyhow, what are you two doing here this morning?"

"We just wanted to be sure everything was all right," Eleanor said.

"Right as rain, Miss Eleanor," Owens said.

"Ready for the big race?" Nathan asked.

"Ready as I'll ever be."

"Remember, today is just Jesse's first Gold Medal event," said Coach Snyder. "There are two more after that—the long jump and the two-hundred-meter race."

"Right," said Nathan. And, he thought, Owens was going to be at risk until the last one was over.

A few athletes at the other end of the hall began shouting and Nathan turned to see what was going on. It was some kind of argument, a loud argument rapidly deteriorating into a fist fight, in fact a serious brawl. Before long, dozens of Olympic athletes were involved and the guides and guards were doing their best to break up the melee.

Jesse Owens stood, to see better. "What's goin' on over dere?" he asked, taking a step toward the commotion.

Nathan put a hand on Owens' arm. "Hold on, Jesse," he said. "Better sit down and stay away."

"He's right, Jesse," Snyder said. "You got other things to think about."

Owens shrugged and sat back down, while Nathan kept an eye on the ruckus and reconnoitered the hall.

Eleanor gave him a questioning look. "Something up?" she asked, out of Jesse's earshot.

"Not sure," Nathan said. "Maybe. Fight might be a diversion. Keep your eyes open."

They both scrutinized the room. "Don't see anything suspicious," Eleanor said.

"Keep looking."

More guides rushed into the hall and inserted themselves between the disputants. The rest of the athletes, saw the skirmish cooling off, began to return to their breakfasts.

Nathan turned to Coach Snyder. "You see that? All the athletes fighting are Asian."

"Oh yeah," said Coach Snyder. "The Chinese and the Japanese. That's been brewing for quite a while. They've been having their own little war, you know."

"War?"

"I mean in China. Japan's been biting off chunks of it for a couple of years now. I guess the athletes brought the fight with them."

"I thought the Olympics were supposed to create harmony between nations," Nathan said.

"That's the intention," Coach Snyder agreed. "It doesn't always work that way."

A loudspeaker crackled on. "Buses to the Olympic Stadium are now available at the main entrance, in alphabetic order according to nation. Athletes will board the bus that flies their national flag. Please be prompt so that all athletes can get to the stadium in ample time to participate in their events."

Owens, his coach, and his teammates rose from the table. Nathan had an idea. "You know," he said to Owens, "we have a car. There's room for you and Coach Snyder. Gotta be better than the bus." And the best way to keep an eye on him, Nathan thought.

"If'n you doan mind, Mr. Novak, I'd jest as soon go on the bus wid my frens."

Nathan turned to Snyder. "It's a convertible, but it has a rumble seat, right Eleanor?"

"It certainly does. I think."

"He wants to be with the team," Snyder said. "I understand. So do I."

Eleanor touched Nathan's hand. "He'll be fine."

They went out to the parking lot. "I'm driving," Nathan announced.

Eleanor tossed him the keys, with a wry smile, and Nathan drove them over to the buses, managing to insert the blue convertible into the line right behind the bus flying the American flag, inspiring angry honking from the next bus in line.

"Pretty pushy," Eleanor observed.

"Just want to keep an eye on him."

"You didn't follow the bus yesterday" She said.

"We were looking for track shoes, remember?"

"Ah."

The long line of buses snaked out of the Olympic Village and headed down the road toward the Olympic Stadium more than a half hour away. It was an agonizingly slow parade of elephants, a poodle in their midst.

Nathan hugged the center line, looking as far ahead as he could and frequently checking the rear-view mirror. It wasn't easy to see past the buses, either coming or going, but he did his best. Fortunately, traffic was practically non-existent.

The caravan was about a mile out of the Olympic Village when the head bus turned slightly to the right at a fork in the road, the others following. Peering forward, Nathan saw an enormous black freight wagon parked in the left fork, a few hundred yards up from the intersection.

But then it wasn't parked at all. The hulking vehicle started up, very slowly at first, but steadily gaining speed, heading directly toward the line of buses. If nothing interfered, it was going to plow through the intersection at maybe forty miles an hour, at exactly the moment the bus with the American flag was crossing it.

In the little blue convertible, Nathan rammed his foot down on the accelerator, earning a yelp of surprise from Eleanor. He swerved out of the bus line, and pulled beside the American team's bus. The truck driver must have seen the buses—and the little car—but his huge vehicle did not slow or waver.

"David, what…" Eleanor saw the truck coming and to her horror, understood what Nathan was trying to do--shield the bus Jesse Owens was riding. The maneuver might have protected the bus, but it put them right in the path of the truck.

Still, Nathan's maneuver had its effect. With the convertible riding shotgun, the driver of the onrushing truck apparently realized that he had no clear path to the bus—he couldn't hit his target. The truck was less than fifty yards away when the driver apparently decided to call it off and stomped on the brakes.

But the truck kept coming, skidding now, tires screeching furiously against the asphalt pavement, the rear end pivoting with lumbering grace, until the vehicle was completely sidewise in the road and still moving, a wall of truck bigger than the athletes' buses, and dwarfing the little blue convertible. It kept coming, like an avalanche, threatening to blot out anything in its path.

Finally, the truck began to slow, its wheels perpendicular to the direction of its skid. It headed toward a seam in the pavement between the forks, the right fork a couple of inches higher than the left. It was still moving at about 20 miles an hour when its tires, eight pairs of them, all the tires on the side nearest the blue convertible and the bus, slammed into the concrete joint.

Six out of the eight exploded and the truck came to an instant and abrupt stop, less than ten feet short of Nathan and Eleanor's car. The truck teetered a moment, then it tipped over in agonizingly slow motion, falling sideways at the intersection with a thunderous crash. The roof split open and thousands of bricks poured onto the road.

Meanwhile the US-flagged bus safely proceeded through the intersection onto the right fork, behind the line of buses that had already made the turn. The little blue convertible did not fare so well, running out of pavement. Nathan lost control of the car and it plunged ahead, into the grassy triangle that separated the two forks, into axle-deep mud and came to an abrupt stop.

Eleanor turned to Nathan and began pounding on his chest in fear and frustration. "You're crazy," she screamed. "You almost got us killed!" Then, suddenly, her arms were around him. She was sobbing and he was holding her.

"Yes. But *almost* only counts in horseshoes," Nathan said, regretting the words before they were all the way out of his mouth.

She pushed him away, pouting. "Nothing funny about what just happened," she warned him. "Nothing at all."

"I know," Nathan admitted.

"What in God's name made you do that?"

"I was just going on instinct."

"Well, would you do me a favor, David? The next time you got an instinct, make sure I'm not around."

"I'll do my best."

She looked at the buses rolling down the road. "Nothing happened to Jesse Owens," she said.

"Yeah. That was the idea." He said, opening the car door. He ran toward the truck. Halfway there, he stopped. In the distance, a tiny figure was running away, down the left fork, beyond pursuit.

"Is the driver okay?" Eleanor asked.

"Oh, he's just fine," Nathan said. He took a look at the convertible's tires, which were half buried in mud. "He got away."

"Got away?"

"Yes." Nathan said. "Wait a minute, you don't think this was an accident, do you?"

"Well, I…"

"Look, it's broad daylight. The truck driver was waiting for the buses, waiting for the one with the American flags. He was intent on smashing into it, destroying it."

"It could have been a coincidence," Eleanor suggested.

"I hope you don't really believe that," Nathan said. "Someone just tried to knock Jesse Owens out of the Olympics, or at least out of this morning's events. And they very nearly succeeded."

"If that's true, what made him stop, David?"

"We did. We got in the way."

For once, Eleanor had no response.

Up ahead a few hundred feet, the US bus had pulled out of line and come to a stop. The doors opened and the American team—Owens and

Snyder included—piled out of the bus and came running over to the little blue convertible.

Jesse Owens—of course—was the first to arrive. "Everybody all right?"

"We're fine, Jesse," Eleanor said.

"That truck driver—was he drunk?" Jesse asked.

"Must have been," Nathan said. "Or maybe the accelerator got stuck."

"Damnedest thing I've ever seen," said Coach Snyder, who had arrived at the convertible along with about forty American athletes. "Could have been a real disaster, but…"

"Luck was on our side," Nathan said, evidently choosing his words carefully.

Snyder gave Nathan a long, appraising look. "Yeah, luck," he said. He didn't sound convinced.

"You want us to have a talk with the truck driver?" one of the athletes asked.

"Long gone," Nathan said. "Guess he didn't want to stick around until the police showed up."

"Anybody called them?" Snyder asked.

"No," Nathan said, "I'll report the accident when we get to the stadium. And speaking of the stadium, shouldn't you be on your way?"

"What about you?"

"Eleanor and I will follow."

Snyder looked at the convertible, sunk into the mud. "How are you going to do that?"

"I'll push it out, I guess."

"There's an easier way," the Coach said. "Weight lifters, shot putters, wrestlers, let's get this baby out of the mud."

Half a dozen well-muscled US athletes took their places on each side of the little automobile. Jesse Owens tried to join them, but Coach Snyder pointed to his shoes and waved him off.

"Shouldn't I get out?" Eleanor asked.

"No need," said one of the weight lifters. "Let's go, guys. On three. One. Two. Three!"

They bent and lifted, at first without result. Then the car suddenly came up, with a loud sucking sound. The athletes carried it to the road as though it were a little red Radio Flyer wagon, setting it down gently on the pavement, facing the right direction.

"Thanks, fellas," Eleanor said, presenting them with a smile that would have weakened the knees of a matinee idol.

Coach Snyder herded the athletes back to the bus and Nathan hopped into the convertible.

"Don't tell me you're going to try to catch up with them," Eleanor said.

"No. I think Owens is safe. For now."

They were back on the road, heading to the Olympic Stadium, when a large black Horch automobile passed them. "Isn't that Oldenburg's car?" Eleanor inquired.

"I'll be damned," Nathan said. "I think it is."

"Another coincidence?"

Nathan watched the automobile pull away from them. "Not very likely," he said.

****

The stadium was three-quarters empty when they got there, and there was no sign of Hitler and his gang. Most of the morning field activities weren't big draws—the women's events, a few of the men's trials. And some of the contests—wrestling, fencing, polo, were being held at other venues. But Hitler—and the crowds—would be at the stadium for the featured events—the races and the hurdles, scheduled for later in the day.

Eleanor and Nathan took their seats in the press box, which was sparsely populated. Richard Helms was nowhere to be seen and neither was Grantland Rice, although his binoculars were stowed under his seat.

Nathan spent the morning with Rice's binoculars, studying the crowd and scoping out the far reaches of the stadium, wondering where the next threat would come from, certain one was coming. Eleanor finally started writing, "some personal observations," she said, which she hoped would keep her employer, the INS, happy and satisfied.

"What will you be personally observing?" Nathan asked.

"Oh, I'll write up my impressions of Hitler and maybe Jesse Owens." She rolled a piece of paper into the typewriter and started to hunt and peck, at the rate, giving her the benefit of the doubt, of one word a minute.

"You never took typing in school?"

"Nope. I'm not much of a cook either," Eleanor said. "Should I be worried?"

"Probably not."

The overcast skies finally dropped off a brief shower just after noon, and then another at two p.m. After that came the crowds, eager to see *Yaycee Ohvens* race in the 100-meter semi-finals and win and repeat the performance a few hours later in the Gold Medal round.

Richard Helms and Grannie Rice got to the press box just as the rain was letting up. Helms gave Eleanor a look evidently intended to be significant and she responded with a noncommittal nod. "Well, you two got here early," Rice told Nathan and Eleanor. "See anything interesting?"

"Not really," Nathan admitted. He'd looked for the sallow-faced man without success. "Kinda dull this afternoon."

"Yeah," Grannie Rice said, looking skyward. "This isn't likely to be a red-letter day."

"What do you mean?" The question came from Helms. "Owens is running for the gold today. You think he isn't going to win?"

"Oh, he'll probably win all right, but he won't be setting any records."

Helms was puzzled. "How do you know?"

Rice pointed to the red cinder track. "It's soaked," he said. "Times are bound to be slow."

Helms turned to Eleanor. "Don't mind him, Ellie. His mother was a psychic."

At about 3:15 p.m., the 100-meter runners trotted out onto the field, Jesse Owens included, and as usual, he was the one who got the cheers. Nathan went on high alert again.

"Look there Ellie," Helms said, pointing at a box just behind them, across the aisle. "Some fellow is waving at you."

Nathan glanced back over his shoulder. "It's Ambassador Dodd and his family."

"And Tommy Wolfe," Eleanor said, waving back.

"Tommy Wolfe?" Rice asked. "You mean Tom Wolfe, the writer?"

"Yes," Eleanor said. "He's the one who's waving."

Helms frowned. "I didn't know you knew each other."

"They met the other day," Nathan explained.

"I see," Helms said. "You certainly do get around, Eleanor."

"Oh, I know practically everybody."

On the field, the cameras started rolling and the runners took their places on the cinder track, digging footholds with tiny trowels. Owens looked calm and confident. Finally, *Herr* Miller raised his pistol. *Auf die Platze... fertig...* BANG!"

They pounded down the track, Owens in the middle lane, striding, gliding over the cinders with grace and power, as though driven by some magical force only he could tap into. He finished first by a good ten meters, to which the crowd responded with great cheers and shouts of Yaycee Yaycee, Yacee!

Nathan kept a close eye on his charge until he trotted off the track and back into the dressing rooms under the stands. Then came the announcement: the winner was Jesse Owens, with a time of 10.4 seconds—good, but a tenth of a second off the record.

"You see?" Grannie Rice said. "The boy's not a mudder. None of them are."

"I'm glad I didn't bet you," Helms said.

"Oh, you'll have another chance," Rice told him. "The Gold Medal heat is just two hours away."

"Don't tempt me." Helms said, laughing. He turned to Nathan. "How about you, old man?"

Nathan regarded Helms. "I'm not going to bet against Owens, not after what I've seen."

Eleanor pointed toward Hitler's box. "Look who's finally honored us with his presence."

Der Führer was taking his seat, followed by a large group of VIP guests.

"Can you identify all those people?" Nathan asked Rice. Nathan recognized most of them from *Triumph of the Will*, but a few faces were new to him.

Rice peered down at the box of honor, less than twenty feet away and one level below them. "I think so," he said. "The woman is Leni Reifenstahl, the movie director. The guy behind her is Julius Streicher. He's the publisher of that anti-Semitic rag, *Der Stürmer*. Next to him is Baldur Von Shirach, the leader of the Hitler Youth. "Then there's the big three—Göring, Goebbels and Heydrich, all dressed up and bemedaled."

Nathan studied Heydrich. No question of it, he was the same man who'd caught Eleanor and him in the cabaret, and the same man Nathan had seen on film in the parade through Munich.

But Rice wasn't finished. "And—I'll be damned—that's Max Schemling. Hey Max!" Rice shouted, waving at a big, square-faced, dark-haired man in civilian clothing.

The man looked up to see who was yelling at him. He spotted Rice, broke into a big smile and waved. "Hey, Grannie Rice, *schon dich zu sehen*! Gut to see you!"

Rice returned the wave. "That's Max Schmeling," Rice told Nathan. "You know, the heavyweight champion of the world, the man who beat Joe Louis last month."

"You're friends?"

"I covered the fight," Rice said. "He's a hell of a puncher—and a pretty good guy, all in all. Of course I was rooting for Louis."

"Of course."

Hitler had noticed Schmeling's interaction. He asked the boxer a question, which Schmeling answered, pointing up to Grantland Rice. Hitler craned his neck toward the press box, nodded curtly at no one in particular and turned his attention back to the athletic field.

Helms gave Rice a smile. "Looks like you got yourself noticed, Grannie."

"Oh goodie," Rice said. "I'm thrilled."

"Do you know the tall one, Heydrich?" Nathan asked.

"Met him."

"Do me a favor, Grannie. Don't wave at him."

"Wouldn't have occurred to me."

****

On the field, it was time for the hammer throw. And in the box of honor, Hitler bent forward, eager for it to begin. This was his favorite event and he was counting on the German athletes to win.

Seventeen athletes from nine different countries lined up to take their turns flinging the "hammer," an iron sphere the size of a cannonball, attached by a wire to a handle. Each man, in turn spun in the sand pit, twirling with all of his might, the hammer driven outward by centrifugal force. At the peak of each man's momentum, he let go of the handle and let fly the iron ball.

After each man had taken three turns, only five competitors had thrown the hammer 51 meters or better. These five each got three more tries.

And sure enough, a squat, heavily muscled, single-eyebrowed German named Karl Hein was the Gold Medal winner, flinging the ball 56.49 meters. And the Silver Medal winner was another German, this one blond and tall, Erwin Blask, with a throw of 55.04 meters.

As the results were announced, Hitler grinned and pounded the table in front of him, elated. "A double victory," he said, "and further proof of Aryan superiority."

"I hope my little film helped," said Leni Riefenstahl, fishing.

"They just had to see how it was done," said Hitler. "I was right to send you to Ireland."

Riefenstahl smiled. As long as she was involved, she didn't mind if Hitler took the credit for the victories.

Hitler leaned toward his Propaganda Minister. "What's next, Goebbels?"

Goebbels ran a finger down the program Hitler was holding. "100-meter semi-finals," he said.

Hitler studied the program. "Owens," he said, shaking his head in disgust. "And Metcalfe. He's also a Negro. Am I correct, Goebbels?"

"Yes, *mein Führer*."

"Both Americans."

Goebbels nodded.

Hitler frowned. "The Americans should be ashamed of themselves, letting Negroes win their medals for them. The brutes are barely one step out of the jungle."

"Yes, *mein Führer*," Goebbels said, angry all over again that he'd failed to derail Owens. "Their primitive physiques are stronger than those of civilized whites."

"Make a note, Goebbels," Hitler said, and Goebbels got out a little notepad. "The Negroes represent unfair competition. They must be excluded from future Olympic games."

Goebbels scribbled down the suggestion, wishing he'd been able to present Hitler with a *fait accompli*—no Jesse Owens to darken his day. But Goebbels wasn't finished. In the days to come, Owens was due to participate in at least two other events. Perhaps he could still find a way to eliminate him.

Heydrich, sitting directly behind Goebbels, leaned forward to join the conversation. "In future years, when Germany is perpetual host of the Olympic Games, we shall certainly bar Negroes," he said. "But today, Owens may win a Gold Medal in this event."

"I won't be shaking his hand," Hitler said. "Can you imagine a newspaper photograph of me smiling and shaking hands with a Negro? It would be mortifying. Fortunately, Monsieur Baillet-Latour's has given me an out. I will honor his request and shake no more hands in public."

Goebbels saw an opportunity to please his leader. "If you wish, *mein Führer*, I can have the German winners brought to the box for your private congratulations."

"Very good Goebbels," Hitler said. "Make the arrangements."

Reichsminister Hermann Göring was sitting behind Hitler, listening to the conversation and silently cursing the incompetent truck driver who had failed to put Owens out of action that morning. The American seemed to have some kind of guardian angel, in this case a reckless fool driving a little blue convertible. Göring burned with frustration, angry at the lost opportunity to gain favor.

After medals were awarded to the hammer throw winners, participants in the 100--meter semi-finals trotted out on the field. The event was an almost exact repetition of the previous heats in which Jesse Owens ran. He glided once again to a ten-yard victory, only slightly slowed by the muddy track. His time was 10.4 seconds, still a tenth of a second off the world's record.

The German spectators rose as one and gave Owens a mighty cheer, shouting Yaycee! Yaycee! over and over again. Hitler, who had remained seated, turned his back to the field and chatted with his cronies, making a joke that drew forced laughter.

At 5:30 came the most important event of the day, the Gold Medal heat of the 100-meter dash. The runners took their places on the track, Owens drawing the far inside lane, generally considered the least desirable position. His red, white and blue shirt—the stripes running diagonally from his left shoulder to his waist—was speckled with mud from the previous heat.

Now the five sprinters crouched into the set position, digging their toes into the cinders. *Herr* Miller raised his pistol once more, calm and focused. *"Auf die Platze... fertig...* BANG!"

Owens instantly took the lead, coming up, out of his crouch, feet pounding the cinders rhythmically, extending his stride to the maximum, flowing over the track like a wave. He hit the tape a good two meters ahead of his nearest competitors. Jesse Owens, a black man from America, had defeated the Aryans and all the others. He had won the Olympics' signature event, and in 10.3 seconds, equaling the world's record despite the spongy track.

One hundred thousand voices roared in unison, the sound ricocheting around the stadium, settling on the athletic field and causing Owens to look up, smile modestly and wave to the crowd.

Up in the box of honor, Hitler had turned his back on Owens and was staring into the stands, icy-faced, trying to locate the source of some particularly loud cheering. It was coming from Ambassador Dodd's box and, more particularly, from Thomas Wolfe. Hitler's eyes met those of the American writer and his lips curled with contempt, then he looked away before Wolfe could react.

After that, Olympics officials hung medals from the necks of the victors while the band played the appropriate national anthems. Owens made a brief statement of thanks and then an Olympics official led him toward Hitler's box—but not up the stairs. Owens smiled and bowed toward *der Führer* and Hitler, stone-faced and without rising, gave him a half-hearted, cocked-armed Nazi salute.

Goebbels and Göring exchanged glances, glowering at each other and at the world. And now, Heydrich noticed the interaction and it gave him pause. He understood Hitler's anger well enough. He shared it. But Goebbels and Göring's reactions puzzled him. They seemed more frustrated than was appropriate, as though they were taking Owens's victory personally. This deserved further thought, Heydrich decided.

****

There was sharp disagreement in the Press Box.

"Hitler definitely snubbed Owens," Helms said.

"No," Rice said, "He gave him a little wave."

Paul Gallico joined the debate. "It was a Nazi salute, junior size," he said.

William L. Shirer came over. "I thought I saw a wave," he said, "but Hitler was turning to talk to Von Shirach and it might have been just a random hand gesture."

"What did you think, old man" Helms asked Nathan.

Nathan shrugged. "Hitler didn't seem happy to me," he said. "I didn't see a wave."

"Me neither," Eleanor piped up.

"Well," Rice said, "That's the way I saw it too and that's the way I'm gonna write it."

Eleanor leaned toward Nathan, so that the others couldn't hear. "You must be really relieved," she said quietly.

"Relieved?" Nathan said. "Why would I be relieved."

"Well, your job is over, right? Jesse is safe now."

"He is? Why do you say that?"

"He's gotten his Gold Medal. They weren't able to stop him," she said. "He won. *We* won."

"He's racing in two more events," Nathan said. "I'm not at all sure he's out of danger. Besides that, my job isn't over until he's back in the good old USA."

"You really take your work seriously," she said, exasperated.

"Eleanor, you're relieved of duty, if you want to be."

Helms stuck his head between them. "What *are* you two whispering about?"

"I was asking Mike for help with my column," Eleanor said.

"Why him?" Helms asked. "He doesn't know anything. He's been a reporter for, what? Five minutes?" He smiled at Nathan. "Sorry, old man, nothing personal."

"Of course not," Nathan said, seething.

"Now I'd be happy to help," Helms continued. "I've written a number of columns."

"Before you started shaving or afterward?" Nathan asked.

At that moment, they were joined by Thomas Wolfe, who'd found his way to the Press box from his spot across the aisle with Ambassador Dodd and his family. "So," he said to Eleanor and Nathan, "A victory for America. Thrilling, wasn't it? I cheered my lungs out. Owens is black as tar, but what the Hell, it's our team and he was wonderful."

"Very white of you," Nathan said.

Wolfe smiled.

Chapter Nineteen

The little blue convertible was waiting for Nathan as he walked out of the *Furstenhof* the next morning.

"How did you spend the evening?" Eleanor asked Nathan as he hopped into the passenger seat.

"Playing poker with the boys."

"Have a good time?"

"Just swell." He didn't ask how she'd spent her evening.

They were silent for the rest of the trip to the Olympic Village, arriving just as the athletes were finishing breakfast. They soon discovered that nothing was amiss, for a change—no missing shoes, no dire telegrams. Owens was on top of the world, wearing his Gold Medal and hoping to add two more to it, in the 200-meter sprint and the long jump. Once more, Eleanor and Nathan followed the American bus to the stadium, but this time, there were no careening trucks brimming over with bricks, or any other attempts to interfere with Owens or anyone else.

The scene at the Olympic Stadium was also pretty much the same as it had been the day before—the place was packed, Hitler there with all his acolytes, a chilly, overcast day, reporters assembled in the press box, hoping for something newsworthy. Nathan scanned the stands for malefactors, Helms chatted up Eleanor and rubbed elbows with Grantland Rice.

"Are you watching Owens?" Eleanor asked Nathan.

"Yes. No. What's he doing."

She pointed to the track. "He's about to run a heat in the 200-meter race," she said. "And he's also doing heats in the long jump."

"At the same time?"

"Just about."

At 10:30, Jesse Owens and five other sprinters took their places at the starting line for the third heat of the 200-meter race. *Herr* Miller said the magic words and fired his starter pistol. Twenty-one and one-tenth seconds later, Jesse Owens crossed the finish line, ten yards ahead of anyone else, and equaling the Olympic record.

"And now he's going to jump?" Nathan asked.

"That's what it says in the program," Eleanor said.

They watched as Owens scurried over to the long-jump venue for the preliminaries. Many sports writers had said this was the event he was most certain to win, based on past performance, a record-setting jump of 26 feet eight inches at a track meet at the University of Michigan. He joined sixteen other participants.

Helms bent toward Nathan. "Now you see, Mike, Jesse's only real competition comes from the other American long-jumpers, and he's beaten them all before."

Rice joined the conversation. "There is one threat," he said. "Take a look at the blond guy in the gray sweatpants and a gray turtleneck. That's Lutz Long. He's a German. And he's definitely a threat to win."

****

At that moment, down in Hitler's box, Goebbels and Göring were also discussing the upcoming long-jump, during a brief truce.

"It makes me sick just to see him standing there," Göring growled.

"You mean the Negro. Owens?" Goebbels said. "Me too. But don't worry, my friend. He won't win this time. He won't even make it past the preliminaries."

Göring threw up a hand. "He's the goddamn favorite, Goebbels," he said. "We both know that. And the…the animal… wins every time he participates. It is infuriating."

"It is," Goebbels agreed. "But he will not win, not this time."

Göring gave Goebbels his full attention. "You seem very sure, Goebbels. You've arranged something haven't you?"

Goebbels smiled. "What do you mean?"

"You've fixed the outcome, haven't you?" It was more an accusation than a question.

Goebbels did his best to sound innocent. "How could I have done that?"

"Don't bullshit me, Goebbels. We've both been trying to sabotage Owens ever since he got here. And until now, we've both failed. Have you finally found a way?"

Reinhard Heydrich, who was sitting next to Göring , leaned over to join the conversation. "Yes, *Herr* Dr. Goebbels, I would very much like to hear the answer to that. I've been watching this dainty little duet of yours—and the *Reichsminister's*—for some time now. I am very curious to see if, at last, you have actually achieved something."

Goebbels offered Heydrich a nervous smile. "I have had to be very subtle, *Obergruppenfurhrer* Heydrich. It had to be done in such a way that we could not be blamed for Owens's failure. But persistence pays off, as you will see."

"He's bluffing, *Obergruppenführer* ," Göring said. "When he says 'subtle,' he means 'weak" or 'useless.'"

"And your methods have been more effective, *Reichsminister*?" Heydrich asked.

"I was twice within a hairsbreadth of success," Göring insisted. "Each time, I was thwarted by accidents no one could have anticipated."

Heydrich shook his head, obviously disgusted. "You two have been working at cross purposes. Perhaps you would have succeeded if you had worked together. But if you had only consulted me, we could have ended the Negro's Olympic chances before he ever set foot in the stadium."

"I am sure you are right, *Obergruppenführer*," Goebbels said, "but I think you are about to see that Owens is all finished here."

"Really?" Göring said. "And just who do you think will out-jump him?"

"There, on the track," Goebbels said, pointing to the blond German near the long-jump venue. "That's Lutz Long, you know, a truly exceptional athlete, the greatest long-jumper Europe has ever produced. Look at that body—perfectly proportioned, lithe but powerful, a symphony of sinew and muscle. He will win the Gold Medal."

"Care to place a wager on that?" Göring asked. There was no mistaking the contempt in his voice.

Heydrich shot Goebbels a skeptical look. "According to the newspapers, *Herr* Goebbels, Lutz's best effort is a full foot short of Owens' best."

"Won't matter," Goebbels said. "Watch. It's about to begin."

On the field, the athletes began taking their turns at the long jump, each getting three chances to qualify for the finals. To qualify, all they had to do was jump the relatively modest distance of twenty-three feet, five-and-a-half inches, which most of them managed easily, getting little attention from the spectators.

Then came Jesse Owens' turn and everyone in the stadium shifted their attention to the long jump. Still wearing his sweat suit, Owens casually jogged down the runway and through the landing pit, evidently trying to get a feel for the terrain. The white-jacketed judge, who had been watching closely, suddenly thrust a red flag into the air, indicating a foul.

Owens stared at the judge in disbelief. He argued as best he could, but to no avail.

"What's he saying?" Göring asked.

"Probably that a practice run is an American custom, which it is," Goebbels answered. "But it is definitely not the custom at European meets—or at the Olympic Games."

"No matter," said Heydrich. "He has two more chances to qualify."

But Owens looked rattled. He lined up for his second try, nervously toeing the start line. Then, he was off, sprinting down the runway, wobbling a bit, perhaps a little unsure of himself. He kicked into the air just before the takeoff strip, his gait uneven and hesitant, and he landed twenty-three feet three inches down the pit—two inches short of the qualifying distance. The judge held up the red flag, but Owens barely glanced at it. He knew. He hung his head and walked back to the start line, completely dispirited.

"Last chance," Goebbels said to Göring and Heydrich. "Just watch what happens."

On the field, Lutz Long approached Owens. They talked briefly, and it looked like a friendly conversation.

Göring regarded Goebbels with suspicion. "What's going on down there?" he asked. "Is this part of your plan?"

Goebbels was staring at the field, frowning. "No it is not," he said. "I have no idea what they're saying to each other."

"Why would Long talk with Owens?" Heydrich asked. "Have they met? Do they know each other?"

"They might have crossed paths at the Village," Goebbels suggested. "But so far as I know they are strangers."

At that moment, Lutz took Owens' sweatshirt and placed it on the ground, just in front of the takeoff strip. He pointed to the sweatshirt and said a few more words.

"Our man seems to be helping the nigger," Heydrich observed, smiling. "Or do you have another explanation, Goebbels?"

Goebbels just shook his head.

Now Owens took his place at the starting line. The stadium went silent, everyone leaning forward to see what would happen. They all seemed to know what was at stake. One more foul and Jesse Owens was out. He would lose his chance at the long-jump Gold Medal.

Owens went into his crouch, then he was off again, sprinting with all the grace and power of a fine Arabian. At the sweatshirt, he gave his kick and lifted off, floating through the air, above the pit, landing twenty-five feet later, nearly two whole feet beyond the minimum.

Goebbels crossed his arms across his chest, and, if it had been physically possible, steam would have shot out of his ears.

"I'm sorry I didn't take that bet," Göring said. "I would enjoy taking money from you."

Goebbels said nothing.

Heydrich lit a cigarette, took a deep drag, then exhaled. "Well, Goebbels, it seems like you have failed. And before you start gloating, Herman, remember that you haven't done any better."

Göring tried a dismissive shrug, but Heydrich wasn't buying.

"And why have you both failed?" Heydrich asked. "Three reasons. First, your efforts have been embarrassingly feeble and namby-pamby. Shoe-stealing. Whose idea was that?"

"How do you know about the shoes?" Goebbels said.

Heydrich looked at Goebbels with open curiosity. "Do you actually believe anything happens in Germany that I do not know about?"

"Well, I thought it was a very clever idea," Goebbels said. "It could have worked."

Göring laughed. "Shoe-stealing? What are we, schoolboys?"

Heydrich regarded Göring with disdain. "May I assume the bicycle accident was your brilliant idea, *Reichsmarshall*?"

"If my man hadn't been interfered with…"

"Ah yes, there's always a reason," Heydrich said. He took a puff on his cigarette, then continued. "The truth is, neither your *Luftwaffe*, *Reichsmarshall* Göring , nor your Propaganda Ministry, *Reichsminister* Goebbels is suited to this task. And neither of you has the right temperament for it. It is, however, well within the Gestapo's purview and capabilities. Perhaps, with my assistance, we can rid ourselves of this black intruder."

Göring and Goebbels exchanged glances. "Are you offering your Gestapo's services?" Göring asked.

Chapter Twenty

Nathan sat back, took a deep breath and relaxed. Owens's encounter with Lutz Long hadn't turned out as he had feared. The German long jumper had no interest in interfering with Owens—quite the opposite, he had helped his American counterpart, so much that Owens might have failed to qualify without him.

"Well, that was nice," Eleanor said.

"International cooperation at its best," said Helms. "It'll make a great sidebar."

"Maybe so," said Grantland Rice, "but that will require some reporting."

"What do you mean?"

"Well, young man, if you're going to write about what just happened with Long and Owens, it isn't enough to report what you saw from a hundred feet away. You'll have to get up off your hindquarters, scurry down to the field, and find out what they said to each other and why. You're up for that, right?"

"Yeah," Helms said. "I am."

"No time like the present," Rice said.

"You're absolutely right," Helms said and headed for the nearest stairway.

"Shouldn't he have thought of that himself?" Eleanor asked. She took a cigarette pack from her purse, got herself a Lucky Strike and would have lit up herself if Nathan hadn't beaten her to it.

Rice watched the little performance with a smile. "You're right, Eleanor," he said, "But some neophytes need a push in the right direction. Besides, I'd rather he go trotting down the stairs than me. He'll be back with the whole story, I'm sure."

"So you're treating him like an errand boy?" Nathan asked.

"I'd prefer the word 'protégé,'" Rice said. "You know it's every veteran newsman's duty to give the rookies a helping hand."

"And sometimes it's hard to figure out who's helping who," Eleanor said, giving Rice a not-so-innocent smile.

"Young lady has me all figured out," Rice said to Nathan. "Better watch out for her, Mike."

"Now you tell me."

"Pay attention, boys," Eleanor said, "the long-jump semi-finals are about to begin."

Now, at 4:30 in the afternoon, the sixteen qualifying jumpers began all over again, each man taking three turns. In his third jump, Lutz broke the Olympic record, with a leap of twenty-five feet, eight and three-quarters inches. An enormous cheer broke out from the crowd. "Lutz! Lutz!"

Owens failed to equal Long's performance on his first two attempts, but on his third, he jumped an inch-and-a-quarter farther than his German counterpart. Once more, the stadium erupted in cries of "Yaysee, Yaysee!" Now it was a duel between the American and the German for the Gold Medal. They each got three turns. But the last two decided it.

On his second run, Owens managed a new Olympic record—twenty-five feet, ten inches. And on *his* second run, Long equaled it. Now it was Owens turn again, his very last chance. He went into his crouch and then he was off, flying down the runway, leaping just before the takeoff strip, legs continuing to pump, coming down in the pit twenty-six feet from the start—beating Long by two inches and again smashing the Olympic record.

It was all up to Long now. He crouched, rose and stumbled. He jumped, nevertheless, but barely cleared twenty feet. For an instant, the crowd was silent. Then, all at the same moment, everyone realized what Long's failure meant. It meant Jesse Owens, the American Negro, had won his second Gold Medal of the Berlin Olympics. The stadium rocked with cheers.

Owens could have skipped his third turn, but he did not. He bolted down the runway one last time and bounded into the air as though he had suddenly become weightless. He hit the pit twenty-six feet five-and-a-half inches from the starting plate, rebreaking the record he had just set. This time, the cheering was practically hysterical.

Even before Owens could pick himself up out of the sand, Lutz Long hurried to shake his hand and throw an arm over Owens' shoulder. Then, clutching Owens' left hand with his right, Lutz turned toward Hitler and raised their arms together in triumph. After that, he and Owens walked off the field, arm-in-arm.

Nathan, Eleanor and Rice simultaneously looked down to Hitler's box. *Der Führer* had turned away from the sports field now and was berating an aide, his face red with anger.

"He doesn't seem happy," Nathan said.

"I guess he was hoping for a different outcome," Eleanor said, sounding innocent.

****

That night, despite Nathan's determined resistance, Eleanor convinced him to take her to the *Sommerfest*. This was Dr. Goebbels huge, elaborate and much talked-of evening gala on the *Pfaueninsel--*Peacock Island—a beautifully-landscaped nature reserve in the middle of Lake Havel, once the playground of Frederick the Great.

"I'm not putting on a monkey suit," Nathan said.

"You don't have to get dressed up," Eleanor told him. "It's a summer festival."

"But, Owens…"

"Owens is at the Olympic Village. Besides that, he's already got two Gold Medals. No one's going to harm him now."

"I wish I were sure of that," Nathan said, but he didn't argue.

They went back to their hotels, changed their clothes, hopping into the little blue convertible and headed out toward the Havel shoreline. Several dozen policemen were stationed there, directing a long stream of Mercedes, Maybachs and Horches, and the occasional Rolls Royce to a huge parking lot. Nathan parked the convertible beside a dark grey Adler Trumpf Junior and they hopped out.

"Looks like we're in pretty high-falutin' company," Nathan observed.

"Well, from what I've been told," Eleanor said, "the cream of Berlin society will be here tonight, plus princes, generals, admirals, ambassadors, athletes, opera singers and movie stars."

"And journalists," Nathan prompted.

"Yes, of course," She winked. "The famous ones, like us."

They merged into the crowd and crossed a quaint footbridge bridge from mainland to island. When they were on dry land again, they passed through a "guard of honor," formed by half-naked female dancers holding flaming torches.

And at the end of this passage stood Dr. and Mrs. Goebbels, both dressed in white, he in gabardine, she in organza, greeting the arriving guests with great charm and panache. Goebbels briefly shook Nathan's hand but lingered with Eleanor, eyes bright, taking her hand to his lips and kissing it.

Nathan and Eleanor then strolled on, through the ancient trees strung with thousands of electric lights forming gigantic butterfly patterns. They stopped at one of the many fountains spouting champagne and dipped their glasses. Then they were approached by a girl dressed as a Renaissance page, who showed them to one of the many dinner tables sitting on the grass, this one occupied by Grantland Rice, Red Knickerbocker and Quentin Reynolds.

"Well, well," Rice said, "I see you found the place."

"All we had to do was follow the Mercedes caravan," Eleanor said.

"Yes," Reynolds said, "the company is a little rich."

"So nice of Dr. Goebbels to seat us with our own kind," Knickerbocker observed.

Rice smiled. "Didn't want us to feel out of place," he said.

Reynolds shook his head, disagreeing. "He wanted to *keep* us in our place, so we couldn't contaminate his guests, or overhear something that deviated from the party line."

"One might think you didn't trust the man," Rice replied, teasing.

Reynolds laughed. "There you go, jumping to conclusions again."

Now came the food, great quantities of Schnitzel à la Holstein, Sauerbraten, Veal Cordon Bleu, Chicken Paprikash, potato pancakes and steaming plates of vegetables, with several bottles of fine German wine at the center of every table. It was nothing short of a feast, a feast for two thousand people.

And as they ate, Goebbels limped among the tables, joking here, complimenting there, exchanging gossip and flattery and generally ingratiating himself. The Reichsminister seemed to love every last one of his guests and they appeared to return his affection, at least to his face.

Then, the dancing began, several bands taking turns. And all around the park-like setting, couples rose to take advantage of the music, Generals and Admirals and Third Reich VIPs tripping what passed for the light fantastic in Nazi Germany.

Nathan, who was no dancer, was nonetheless steeling himself to approach Eleanor when *Reichsminister* Goebbels moved in on her. Bowing and smiling. "Good evening," he said, looking at Eleanor. "I am Josef Goebbels, your host. I didn't catch your name when you arrived."

"I'm Mike Novak, of the *Cleveland Plain Dealer*," Nathan began, "And this…"

"I'm Eleanor Holm, of the INS.

Goebbels took her hand and kissed it once more, while simultaneously bowing and clicking his heels, no small feat on the luxuriant grass. "*Fräulein* Holm," he said, almost purring.

"I have heard of you." Then he turned to Nathan. "May I have this dance with your beautiful lady?"

"She is a beautiful lady," Nathan said, "But she's not *my* beautiful lady. I'm afraid you'll have to ask her."

" *Fräulein* Holm?" Goebbels said

Eleanor flashed a look at Nathan, half-surprised, half-panicked, but he couldn't help. He shrugged almost imperceptibly.

"I would like that very much, *Reichsminister* Goebbels," Eleanor said with as much sincerity as she could manage.

The band struck up another tune and Goebbels swept her away, despite his limp, holding her close, smiling seductively, whispering in her ear. Nathan watched with some dismay, helpless but not overly concerned. Goebbels would bring her back after a dance or two and she would have a great story to tell.

That wasn't what happened. Goebbels held onto Eleanor dance after dance, steadily moving through the other dancers and away from him toward some green and yellow striped tents that had been put up far from the tables. After a bit, Nathan realized he could barely see them.

He went up on his tiptoes and craned his neck. When that failed, he stood on a chair. A flash of dark gold hair caught his attention. They were quickly moving toward the tents. And then, without making a conscious decision, so was he, taking the direct route through the dancing couples, annoying several as he jostled through the crowd.

Nathan spotted *Reichsminister* Goebbels and Eleanor Holm walking toward the tents, he purposefully, with a tight grip on her arm, she trying—as politely as possible—to extricate herself, laughing, flirtatiously protesting.

"Oh there you are," Nathan called out when he got within shouting distance. "I've been looking for you."

"Oh hi, Mike," Eleanor said gaily. "We were just…"

"I'm going to show the *fraulein* the beautiful view from the other side of the island," Goebbels said.

"I'm afraid there won't be time for that," Nathan said. "Eleanor just got a message from her editor. He needs a column from her by midnight. We'll have to leave now."

Goebbels looked at Nathan with undisguised malevolence. "I'm sorry you saw fit to interrupt us," he said. There was nothing threatening in the words, but the tone of voice was another story.

Nathan shrugged. "Well, you know how it is, *Reichsminister*, we journalists are always at our editors' beck and call."

"Perhaps another time," Eleanor said, detaching herself and giving Goebbels a smile in consolation.

"Perhaps," Goebbels said with just a hint of anger. He knew there would be no other time. "But it was very nice to meet you, *fraulein*." Then, as an afterthought, "and you too, *Herr…*"

"Novak," Nathan said. "Mike Novak."

Goebbels gave him a look, as if he were trying to fix the face in his memory. "Yes. *Herr* Novak."

Nathan took Eleanor's arm and they walked away from Goebbels as quickly as they could without seeming to flee.

"Thanks," she said. "I thought he had me."

"What was he trying to do?"

"Get me into one of those tents," she said. "And once we were out of sight…"

"I see."

"You came along just in time."

"Bodyguard instinct," he said.

They were halfway to the pontoon bridge when they were intercepted by a tall, blond, long-faced man in an immaculate black uniform. Nathan recognized him instantly—this was *Obergruppeführer* Reinhard Heydrich, director of the Gestapo. And he had recognized them first.

"Ah, my friends from the cabaret," he said with an icy smile. "I trust you've been staying out of trouble."

Nathan decided it would be better not to play coy. "Hello, Director Heydrich. We're spending most of our time at the Olympic stadium, actually."

"So." Heydrich said. "You found out who I am."

"I saw *Triumph of the Will* last night, and there you were."

"Yes. Wonderful film, wouldn't you say?"

Nathan paused for a moment, searching for the right word. "Remarkable." he said.

"But you have the advantage. Your name has slipped my mind."

"Novak, Mike Novak," Nathan supplied. "I'm that newspaper reporter from Ohio."

"Of course. And Eleanor…Jarrett, I believe. I don't know why, but I'm better at remembering women's names than men's." He produced a self-deprecating chuckle. "Are you enjoying the *Sommerfest*?"

Eleanor dipped into her extensive repertoire of smiles, found one that was friendly, but not quite flirtatious and she bestowed it on Heydrich. "I think it's the most beautiful soireé I've ever been to," she said. "Dr. Goebbels really knows how to throw a party."

"He'll be happy to hear that you think so," Heydrich said. "And will the two of you be at the stadium tomorrow?"

"Of course," Nathan said. "Wouldn't miss a single event."

"We're not tourists, you know," Eleanor said. "We're journalists."

"Yes," said Heydrich. "So I am reminded."

Suddenly, the entire sky lit up with a rainbow of flashing and blinking colors, the bright burst followed by a huge boom, as if lightning had struck only a few feet away. Nathan threw an arm around Eleanor as many of the other party-goers crouched down or ducked behind trees.

Heydrich seemed totally unfazed. He smiled tolerantly at Nathan and Eleanor. "Just fireworks" he explained. "A little surprise from Dr. Goebbels. Nothing to worry about."

As he spoke, a dozen more explosions erupted in the sky, one after another, turning twilight into midday, if midday included brightly fiery reds, greens and blues.

"If I didn't know better," Nathan said to Heydrich, over the noise, "I'd say that was artillery fire and that an invasion was about to begin."

Heydrich laughed. "No, my friend, not this time." He looked at Nathan for a moment, sizing him up, then glanced at Eleanor and bowed. "Enjoy the party," he said, walking away.

"*That* was the head of the Gestapo?" Eleanor asked.

"The very same."

"He knows."

Nathan considered her. "He knows what?"

"He knows you're not who you pretend to be," Eleanor said.

"What makes you think so?"

Eleanor thought a moment. "His manner," she said, finally. "He acted like he was toying with us."

The sky lit up again, the sudden brightness followed by another man-made clap of thunder, and then another, and another. The partygoers seemed more dismayed than entertained.

"Let's get out of here," Eleanor said.

"To where?"

"Hmmmm...." She slipped Nathan a mischievous smile. Nathan smiled back, surprised but pleased.

Then it was back over the footbridge, into the little blue convertible and back to the city. It didn't occur to either that anyone might be following them.

Chapter Twenty-One

On Wednesday morning, August 5, 1936, they woke up together, in her room at the Adlon. Eleanor stretched, yawned and put a question to her bedmate.. "Do we really have to go out to the Olympic Village again, David?"

"You don't. But I do."

"You do? Why?"

"Well, because he's running in two more events today, the 200 meter semis and the Gold Medal round. So I'm still on the job. You can sleep in and show up at the stadium later. The 200-meter semis are set for 3:30 this afternoon."

"Oh, I suppose I'll go with," Eleanor said. She slipped out of bed and headed toward the bathroom, stark naked and, Nathan thought, very nearly perfect.

Nathan looked at her until she closed the door, then rolled out of bed, checked his watch and got dressed. There would be other nights, he promised himself.

****

They drove out to the Olympic Village in the little blue convertible, Nathan behind the wheel this time. Despite that, their visit was completely uneventful. Nathan was on the alert, but no emergency or threat presented itself. Owens and Snyder were in a fine mood and looking forward to the day's races.

After lunch, Nathan and Eleanor followed the US bus to the Olympic Stadium, encountering no out-of-control brick trucks on the way. They said goodbye to Owens as he entered the stadium dressing rooms and headed for the press box.

They were passing Ambassador Dodd's box when Thomas Wolfe spotted Eleanor. "Well, there you are," he said. "I looked for you last night."

She looked back at him, Nathan waiting. "I went to Goebbels party," she said. "The one on the island."

Wolfe stood, trying to engage her. "Really?" he said. "I was there too, but I didn't see you."

"I guess we were just ships passing in the night," she told him, smiling.

"Maybe I'll see you later," Wolfe said.

"Well, you never know." The smile was briefer.

They left Wolfe behind and found their way to the press box, where they were greeted by Richard Helms, who was studying that day's edition of *Der Angriff*, a hard-core Nazi newspaper. "Can you translate this, old man?" he asked Nathan, pointing at an article about the Olympics.

"Sorry," Nathan said. "It's Greek to me."

"German, you mean," Eleanor said.

"Grannie?"

"No speaka da German," said Grantland Rice, who was sitting next to Helms.

"Here, let me see that," said Quentin Reynolds. He looked at the newspaper. "You sure you want to hear this?" he said. "It's pretty nasty."

"I'll grit my teeth," Helms offered.

"Okay, here goes: 'If America didn't have her black auxiliaries, where would she be in the Olympic Games? For then, the German Lutz Long would have won the long jump, the Italian Mario Lanzi the 800-meters run and the Hollander Martin Osendarp the 100-meters.'"

"Nasty indeed," Eleanor said.

"But not surprising," said Nathan. "I'm sure Hitler isn't pleased that the Olympics have become a showcase for those he considers racial inferiors."

"That's true," Rice said, "although you have to admit that this Olympics hasn't been a triumph for white American athletes."

Nathan spent the rest of the afternoon searching the stands again for anyone suspicious. Before long, he saw the sallow-faced man again, the one who reminded him of Peter Lorre.

Either this guy was a villain of some kind, Nathan decided, an assassin perhaps, just a sports fan or nothing more than an ordinary tourist. It was maddening, not to be able to figure him out. But the man was simply sitting in the stands, watching. So Nathan watched him.

The others concentrated on observing the 200-meter trials. And even though the track was muddy from repeated rain showers and the temperature hovered at about 12 degrees C., Jesse Owens did not disappoint. He won the first trial, and Mack Robinson, older brother of the notable high school athlete, Jackie Robinson, tied with Canada's Lee Orr in the second heat. At 6 p.m., these three would be competing for the Gold Medal, in what, apparently, would be Owens' last event of the Olympic games.

Just before 6:00, the six competitors gathered at the 200-meter starting line—Owens, Robinson, Orr, two runners from the Netherlands and one from Switzerland. They took their places, digging footholds in the soggy track with their toes.

Now, throughout the stadium, all eyes turned to the six sprinters. Standing just behind *Herr* Miller, Leni Reifenstahl signaled her crew to roll camera. *Herr* Miller raised his pistol. *"Auf die Platze… fertig…* BANG!"

And they were off. Owens broke out in front, Mack Robinson right on his heels and Tinus Osendarp of the Netherlands two steps behind him. Despite the mud, the wind and the chill in the air, they flew toward the finish, Owens steadily pulling away.

Jesse Owens crossed the finish line well ahead of his competitors, in—according to the giant stopwatch mounted on the stadium pillar— 20.7 seconds, a world record, and enough to trigger a tumultuous reception from the stadium's 100,000 spectators, along with thunderous shouts of *"Yaysee! Yaysee!"* repeated over and over again.

In the press box, Grantland Rice was the first to start typing, and Richard Helms, who was sitting right next to him, bent over to see what was coming out of the typewriter. "Read it out loud," Eleanor suggested. She gave Rice a winning smile.

Rice sighed, helpless, and read. "Jesse Owens looked like a dark streak of lightning. His final performance in breaking all records for the 200 meters under miserable conditions, with a rain-soaked track, left the athletes of fifty-one nations goggle-eyed with astonishment."

"Has anyone ever won three Gold Medals in a single Olympics?" Nathan asked.

"Actually, several have accomplished that," Helms replied. "As I recall, the first was Morris Kirksey in 1904."

"Three?"

"Yes, two in track and one in rugby. And he wasn't the only one, Gustaf…"

"Yes, Dickie," Eleanor said. "You've proved you have a remarkable memory."

***

Hitler and most of his guests abandoned the box of honor as soon as the race was over, not wanting to see Jesse Owens receive still another Gold Medal. Göring and Goebbels were about to leave, but Heydrich stopped them. "I think we have something to discuss," he said.

"Such as how the nigger has humiliated us?" Goebbels asked.

Heydrich lifted an eyebrow. "Such as how we can get rid of him," he said.

Göring laughed bitterly. "What good would that do us? He's already won three Gold Medals. Are we going to order him to give them back?"

"His very existence is an insult to the Third Reich," Heydrich said. "As long as he walks the Earth, he mocks Aryan superiority. I cannot tolerate that."

"Well, he's run his last event," Goebbels pointed out. "He probably won't come to the stadium again. We won't be able to get to him."

"That may not be the case," Heydrich said.

Göring looked at him sharply. "What do you mean?"

"I have looked into this," Heydrich said. "Back in America, he often runs in the 4 x 100-meter relay."

"But he is not scheduled to run in the relay this time," Goebbels said.

"Not yet," Heydrich said.

Göring scoffed. "Even you can't put him in the race, Director."

Heydrich smiled, then lit a cigarette. "No." He took a puff. "At least not directly."

"What are you hinting at?" Goebbels asked.

Heydrich puffed on his cigarette again, considering the question, not answering.

"With our luck, it wouldn't matter," Göring said. "The man lives a charmed life."

On the field, Jesse Owens, Mack Robinson and Tinus Osendarp mounted the honors podium. The stadium orchestra launched into the national anthem of the United States of America.

Göring, Goebbels and Heydrich paused to watch, faces set in stone, as the Olympic official hung the Gold Medal around Owens' neck, and the spectators once more broke into excited applause.

"The *Reichsminister* has a point, *Obergruppenführer* Heydrich," Goebbels said, after waiting for the noise to subside. "The nigger can do no wrong."

"What's worse," Göring added, "is that we can't seem to lay a hand on him."

"Do you know why you've failed?" Heydrich inquired mildly.

Goebbels shrugged, "Bad luck."

"Or simple incompetence," Göring said. Then he smiled at Goebbels. "Yours, I mean. Not mine."

Goebbels smiled back. "Of course."

The *Reichsmarschall* noticed a spot on the bulging left pant leg of his powder blue uniform. He frowned, pulled out a brilliantly white handkerchief and, trying to be inconspicuous, attempted to rub out the blemish. When that failed, he moistened the handkerchief with his tongue and tried again. To his consternation, the spot grew larger.

Heydrich watched Göring with the sort of fascination a child feels when he sees a rhinoceros at the zoo. "Now, now, gentlemen," he said, after Göring's failure to restore his pant leg to pristine condition, "Your inability to get rid of Owens has nothing to do with bad luck or incompetence. You've been fighting an invisible enemy."

"I hope you're not going to say 'fate,' *Obergruppenführer*," Göring said.

"No," Heydrich said. He took one last puff on his cigarette, dropped it to the floor and crushed it with an immaculately polished boot. "I'm going to say 'bodyguard'." He let the word fall into the conversation like a lump of coal.

"The Americans brought no bodyguards," Goebbels said. "I personally checked the team list—unless you think Owens' coach is acting in that capacity."

Heydrich shook his head. "He's just a coach."

"But the Gestapo is providing all of Olympic security," Göring said. "You're not telling me that one of your own men…"

"Pardon me, *Reichsmarshall*?"

"No, of course, you're not suggesting that," Göring hurried to say.

Goebbels was mystified. "Then who…"

"I'll show you," Heydrich. "I'll point him out right now, if you'll promise to look discreetly, and not to call attention to yourselves."

It was Göring's turn to be mystified. "What? He's here? Within view?"

"He's about 10 meters feet away," Heydrich said.

Göring was astonished. "Where?"

"Show us!" Goebbels demanded.

Heydrich was gazing at the sports field now, watching the sprinters coming down from the honors podium. Göring and Goebbels did the same, trying to figure out who he was looking at. "*Reichsmarshall* Göring," Heydrich said, "keep looking at me for a moment. *Reichsminister* Goebbels, look up and behind us, at the press box."

Goebbels and Göring exchanged skeptical looks, but they did as he asked.

"Now, Dr. Goebbels. Do you see the pretty blonde girl at the near end of the row of reporters?" Heydrich asked.

"Yes," Goebbels said, frowning, "Eleanor Holm. The American swimmer who was dismissed from the team."

"Very attractive," Goring reflected.

"All right. Now notice the young, dark-haired man sitting beside her."

Goebbels gazed at Nathan, eyebrows knit. "Yes. They were both at my party last night," he said. He was not happy with the recollection.

"Indeed they were," said Heydrich, "I spoke to them. Now look away from them, Dr. Goebbels. It's *Reichsmarschall's* turn."

Göring twisted himself backward and craned his neck so he could see the press box, no easy feat given his bulk. Then he looked back at Heydrich. "I've seen them as well," he said. "They were at Templehoff when Lindbergh arrived."

"Well, that man is Jesse Owens' bodyguard," Heydrich said.

Both Goebbels and Göring briefly glanced back at Nathan again.

"Are you sure, *Obergruppenführer*? I'm familiar with that man," Goebbels said. "He's a reporter for some provincial American newspaper."

Göring turned to Heydrich. "If he's Owens' bodyguard, why isn't he with Owens? What is he doing in the press box?"

"Maintaining his journalistic identity, I would guess, while Owens is safe in the locker room with his teammates," Heydrich said. "But according to our telegraph office, this so-called journalist has never filed a single story. Don't you find that curious?"

Goebbels crossed his arms across his chest, unconvinced. "*That's* your evidence?" he asked. "I can think of all kinds of explanations—

filing by mail or telephone, for example, or asking someone else to file for him."

Heydrich nodded thoughtfully. "That is true. Still, I found his lack of filing very suggestive," he said. "So I talked to some of my men last night, did a bit of investigating, and found there are many other reasons for suspecting him."

"As I recall," Göring said, "When Lindbergh flew the Junkers, that man was one of the passengers. If he is Owens' bodyguard, he was certainly neglecting his duties."

"Unless he was preserving his cover," Heydrich said. "If he hadn't shown up, we might have asked ourselves if he were really a journalist."

"You said you had many other reasons for suspecting him," Goebbels prodded.

"One of you—I am not sure which—sent Owens a distressing, but fictitious telegram asking him to come home immediately because of a family illness." He looked expectantly at Göring, then at Goebbels.

"My doing," Goebbels admitted.

"Yes, *Reichsminister*, and it was our friend in the press box and his female companion who determined it was phony and reassured Owens that all was well at home."

"How do you know that?" Göring asked.

"We have eyewitnesses," Heydrich said. "And that night, one of you arranged to have Owens shoes stolen—his only pair."

"That was also me," Goebbels said.

Göring laughed. "Shoes? You had his shoes stolen, Goebbels? Did you think no replacements could be found in all of Berlin?"

"They were very special shoes."

"And guess who found the replacements for them, Dr. Goebbels," Heydrich said.

"No!" said Goebbels, thoroughly perplexed.

"Yes. My man spoke to the owner of the shoe factory."

"Did you really think shoe-stealing would work, Goebbels?" Göring said.

"Did you think attacking Owens with a man on a bicycle would work?" Heydrich asked Göring. "That was your operation, wasn't it?"

"Well, yes, at least my man was responsible."

"Following your orders?"

Göring paused a moment, then spoke, softly. "Yes, *Obergruppenführer*."

"A bicycle?" Goebbels asked with contempt. "And you're criticizing me?"

"It would have worked," Göring said, "if a stranger hadn't interfered."

"A stranger whose description, oddly enough, matches that of our friend in the press box in *every* particular," Heydrich said. "Quite a coincidence, wouldn't you say?"

Göring straightened one of his chest medals, saying nothing.

"I also spoke to one of your drivers, *Reichsmarshall—a* fellow who had an accident with a brick truck. He claims he was sent to crash into one of the Olympic buses, the American one. Is that right?"

"I'm still not sure why that failed," Göring said.

"Ah," said Heydrich. "I think I can explain. I spoke to your truck driver. He told me that at the last instant before a collision, a little blue convertible inserted itself between his truck and the bus, screening the athletes from an impact. The truck driver hit his brakes instead of crashing into it, since the car wasn't his target."

"It's almost as though fate…" Göring began.

"According to the truck driver's description, our reporter friend was in the vehicle with the young lady," Heydrich interrupted. "She rented it when she arrived in Berlin."

Neither Göring nor Goebbels uttered a word, but both, one after another, turned back toward the press box for another glimpse at the man in question.

"The man's name—at least the name on the passport—is Michael Novak. But my office has checked with the newspaper he purports to work for. They've never heard of him."

"So he's an agent," Göring said, coming to the obvious conclusion.

"Almost certainly," Heydrich agreed. "And a very capable and highly resourceful one. If we expect to rid ourselves of Jesse Owens, we're going to have to deal with Novak first. And not with stolen shoes or bicycle accidents. The job must be given to an assassin."

Göring and Goebbels were both silent for a moment. Then Goebbels had a thought. "What about the girl?"

Heydrich put a hand to his chin and considered the question. "Oh, I don't know.

I think that's an opportunistic association, probably for both of them. She's certainly no agent and therefore, no danger to us. Besides, she is very pretty, no?"

"Yes," Goebbels said. "But Novak…".

"He will die," said Heydrich. "So will Owens. They will both be dead by sunset tomorrow, I guarantee it. If you both agree."

"I'm not sure I do," Goebbels said. "If Owens is murdered here at the Olympics, the Third Reich will be forever disgraced. It will nullify all of our efforts to seem welcoming and hospitable. And the death of an American reporter, well…"

Heydrich smiled. "You are being unnecessarily cautious, Goebbels. The question you raise is easily dealt with. The killer will be an escaped mental patient, or a Jew, or whomever it is convenient for us to blame, perhaps a Czech or a Pole trying to sabotage our wonderful Olympics. If you'd thought that out clearly, Owens would already be dead.'

"I'm not sure…" Goebbels said.

"That's the problem," Heydrich observed. "You were reluctant to take decisive action."

"I was thinking of Germany's reputation," Goebbels countered.

"I understand that," Heydrich said, "and your caution is admirable. But the problem is easily dealt with. The killer will be shot by a heroic German soldier while attempting to flee the scene. It will be a terrible tragedy, but no one will blame the Third Reich. Thanks to you and your wonderful propaganda, *Reichsminister* Goebbels, the world will sympathize with us, and mourn Owens and we will join them with unquestionable sincerity."

Goebbels, trapped, smiled weakly.

"You're sure you can get Owens back into the stadium tomorrow?" Göring asked, then immediately regretted the question. "I mean, I know practically nothing is beyond the Gestapo's abilities. Still, your influence over the American coaches…"

"I will make a telephone call," Heydrich said.

Chapter Twenty-Two

Nathan and Eleanor played, had breakfast in bed, then played a little bit more, having gotten the hang of each other. Afterward, Nathan looked at his watch. "Gotta get dressed," he said.

"In God's name, why?" She was sitting up, clutching a puffy comforter around her.

"Well, it's time to go out to the Olympic Village, check on Jesse," Nathan said. "In fact, we're late." He slipped on a shirt.

Eleanor groaned. "Surely the danger is over, David. He's won his medals. He's with his teammates. The Village is well-guarded."

Nathan was not convinced. "I'm on duty until he's back in America, remember." He stepped into his pants and pulled them up.

"Well, I'm not going," Eleanor said. "You do whatever you want. Take the car."

"What will you do?"

Eleanor shook her head, her hair swinging, then falling back into place. "Oh, I don't know. I'll keep busy somehow."

Nathan put on his sport jacket. "Guess I'll see you tonight, then."

"Okey dokey."

He took a couple of steps toward the door, stopped and took a deep breath. "How about a compromise?"

"I'm listening."

"We stay here this morning, head out to the stadium this afternoon."

"To see the games."

"Yes, just to see the games."

He took off his sport coat.

****

Rudolph Theilmann, a Gestapo *Kriminaldirektor* and the 1932 Silver Medal winner of the 600-meter rifle shot competition, arrived at the Olympic stadium soon after sunup. He was carrying two pieces of black leather luggage, one a tube about six inches in diameter and almost as long as he was tall, the other a fat little bag in which an athlete might keep his gymnastics clothing and shoes.

The tube contained a Mauser GeWehr 98 bolt action rifle fitted with an internal magazine holding five cartridges. A leather sling was attached to the rifle by two metal swivels on the bottom of the stock. The tube also contained a Zeiss six-power telescopic sight and a tiny folding tripod. There were no additional cartridges. Theilmann was sure he would have no need for them.

The fat little bag contained cigarettes, sandwiches, bottled soft drinks and reading matter—several magazines and a novel, *Berlin Alexanderplatz*, by Alfred Doblin. A page about a third of the way into the book was folded down. Theilmann knew he would be waiting here for a long time. He'd learned it was essential to keep his mind occupied.

Theilmann himself was something of a freak. In most respects, he was an ordinary-looking barrel-chested man of medium height, blue eyed, with longish and limp blond hair. It was his arms that were strange. They were so short he had to bend sideways at the waist left or right if he wanted to reach deeply into a pocket. As a result, he kept his side pockets empty and used those in his blouse to carry cigarettes and coins.

Theilmann's abnormality had not affected his shooting abilities. Indeed, he had found a way to wrap the leather gun sling around his arms in such a way as to give him exceptional stability. Other marksmen, jealous, said it was the secret to his success, and tantamount to cheating. Because of his skills, he'd been Heydrich's first choice to lead an execution squad during the Night of the Long Knives, in 1934, which wiped out all of Hitler's domestic competitors.

Now, the Hangman, as Heydrich was known throughout the Gestapo, had selected Theilmann to do another service. The shooter's task: to eliminate the American reporter known as Michael Novak and to slay the Negro sprinter, Jesse Owens. He had no special feelings about this. A job was a job. Except for the crowd and the location, it was entirely routine.

From a technical standpoint, Theilmann's problem was how to target someone in the stands and someone on the field so he could kill them in quick succession. The answer was simple enough: find a spot on the roof that commanded a view of both. He stood in the infield for a moment and surveyed the stadium's upper level. One location appeared ideal, a spot beside the stop-watch tower.

Theilmann climbed the stairs, flight after flight. At the highest level, a ladder led to a roof hatch. He climbed that too, and popped the hatch without difficulty. He found a likely spot just an arm's-length from the tower, far enough back from the roof's inner edge that no one would notice, at least no one who wasn't looking for him, no one who didn't know what to look for amidst the roof's drainage pipes and ventilation shafts.

He crouched on the concrete roof and stowed his pieces of luggage, then he unsnapped the tube and pulled out the rifle. *His* rifle—the weapon on which he had lavished a lover's attention and which had rewarded him with medal after medal, as well as an assortment of fleshly trophies, or at least the memory of them.

Theilmann fastened the telescopic sight to the rifle and attached the tripod.

He kneeled, then stretched himself into the prone position and took several sightings of his prey through the telescope, making small adjustments on the gun each time. Finally satisfied, he left the rifle in place, pulled the book from the fat little satchel, leaned back against the tower and immersed himself in the story, which was about a murderer newly released from prison.

****

Nathan and Eleanor took their seats in the press box just before 3 p.m. The stadium was filled to the brim.

"You almost missed it, old man," said Richard Helms.

"What, the relay race?" Nathan asked.

"No, the *fuss* about the relay race."

"What fuss?" Eleanor asked.

Grantland Rice leaned over to join the conversation. "You haven't heard? Two sprinters have been kicked off the team…"

"Which means that Jesse Owens has a chance for a fourth Gold Medal," Helms said. "When's the last time that happened? Never, that's when. Not once."

Nathan was surprised. "So Owens is running again?"

"That's right," Rice said. "He and Ralph Metcalfe are replacing Marty Glickman and Sam Stoller. No one knows why."

"From what I hear," Helms said, "the Germans have secretly assembled the fastest relay team anyone's ever seen, so the Americans felt they needed their very best men to compete."

"Which, of course, is pure nonsense," Grannie Rice said. "No German sprinter has even placed in the other races. The Americans have always been a shoo-in, even with Glickman and Stoller. Something else is going on here."

Eleanor raised an eyebrow. "Like what?"

"Like politics," said a good-looking young man wearing a USA sweatshirt. He smiled, and it was a broad, full-faced smile.

"Hi Marty," Grannie Rice said. "We were just talking about you. Marty, I think you know Eleanor Holm. The man to her left is Mike Novak, *Cleveland Plain Dealer*, and the fellow on her right is Richard Helms, who, I think, is working for United Press these days. People, this is Marty Glickman, until today a member of the US 400-meter relay team."

Smiles were exchanged, hands were shaken.

"What you said, Marty," Helms said, "about 'politics.' What did you mean?"

"I'm talking about racial politics," Glickman said.

"I'm not getting it, Marty," Helms said.

"Sam Stoller and I are the only two Jews on the American track team," Marty said. "And we've both been replaced by Owens and Metcalfe."

Rice spoke up. "I've heard your coaches are worried about the German relay runners."

"That's bullshit, Grannie," Glickman said. "And you know it."

Rice shrugged. "So tell me the truth."

"The truth is that Hitler didn't want to see two Jews standing on the victors' podium," Glickman said. "He passed the word to Avery Brundage. Brundage agreed to accommodate him, so he passed the word down to our head coach, Lawson Robertson."

Nathan considered this. "But if he doesn't get two Jews, he's gonna get two Negroes instead—if the US wins, that is. That doesn't make any sense."

"I don't think so either," Glickman said, "but evidently *der Führer* would rather America's 'black auxiliaries' get the medals than a pair of Red Sea pedestrians."

Rice had begun scribbling on a notepad. Now he looked up. "Robertson told you that?"

Glickman laughed. "Hell no. He said, 'We were hoping to give both of you a chance, but we can't take the Germans lightly.' He said, 'personally, I'd like to let you run, but we're here to win medals.'"

Rice was scribbling furiously now. "Was Jesse Owens in the room, Marty?"

"Yeah. We were all sitting there together. And Jesse stood up and objected. He said, 'I've got my medals, coach. Let Marty and Sam run."

"How did Robertson react to that?" Nathan asked.

"He pointed his finger at Owens and said, 'You'll do as you're told.' And you know Jesse—he's no troublemaker. He just sat down."

"You didn't object?" Eleanor asked.

"Oh, I objected all right," Glickman said. "I told him it was ridiculous—the Germans weren't hiding any experienced world-class sprinters. They were no threat to us. I said, if you drop us, there's going to be a furor back home—we're the only two Jews on the track team."

Nathan and Eleanor exchanged glances. "How did he answer that?" Eleanor said.

"He said, 'That's *my* worry, not yours.' And that was the end of it."

By this time, several other newsmen had joined the little group, curious about Glickman because of the relay participant switch.

"Would you mind if I quoted you?" Quentin Reynolds asked.

"I hope you do," Glickman said. "I hate to be a complainer, I really do. But Stoller and I have trained for months. We've run the relay dozens of times. Owens hasn't. Who knows if he'll be able to hand off the baton without dropping it?"

Well now, Nathan thought, looks like my job isn't over yet. He reached for Rice's binoculars and began scanning the stands, going from the bottom up. He congratulated himself on having decided to wear his shoulder holster this morning. A bodyguard without a gun wouldn't be much use.

"You always seem to be looking, old man," Helms said. "What are you looking for?"

"Trouble," Nathan said. Then he laughed. And kept scanning.

Eleanor fixed him with a skeptical look. "It was a last-minute change, you know."

On the field, Olympic officials and camera crews were setting up for the 4 x 100-meter relay. Fifteen nations had entered the competition, but only five teams had made it to the finals—the US, Italy, Germany, Argentina and Canada. Now, twenty athletes—Jesse Owens included—were milling around the track, checking the surface, taking a few steps on their lanes.

Nathan edged his binoculars up one row and scrutinized the next batch of spectators. If anything, he thought, the stadium was more packed than before, filled with ordinary workingmen and sometimes their *Frauen und Kinder*, with students and shop clerks playing hooky, with tourists, mainly European but here and there an American, and with an unusually large proportion of young men in uniform, unusual that is, anywhere but Nazi Germany. As for the sallow-faced man, he was there all right, sitting by himself just where he'd sat yesterday, reading his program and looking pretty damn harmless.

Nathan saw nothing out of the ordinary, just thousands upon thousands of people here to watch the world's finest athletes, to make memories for themselves and their grandchildren. They were gazing at the field, studying their programs, chatting with each other, making friendly bets, and munching on sausages from home.

He tilted the binoculars up another level and scanned the next set of spectators, who were, but for their faces, duplicates of those sitting below them. It was almost noon, a bright, sunny day for a change, and they were dressed for it, in short sleeve shirts and summer dresses. From a cop's point of view, they could all be described in a single word: innocent.

Except—oops, on the third tier, Nathan spotted a purse snatcher, a wiry young fellow, dark-haired, furtive, couldn't have been more than sixteen or seventeen. He was sizing up a mark and simultaneously checking out an escape route—the nearest stairway.

His mark, Nathan realized, was a hefty housewife in a bright, flowered dress, with an even heftier husband on her left. Instead of putting her black leather purse between them, she had made the common error of putting it beside her, on her right.

The would-be thief moved down the row toward the purse, the woman and the stairway, excusing himself as he went, head swiveling like a searchlight to make sure no one was looking. His idea. Nathan realized, was not to spring like a cat and flee, but to slip by, like a ship in the night, lifting the purse and sliding it into his open jacket, moving on smoothly, down the stairs, probably to a men's room to count the loot and get rid of the evidence.

Nathan could do nothing about this little drama but watch. He was, after all, some three hundred feet away. He knew he had other fish to fry, but what he was watching had him riveted. It wasn't often that he saw a crime as it was happening, even a petty crime like this.

Now the boy was even with the purse. His hand crept toward it. Husband and wife were oblivious. The thief's fingers curled around the handle as he took another step. The bag rose as he walked. He was past the housewife, who had noticed nothing. He was past her husband, who—the husband's hand shot out and grabbed the boy's arm, the one holding the purse, abruptly halting his progress.

The boy's fake nonchalance now gave way to sheer terror. He stood there, in the husband's iron grasp, while the outraged wife retrieved her purse. As Nathan watched, unable to suppress a grin, the husband stood and signaled to a nearby usher. The usher called over another of his kind and quietly took the thief into custody.

"What do you see up there, old man?" Helms said, puzzled.

"Not much," Nathan said. "Just observing the huddled masses."

"I see," Helms said with disdain. "Slumming."

Nathan shrugged and resumed scanning. More *burghers*, house *frauen* and their *kinder*, more soldiers, more tourists, more college boys. No one of any particular interest. After inspecting the stadium's top tier, he instinctively checked out the roof, as much as he could see of it.

Of course, he had done all this before. He'd been doing this for five days, searching for trouble and not finding it. Looking at all those stolid, square German faces, again and again, the same faces in different places, different faces in the same places. It was not an easy job, scoping out a full stadium day after day, looking for God knows what.

Now Nathan swept the binoculars along the edge of the stadium roof, seeing nothing but concrete, nothing he hadn't seen again and again, day after day. He scanned past the flagpoles on the left, the vent about ten feet beyond them, the drainage pipe about twenty feet farther along, the stopwatch tower, the little vertical pipe a few yards down…

Wait, stop. What vertical pipe? Nathan trained the binoculars on the little protuberance. Had he seen it before? No, he decided, he had not. It was a new addition to the scenery. He refocused the binoculars and studied the object. It looked almost like a rifle barrel. A rifle barrel with a telescopic sight. And as he watched, it was lowered until it was pointed directly at him.

Nathan hit the floor. Almost simultaneously, the back of his chair—the chair he'd been sitting in only an instant before—blew apart with a bang. The middle slat shattered into a dozen pieces, sending wooden shards in every direction.

"What the hell, Mike!" Helms yelled, after a splinter bounced off his chest. "You broke the damn chair…" But Nathan was off and running. He knew he'd just escaped with his life. He also knew who the next target would be.

Just before he got to a stairway, he glanced at the field. The athletes stood around, stretching, chatting, kicking at the turf, having mistaken the rifle's crack for a starter's gun. Jesse Owens was in the midst of them, presenting a very poor target. But when they all lined up for the start, he would be totally exposed.

Nathan vaulted up the steps, swung around, and took the next stairway in three bounds, and the stairway after that two steps at a time, He had one level left to go, but the shooter was almost exactly on the opposite side of the stadium. There was going to be some running once he got to the roof, and probably some shooting.

At the top tier, four levels above press box level, Nathan paused for a moment. How was he going to get to the roof? He looked desperately for a ladder or stairway but came up empty. Has to be one by the stopwatch tower, he thought. Technicians must have a way to get to the clockworks.

Nathan ran along the stadium's top tier, trying to find the roof entry and watch the sports field at the same time, past rows of spectators who barely noticed him. *Herr* Mueller was loading his starting pistol far below. How long would it be until the athletes lined up, waiting to hear him call out the count?

Halfway around the stadium, Nathan spotted a ladder leading to a roof hatch. It was just a few feet from the stopwatch tower. He could climb the ladder and pop through the hatch, but if he did, he'd be right on top of the assassin, too close for comfort.

Then, up ahead, on the far side of the tower, Nathan noticed a second ladder and roof hatch. If he chose this route, he might be able to surprise the assassin and take him from behind, before the man realized he was being attacked.

He glanced down at the athletic field. The runners were hanging around the starting line now. In a few seconds, they'd be taking their places. Then they'd crouch down, dig their toes into the cinder track, and position themselves for the fastest possible start, holding themselves still until they heard the starter's pistol.

If he were the guy on the roof, Nathan thought, that would be the ideal moment to shoot. At that instant, and that instant only, Owens would be motionless, waiting for the crack of the starter's pistol. If the assassin fired then, as Nathan was sure he would, the rest of the runners might take off at the shot, mistaking it for the starter's signal, leaving Jesse Owens dead in his tracks.

Nathan chose the more distant ladder and clambered up it like a monkey. Fortunately, the steel hatch was unlatched. Just before pushing it open, he unholstered his revolver. He put a hand against the hatch and gently pushed, doing his best to be quiet. It opened just a crack and he took a peek.

From where he was, Nathan couldn't see the assassin. The tower blocked his view. But the roof was broad and the tower was narrow. It would be easy enough to walk around it. He pulled himself up onto the concrete roof and carefully closed the hatch.

The concrete was rough, pebbly, crunchy to the footstep. Nathan wanted to run—he *had* to run—but he did not dare. Instead, he walked as quickly and as quietly as he could. He stopped at the edge of the tower and peered around it, showing as little of his face as possible.

The man looked like some kind of stadium worker on a break, a janitor maybe. He was lying on the roof, on his belly, cradling a rifle, eye to the telescopic sight, one stubby arm wrapped around its leather sling, the other at the trigger guard, finger hesitating in mid-air.

Nathan glanced at the field. The relay runners were taking their places. There was no time for thought. He raised his revolver. "Hey!" He shouted at the assassin, who suddenly looked up, completely startled. "Get away from the gun."

The assassin grinned and put his eye back up to the telescopic sight. His hand moved back to the trigger. Nathan fired once, catching the assassin in the left temple, at about ear level. He slumped to the roof. Nathan took a long look at the dead man, thinking about what would have happened to Owens if he'd delayed or missed the shot, telling himself it had been a very close call, too close. Then he took the rifle from the dead man's hands.

Then, awakening to the crowd's clamor, he looked out at the field and was amazed. Evidently, his revolver and the starter's pistol had fired simultaneously, for the sprinters were all off and running their hearts out. Jesse Owens was in the lead, as usual, his legs pounding the cinders, his arms pumping furiously, and one hand holding the baton in a death grip.

Nathan sat on the roof, watching the race and removing the rifle's cartridges and flinging them, one by one over the roof and into the grassy field beside the stadium. On the track and running with consummate grace, Owens flawlessly slipped the baton to the next American sprinter, Ralph Metcalfe, giving him a four-yard lead.

In the next 39.8 seconds, three other US runners took the baton and ran with it, the American anchor runner, Frank Wycoff, crossing the line twelve yards ahead of the second-place finisher, an Italian runner. The Germans came in third. Once more, the crowd went wild, despite their countrymen's loss, with more shouts of "Yaysee, Yaysee!"

Nathan turned his attention to the crumpled figure on the roof. The pool of blood at his head was slowly spreading over the concrete. What should he do with this one? Fortunately, no one could see the guy up here—neither the spectators in the stadium, nor anyone who happened to be standing outside or walking by. And there was no dirigible flying overhead, watching from above.

He could waste time—and increase the chance of being caught—by looking for a place to stow the body. Or he could simply leave the dead man where he was. That would do, Nathan decided. It would be hours, if not days, before anyone found the assassin, although his failure to kill Owens had no doubt already been noticed by whoever had put him up to it.

On the field, the American team climbed onto the victors' podium. The orchestra struck up the Star-Spangled Banner. Olympic officials hung gold medals from the necks of the four US sprinters and of course everyone in the stadium rose and cheered. Nathan took a deep breath, climbed down from the roof and started back toward the press box. He still had a little business to conduct.

Helms was the first to spot him and was ready to tease. "Novak, where have you been, old man? You missed the relay."

"Bathroom, old man," Nathan said, a little more sharply than he meant to. "I saw the race from back there." He waved a thumb over his shoulder, toward the rear of the tier.

"Everything all right?" Eleanor asked. Her voice was tight with concern.

It was Nathan's turn to smile. "Problem solved," he said. He pointed his index finger toward her, cocked his thumb and fired off a pretend shot.

"Really?" She said, horrified.

Nathan nodded.

"You're not hurt, though?"

"Totally unharmed," he said.

Eleanor reached into her bag of smiles and donned one that was small, sweet and genuinely affectionate. "When you bolted out of here, I thought…"

Helms intruded. "What in the world did you do to your chair, old man?" he asked. "The back practically exploded—and then you ran off. I thought you might be hurt."

Nathan stood looking at his chair. "Damnedest thing, Helms. Some flaw in the wood. Just snapped and landed me on the floor. The middle slat simply shattered."

"Yes I know," Helms said. He picked up a broken piece. "Look at this. If I didn't know better, I'd think that was a bullet hole."

Nathan chuckled. He took the shard and examined it closely. "Loose knothole," he declared. "Not the usual fine German craftsmanship. I should probably complain to someone." He pocketed the evidence.

"Not to *Eydrich-hay*, I hope," Eleanor teased.

Nathan cocked an eyebrow. "No. I'm hoping we don't run into him again."

Helms leaned toward Eleanor. "What are you two talking about?"

She ignored him, speaking instead to Nathan, flirting no less "So, what now?"

"I was hoping…" Helms said.

Nathan shrugged. "I don't know. Dinner?"

Eleanor pondered the suggestion briefly. "Room service," she said. "My room."

"Well, then. "Helms turned toward Grantland Rice. "Poker tonight?"

"I'm sure someone will be playing," Grannie said.

Chapter Twenty-Three

Still half asleep, David Nathan rolled over and reached toward the other side of the bed. He'd expected to find a warm, willing, female body. Instead, his hand hit a large brown leather suitcase. Eleanor was standing beside it, stuffing it with her belongings. She was fully dressed.

"I did something wrong?" he mumbled.

She laughed. "On the contrary," she said. "You were excellent."

Nathan pulled himself up on an elbow. "Then what's with the suitcase? Closing ceremonies aren't until this afternoon."

"I'm not going to closing ceremonies," Eleanor said. "I've had enough of Hitler and his crew."

"Yes, but what's the hurry? The boat train doesn't leave until tomorrow morning."

"I know," Eleanor said. "But *my* train leaves in an hour."

Nathan was alarmed now. "Your train? You're not going back to America tomorrow on the SS *Europa*?"

She unceremoniously rolled up last night's negligee and tossed it into the suitcase. "Oh, I'll go home eventually, I suppose," she said. "Art is getting a little antsy."

"Art?"

"Art Jarrett. My husband?"

"Oh, *that* Art."

"Yes. Anyhow, I figured as long as I'm in Europe, I might as well get a look at the place. Paris first..."

"First?"

"Yes. Then Rome, Vienna, maybe Prague."

Nathan was thoughtful. "So I guess..."

"That this is goodbye," She said, "Yes."

Nathan propped himself on the headboard. "Eleanor, do you think we'll ever, you know..."

"See each other again? She gave him a fond and tolerant smile. "Could happen. You never know, do you?"

"I wish you'd stay now and go back to America with me," Nathan said.

"Of course you do, David. I do too, a little. But, well, all good things..."

"Still..."

"Let's resist getting sentimental about it, David. Okay?"

"Sentimental? Heaven forfend!" Nathan said, forcing a smile.

Eleanor smiled back.

"Hey," Nathan said. "Would you mind standing there for a moment?"

"What? Why?"

"I just want to look at you."

She stood at the bedside and posed mischievously. He looked.

Nathan was trying to think of something else to say when someone knocked at the door.

"That'll be the bellhop," Eleanor said. She opened the door and found herself face to face with a dark-haired young man wearing a little red round cap and a fussy, multi-colored uniform that might have better suited a toy soldier. He clicked his heels and bowed sharply, and she invited him in.

"I'll just be a minute," she said. She searched the room, found one silk stocking behind a chair and kept hunting for the other one.

Nathan stuck a hand under the sheet and fumbled around a bit, at last coming up with its mate. "This what you're looking for?"

Eleanor gave him a naughty grin. "How in the world did it get under the sheet?"

"You don't remember?"

"Vaguely," she said. She tossed the stockings into the suitcase and snapped it shut, then motioned to the bellhop, who took charge of it, studiously ignoring the scene.

"Nothing I can say to keep you here?"

She bent down. The kiss lasted long enough to cause the bell hop to cough and turn his back. "Time to go," she finally said, breaking it off.

Eleanor turned and walked out of the room, the bellhop scurrying after her. Just before the boy closed the door, she turned back and presented Nathan with an utterly spectacular smile, her very best.

And just like that, he thought, she slipped away from him—as if he ever had her in the first place.

***

Having nothing better to do, Nathan decided to go out to the Olympic Stadium to see the closing ceremonies. He ended up wishing he hadn't. Half the foreign press corps skipped it, sleeping off a hangover, he figured. Berliners weren't much interested either—the stadium was two-thirds empty. Many of the athletes failed to show up for the final march around the track. So it was mostly band music and speeches in German, hour after hour of each.

That night, Nathan had dinner at the *Furstenhof* with some of the American newsmen, then crammed his clothes into his beat-up black suitcase and went to sleep early, feeling bereft. The next morning, he was up with the sun. While he was getting dressed, he picked up his shoulder holster and hesitated. Guard duty was over—of that he was sure. But he was still in Germany. He donned the shoulder holster, then his jacket.

Downstairs, Nathan had breakfast with Quentin Reynolds and Grantland Rice. Then the three of them grabbed a taxi, stowing their suitcases in the trunk. They headed to the Lehrter *Bahnhof*—the Berlin train station that served northern Germany and beyond.

What lay ahead was another fast trip on the "Flying Hamburger" express train to Hamburg, where he would board the *SS Europa* for the trip home. But there would be no train trip until he passed through German passport control, at the departure gate.

It looked pretty simple. All he had to do was show his passport, get it stamped, move through the turnstile and get on the train. Half a dozen people were waiting in front of him and a couple dozen more behind—most of them foreign journalists. And the line was moving pretty quickly.

Then it was Nathan's turn. He put on his best blasé, business-as-usual, this-is-all-routine expression and handed his passport to the guard, a clean-shaven young man with steel-rimmed glasses who was too bored even to glance at him. At first. Then he read the name on the passport. "Michael Novak," he said. "Hew Hess Say."

"That's me," Nathan said.

The guard finally looked up and smiled, as though he had discovered something delightfully unpleasant about Nathan's passport, a cat who had unexpectedly found himself with a particularly vulnerable mouse. The guard paged through Nathan's passport. "Novak," he said thoughtfully, pretending to jog his memory. "Novak.

That name is familiar." He checked a list on his clipboard, sliding a finger down the names. "*Ja.* Here it is. Novak."

Nathan tried to get a look at the list, but failed. This wasn't good.

"You will report to the office," said the guard, pointing to a door at the corner of the waiting room.

"Why is that?"

"Routine inquiry," said the guard. He was still smiling that obnoxious smile.

"I don't have much time," Nathan said. "I have a train to catch."

"I'm quite sure it won't take long, *Herr* Novak."

Nathan looked at the turnstile and considered his options. They couldn't have connected him with the dead body on the stadium roof. Still…

The guard cocked his head expectantly and stepped back, letting Nathan see his holstered pistol. "Do you need an escort?"

"No," Nathan said. "I can find the way."

The guard handed back Nathan's passport. They nodded at each other and Nathan walked toward the office, suitcase in hand, feeling the guard's eyes on his back. He kept telling himself they had no reason to detain him. They couldn't have known what happened on the stadium roof, or on the stairway of that restaurant building, or what he was doing here. And yet…

He knocked gently on the office door's frosted glass window.

"Come," said someone inside.

Nathan opened the door to find himself face-to-face with the very last person he wanted to see: Reinhard Heydrich, tall and elegant, dressed in a black uniform. The *Obergruppenführer* was sitting behind an old wooden desk, gazing at him with those pale blue eyes of his. The room was otherwise empty.

"Ah. *Herr* Novak, isn't it? We meet again." He did not invite Nathan to sit.

"Hello, *Obergruppenführer*," Nathan said. "It's a coincidence, I hope." He couldn't believe that the Director of the Gestapo was here merely to intercept an American journalist, or what he thought was an American journalist.

Heydrich laughed. "Ah yes, a coincidence. Well, I thought it would be polite to say goodbye," he said.

"And ask me a few 'routine' questions, no doubt," Nathan said.

"No doubt."

Nathan made a show of checking his watch. "I don't have much time," he said. "I'm catching the 'Flying Hamburger'."

"Yes, I know," Heydrich said. "And at Hamburg, you'll board the *SS Europa* for the voyage back to America."

Nathan didn't like this at all. "You know my travel plans?"

Heydrich shrugged. "Just an educated guess."

"Well, you're right," Nathan said. "Now, how can I help you, *Obergruppenführer*?"

"Please show me your passport," Heydrich said, extending a hand.

Nathan handed over the passport, trying to be offhand about it.

Heydrich leafed through the document, carefully examining the photo pasted inside, then looking back up at Nathan, comparing. He held a page close to his desk light, looking for watermarks. "This is really very well done," he said. "It appears completely genuine." He made some notes on a desk pad and handed back the passport.

"It ought to. I got it from the United States government."

Heydrich considered that. "Ah. Well, that would explain it," he said, giving the phrase an ambiguous twist. "Michael Novak—that is your real name?"

"So my momma told me." Nathan had conducted many a police interrogation, sitting on the other side of the desk. He knew exactly how to handle this line of questioning.

"Your background is Czech? Serbian?" Heydrich pulled out a small gold lighter and lit a *Neue Front Zigarette*.

"Mixed, but mostly Czech." Nathan was surprised by this question. Did Heydrich know more than he was saying, Nathan wondered? And if so, could this be a preamble to something really unpleasant?

"Did you know your name comes from the Czech word *nový*?" Heydrich smiled when he asked the question.

"My Dad died when I was five years old," Nathan improvised. "He never talked much about the old country, at least not that I recall."

"Understandably," Heydrich replied, nodding gravely. He took a puff of his cigarette. "You know, that word—Novak-- usually means 'new man'—a convert to Christianity." He paused while the words sank in.

"Well you'd know more about that than I would," Nathan said. He realized Heydrich was trying to sweat him, with ominous hints and implications. And the *Obergruppenführer* was employing the technique with enough skill that Nathan could feel his underarms getting damp.

"Have you enjoyed your stay in Germany, *Herr* Novak?"

"Yes, very much," Nathan said. "Of course, I've been working—reporting on the Olympics. As you know."

"Of course," Heydrich said, as though he knew there was more to it, "You're employed by a newspaper in—where was it?—oh yes, Cleveland, in the state of Ohio. I am correct?"

"You have an excellent memory, *Herr Obergruppenführer*."

"Did you have a chance to see much of Berlin—that is, other than your adventure in the…cabaret? And your evening at Goebbels' party?"

"Those were the highlights," Nathan said. "Other than the Olympics themselves, that is. And my flight with Lindbergh."

"I heard about that," Heydrich said. His cutting, high-pitched voice was a challenge to Nathan's self-control. "Wonderful flyer, an Aryan man of many virtues."

"Yes. We Americans come in many varieties," Nathan said. "At any rate, I'm sure Germany also has some wonderful pilots."

"A few," Heydrich graciously allowed. He studied Nathan for a moment. "May I ask question?"

Nathan hesitated, then shrugged. "Why not?"

"You're a Jew, aren't you?"

"What leads you to think so?"

"I can always tell. You people have a certain subtle arrogance."

A nasty little rejoinder popped into Nathan's mind, and while he was asking himself if it were safe to say it, he heard the words coming out of his mouth. "They say the same about you, *Herr Obergruppenführer*." He smiled modestly, hoping that would soften the remark.

Heydrich laughed. "But not to my face.".

"Me neither," Nathan said. "I'm a reporter. I just reported what I heard."

Heydrich produced a terrifying grin. "Of course you were. I understand. I thank you for the information."

Nathan's eyes met Heydrich's. "As it happens, Obergruppenführer, I'm not only Jewish, I am a Bar Mitzvah boy. If that matters. How did you know?"

"You haven't figured out how to hide your racial characteristics."

"Why would we want to hide who we are?"

Heydrich was silent for a moment, as if choosing his words carefully. "Well, there are good reasons these days."

"That may be true in Germany."

"America is different?"

"I like to think so," Nathan said.

Heydrich nodded, dismissing the subject. "Tell me, *Herr* Novak, are you taking any contraband out of Germany?" He waved a finger at Nathan's suitcase, then took one last puff of his cigarette and ground it out in an aluminum ashtray.

"Contraband? What kind of contraband?" Nathan realized Heydrich was just tightening the screw, but he'd have to put up with it.

Heydrich shrugged. "Currency, for instance. We have strict rules about foreign nationals leaving Germany with more than ten thousand R.M. "

Nathan couldn't help smiling. "You're kidding, of course."

"It's a routine question, *Herr* Novak." There was no return smile.

"Well, I doubt I have 100-R.M. with me."

"I see," Heydrich said. He made another note on his desk pad. "Any other contraband?

"Such as what?"

"Such as precious stones, fine art, objects of archeological value.

"Nope," Nathan said. "But you're welcome to paw through my suitcase if that would please you." He found himself thinking of the revolver in his shoulder holster. Was this going to turn sour now, at the very last minute?

Heydrich met Nathan's eyes and held the gaze for several seconds. "It will not be necessary to search your effects," he said. "I trust you."

"Thanks for the vote of confidence," Nathan said, trying not to sound relieved.

Heydrich paused, made more notes, then looked up at Nathan again. "*Herr* Novak, are you armed?"

Nathan gave him a non-answer. "What would a newspaper reporter be doing with a gun?" he said.

"Yes, of course, silly question," Heydrich said without conviction. "Tell me, *Herr* Novak, what did you do to Rudolph Theilmann?"

And there it was.

"Who?" Nathan said. He tried to look puzzled.

"The man I sent to kill Jesse Owens. And you. *That* Rudolph Theilmann." Heydrich smiled slightly, lips closed. "He's missing."

Nathan recognized Heydrich's technique: the shock question, meant to upset, confuse and undermine the prisoner's resistance. In Nathan's experience, it often got confessions from weaker men. But he knew a way to turn it back on the interrogator.

"You have a very peculiar sense of humor, *Obergruppenführerr*," Nathan said, managing a fairly convincing chuckle. "Unlike most Germans, I must say."

Heydrich looked at Nathan so intensely that he felt his mind was being probed. Nathan returned the gaze in kind, although it took everything he had. The man on the other side of the desk was no gangster, no crime boss, not even a run-of-the-mill murderer. This man was evil to his core.

Nathan could see the Lugar in the holster at Heydrich's waist. Could he beat his adversary to the draw? And even if he did, could he fend off the gate guard, who would come running at the sound of a shot, along with the other soldiers probably on duty in the station or nearby? He took a deep breath and got ready.

"Sense of humor," Heydrich said at last. "Yes. Others have made the same observation." He broke the gaze, glanced down at his pad and scribbled something. The game—if that's what it was—was over. "Tell me, *Herr* Novak, will you be returning soon to Germany?" His voice betrayed nothing.

Nathan waited as long as he could before he answered, hoping his voice would be steady when he spoke. "I have no plans to come back, *Obergruppenführer*," he said. He looked at his watch again, pretending impatience.

"Oh, I think you'll be back," Heydrich said. "I have a feeling our paths are destined to cross again. Oh, and don't worry about the train. You have plenty of time."

"No offense, *Obergruppenführer*, but I hope this is a final goodbye."

Heydrich was simultaneously perplexed and amused. "You don't find me a companionable fellow, *Herr* Novak?"

"That wasn't my point," Nathan said.

"Yes, I understand." Heydrich nodded, then stood. "Well then, *Herr* Novak, I guess this is goodbye. Or should I say *auf weidersehen"?* He offered a hand, which Nathan declined. Heydrich shrugged and smiled, snake-like.

Nathan walked out of the little office, knowing the Gestapo director was watching him. At the gate, the guard waved him through with barely a glance and he continued onto the train platform, boarding the 'Flying Hamburger' directly. He had ten minutes to spare before it left.

The train was filled with reporters and athletes, most of them American. Jesse Owens and several of his teammates were not on board—they were on a brief European exhibition tour. Nathan looked for Helms, but he must have been in the next car up. There was an empty seat next to Red Knickerbocker, so he took it.

"Ah, the neophyte newsman from northern Ohio," Knickerbocker said. "Had enough of Germany?"

"Too much, actually," Nathan said.

Knickerbocker laughed. "I'm with you there, Mike. But I'm bringing some of it back with me." He patted his stomach. "This was your first visit, right?"

"And my last, I think," Nathan said. "Gives me bad dreams."

Knickerbocker laughed again, ruefully this time. "I know what you mean. *Herr* Hitler and his friends don't sit well with me either."

"Well, at least Owens won his medals," Nathan said. "He was the star of the games. Even the German people loved him. I'm sure Hitler wasn't pleased by that."

Knickerbocker nodded thoughtfully. "Is that how you're going to write it—Jesse Owens was the star of the Olympics?"

"I think it's the best angle, don't you?"

"I suppose so. Especially for the good folks of Cleveland, Ohio, which, I believe, is his hometown. Your editor will be pleased, I'm sure."

"You have a better idea?"

The train gave a couple of toots and began moving out of the station, quickly picking up speed.

"I do. But I won't be able to get it into print. Not on the sports pages, and the sports pages are my domain, young man."

"What's your angle?" Nathan asked.

They were moving swiftly through the Berlin suburbs now, farms and forests ahead.

"Well, I'd write it this way," Knickerbocker said. "For all the spectators at the Olympic Stadium and sports fans around the world, the star of the Olympics was America's remarkable Negro sprinter, Jesse Owens. But the real star was not an American and not an athlete. He was a German politician, name of Adolf Hitler." He raised an eyebrow and looked at Nathan, inviting a comment.

"Well, that's certainly an interesting way to put it," Nathan said, "but what do you mean?"

"Okay," Knickerbocker said, "Second graph: Adolf Hitler managed to use the Olympic Games to convince the world that all of Germany was united behind him, that the Nazis were a civilized political group and that the Third Reich could be trusted to act responsibly on the world stage. It was a masterly performance by *der Führer* and his minions. And that's what it was, profoundly: a performance, a stage play with no resemblance whatever to reality."

For a moment, Nathan just stared at Knickerbocker. "Are you going to write that?" he finally asked.

Knickerbocker sighed slowly. "Why bother? No one's going to print it. We're all playing nice with the Krauts these days. Don't want to stir 'em up, make trouble. Neutrality in word and deed, that's the slogan. Those are our marching orders."

"Who from?"

Knickerbocker shrugged. "The newspaper owners. Washington."

"Not Roosevelt," Nathan said.

"No. But he's busy trying to get Social Security, the Works Progress Administration and the Labor Act past Congress—and the Supreme Court. He can't afford to pick any battles with the isolationists or the Conservatives."

"One can hope," Nathan said.

"One can hope. But there's trouble coming, young man, and we'll be in it, like or not."

"I hope you're wrong, Red." Nathan said.

"God, so do I."

****

The train arrived in Hamburg just after noon and Nathan walked directly to the docks, where the *Europa* was berthed, taking on passengers and supplies. The sooner he departed German soil, the better, he thought.

The customs inspection at the ship was brief and cursory, as it had to be, given the hundreds of boarding passengers. No Heydrich this time, Nathan noted with relief.

He was standing in line at the gangplank, waiting to board the big ship home, when a big black Horch pulled up nearby and Karl Oldenburg hopped out. He made his way over to the departing American. Oldenburg was wearing a pearl-grey homburg and dressed to the nines, as usual, as if headed to a fancy cocktail party.

"Good morning," Oldenburg said. "I wanted to catch you before you departed."

"Good morning, *Herr* Oldenburg," Nathan said, "to what do I owe the pleasure this morning?"

"Just a parting gesture," Oldenburg said, looking around. "Where is the lady?"

"Hard to say," Nathan told him. "Off on a European tour."

"Ah," said Oldenburg. "Women."

"Indeed," Nathan said, shrugging.

"I hope you enjoyed your stay in Berlin," Oldenburg said. " It must have been very pleasant to watch your countryman win all those Gold Medals."

'I did…and it was. But tell me, *Herr* Oldenburg, I wonder if you would answer one question before I leave."

"Of course."

Nathan locked his eyes on Oldenburg's. "Okay. Enough of this little charade. Tell me, what is your game? It can't matter anymore."

"I'm just a messenger," Oldenburg said.

"A messenger?"

"Yes, Mr. Nathan, and I have a message I'd like you to convey to Mr. Roosevelt."

"I think you have the wrong person. My name is Kovaks."

Oldenburg ignored the correction. "When you next see your President, please tell him that Mr. Churchill sends his best regards and his congratulations."

Nathan just stared, dumbstruck.

"And if I may, I'd like to add a personal note. I very much admired the way you handled yourself here. FDR chose the right man."

"Who are you?" Nathan finally managed.

Oldenburg smiled again. "Winston calls me his Scarlet Pimpernel."

"Scarlet Pimpernel? Wasn't he a fictitious British secret agent from before the war?"

Oldenburg thought a moment. "There's some dispute about the fictitious part," he said. He shook Nathan's hand, hopped back into his enormous automobile, then looked back toward the American. "So you've lost?"

Nathan managed a rueful chuckle. "Lost Eleanor? I never had her, not really."

"Yes. Well, better luck next time," he said, sounding sympathetic. And he drove away with a little wave, which Nathan awkwardly returned, looking thoroughly bemused. The Scarlet Pimpernel, of all things, he thought. He'd had a backup and he'd never guessed it.

And now the passenger line began to move forward. Nathan hesitated a moment, then shrugged and walked aboard the giant ship. A steward directed him to his tourist-class stateroom, which—thanks to the largesse of the US government—turned out to be relatively large and comfortable,

Off came the tie and jacket. He laid down on the bed for what he expected to be a few minutes. Four hours later, he was awakened by the low thrumming of *Europa's* powerful steam engines. They were moving, leaving Germany behind.

Nathan roused himself. He wanted one last look at the place. He found his way up to the promenade deck and walked aft, as far as he could, past a number of passengers wandering around with drinks in their hands, quietly chatting.

He dragged a teak deck chair to the rail, sat down and gazed into the gathering dusk, toward the twinkling lights of Hamburg, watching Germany disappear into the night.

After a bit, Nathan felt a hand on his shoulder. "Enjoying the view, old man?" asked Richard Helms.

"More with each passing mile," Nathan said.

"Yes," Helms said. "You never seemed comfortable in Germany."

"You could say that."

"One thing I don't understand," Helms said.

"What's that?"

"Did you ever file any stories?"

Nathan thought a moment. No harm in telling him the truth, not now. "Wasn't my job," he said.

"Really?" Helms said, confused. "Then what was?"

"I'm actually a cop on detached duty. My job was to look after Jesse Owens," Nathan said, enjoying the look on Helm's face.

"A cop? I never suspected." Helms said. "Some journalist I am."

Nathan decided to be generous. "Well, you didn't have any reason to doubt me, Dick," he said.

"But that was an easy job, looking out for Owens. He wasn't in any danger. Germany loved him, except for Hitler and his buddies I mean."

Nathan shrugged. "Maybe so. But they didn't want to take any chances."

"They?"

"Look, I'm just a cop, following orders," Nathan said. "I don't know how far up the chain the orders came from."

"Well, I envy you," Helms said. "Skullduggery is a lot more interesting than sports writing."

"Not always, Dick, not always."

Helms pulled up a desk chair and sat down next to Nathan. "Whatever happened to Eleanor? I haven't seen her aboard the ship."

"Off on a European tour," Nathan said.

"I thought the two of you were an item."

"Mostly in my imagination."

Helms laughed. "For a time, I hoped she and *I* might be the item."

Nathan looked up to see Thomas Wolfe standing at the rail, gazing at the fading lights of Hamburg, notebook under his arm. "Hello, Tom," he said.

Wolfe looked around. "Mike…Novak, right?"

"Right. Nice to see you."

Wolfe thought a moment. "You were with Eleanor last time I saw you, right?"

"Right," said Nathan. "Not anymore."

"Too bad. But then she's very, ah, elusive, wouldn't you say?"

"Good word," Nathan admitted.

"So, other than that, how was your stay in Germany, Novak? Did you enjoy the Olympics?"

"They were very, um, interesting," Nathan said. "You?"

"I was just writing about them," Wolfe said.

"Care to read us a few words?" Helms asked.

"Well, it's still rough—it's just notes."

"Wouldn't mind hearing a famous author's rough notes," Nathan prompted.

Wolfe gave him an aw-shucks smile then opened his notebook. "Germany did not send a team to the Olympics," he read. "Rather, the entire country acted as the team. The whole united power of Germany's enormous organizing and disciplining genius went into the effort."

He looked up, inviting comment.

"Very true," Helms said.

"Good way to look at it," Nathan said. "Please go on."

"No one really knows how strong America is," Wolfe continued, reading from his notebook. "We are a loose-joined, shambling and disengaged people. But from the effort of these games, some idea may be gained of Germany's power. It was enormous, and it was collected in a single stroke as compact as the blow of a fist. An ominous blow."

"By noon each day, all the main approaches to the games were walled in by troops. They stood at ease, young men, laughing and talking with each other—the leader's bodyguards, the Schutz Staffel units, the Storm Troopers. Then, suddenly, the sharp command and instantly there would be solid smack of ten thousand leather boots as they came together with the sound of war." Wolfe looked up from his notes.

"Good image," Helms said.

"After experiencing life in Nazi Germany," Wolfe went on, "I saw an entire nation infested with the contagion of an ever-present fear. It was a kind of creeping paralysis that twists and blights all human relations."

"And here I thought you were a big fan of Germany," Nathan said. "You know, from what you said at the Dodd residence."

"I have loved Germany," Wolfe said. "This was my sixth visit. I love the people and I love the traditions. But the Germany I see today is not the Germany I knew. It is being systematically poisoned. I'm heartbroken by what it's becoming and I intend to do what I can to warn the world."

"I hope the world listens," Nathan said. "But I'm not optimistic."

All three men were looking out toward Hamburg now. One by one, the weaker lights flicked out. And finally, the darkness was complete. Nathan thought of Heydrich's ominous goodbye. It contained a truth

Nathan couldn't deny. Someday, somehow, for some very good reason, he knew he would have to return to Germany.

Author's Note

JESSE OWENS

After Jesse Owens' triumph in Berlin, the world seemed to open up to him. He was, briefly, a national celebrity. Comedian Eddie Cantor offered him $40,000 a week for ten weeks to appear with him on Broadway. A California orchestra offered him $25,000 a week for ten weeks to tell jokes before they stepped on stage. And there were coaching offers as well.

None of this turned out. After the Olympics, Owens tried many times to cash in on his fame, putting his name on a string of dry-cleaning stores, running a barnstorming black baseball team, racing against horses in exhibitions, working as a physical education teacher in the Illinois school system, as a disk jockey and as the president of a boy's club.

Owens died in 1980 of lung cancer at the age of sixty-six. The long jump record he set at the 1936 Olympics was not broken until 1960, by Ralph Boston. Not until 1984 were Owens' four Olympic track and field victories in a single year were equaled, by the US athlete Carl Lewis, whom some called "the second Jesse Owens."

JESSE OWENS

ELEANOR HOLM

In 1932, at the Los Angeles Olympics games, Eleanor Holm won the gold medal at the women's backstroke event. She was 20 years old. In 1936, she was kicked off the team for drinking. The International News Service immediately hired her to report on the Olympics.

At the time, Eleanor was married to the American band leader Art Jarrett, and sang with his band in Hollywood nightclubs. During the Olympics, she attended several Nazi bigwig parties and was generally treated as a celebrity. Hermann Göring gave her a sterling silver swastika pin, into which she later had inserted a star of David diamond.

Holm's contact with the fictional character David Nathan is a product of the author's imagination, although the author would like to think that's just what she would have done if "Outrunning Hitler" had been non-fiction He imagines she would have been amused by her inclusion in this book.

In 1938, Holm played the female lead in the Technicolor Hollywood film "Tarzan's Revenge, which includes swimming scenes and can still be found on Youtube. In 1939-40, she appeared in the Aquacade show at the World's Fair and fell in love with the show's manager, Billy Rose. She soon divorced Jarett and married Rose. As time passed, she would marry twice more. In 1999, Eleanor met President Clinton at a White House reception. She died at the age of 91.

ELEANOR HOLM

RICHARD HELMS

Richard Helms, who is used fictitiously here, was born in 1913 into a family of means and international connections. He grew up in smart suburbs of Philadelphia and New York. One of his brothers described their youth as "conventional upper-middle class, well educated, well traveled, interested in good schools and sports, and with a social life centering around the country club." Helms took part of his schooling at academies in Switzerland and Germany and became fluent in French and German. In 1931 he entered Williams College and majored in literature and history. He became class president and head of the school paper, and was voted "most respected," "best politician," and "most likely to succeed." After graduating in 1935, Helms set out to be a journalist and newspaper owner, and by age 23 was a European correspondent for United Press International. He advanced from writing obituaries of English celebrities to covering the 1936 Summer Olympics in Berlin—the so-called "Hitler Games".

In 1942, Helms joined the US Navy Reserve, received a commission as a lieutenant, and worked in the Eastern Sea Frontier headquarters in New York City, plotting the locations of German submarines in the Atlantic Ocean. On finishing OSS "boot camp," Helms began what he would spend most of his intelligence career doing: planning and directing espionage operations from an office in Washington. The OSS soon became the CIA and Helms worked his way up the espionage ladder until, in 1966, he became the director of the spy agency, a position he held through most of the Cold War, He died in 2002 at the age of eight-nine.

RICHARD HELMS

THOMAS WOLFE

When Thomas Wolfe returned from Germany, he wrote a story called "I Have a Thing to Tell You," an indictment of the Third Reich, which became a part of *You Can't Go Home Again.* Some of this is quoted in the book. The critical nature of this story made him *persona non grata* in the eyes of the Nazis. He never again returned to Germany. He died in 1938 of tuberculosis of the brain, at age of thirty-eight.

MARTY GLICKMAN

If you're old enough, you may remember this name. After the Olympics, Glickman returned to New York and gained fame as an announcer of the New York Knicks basketball games.

MARTY GLICKMAN AND SAM STOLLER

REINHARD HEYDRICH

Reinhard Heydrich, also used fictitiously here, became one of the main architects of the Holocaust, chairing the January, 1942 Wannsee Conference which laid out the plans for "the final solution" to the "Jewish problem" – that is, the deportation and extermination of all Jews in German-occupied territory. He was wounded in an assassination attempt late in May, 1942 and died a few days later.

CARL "LUZ" LONG

Carl "Luz "Long was a German long jumper who competed at the 1936 Berlin Olympics, winning a silver medal behind Jesse Owens. Jesse Owens and Luz Long were friends, despite the circumstances of the 1936 Berlin Olympics and their different backgrounds. Their friendship transcended sports, race, and the political climate of the time. Long even offered Owens advice during the long jump competition, helping him qualify for the finals, where Owens ultimately won the gold medal. Carl "Luz" Long was wounded in Sicily on July 10,1943, during the Allied invasion of Sicily in Operation Husky (July 9 – August 17, 1943). He died on July 14 in a British military hospital there.

JESSE OWENS AND LUZ LONG

**David Nathan and Eleanor Holm,
as AI might imagine them.**

Final Observation

Because of World War II, no Olympic games were held in 1940 or 1944. They resumed in London in 1948, but did not return to Germany until 1972, when they were held at Munich. At that Olympics, eleven Israeli athletes were massacred by Arab terrorists.